DRAGONSIN

Descendants of Twilight: Book 1

BY

C. M. SUROWIEC JR.

Hardcover: 979-8-9859622-2-2
Large Print Paperback: 979-8-9859622-1-5
eBook: 979-8-9859622-0-8
Trade Paperback: 979-8-9859622-3-9

Dev / Copy Line Editor: Marie Still
Assistant Editing: Erin Bledsoe
Proofreading: Quata Diann Merit
Cover Art Design: CM Surowiec Jr
Cover Art Illustration: luv_draft
Map Enhancement: Khayyam Akhtar

CMSurowiecJr.com

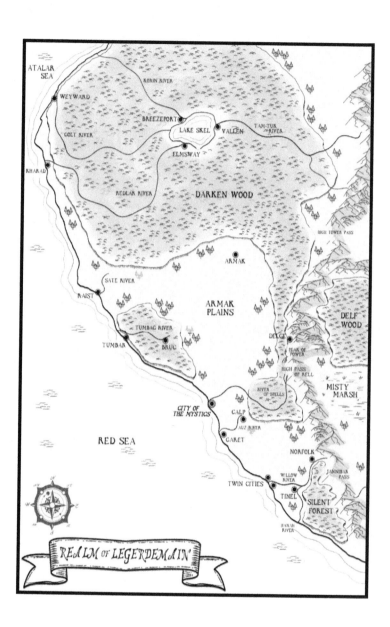

REALM OF LEGERDEMAIN

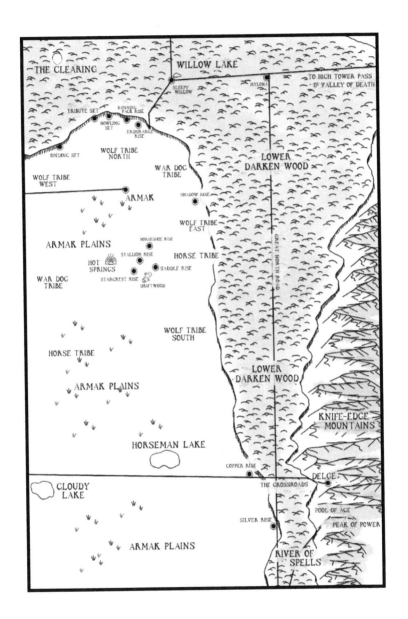

THE CLEARING   WILLOW LAKE   TO HIGH TOWER PASS & VALLEY OF DEATH

SLEEPY WILLOW

AYLONA

TRIBUTE SET   RUNNING PACK RISE

HOWLING SET

ENDURANCE RISE

BINDING SET   WOLF TRIBE NORTH

WAR DOG TRIBE

LOWER DARKEN WOOD

WOLF TRIBE WEST

SHADOW RISE

ARMAK

WOLF TRIBE EAST

ARMAK PLAINS

HORSESHOE RISE

STALLION RISE

HORSE TRIBE

HOT SPRINGS

SADDLE RISE

WAR DOG TRIBE

STARCREST RISE   DRIFTWOOD

GREAT NORTH ROAD

WOLF TRIBE SOUTH

HORSE TRIBE

LOWER DARKEN WOOD

ARMAK PLAINS

KNIFE-EDGE MOUNTAINS

HORSEMAN LAKE

COPPER RISE

DELGE

CLOUDY LAKE

THE CROSSROADS

POOL OF AGE

SILVER RISE

PEAK OF POWER

ARMAK PLAINS

RIVER OF SPELLS

~ v ~

My debut release is dedicated to those that supported me every step of the way:

MY FAMILY

EROGOTHIAN CALENDAR

1. First Twilight 1/24 - Terashan's Twilight	**2.** Progression	**3.** Breeze
4. The Initiate 4/4 - Terashan's Twilight	**5.** Harvest	**6.** Rhomerian 6/14 - Terashan's Twilight
7. Anuberis	**8.** Oderian 8/24 - Terashan's Twilight	**9.** The Holy One
10. Gathering	**11.** Sendarian 11/4 - Terashan's Twilight	**12.** Final Harvest
13. Last Twilight 13/14 - Terashan's Twilight		**14.** Festival

- **30 days in every month**

DragonSin

1

Green Sunrise

The last remaining torch in the village extinguished, and with it, TetraQuerahn's fun came to an end as quickly as it began. He landed heavily in the horse corral behind the humans. The ground trembled beneath his girth, as green smoke billowed from his nostrils. His piercing white eyes scanned the area before he issued a deafening, ancient roar. The dragon's tail swooshed back and forth, splintering wooden fence posts and rails while frantic horses cantered past him, racing for freedom. Today they were safe; he wasn't here for horse meat.

The three-hundred-year-old monstrosity could not contain his grin, his throat vibrated with glee. The acrid smell of burnt chlorine hung in the air, and behind the two huddled humans lay the remnants of the first explosion.

A brutal rampage flitted through his mind, crushing humans, crashing fences, demolishing the barn. He reconsidered. Was it worth sacrificing his immediate needs? TetraQuerahn approached the vermin slowly, scraping his claws on the ground, fanning his wings, preparing to rejoice when the human's dragon fear intensified.

The *whooshing* from his wings echoed off the buildings.

A man stopped cradling a young girl before turning to face him. Her broken, lifeless body returned to her landing position after the explosion, bent over backward on the split-rail fence.

"Light . . . the . . . torches!" said TetraQuerahn, his gravelly voice drenched in malice. Thick strands of saliva dripped from his mouth, hitting the ground with a hiss.

"No," the injured man choked, clutching his chest in agony, blood frothing on his lips.

TetraQuerahn's head pulled back, unaccustomed to defiance. "You will die a slow death."

"You don't frighten me anymore. I am already—" The horse rancher seized with a coughing spasm.

"Otec, we need to leave now." A woman staggered around the corner of the barn, struggling to keep her balance.

The rigid brow of the dragon lifted when a tear rolled down the cheek of the one called Otec. *Are you going to restrain yourself or look back over your shoulder?* He briefly searched the night sky, wishing the twins could share this moment with him.

The green behemoth craned his neck downward, placing his snout two feet from the man's face to relish every micro-expression. "Now, do I scare you?" He chortled in response to the human's countenance.

"No, Shay! Run!" the rancher bellowed before another bout of coughing overwhelmed him.

The woman pulled back her shoulders, replying calmly, "There is no reason for me to run . . . we will face this calamity together."

TetraQuerahn growled in her direction. "So brave now! Ten minutes ago, you were shaking on that porch over there, paralyzed by fear."

Her gaze fell upon the young girl's body. "That woman had something to lose." She maintained her course fixing him with a frosty glare. The woman sauntered past the epicenter of the explosion with her hands daintily clasped at her abdomen.

No tears. He stomped. *No fear!* He clenched his teeth.

"Shay, you're bleeding!" the man exclaimed in a shaky voice.

TetraQuerahn examined her, noting the blood dripping from her hands. "Have you returned to mourn the dead or join them?"

His lips curved up, releasing a tiny cloud of gas. The mist swirled around Otec's shoulder. A large, yellow-tinged blister erupted where the gas brushed his skin. The rancher responded with a piercing scream.

"Give me a moment to finish with this one." His voice lowered to a snarl; his fangs bared. "Or you can help me, and I will leave your farm to find my entertainment elsewhere."

The woman, now standing next to the man, did not respond. Instead, her unwavering eyes stared at the dragon while tracing her finger on the top rail of the wooden fence.

"No deal? Pity," TetraQuerahn said light-heartedly. "Now, where were we? Oh yes, lighting . . . the . . . torches!" He growled the last part with eyes bulging from his horrifying face.

The woman shook her head in defiance. "There will be no more torches. Your terror is over!"

"Shay!" wheezed Otec, reaching for her with a trembling hand, then quickly turning to vomit blood.

The dragon's tongue flickered in and out of its mouth rapidly as he sniffed around the man's head. "No, it would appear my fun is only beginning."

The human wiped his mouth before pleading, "I will light a torch if you let her go." He whispered to the woman, "Shay? Save yourself."

The woman removed the remaining blood-soaked hand still covering her abdomen. "Otec, remember your pledge to me? 'Even wild horses could not pull us apart.' I will die holding your hand."

TetraQuerahn studied the amusing scene before him. "Die? That's a bit premature. Before this is over, you will beg for a quick death."

She grabbed the rancher's hand, half rotated her body, and peered over her shoulder. A large shard from the detonated wagon had impaled her forcefully, driven deep into her belly. Fourteen inches of the wooden stake protruded from her back.

She slowly twisted back to the front. "Awwghh!" Her knees buckled; her face turned white. The female released her grip on the man's hand to catch herself on the fence rail.

Wide-eyed with mouth agape, Otec reached over and grabbed her hand on the railing. "It's not bad. Cymm can help you."

The color returned to her face. "Let's finish this so we may start a new journey."

TetraQuerahn's eyes darted between the man and woman, attempting to speak several times, but to no avail. He considered himself a master of manipulation, but his smirk had disappeared. He slammed his tail into a canopy covering for the horses, sending pieces flying everywhere.

The sky began to lighten, and with it, his frustration grew. His fury erupted in another roar, and two cries answered it from above.

"*You* should be afraid . . . dragon!" Shay shouted, putting an end to his tantrum.

He chuckled. "Me? That is funny. Too bad you'll be dead soon. Otherwise, I would take you back to my lair to watch the finale of this humorous performance."

Dawn continued to break as she replied, "I would have enjoyed that too. Watching death come for you." A chill crept up TetraQuerahn's back, his muscles twitched. He glanced behind him.

"Not now, half-wit. Death *will* come for you, but in your lair, while you sleep."

Two dark shapes glided through the village like crop-dusting planes, laying down a toxic haze of chlorine gas intending to kill everything. He would join them soon.

TetraQuerahn's nostrils flared, and his inner eyelids pulsated. "I will not listen—"

"Before you die, if you get the chance, make sure you ask for the name of your executioner," Shay hissed at him. She looked at the rancher for support, but his unseeing eyes had glazed over, and he was unresponsive. Her next breath caught in her throat.

"You have two bodies to carry now. Are you sure that is a good idea in your condition?" He sniggered, enjoying his joke.

She squeezed Otec's hand until her knuckles turned white and let out a venomous, "His name will be Cymm Reich!"

"Enough!"

"Say it!" she commanded, drawing strength from an unknown source.

TetraQuerahn breathed in deep, his gas billowing forth. "I have heard enough of your blathering!"

"Cymm Reich, say it . . . Cymm. She stared up to the southeast, screeching in pain. The mighty dragon followed her gaze.

The sun peeked above the Knife-Edge Mountains. The toxic clouds masked it beneath a green hue. The emerald monstrosity thought, *What a wonderful sight — a Green Sunrise.*

2

The Hunt

(Six Days Earlier)

Cymm entered his sister's bedroom, depositing a large apple on her nightstand before leaning over and kissing her forehead while she slept. "I am sorry, Bria," he whispered. "Double chores for the next ten days. I owe you more than an apple."

Prior to Cymm turning to leave, one of Bria's eyes blinked open. "Yeah, you do. Maybe I'll go hunting and retrieving when you get back, and you can do my chores."

"If only you were three years older, like me." Cymm shook his head, taunting her.

"Two years and twelve months, orc breath," Bria retorted. "Now get out and let me sleep," she exclaimed, nestling back into bed with a deep, gentle sigh.

When Cymm entered the kitchen, the fragrant scent of freshly baked berry bread assaulted his nose, making his mouth water. He grabbed a huge slice and kissed his mother, Shay, on the cheek before heading out the door.

"Tell your father to come inside to eat breakfast with me," she called to his back.

"Um . . . hmm," he said with his mouth full as the door swung closed.

His father, Otec, already in the barn, struggled to get Cymm's horse ready. The young man hustled over to the opposite side of the horse to feed the saddle's belly strap underneath to his father.

"Here you go." He walked around to pat his father on the back.

"Thanks. Be careful out there," Otec replied.

Talo Reich, Cymm's cousin, appeared in the doorway leading his warhorse. "Are you ready? Where's Old-Man Semper?"

"Right behind you, orc-brain," Semper called out, an old man of eighty or ninety, astride an imposing warhorse. He dismounted with vigor, then smacked Talo on the arm with his gloves.

"Don't forget the Knights of Kharad need two dozen warhorses by Terazhan's Twilight. We have a lot to do when you get back. You and Talo need to test each horse's response to verbal commands, visual signals, clicks, and whistles," Otec said.

"Terazhan's Twilight? How—" Talo started to ask.

"You know, when the four moons are in the sky at the same time," replied Cymm.

"You really are an orc-brain," stated Old-Man Semper with a dour disposition.

Talo rolled his eyes. "Why do I bother? How did it get named after your god?"

Laughter and commotion suffocated his question. Old-Man Semper puckered his lips and nodded his head in approval. "The Knights of Kharad? I guess everyone has come to realize your warhorses are the biggest and the strongest in the realm."

"In the twenty years we've run the farm, this is the best year Shay and I have had. We turned business away after promising our two-year-old colts and fillies," Otec said, while making one last check of the horse's rear hooves.

"Alright, let's get a move on before the rest of the village awakens." Old-Man Semper winked at Otec. "Don't worry, I got 'em."

"Have fun while the rest of us are working twelve-hour days taking care of the horses, feeding the farm animals, making repairs, tending the crops, and—" Otec teased.

"Bye, Father! Mother has summoned you for breakfast," Cymm winked at his father, then raised his eyebrows toward his cousin.

"Bye, Uncle Otec!" Talo quickly urged his horse forward before his uncle had the chance to reply.

Five minutes later, he peeked back at his village, Stallion Rise, resting peacefully on top of a small knoll in the Southern Armakian Plains. Most horse villages were the same, laid out in the shape of a wagon wheel, the buildings at the hub, and the farmland spoked out in seven pie-shaped pieces.

The three-story bell tower—its only unique feature—protruded from the center of the village.

The small band of hunters rode south through the grasslands for two days before happening upon a rare grove of trees.

Cymm pointed at the trees. "Looks like we found camp."

Semper grunted at the trees. "All this natural beauty tainted. I can't wait to cut them down."

"Shhh! Two antelope," Talo whispered over his shoulder. He had his bow out, an arrow nocked. Cymm squinted in the direction the arrow pointed, nothing was visible in the tall grass. Talo urged his horse forward. The sharp *twang* of his bowstring cut through the silence. The arrow pierced its eye, and the antelope fell dead. The thud on the ground sent the other animal fleeing.

Fizzztt. Cymm's projectile buried into its hind leg, significantly slowing it down.

Fizzztt. Talo finished it off moments later.

"Are you saving your arrows?" Cymm ribbed Old-Man Semper.

Talo smirked, slinging his bow over his shoulder.

The old man shot a glare at Talo. "What in the nine hells are you smiling about? Now we got two antelope and no preserving berries!"

The expert archer's enjoyment disappeared. He grumbled while dismounting and kicked at the tall grass on his way to the dead animal.

A cloud passed over Cymm's face. "Why you gotta do that?"

The antagonist stared him down with nostrils flared. "Let's go. We got a lot to do."

They threshed a circle in the tall grass, then built a fire. The camaraderie slowly returned over the next few hours as they butchered the meat, made meat-drying racks, chopped more firewood, and set aside fence rails. After a late dinner, they turned in, but Semper lingered by the fire, surveying the plains.

Cymm, unaware he had fallen asleep next to the fire under the stars, abruptly awakened from his slumber when Semper nearly ripped his arm from its socket. His eyes now wide open, he followed Semper's pointing finger past the fire. "We got company," hissed Semper.

Cymm propped himself up on his elbows, peeking past his toes to the other side of the fire. Red eyes glinted among the tall grass.

Semper was already shaking Talo.

"Wolves. How many?" asked Cymm quietly.

Semper shrugged.

Cymm drew his sword, and it clanged off both sides of the scabbard from shaky hands. His cousin's bow creaked behind him, the sound giving him some comfort. Still crouching, he waited for the signal from Old-Man Semper.

With a nod, they charged the closest wolf as it lunged at the old man; Semper dodged left and skewered it through the neck. Meanwhile, Cymm slashed its side, ripping through matted fur and exposing ribs. The creature fell to the ground with a dying yelp.

A wolf came crashing out of the tall grass, claws and teeth bared.

"Cymm, watch out!" Semper pivoted to defend the young man's exposed flank too late.

Cymm barely had time to rotate his head when it collided with him, and they collapsed to the ground. He grabbed the wolf's neck with both hands fighting for dominance and to keep its fangs away from his face.

He rocked back and forth, but the beast did not fight back.

With a breathless huff, he heaved the carcass off himself. The old man's visage changed from horror to relief. He slowly rose next to the crumpled body of the wolf, an arrow protruding from its side.

Cymm slowly rotated his right shoulder with a wince. "Nice shot."

Old-Man Semper gave the archer a nod of respect.

"I always got your back. Heads up." Talo pointed with his chin and notched another arrow.

Four more wolves entered the little clearing with menacing growls.

"Cover me," Old-Man Semper yelled, running away from the wolves.

Cymm stepped back toward his cousin, and the wolves stalked closer, wary of the fire.

A horse whinnied, before the elder Plainsmen stormed past them, crashing into the wolf pack with iron-shod hooves and swinging steel. Talo released the arrow he had notched, striking one of the confused wolves in the rump. Cymm charged with his sword held high, issuing a lively battle cry. The remaining wolves scampered off howling into the dark grasslands.

"Alright, back to bed," instructed Old-Man Semper dully, irritated the wolves had disturbed them.

"Yeah, right. How are we supposed to sleep after that?" asked Cymm. Talo nodded in agreement.

Semper opened his mouth to argue, then reached up, grabbed meat off the drying racks, and tossed them each a large dry piece before grabbing one for himself.

After they had eaten their fill, the elder said, "It's time. I will gut the wolves while I finish my watch."

The young men did not argue and returned to their bedrolls. Cymm still had adrenaline coursing through his body, but with a full belly, he fell fast asleep.

∞∞∞∞

They continued to hunt and collect stray horses for the next four days. The wolves never bothered them again. After collecting four antelope, two wolves, and a buffalo, they decided to head home early on the seventh day of the hunting trip. The stray horses were laden with meat slathered in preserving berries and wrapped in the animal's skin.

The day after they started their journey home, a village appeared on the horizon.

"Getting close. Only a few hours left," Cymm said.

"I want to hunt more often. This is the best we have ever done," boasted the archer.

Old-Man Semper nodded. "This meat will really help both our families make it to Harvest, and a dozen stray horses is the most I've seen anyone retrieve."

"Bria would kill me." Cymm's body shook with laughter. ". . . but it sure would be fun. What about these strays from other villages?"

"Let's return the one for Star Crest Rise up ahead. The others we need to carry the meat and fence poles." The elder Plainsmen casually swayed in his saddle and chewed on one end of a long strand of jerky.

"Is that the mid-color blue?" asked Talo.

Colors ran through Cymm's mind. Every horse's mane was temporarily color branded with three stripes representing the tribe, the village, and the house to help identify its rightful owners.

Semper stared at him, shaking his head in disappointment, but Cymm nodded to confirm.

Talo's eyes flared briefly. "Do you think Auntie Shay will have some berry bread baking when we arrive?"

"I don't know, but my stomach just rumbled at the thought of it." Cymm patted his belly and licked his lips.

"Talo, maybe next time I will take your sister hunting, and you can stay home and bake." Old-Man Semper fixed him with a final gaze and urged his horse to canter ahead.

The two cousins shared their feelings with their eyes, but patiently waited for him to get out of hearing range.

"What in the nine hells was that about?" Cymm asked.

"What is it ever about?" Talo replied, causing them both to laugh.

"You should have asked him if he has any elvish blood in his lineage." He received a dirty look from Talo. "Or asked him what his real name is?" Cymm asked mischievously.

Talo reached down, grabbed a handful of grass tassels, and threw them at him. "You know he attacked my father for that elf comment. Why do you continue to bring it up?"

"Bah! A little spilled beer. No one got hurt. Not even the ancient one. He charged your father, tripped, face-planted, fight over." Cymm winked at his cousin.

They caught up to their crotchety mentor as they entered the outskirts of Star Crest Rise. Semper led the way to the village center, dismounted like a forty-year-old, and helped himself to the town's well water.

A local called out, "Hey, Old-Man Semper. Looks like you got a bunch of strays there. Any for our village?"

"Don't you know your own colors? What kind of Plainsman are you?" Old-Man Semper scolded.

The boys shifted the load to free up the horse while the elder collected three copper coins.

Another man came running over. "Old-Man Semper! How's your village?"

He ignored him while putting the coins away, then glared at him. "What are you talking about?"

The rancher scrutinized the cousins, the horses, and the old man. "How long have you been out on the grasslands?"

"Over a week. Make your point before I beat it out of you." His mentor practically growled the last few words.

"Three days back, dragons attacked Stallion Rise. We heard it was horrible." The man cringed while sharing the grave news.

The young men were bringing the horse forward, but Cymm froze in place. "What? When?"

"Why would they attack? What do we have that a dragon would want?" Talo shook his head, trying to make sense of the news.

Semper fumbled his coin bag, struggling to think. "Get on your horses!" He ran and vaulted onto his own, preparing to turn and leave. "We have to go now!"

Finally, a thought brought Cymm from his stupor. "Bria!" He rushed to his horse with clenched fists.

When the youngsters caught up, the elder yelled, "Our bounty will slow us down! Cymm, you ride ahead and see if you can help."

The lump in his throat had grown so large he couldn't speak, so he nodded, then rode hard for Stallion Rise.

Less than an hour later, his village came into view floating on a sea of grass, propped up by a knoll. The first wave of death and decay rolled past his nose, as he cantered by a bloated horse with hooves in the air.

He rode his mount hard until he arrived at the first house. With a click and a whistle, the horse immediately slowed to a walk. The beast was blowing hard and lathered, but Cymm barely took notice. A tear rolled down his cheek as he gaped at the body of Syra, his childhood girlfriend. She lay in the road, grabbing her throat. Small yellow blisters marked her hands and face. Two more bodies lay on the ground in front of the home, collapsed through the doorway. He knew the family well. They were her mother and younger sister, but their faces and bodies were so distorted by the yellowish-green boils, he could not be certain.

A lump returned to his throat as he made his way toward his home; death and destruction were everywhere. The noise from thousands of bird calls steadily increased. Crows, ravens, and vultures were feasting then dying by the hundreds, poisoned by the very corpses they gorged on.

"They are okay. They are okay. Terazhan, please make them okay," he pleaded desperately. His home came into view, intact and untouched. He sighed in relief. "Terazhan be blessed!"

He rounded the corner of the barn and brought his horse to a halt. Shards of wood lay strewn over the barnyard. He dismounted, picking his way carefully through the debris toward the depression in the ground. The remnants of the wooden wagon and the manure it held lay scattered in a circular fashion.

"What could have caused this?" Cymm continued scanning the area until his gaze fell upon the bodies by the horse corral. "No!" He rushed over to the fence, his hope dissipating with each step, like the mist on a hot summer morning. "No!"

A few crows took notice and flew to the top of the barn while the rest continued to peck ravenously at the corpses. He swung at a bird pecking his sister's eye socket, but his all-consuming sorrow caused him to miss and nearly fall.

"They're dead. All dead." His mother and father were slouched against the lower split-rail fence, still holding hands. The same hand his mother had accidentally sliced open while making dinner a few years back, and Cymm had tended to her wound.

"Terazhan! Why?" he bellowed. His sister hung on the top fence rail like laundry on a clothesline. The leather thong necklace she wore appeared to be choking her. The heavy copper medallion attached to it hung from the back of her neck, almost touching the ground. "Bria, I am so sorry . . ." he sobbed, struggling to breathe. He fell to his knees, his anger and grief erupting in a scream of frustration. "I am so sorry. I should have been here for you like I promised." He recalled the times Bria came fishing with him at the pond, especially when they saved the beautiful white dragonfly. They would never go fishing again.

His rage came fast and sudden, crying out in agony toward the sky. The cacophony of birds cawing swelled in reply. He lowered his face into his hands and clutched his head, swaying back and forth.

"They can't be gone. They can't be gone," he whispered to himself. Maybe he was still in his bed, slumbering away, and this would all be over soon, but the nightmare continued. No matter how hard he tried, he couldn't wake up.

He blinked through his flooded eyes, bringing objects in and out of focus until something caught his eye. Something on the fence rail didn't belong. *What is that?* He moved closer for inspection. On the top rail was a "painted" red heart.

Footsteps and a low, guttural moan sounded behind him. A glance over his shoulder revealed the arm of a grotesque monster reaching for him. *This is real. This nightmare is really happening. There is no waking up.*

He lurched backward, too late to unsheathe his sword. The creature lunged for him, and he braced for impact. His assailant tumbled to its knees next to him, then pulled its hands back as if in prayer. The moaning guttural noises returned, much louder and filled with emotion.

Is it crying?

He recovered and leaned in close to inspect the creature. *It is wearing remnants of farm clothes,* he thought. *It must be human, a farmer or rancher maybe.*

"Are you . . . from this village?"

It nodded, the yellowish-green pustules covering its body rubbed against each other, producing a sickening squishy noise. Some were the size of a corn kernel; many were as big as an apple. The largest pustule, bigger than a dinner plate, enveloped the farmer's throat and lower jaw. Bearing the resemblance to a bullfrog, with one eye swollen shut, and the other bulged out of its socket. Both were surrounded by the ghastly colored fluid, pulling the skin so tight they could burst at any moment.

Who are you? He hugged the farmer like a newborn baby, trying not to rupture the boils. *How can you still be alive?* He immediately placed both his hands on the farmer's face, one on each swollen, puss-filled cheek. "Terazhan, I call upon you to grant me the power to heal—"

3

A Force of Nature

L ykinnia instantly traveled to Darken Wood for the fifth day in a row. Her golden, ethereal form hovered next to the five-foot egg sac, scrutinizing it for any sign of movement or hatching.

"Hey, little guys, can you hear me?" She giggled and covered her mouth with a cupped hand. "I guess I better get used to speaking your language." She switched to the language she had created and planned to teach them. "You should have hatched already. Is everything alright in there?"

She had many interests, but she especially enjoyed studying mutations and creations. Her research and experimentation in this region of the forest over the past many years had resulted in several new species and variations.

A *tic, tic, crack* sounded from the egg sack; she could feel a tremor run through it. Well, not actually. She could not "feel" anything in her ethereal form, but she liked to imagine how it would feel. She twirled excitedly; her aura pulsed like a rapid heartbeat. She flitted around the ovular egg sack, examining it for movement. The egg sack was fibrous, with hardened foam filling the gaps. After several agonizing moments, a dark brown head popped out like a worm, then rested.

"Take your time my little trailblazer." She clasped her hands together, shaking them vigorously.

A second, dark brown head popped out several inches away, the first already wriggling its way out. Six inches of the light tan body, which contrasted sharply with its head, had emerged before springing out of the hole and clinging to the egg sack. It remained stationary, breathing heavily.

"Hello there! Aren't you a beautiful little creature?" Her eyes swung to the side as three more heads burst out, beginning the same journey. She hovered close to the first insect while it dried itself by vibrating rapidly. One leg finally unglued and separated from its body like a spring. Five additional heads erupted, then six more, all while other nymphs wriggled free and clung to the sides of the sack.

In a matter of ten minutes, the incubator evolved from dormant to a flurry of activity. Six-legged creatures were crawling all over the sack, each other, and more were emerging.

She sighed deeply, tilting her head to the side. "I see you are still leading the pack. Are you drying your wings now, my little friend?"

A bird swooped in, snatched her trail-blazing friend in flight, then flew to the closest tree. It immediately began dissecting and eating the six-inch insect.

She froze with her mouth agape. Gently she shook her head, scanning the vicinity. Dozens of birds had gathered, roosting in the trees surrounding her. Two more swooped in and departed with a nymph in its beak. She scolded herself for being so consumed with the event that she was oblivious to the imminent danger threatening the hatchlings.

Six more birds took wing, gliding in for an easy meal, apparently no longer afraid of her. A few more successfully absconded with lunch. The birds cawing and squawking rose to a clamor. Dozens were now in flight.

"No!" Her anger erupted in a piercing scream, and the intensity of her image flared in a bright flash. Most of the birds veered away or left, but the rest remained in place, watching.

Lykinnia ran her hands through her hair frantically and sped to the forest floor. She zoomed around, focused on finding the answer to her problem, then raced back to the hatchery.

A feeding frenzy was in full effect; birds were picking off her nymphs rapidly. She screamed and flashed again, pausing the flurry of action.

4

Cymm

Cymm was born on the fourteenth day in the month of Rhomerian in the 382nd year in the Age of Dragons. His father, Otec, built a home for his family on the other side of the Reich barnyard, across from the home his uncle inherited. It was a mudstone structure with a thatched roof constructed from thick, hollow prairie grass, perfect for channeling the rain toward the house's edge.

On the day he turned ten, he entered his neighbor's barn crunching on an apple. "What cha doin' Old-Man Semper?"

"Keeping my sword sharp in case trouble comes a-knockin'," he grumbled.

"What kind of trouble?" Talo peeked around the door frame, also gnawing on an apple.

"Bah. I should have known you'd be skulking around spying!" yelled Old-Man Semper wagging his finger with a contorted face.

About to leave, Talo pouted. "See, I told you he doesn't like me!"

Cymm was more than two years younger than his cousin, but they were nearly the same size. He fed the rest of his apple to a horse in the closest stall. "Hold up Talo. Old-Man Semper, we want you to train us to become part of the town militia," he said in a matter-of-fact tone with his hands on his hips, chest puffed out.

The old man stared at them for ten long seconds before he burst out laughing. He leaned forward, still chuckling. "First of all, we don't have a militia, and second, what in the nine hells could you two half-pints do if trouble did come a-knockin'?"

Cymm stood his ground, locking eyes with the old man. "If you train us, we will have a militia, and as far as I reckon, anyone that likes ale knows two half-pints are better than no pints."

The old man whacked his knee with his hand and roared even louder.

Cymm cast a smile at Talo with a double eyebrow raise. His cousin smirked back with a look of admiration, patting him on the shoulder while they waited.

Old-Man Semper stroked his chin. "Alright, alright." He turned his back on the boys, and the sound of his voice became jovial. "To cover my horse's hooves, your parents have to agree."

They replied in unison, "Really?"

"Four days a week, no exceptions, with bows and spears," he said, turning back to face them.

"What about swords?" asked Cymm.

"Maybe in a few years." He returned to sharpening his sword, but not before shouting, "Now get out!"

Six months went by. Semper's barnyard had become a training ground, replete with archery targets and grass mannequins.

"Four center-eye shots in a row. I need a break." Talo's bragging accompanied a strut resembling a wounded chicken.

Old-Man Semper scolded Cymm. "Concentrate! Look at your shot group!"

"Me? You should talk! You haven't hit a center-eye all day," he scoffed, pointing at the old man's target.

Fizzztt . . . Fizzztt. An arrow struck each target. "Now you both have a center-eye shot," yelled Talo as he ran for the exit and his horse.

Cymm and Semper looked from the targets to each other before dropping their bows to chase Talo.

"You better run, boy!" yelled Old-Man Semper.

∞∞∞∞

Festival, or the fourteenth month of the year, arrived, and with it the nightly parties at every Plainsman village to celebrate the end of another year.

Old-Man Semper stood by the bonfire in front of more than two hundred people. "Alright, settle down!"

"Special occasion? You're usually quiet by the keg," Zeke Darkmane scoffed.

Semper fixed a fiery gaze on him until the man shifted uncomfortably. "Maybe *you've* had too much of the keg. Let me know if you want to continue this conversation." Zeke remained silent. "Cymm, Talo, come up here." He waved for the boys to join him. "These two young men have been training for eight months, and their skill with a bow is quite impressive. Therefore, after speaking with each head of household, you both have been promoted to Militia Archers."

The cousins stood tall with heads held high. Boisterous applause and cheers rang throughout the night.

"Also, we are presenting you with this gift for your hard work and dedication." He handed each boy a dirk dagger. They beamed as they admired the daggers, basking in the praise from their neighbors.

Semper cleared his throat. "Never to be drawn against a fellow villager."

Both glanced up, nodding energetically.

"Lastly, a new training phase will begin tomorrow, hand-to-hand combat, with daggers and spears." Semper held up wooden daggers and spears without points. "Now, let the party begin!"

Cymm grabbed hold of Semper's arm, turning him. "Thank you."

A rare smile appeared on the elder's face. "You deserve it, half-pint."

"What about swords?" Cymm pressed, not letting him forget about his initial request.

Old-Man Semper stared at him in reply, then shook his head slightly before heading back to his farm.

The month of Festival ended, and with it, the year 392 AoD. The new year proved to be more challenging for the Reich family. Nightmares became a regular occurrence for seven-year-old Bria. On this night, her terrified scream echoed through the house and carried across the village.

"Oh, Cymm," Bria sobbed, hugging her brother tightly, trying to explain her nightmare. "It was awful. I couldn't get away!"

Her mother walked into the room. "What was it?"

Bria nestled into her brother's chest, still shaking. "I don't know, but it was huge, green, and had moss hanging from its chin. At least I hope that was moss. That's when I screamed and woke up."

He returned her hug, stroking her hair. "Bria, you don't have to be scared. I will protect you with my new fighting skills."

She frowned in response. "How orc-face?"

"Bria! Watch your mouth!" chastised her mother.

"Sorry, Mama." The young girl reached out for a hug.

Cymm stood and gazed lovingly at their embrace while a warm feeling tugged at his heart. He considered the skills he'd learned over the last year and how far he'd go to use them against anyone who dared to hurt his family. "Bria, I will always be here to protect you."

"You promise?"

"I do," he replied for the third time this week alone.

Usually, the day after a nightmare, his sister attended his training session, and today was no different. She sat in her usual spot on the fence rail while her cousin pulled on her shirt sleeve, stomping her feet.

"Come on, Bria, let's go play," whined Cela.

"Nah. Go ahead. I'm watching my brother," she replied, disregarding her completely.

"Aww, whatever!"

Cymm walked over after she departed. "You should go play with her."

"Nah, this is more fun, especially when you knock Talo on his butt." She giggled and bit her lower lip.

"I am going to tell him what you said," he teased, hoping to get a reaction.

"I don't care!" She had sass in her voice and shook her head.

With each passing month, the frequency of Bria's nightmares diminished, but her presence at Cymm's practice did not.

∞∞∞∞

Two and a half years went by, and her nightmares were long gone.

On this day, Cymm's mother and father woke him up early. "Happy lifeday!"

"Huh?" He rubbed his eyes. *What time is it?*

His mother had a spring in her step. "It's a very special day. It's your coming-of-age day!"

Bria ran into the room and jumped on his bed. While on hands and knees, she inspected him closely. "Are you sure, Mama? He doesn't look thirteen to me, maybe twelve."

A scream followed by a squeal replaced her suspicious scrutiny.

Cymm tickled her again.

"Yes, I am sure darling that he is not too old for his own treatment." Shay dove onto the bed to tickle him.

"Alright, alright." Otec tried to break it up, but Cymm pulled his father into the mayhem by his wrist. The bed collapsed with a *thud*. They paused, examining each other, searching for injuries. When none were found, they folded into another fit of laughter.

Even on his special day, he had chores to do, so he knocked them out as quickly as he could. When he entered the barnyard, his footsteps halted at the sight of Old-Man Semper leaving Uncle Daro's house. *That's weird. They don't get along.*

Then his father walked out. "Cymm, go find Talo and come inside." His father's deep voice and unblinking glare unnerved him.

Cymm's eyebrows knitted together. *What did I do, or was it Talo? This can't be good. Father looks so stern!* His stress continued to magnify as he searched for his cousin.

Fifteen minutes later, both stormed through the door in a huff. Every Reich family member was present, staring at them quietly. You could cut the tension with a dagger.

"Cymm, you turned thirteen today, and Talo, you were thirteen more than two years ago. You are both men in the Reich family," Otec shifted his eyes from his brother to his wife.

Shay tousled her son's hair. "Stop torturing them already."

Cymm breathed a sigh of relief, but the knots between his shoulder blades remained.

Otec paused. "My brother and I have given Old-Man Semper permission to train you both to fight with a sword!"

The young men slowly swiveled their heads with mouths agape. They started yelling, bumping, and jostling each other.

"They don't look like men to me!" Bria exclaimed.

Cymm paused and snapped a gander her way. He charged her, causing her to scream, and the chase began. Talo and the other children joined in while the adults opened the front door and pushed them outside.

Later that day, they arrived early at Semper's farm for training.

The elder emerged from his barn with a frown. "I bought three wooden swords to use for practice. Training will also begin with metal-tipped spears." The two boys started pushing and shoving each other. "Don't be fools! Both weapons can seriously hurt you!"

The reprimand severed the invisible strings lifting the corners of each boy's mouth, and they stood up straight.

A couple of days later, the village bell tower rang in the middle of training. Semper's barn blocked their view, so they moved toward the gate to check it out.

The old man grabbed his real sword after kicking the dirt. "There better be an emergency this time, or I'm gonna tear that bell down and throw it in the well!"

The cousins pursed their lips, issuing their own unique whistles. The horses came galloping over, passing their mentor as he swung into his saddle. Screams blared before they reached the corral gate. Semper flashed his eyes in a panic. "Move it! This ain't no drill." His horse lunged forward, riding around the corner, out of sight.

Time slowed for an instant as they observed each other, sharing unspoken words of doubt and fear. Talo swallowed hard; Cymm fidgeted with the bow slung over his shoulder. Then all hell broke loose, starting with their horses lurching forward. The magnitude and frequency of the screams intensified. Cymm's heart pounded so hard, he thought it would erupt from his chest. They rounded the corner of the main house at the Wither Farm, reining their horses abruptly to avoid hitting Semper on his horse.

"What in the nine hells is that?" croaked Cymm.

5

Nature versus Nurture

Lykinnia could feel her material body calling to her ethereal form—a warning her time was short.

"Follow me, little ones. This way!" She hoped the remaining nymphs recognized her voice from the past few months.

"Bad birds! No!" She flashed brilliantly again.

Inside she seethed, but she continued to lure them toward the barren forest floor with a calm voice. Many baby insects leaped, following her voice. Some plummeted to their death because their wings had not released or dried sufficiently. Still others were coasting to the ground unharmed.

A small group of survivors formed, and she led the band to the closest underbrush almost a hundred feet away. The insects skittered, jumped, and flew after her, then hid among the leaves of the undergrowth.

She retraced her steps. An accumulation of the dead and wounded lay on the ground directly below the sack; a stabbing pain in her stomach made her look away.

Her head throbbed, and an ache accompanied each pulse. *It will get much worse if I don't return soon.* She called to the rest of the nymphs on the egg sack, causing more to plunge to the ground before their wings dried.

Lykinnia couldn't wait for them to gather. The pain in her head had escalated significantly. She proceeded straight for the underbrush, calling to those on the ground in a desperate plea to lead them to safety. The first group was tightly packed, but this time, the insects stretched out in a long-disorganized line. She clenched her jaw in defiance as the pain reached excruciating levels. Two more deep breaths brought her closer, but time had run out. Succumbing, she released her ethereal body to return home, leaving the second group stranded on the barren forest floor.

6

Trouble Comes a Knockin'

The veteran shook himself out of a daze. "That big thing is an ogre. The others are orcs."

"Orcs!" The boys laughed at the derogatory term the Plainsmen used. Blood spurted from the neck of one of the Wither's women. The laughing ceased and they quickly sobered; death was all around them.

In addition to Cymm's dry mouth, uncontrollable tremors assaulted his body, leaving his horse in an unusual state of flightiness. He yearned for his cousin's support, but Talo's face had turned milky white, and his mouth hung open. He looked to his other side, seeking reassurance from Old-

Man Semper, but his mentor sat stoic, frozen in place on his horse.

The young man surveyed the battle, trying to muster the courage to use his training. His fear became a raw, living thing, punching through his chest, grabbing his heart, and squeezing. Many of the Wither family were dead or maimed. The Darkmanes and Softtails were not fairing much better after joining the cause.

Cymm opened his mouth to speak—

Fizzzztt.

One orc fell dead with an arrow in its eye. He swiftly looked back at Talo. The bowman's color had changed from the white of fear to the red of deep fury. Tears streamed down his face while he alternated between growling and whimpering.

Talo nocked his next arrow with sadness in his eyes. "They are dead," he whispered to himself darkly, then fired another arrow. "They are dead."

Cymm's attention returned to Old-Man Semper whose sullen face turned toward him briefly before charging into battle on his warhorse, heading straight for the ogre.

The brute towered above everyone at nine and a half feet tall. His head was bald and bare like the rest of his body from the waist up. He prominently displayed his yellow-gray skin, wearing only a necklace of teeth around his thick neck, a copper nose-ring like a bull, and crude buffalo skin breeches that barely extended to his knees. Although the monster was frightening, the huge seven-foot-long wooden club he carried was terrifying. Bone fragments encrusted the barrel, which added cutting to the bashing damage it delivered.

"Smash and stomp! Ha! Ha! Ha!" The ogre swung his club, and kicked at anything moving, including orcs.

Cymm forced himself to enter the fray. *Everyone needs you to be strong. Now help!* he berated himself. His arrow beat a steady rhythm against the stock of his bow as he tried to notch it. He pulled back on the bow with trembling hands, took a deep breath, aimed, then released.

Fizzztt.

His arrow slammed into an orc, joining another already protruding from it, but his sunk deeper. The creature fell to its knees with a resounding thud, then crumpled to the ground. At the sight of the fallen enemy, Cymm's fear subsided, and he notched another arrow.

Semper urged his warhorse into a gallop, careening from one side to the other. He left a laceration stretching from the ogre's shoulder across his back as he rode past.

He took another deep relaxing breath, allowing his battle training to guide him.

"I got the one on the left," he said to his cousin.

Talo's crying had ceased, but his clenched jaw was still crimson like the moon Phoenix. He muttered something to himself, but Cymm couldn't discern a word of it. Arrows were ripping off the end of Talo's bow, but none were landing. Many buzzed past their fellow villagers, distracting them, giving the orcs an advantage.

"Talo! Focus! We need you!" His cousin looked through him, still in a daze. "Talo, take your time and call your shot, just like at Semper's farm."

The young archer nodded and yelled, "Tallest orc . . . center-eye."

Fizzztt. The creature fell dead with an arrow through its eye.

"One more arrow, then shift thirty yards to the right," Cymm yelled, trying to replicate their training sessions. Semper insisted they never engage in hand-to-hand combat and to absolutely never get off their horse.

The young leader was also having success with his arrows, targeting the ones his cousin wounded.

"Semper hit the ogre again!" Talo nocked his next arrow. "The one on the far left."

Their next arrows released at the same time and hit two orcs. Then they hit two more, and the remaining enemies took notice. The raiders charged the bowmen, but the farmers with pitchforks and axes intercepted the invaders. They clashed. One farmer buried his axe in an orc's chest while they grappled. Other villagers were swinging, pushing, grunting, with faces stretched in fear and fury.

Talo's next arrow pierced an orc's throat. It choked, clawing at the arrow until Cymm's arrow sailed in to finish it off.

"Shift back!" Cymm's horse walked backward upon command.

The dead orc count mounted, numbering more than the humans lying on the ground. Semper swung his horse around and charged again, feinting to the left, driving to the right. The ogre delayed his swing, then swung the opposite direction, spinning his body. The massive club connected solidly with the chest of the warhorse. Bones cracked, and the horse shrieked. It swayed on unstable legs until its front limbs buckled.

The old man's forehead struck the back of his sword as he lurched forward from the jarring impact. He cried out in pain, fumbled his sword, and it fell to the field. Simultaneously, the horse collapsed, pitching Semper over its neck, both barreling to the ground.

His mentor struggled to stand, but his right ankle buckled at a ninety-degree angle, and he fell to his knees. Semper held his side and chest with both hands while the severe cut on his forehead bled profusely into his left eye.

The ogre walked over to the injured horse, raised its club high with a stupid grin spreading across its face. The monster issued a boorish laugh before the massive club descended, smashing the magnificent beast again.

"Horse dead." Still giggling like an idiot, the ogre stepped over his latest victim and followed Semper as he crawled toward the barn wall. "Now your smash turn!"

"No!" yelled Cymm, firing an arrow at the ogre, but it ricocheted off the barn wall. The dim-witted monster now fixated on him. He patted the riding horse and whispered, "We gotta save the miserable old goat." Then he urged it to charge ahead.

The ogre hoisted its club, issuing a booming roar.

The horse dug its hooves into the earth abruptly, and Cymm lost his balance. He slid down the equine's neck to the ground, ten feet from the dead warhorse. The ogre chuckled, turning back to finish the old man.

While Cymm sprawled on the dirt, he pounded it with his fist. His mentor fixed him with the same deadpan gaze he gave before charging the ogre. In frustration he swung at the ground again, hitting Semper's long sword.

Fizzztt.

An arrow whizzed over his head, sinking into the behemoth's shoulder.

He lifted his fists in the air. "Yes!"

The ogre turned abruptly with a roar, its body shuddering.

No more stupid laughing! Cymm grabbed the sword, prepared to do something stupid himself.

Semper sat up, shoving his back against the barn wall. His eyes were now insanely wide after seeing him pick up the fallen sword.

The old warrior unsheathed his dagger without hesitation, hollered, swung, and drove it deep into the ogre's right calf.

Howl!

The ogre grimaced, then hobbled back around to Semper, and swung its club straight down toward his head. The old man closed his eyes and half-heartedly lifted his arms. The ogre's club slammed into the barn wall several feet above the Semper's head where it lodged between two bricks.

Fizzztt! Another arrow hit the ogre in the back while he struggled to free the club. He heaved, snarled, howled, then thrashed in a fit of rage. He lifted a massive foot and stomped on the old man's chest. A sickening *crunch* echoed through the barnyard. Semper cried out in agony, not seeing the ogre lift its foot for another stomp.

Cymm commanded, "Don't even think about it."

He stood on top of the triple-stacked hay bales on the ogre's right flank, towering over the creature by almost a foot. The ogre was in a precarious position, leaning back, strenuously pulling on its club with muscles bulging and one foot raised above the old man. The young man had Semper's sword cocked back like he was threshing hay for the horses. When the ogre rotated its head to determine the source, he was already swinging.

Blood spurted from a large gash in its neck. The beast released the club, grabbed its throat with both hands, trying to hold it together. The monster opened its maw to roar, but only a raucous gurgle sputtered out accompanied by frothy blood. It staggered backward with wide eyes, then collapsed next to Semper's warhorse.

The farmers cheered loudly. The story spread immediately throughout the Horse tribes becoming a tale they told to their children for centuries to come.

Cymm immediately jumped down and crawled over to his mentor, still breathing but barely hanging on. "Semper needs help! Who can help him?"

Talo raced over with several villagers. "The orcs have all been killed," he reported. "What can we do?"

"I don't know . . ."

Semper grabbed his arm roughly, causing him to jump. "Find . . . hardre . . ." he said faintly. His wheezing sprayed flecks of blood upon his lips.

"Hardre? What is *hardre*?" Cymm asked, but the old man was no longer awake.

Cymm's and Talo's fathers pushed through the gathering crowd.

"Back up. Back up," Otec said.

Talo's father, Daro, addressed the crowd. "Let's get the wounded into the Wither's home."

"Father!" yelled Cymm. "What is *hardre*?"

Otec shook his head, still trying to get the crowd to work together. "What is it, Cymm?"

"What . . . is . . . *hardre*?" He annunciated each word this time.

With his focus still on the crowd, he responded, "Not *what*, but *who*. *Who* is Hardre? He is a cleric that travels through the plains begging for food."

"A cleric? You mean a healer?"

"Yes, now help clean up this mess so I can try to help Semper," Otec commanded. Four men hoisted his mentor and carried him into the house.

He grabbed Talo's arm and pulled him to the side. "We need to find Hardre like Old-Man Semper said. My father told me he is a healer."

The boys asked every adult in the area if they knew where to find him, but no one could help. Cymm put his hand on the back of his neck. The panic slowly seeped in, growing worse with every shrug or dismissive nod. Nobody could give him the answer he needed–the answer that might save his mentor's life. Where is Hardre?

From behind, someone grabbed him firmly around his waist. "Bria, you shouldn't be here!"

She hugged him tightly, swelling with pride. "You really can protect me!"

His cheeks flushed from the effort to untangle himself from her. He didn't have time for this, even if her small arms brought him momentary comfort. "Let go. I need to help."

Bria let go immediately, walking over to the ogre, leaving him awestruck by her courage. Bria murmured to the ogre before she reached down, wrapped her three largest fingers around the nose ring, and heaved.

A sickening *Pop* resounded, making his skin crawl as it ripped through the cartilage. She polished it on her pants, then walked inside the Wither's home.

With the grimace disappearing from his face, he returned to questioning the villagers. His discouragement continued to mount until a villager named Sero told them Hardre was in Star Crest Rise a little over a month ago.

Cymm clapped his hands, uttering words in a speedy jumble, "One hour to get to Star Crest Rise if we ride fast."

Talo trembled nervously. "Maybe we should tell . . . tell . . . Old-Man Semper's family what we know and do what your father told us."

He shook his cousin by the shoulders. "Do you want to put Semper's life in anyone else's hands? Will anyone else try as hard to find Hardre?"

"Ah Cymm."

"I am leaving my house in twenty minutes, with or without you, and traveling light," he yelled over his shoulder, while rushing inside the Wither's home.

"Father," he said. "Father! Please spare me a moment. I'm in a hurry."

Otec dismissed himself and followed his son outside. "What is so important, Cymm? Don't you see how many have been injured? I don't have time for this."

Cymm shifted nervously from side to side. "I'm leaving immediately to find the healer. He was seen about a month ago in Star Crest Rise."

His father firmly crossed his arms over his chest. "Oh really? Who is riding with you?"

"Well, Talo might go with me . . ." he trailed off, realizing how silly he sounded.

"A young man with thirteen lifeyears out on the plains by himself? Does that sound smart to you? Bandits, orcs, wolves, or a dozen other things could end your ride before it started," scolded his father. "I have too many people I need to worry about right now, without adding you to the list."

He stuck his chin out defiantly toward his father. "I will not let him die! I have to try!"

Otec sighed, thinking long and hard while tapping his chin. "No, *you* don't—Daro."

"No, not Uncle Daro." Cymm hung his head. *Great, I got Talo in trouble too.*

"Silence," his father said under his breath.

Daro leaned out a window. "Yes, brother?"

"Find two men to ride with us. We leave for Star Crest Rise immediately." Otec directed before his brother withdrew into the window.

"Father, what is going on?" His eyes contained both hope and confusion.

"When you asked about Hardre earlier, I told your Uncle Daro we might be searching for him. You were trusted to make the right decision and talk to us before running off."

Cymm stared, still trying to piece everything together.

"So now, there will be six of us riding for Star Crest Rise. Are you sure he is there?"

"Thank you, Father!" Cymm replied, giving his father a giant hug. "Yes, Sero told me he saw him there a month ago."

"No time to waste. Go get ready. Remember to reload that quiver of yours. I will be right behind you!" Otec returned to the house.

Less than twenty minutes later, six riders departed the Reich farm riding southwest. Cymm's calculation was accurate, and they rode into the center of Star Crest Rise about an hour later.

Many villagers stopped their daily chores and warily approached to find out what was going on. News of the attack at Stallion Rise agitated the farmers; they rallied together to find someone with information about Hardre. He had departed the village many weeks earlier, heading for Saddle Rise.

"Saddle Rise?" Daro shifted his weight. "That's a three-hour ride back to the east."

"Well, we should arrive around sundown," replied Otec, but then he whispered to Uncle Daro, "This course will take us right through the Driftwood."

A shudder fell over Cymm. The Driftwood was a rough section of the plains where rock outcroppings of all sizes erupted from the ground. When the dark brown rock protruded above the height of the grass from afar, it appeared to be a piece of driftwood floating on a sea of green.

When they first entered the Driftwood an hour earlier, the pace had slowed considerably. The horses and riders intently searched the ground for treacherous terrain, but fortunately, Daro peered ahead. "Wolf to the right!"

A wolf had positioned itself on top of a large brown rock; his uncle clicked and whistled lightly to calm his own horse.

Otec scanned the perimeter. "The same direction until we know how many there are."

A trained warhorse could have handled several of these wolves, but they chose light horses to travel quickly.

Another wolf emerged on the left, perched on a different rock that rose above the grasses.

"Daro, lead us to the right! Do not go between those two big ones! Cymm, Talo, ready your bows," barked the head of Reich household.

"Yes, brother. Everyone, stay close!" Uncle Daro yelled.

The rider's heads swiveled, scanning from side to side.

Moments later his uncle cried, "Two wolves on the—"

A haunting howl came from behind them sending a chill down Cymm's spine.

His uncle's voice trailed off strangely. Cymm whipped his head around seeking guidance from his father, but the elder's face had drained of color, a sight he'd never seen before.

"What's wrong?" he asked.

"It's a blood wolf."

7

Nature Calls

lthough Lykinnia returned to her body an hour earlier, her senses had not yet fully recovered. Exhausted, she had planned to lie there under the altar and recuperate next to the Pool of Age, but the distinct scuff of sandals on pebbles alerted her. Terazhan approached. She grasped the edge of the pure white quartz altar and smiled in her weary condition at the intricate carving on the base and legs. The teenager knew she wasn't allowed to use any of its special powers; she was only permitted to pray.

Oh great! He is with Solar, and they are coming to the altar. She had played this game before, but never with her head throbbing. She cast an invisibility spell on herself, stumbled toward the closest tree, and sat with her back against it.

Terazhan strode by fully robed in white with his cowl drawn tight, while Solar was scantily dressed, surrounded by a golden aura.

She held her breath, not daring to move a muscle.

The men approached the magnificent altar side by side, Terazhan slightly taller than his nine-foot-tall companion. Solar discreetly turned his angelic face toward her, waved, then returned to his previous demeanor and the discussion at hand.

She pouted internally and vowed to pluck a feather from his magnificent wings.

"The young boy's aura is quite impressive. I have not seen anything like it since . . . since . . . Melcorac," Solar whispered the last part, more in reverence than secrecy.

"Are you certain? That is quite the comparison and a bold statement," replied Terazhan, deep in thought.

Solar began weaving the fabric of space over the altar until a scrying window appeared. "Yes, quite certain. I also discovered he's traveling now to find a cleric, one who worships you."

The process was quite loud, providing Lykinnia a distraction to slip away and return to her quarters on the far side of the plateau. She needed sleep; her body could not handle another flash travel right now, even if the altar allowed it. Her thoughts returned to the nymphs. *They are probably so scared. I left them in a dangerous spot.*

Her living space consisted of one room carved into the cleaved face of the mountain. In it was everything she owned, a bed, a table, two chairs, and many bookcases. She didn't light a candle; she closed the door, took off her sandals, and collapsed on the bed.

When she awoke, her headache had subsided. In her haste, she skipped breakfast and snuck back out to the Pool of Age. She temporarily enjoyed the serenity, listening to the gentle waves in the pool lapping against the raised platform where she stood. Placing both hands on the altar, she invoked its ability to send her ethereal form back to Lower Darken Wood.

8

Blood Wolf

"**M**ore wolves from the back! We need to pick up the pace a little!" Otec's voice cracked mid-sentence.

His father brought up the rear with Cymm immediately in front of him. He swung around to ride backward as he had done many times.

"This is no time for games, Son," his voice cracked again.

"I know, Father. I will protect your back." He nocked an arrow and made a silly face. If he could make his father smile, maybe things weren't as bad as they seemed.

Otec let out a humored scoff. "Who would have thought the time you wasted learning to ride like this would actually come in handy."

The blood wolf released another howl. It was closer, and his father's countenance appeared grave once again.

The grasses were tall, chest-high on a human, and hid all the other wolves, but each time the blood wolf leaped, his black head appeared among the grass tassels. An intense fire burned in its eyes—scarlet sclera surrounded by pools of darkness. The beast was clearly ahead of the pack and gaining ground.

Fifty feet away. Cymm now understood why fear had consumed the adults.

Cymm released the arrow without hesitation, but his horse swayed, and the arrow zipped through the air above his target. He quickly nocked another while calling over his shoulder, "I may need help back here, Talo."

"You know I can't ride backward. Besides, we have two wolves to . . ." Talo grunted, and the twang of a bowstring rang out, ". . . deal with." A wolf shrieked and whimpered in pain.

Cymm timed his next shot with the rhythm of the horse's gait. To his relief, it sailed true hitting the blood wolf in the shoulder. Undaunted, it continued to leap and bound, closing the gap.

"Father, I don't think I can kill this thing," he said uneasily, nocking another arrow. The rest of the pack trailed, but their labored panting kept increasing in volume.

Forty feet. Black fur glistened in stark contrast to the green blades. His next arrow sprang from the bow, ripping through the beast's ear, but again it was unfazed.

Every arrow he launched at the menacing beast left his hands shaking.

"Daro, see the driftwood up ahead?"

"Yes, brother, go around them," he replied.

"No, go through the middle!" Otec began fiddling with a large saddlebag, and Daro immediately changed the direction they were heading.

Twenty-five feet. The fading sunlight illuminated a red tinge among the glistening wetness of the beast's black fur, now matted with blades of grass and seeds. Another arrow hummed until it struck the wolf's chest.

His father had one buckle undone, already working on the second. Cymm reloaded. *What are you doing Father? Stop wasting time on that saddlebag.* The bowstring almost slipped off his sweaty fingers. The fear—so raw and unforgiving—had returned, filling his entire body. An avalanche gaining momentum inside him, it roared in his ears, attempting to break him.

Ten feet. The wolf's eyes—now visible, menacing red orbs with black pupils and no iris—stared back at him. *Is that the sheen of blood on its coat?*

The smell of the creature filled his nostrils, and his stomach lurched. A putrid smell of decay. The blood wolf launched itself in one mighty leap at the hindquarters of his father's horse with claws and teeth bared. Bone-white incisors clearly visible against a black backdrop of its body, sent an eerie chill through him.

"Father, watch out!" He fired his arrow, and it entered the wolf's open mouth and exited the side of its neck. The beast emitted an ear-piercing yelp and fell several feet short of the horse.

The blood wolf shook its head violently, trying to dislodge the arrow stuck in its mouth. Giving up, it gave chase, spitefully biting down hard on the shaft, snapping it in half.

Twenty feet. The rest of the pack materialized behind their leader, attempting to overtake him. However, the relentless blood wolf leaped to the front, closing the gap again.

Cymm reached to his quiver.

The driftwood loomed overhead.

"Turn around, Son, and get ready to ride," Otec demanded while dumping the contents of his saddlebag directly behind him. Metal tinged against metal as scores of caltrops fell to the ground creating a dangerous carpet of spikes between the driftwood.

The monstrous wolf covered a lot of ground with each bound. His father breathed in sharp as the beast almost cleared the minefield. Its body compressed to push off and leap forward, but the brute collapsed with a pitiful howl. It stared at Cymm with hatred, stood immediately, and attempted to give chase, but the effort ended with another yelp.

The growls and snarls of the wolf pack transformed into cries of pain as they too met the field of caltrops. Otec cringed. "Let's go! Pick up the pace!"

Cymm reluctantly rotated his upper body, heart pounding in his chest; only a handful still pursued them, the sound of whimpering drifting further away.

Every rider straddled their saddle as they galloped through the Driftwood. The horses instinctually compensated for the unseen rough terrain. *How long can we continue at this pace before a horse goes down?* The edge of the grasslands appeared in the distance, and Otec finally slowed the pace. As they exited the Driftwood, everyone formed a circle around their leader.

Cymm, positioned his horse next to his father's. "What were those things you dropped?"

"They are called *caltrops*. Four sharp points are formed into the shape of a pyramid. Typically, three sides touch the ground and force the fourth spike straight up in the air. They are wicked devices capable of stopping a horse. The upright barb buries itself deep into the hoof. I do not like to use them, but we didn't have a choice," Otec answered with an audible sigh.

"That pack was large and well organized," Daro said from the other side of Otec. "We need to gather a group of hunters, come back, and clear them out. May need a few villages to help."

"I knew something was amiss when they tried channeling us in a specific direction, but I never would have thought the leader was a blood wolf," said the head of the Reich household.

Recalling the wolf, Cymm uttered, "That wolf's fur was soaked in blood."

"It is unknown how the disease spreads, but once a wolf or dog gets it, they turn savage and feral. Blood seeps from their pores like sweat, causing an insatiable appetite. I would guess he is eating an injured wolf now. Let's be glad that creature didn't begin its life as a dire wolf. Those wolves are almost a foot taller at the shoulders."

"By Melcorac's Hammer! That would make them almost as big as a horse," the young man exclaimed.

Uncle Daro issued a deep grunt. "Maybe these horses, but nowhere near the size of our warhorses."

They rode into Saddle Rise to the alarm bell ringing. They were met with pitchforks and axes held high by a hostile crowd.

"Bandits!" a villager yelled.

Otec raised his hands. "Hold up! We are from Stallion Rise! We need help!" Several horses pranced in place, pulling at the reins to leave.

"Turn around and get out!" said a different villager.

At least twenty agitated villagers barred their way. "This is your final warning!"

Otec started to turn his horse. "We were attacked by orcs and an ogre. Many are injured."

No one replied, but several villagers pointed back the way they came.

Each rider pulled their horse around, following Otec out of the village.

Everyone except Cymm. "Are you afraid of children too?" Cymm stared down the biggest of the troublemakers. Smirks appeared on many faces; two villagers laughed out loud.

An old woman holding a battle-axe yelled, "I like him!" She pushed to the front of the crowd. "What do you need, Hon?"

"We are trying to find Hardre Ironcore." Cymm tentatively watched his retreating party; they finally noticed he was missing.

Another villager said, "He left a week ago for Horseshoe Rise."

The old woman stroked her chin. "I'll tell you what. Since it's getting late in the evening, you and your friends can stay in my barn."

"Thank you, but—" Cymm began.

Otec's horse pushed up next to his. "Thank you! We will be out at the crack of dawn."

"Father, we can't wait. We . . ." He received a stern look and fell silent. His gaze darted to Talo, then moved furtively through the rest of the party. Not one ally. His shoulders slumped with a sigh.

When they arrived at the barn, Cymm could not hold his tongue. He jumped up on a hay bale before he spoke. "Old-Man Semper . . . that's what everyone calls him because no one knows his first name. Maybe it doesn't matter. After all, he is a crotchety old fool, and most of the village doesn't like him." Talo wrinkled his nose at the last part.

Cymm had everyone's full attention. Surprisingly, no one said a word, not even his father, so he quickly continued. "This shouldn't surprise anyone. He is mean, stubborn, and picks fights over the smallest of slights like with you, Uncle Daro. He doesn't wave or say 'hello', rarely lends a neighborly hand, and misses many of our village festivals."

His voice increased in passion and volume, as he surveyed each adult. "I wonder how he feels about you." "He probably doesn't like you very much either. And yet, he answered the call of duty. Yes, he did. As soon as that bell rang, he was first on his horse. Talo and I could barely keep up with him. But he knew his duty and rushed to help, not knowing or caring who was in trouble." He glanced down in thought, pausing for a moment.

"When we rounded the corner of the Wither's home . . ." he paused recalling the day, ". . . that monstrosity caused us all to halt. It towered over our fellow villagers wreaking havoc."

Talo gave him a sideways glance.

"Old-Man Semper must have been thinking, 'why am I risking my life for people who hate me?' And yet, he answered the call, performing his duty to the best of his ability. Now he lies in bed close to death, as do several others. He is counting on us to respect his sacrifice and find him the help he needs. The bell is tolling, and I have one question for each of you: Will you answer the call and perform your duty?" Cymm anxiously awaited a response as he stepped down from his hay bale.

Talo's eyes twinkled while he studied everyone. Uncle Daro patted his brother on the shoulder, then whispered in his ear. Otec's hands were on his hips, and he shook his head from side to side, beaming. One tear slowly crept down his cheek like a slow meandering stream through the flatlands. The other two villagers shook off their weariness and now waited with wide, eager eyes.

"Well, you heard the boy." Otec cleared his throat. "I mean, young man. Are we going to answer the call?" Three riders immediately mounted their horses while his father and uncle approached.

"Well said Ogre-Slayer." Uncle Daro placed a hand on his shoulder, then walked back to the others to mount his horse.

His father embraced him, resting his forehead against Cymm's. "When did you become so wise?"

Cymm replied with a dubious smile, "It was inevitable being surrounded by all of you scholarly sages."

Otec held his belly, laughing deeply. "Scholarly? Sages? All of us horse farmers combined couldn't read a book. And for the record, Semper is a crotchety old son-of-a red dragon."

They rode out of the village in the dark, bound for Horseshoe Rise, three hours away.

The largest moon, Phoenix, had already risen an hour earlier, but the deep crimson light did not assist their visibility; it only enhanced the dark shadows. Cymm squinted. "I can't see anything, Father. Are the horses safe?"

Otec took a drink from his waterskin. "Yes, we will keep this slow pace until Primordian rises in about an hour to brighten our way."

"That's the second largest, but the brightest moon," Cymm said. His father nodded.

"What about the other two moons, Plover and Pulse?" asked Talo.

"They won't be seen this night," replied Otec.

"At least we don't have to go through the Driftwood again," Daro said, shuddering.

An hour after midnight, they saw the torches of Horseshoe Rise flickering on the horizon ahead. Most villages in the Horse Clan didn't have a formal night watch, but the barks and bays of the farmer's dogs alerted the village of their arrival.

An alert farmer stepped off his front porch, sword in hand. His eyes flitted to the alarm bell before returning to the weary group of travelers. "State your business."

"I am Otec Reich from Stallion Rise. There has been an attack on our village leaving many wounded. We are trying to find the priest, Hardre Ironcore; he traveled this way a week ago," Otec said calmly with respect.

The farmer scrutinized him. "You will find him at the third barn on your left. Be on your way." He slammed the door behind him.

Cymm couldn't hide his excitement. "We found him? Let's go!"

"Otec, he had a sword," Daro said with a bewildered expression.

"I saw. Take care and keep a close watch. It's too late for visitors." Otec's eyes were already shifting from side to side.

They rounded the corner of the third barn to find ten men and women with pitchforks, axes, and crossbows.

The oldest among them yelled, "That's far enough. State your business!"

A dozen horsemen rode up behind them, blocking their exit, including the helpful farmer who gave them directions.

Cymm's elation quickly dissipated when a crossbow bolt zipped past his father's face. *By Ledaedra's bones!* he cursed.

9

Let Nature Take Its Course

Lykinnia returned to Lower Darken Wood feeling rejuvenated until she approached the tattered egg sac, and her heart rendered anew. It barely clung to the branch it was previously secured to. Ravenous birds had shredded it to root out any remaining nymphs.

With pursed lips, she closed her eyes momentarily, desperate to open them to the thriving hatchery she'd spent almost two years creating. "Three hundred eggs," she muttered to herself.

She zoomed down to the forest floor, retracing her prior path. The dead and injured had already been devoured.

The amber, ethereal figure raced to the oasis of greenery, zipping over the barren forest floor. Her panic deepened while she frantically searched. *None of them made it through the night? None?*

The undergrowth covered a circular area roughly fifty feet in diameter. Sunlight streamed past the remnants of a decaying tree, sustaining the vegetation. Her heart continued to race while she choked back the tears. *None!*

Maybe they are hiding? She took several deep breaths to focus her mind, then hunted for predators. With none to be found, she called to the nymphs. A creature appeared less than three feet in front of her face. Its light green body blended perfectly with the underside of the leaf it gripped. *One!*

It hovered in front of her for a moment, then tried unsuccessfully to land on her, passing right through her spirit form.

Two! Three! Lykinnia began humming, then abruptly stopped, scanning the area around her.

"Too much noise! We will need to be careful until you are big enough to defend yourselves," she said in the high-pitched shrill language they had yet to learn.

The nymphs continued to gather around her, and she gleefully counted thirty-three. Not exactly what she was hoping for, but better than the dark thoughts she had only a few minutes earlier.

"You look so cute. Your little gossamer wings keeping you aloft. Hopefully, your natural instincts will serve you well and protect you. I will help as much as I can. However, it will have to be in this form because I am forbidden from leaving my home, the Peak of Power. We—"

A bird cawed in the distance, and the nymphs dispersed like a school of fish escaping a barracuda.

10

Hardre Ironcore

Otec held his hands out in defense. "Whoa! Whoa! Whoa! We are from Stallion Rise and need help. A huge ogre attacked—"

"Otec? Daro? What are you doing here so late?" the leader asked in a you-should-know-better tone.

Otec dismounted and took a few steps forward with his hand extended. "Cadd? It's been like fifteen years since those Festival days!" Two younger men blocked his path.

"More like twenty." With a nod from Cadd, everyone dispersed, shuffling back to bed or wherever they came from.

Cadd motioned for them to follow him while he walked toward the horse barn.

"Earlier today, we had an attack at the Wither Farm. An ogre, joined by many orcs, killed and injured many villagers. Rumors persist that Hardre is a healer," Otec explained.

After entering the barn, Cadd spoke into the darkness, "Hardre, these people are looking for you."

Both boys were in the back row behind all five adults. Cymm struggled to catch a glimpse; determined to see, he climbed the dividing wall of the nearest stall.

A short, broad figure emerged from the corner stall holding a two-handed Warhammer across his chest. He eyed Cadd with a dismissive huff. "Yeah, I know them. They are from Stallion Rise." A muscle twitched in his jaw. "What do you want?"

He was clean shaven up to the crown of his head. He braided the remaining jet-black hair at the top into a long ponytail pulled back at the crown.

"Well—" Otec shifted uncomfortably in the awkward silence.

"Can you actually heal people?" Cymm asked bluntly, unaffected by the dwarf's attitude.

The dwarf scowled. "Haven't you heard of Terazhan?"

Dogs barked in the distance.

Hardre's brow creased as his head cocked for listening. He exchanged unspoken words with Cadd, sending Otec's old friend bolting out the barn door.

The dwarf gestured to the door. "Get out!" With a mix of fear and fury on his face, he disappeared back into the darkness.

Outside the barn, the barking of dogs echoed throughout the village. Nearby, a distinct yelp caught their attention. Except for their horses, the barnyard was vacant. Cadd had disappeared. The moonlight barely penetrated the dark, barren windows of the surrounding houses.

The steady beat of many horses' hooves reverberated in the still night, drawing closer. Instinctively, Cymm unslung his bow, but his father grabbed his shoulder angrily. "No!"

Cadd stepped out of the shadows near the main house when the riders arrived. A horseman announced, "We lost them! There were four of them; two are dead, and two got away."

Noise erupted in the barn—grunts, groans, metal clanging against metal. Cadd listened in silence for a moment, then raced for the door only to find it barred from the inside.

"They are in there with Hardre! Get this door open!" Cadd barked with flailing arms.

The battle continued in the barn while several men threw themselves at the double doors.

Cadd pointed at the window above the entrance they were bashing, "It is too small to crawl through, except for maybe one of the boys."

"Then go get one of your boys," replied Otec with his back to the door, oblivious to the fact that Cymm was already climbing. The sounds of fighting began to slow and ceased altogether as the young man's hands grasped the windowsill.

"Cymm, get down here!" his father roared, trying to grab his ankle, but Cymm pulled himself up, placing one arm over the sill. Darkness shrouded everything; labored breathing emanated from the last stall in the barn.

"What's going on in there?" Cadd whispered up to him.

Cymm shrugged his shoulders, intentionally avoiding his father's glare below. A deep singular breath followed by a groan drew his attention back. It reminded him of his father hammering in a fence post. *Splat.* The wet sound mixed with bone crunching reminded him of the ogre standing over Semper's warhorse, and the pounding impact of the monster's mighty club. His stomach churned.

A voice began speaking in a language he didn't recognize; then a warm amber light exploded from the corner stall illuminating half the barn. The light consumed the darkness, revealing a motionless bloody body on the floor.

The darkness returned in seconds, and a gruff voice called out, "Cadd, I'm alright."

The dwarf unbarred the door and men rushed inside. Once the torches were relit, and the barn thoroughly searched, the energy level subsided.

Hardre gave the Stallion Rise group the evil eye. "What are you still doing here?"

Otec corralled his son with an outstretched arm. "We should go."

Everyone from Stallion Rise headed for their horses, except Cymm. He spun out of his father's arm and rushed straight for Hardre.

Otec attempted to grab him. "What has gotten into you today?"

"What is your problem?" the boy said, pointing his finger in the dwarf's face. "We need your help, and you apparently have the ability, yet you won't hear us out. What kind of god do you worship?"

The dwarf turned as red as the moon Phoenix and wrung his hands on the shaft of his Warhammer, making his muscles bulge through his shirt. The cold, dead stare told Cymm he might have pushed him a little too far.

Cadd put his hand on the dwarf's shoulder. "He was willing to help you."

"Pfff, how?" Hardre's eyes rolled.

Cadd pointed above the barn door. "He was halfway through the window when the fighting stopped."

The dwarf's face softened, and he exhaled sharply.

Cymm dove in, unrelenting, "We have many injured from the attack on our village, and Old-Man Semper sent us to find you."

The dwarf's eyes widened suddenly, "Semper sent you? Why didn't he come himself?" The answer registered before Cymm could open his mouth. "What happened to Semper?"

Hardre began tapping his foot.

After a long pause, Cymm finally replied, "He got into a fight with an ogre, took a hard fall from his horse, then the beast stomped on him."

Talo sneaked up blaring, "The ogre would have stomped him again, except Cymm took him down using Semper's sword!" He motioned toward his cousin with his hands swinging an imaginary sword. "Almost cut his head clean off!"

The stocky dwarf, barely standing four foot ten inches tall, nodded and pursed his lips. He inspected Cymm from his boots to his hair, then started speaking rapidly, "How long ago did you leave him? Do you think he is still alive?"

"He faded in and out of consciousness as we left eleven hours ago," replied Otec.

The dwarf moved swiftly toward his pony; the change in his demeanor so quick it made Cymm wonder how deep his history went with Semper. "I'm already packed. We need to leave now!"

The brothers said their goodbyes to Cadd then hurried to their horses.

Talo grabbed Cymm's arm to slow him down. "Did you see the look on Hardre's face when your father said Semper was losing consciousness?"

Cymm scratched his head, deep in thought.

Still speaking confidentially, Talo asked, ". . . and who attacked him?"

Cymm gave a distracted, *"Hmmphf."*

Talo kept going. "I heard the men talking, and they said he killed two dwarves in the barn."

The rest of his cousin's comments faded away. The amber glow in the barn continued to beckon him, pulsing in his mind. A vague memory from a few years earlier—of a white dragonfly—flooded his thoughts.

Talo shook him out of his trance. "Come on! Everyone is leaving."

As soon as they passed the last farm in the village, the priest chanted, and light as bright as day engulfed them. The horses whinnied in fright; their riders gasped in surprise.

With the extra light, they moved considerably faster. Several predicted they might be home before sunrise.

Cymm rode next to Hardre. "My cousin Talo and I have been training with Old-Man Semper for a couple of years now. We are members of the militia."

"Why do you call him *Old Man*? Very disrespectful." The dwarf had a dour expression.

"He insisted we call him that. How do you know him?"

"We go back many years before he became a farmer and I a disciple of Lord Terazhan," the priest answered cryptically.

Cymm's desire for answers intensified. "Where are you from?"

"I was born and raised in the city of Delge in the Knife-Edge Mountains, a little over twelve days ride from here. You will find most mountain dwarves in this realm hail from the same place."

"Did you meet Semper in Delge?"

The dwarf shifted uncomfortably in his saddle. "So, you attacked and killed an ogre? That is quite a feat for any man, let alone a young man like yourself."

Cymm nodded, his open mouth ready to reply, but the dwarf nudged his pony ahead. As Hardre moved away, his ponytail swayed side to side in complete harmony with the tail on the pony he rode. Cymm could not contain his giggle.

They arrived at the Wither Farm with the rising sun. Cymm and Talo quickly dismounted and raced into the house. Many villagers still crowded the gathering room, but the conversations stopped abruptly when they entered.

Cymm skipped the pleasantries, blurting out, "How is Semper?"

Zeke Darkmane spoke in a hushed tenor, "Not good. He stopped breathing twice during the night, but that stubborn old goat refuses to die."

Hardre listened in silence, his distraught face revealing strong emotions. In a sudden flurry of movement, he pushed through the crowd, rushing into the side room where Semper lay. The dwarf, with a touch of insanity in his eyes, placed both hands on Semper's chest without delay. "Lord Terazhan, Lord of Healing, I humbly request your help to heal my brother!"

A golden aura began to emanate from Semper's prone body. The soft glow initiated in his chest, then radiated throughout his body to his extremities before surging forth, engulfing the room. Instantaneously, he drew a deep breath, then let out a cough and a whimper.

Cymm's chest swelled as the hypnotic feeling returned.

The Armakian Plainsmen stood there slack jawed and silent.

The priest rolled his neck in a circle, a satisfied smile spreading across his face. He stared at Semper with a loving expression, unconsciously spinning the ring on the human's index finger. "I had to pull him back from Death's Door, and now he needs to rest."

Cymm's stomach filled with sweet relief. The healing event replayed in his mind.

Talo spoke first, "So, he will be alright?"

The priest responded exuberantly, "Yes. Now, who else needs the healing power of Terazhan?"

His father and uncle exchanged surprised glances, then immediately led a smaller group to the patients with life-threatening injuries. Exhaustion fogged Cymm's mind and body, compelling him to find a quiet spot to sit down.

Hardre returned a few minutes later to the main room. "When my power returns tomorrow, I will heal the others. I should be able . . ." Cymm promptly fell asleep.

Cymm woke a little before dinner the following morning and took a mental inventory of the past two days. His memories came rushing back. *Wow, what a trip. That was the best day ever.* He took a deep breath and sighed. *I wonder how Old-Man Semper is feeling.* He hopped out of bed, got dressed, and ran for the door.

"Where are you going, hot foot?" his fatigued and disheveled mother asked.

"Oh, Mother, you know where I am going," he said, rolling his eyes.

His sister joined them with a smile on her face, toying with the trophy around her neck. "To fetch Momma some water from the well?" She had polished the ogre's nose ring to a sheen, wrapped it with a thick leather thong, and tied it behind her neck.

"Stop teasing! Can I please go? I will be back in time for dinner," he begged.

"I was very worried about you and your father yesterday."

"Mother?" Cymm pressed.

Shay brushed his hair to the side. "Drag your father back as well. He is already there."

Cymm didn't bother saddling his horse; it would take too long. He ran, without stopping, all the way to the Wither Farm, more than a mile away. Several people called out to him as he passed, and a small crowd gathered when he entered the Wither's home. Villagers patted his shoulder or back while others shook his hand vigorously.

Kala Wither, tried to speak, but the words caught in her throat. She gave up and resorted to hugging him fiercely.

He gazed at them all, trying to force the corners of his mouth up, but he found the attention surprisingly unnerving. His father leaned in to whisper in his ear, "The life of a hero has its advantages and disadvantages. We can talk more when we get home."

Cymm nodded slowly then gently pushed his way to Old-Man Semper. Hardre was in the room administering to the patient who was sitting up, wide awake.

"Old-Man Semper! You're awake? How do you feel?" His words were nearly incoherent.

The old man's face brightened, and he vigorously motioned for Cymm to approach. He shook his hand firmly and would not let go. Talo entered the room soon after to complete the grand reunion.

When Semper finally spoke, he said, "I guess two half-pints are better than no pints after all!"

They shared a laugh, but Semper began coughing uncontrollably, a small sputter of blood soaking his lips.

The dwarf interrupted the reunion with a thunderous voice that carried throughout the house. "Alright, everybody out. He needs more rest and another dose of Terazhan's almighty healing."

Cymm lingered at the doorway, excited to see the spectacular healing event again. He was not disappointed—it was magnificent. Quite suddenly, it dawned on him that the golden light inside the barn after the attack must have been him healing himself.

Hardre turned his attention from Semper to Cymm. "Care to join me outside for a breath of fresh air?"

Cymm flinched in surprise but fell in next to him. "What does it feel like? The golden aura you bring forth?" Cymm asked, testing the dwarf to see if the animosity he showed yesterday still existed.

"It's hard to explain, but it feels fantastic! My entire body tingles, and I feel like I'm about to leave my body or something like that," the priest struggled to explain.

The young man's vision of his future flashed through his mind. With eyes shining and hope swelling, he took a chance. "I want to become a healer like you. Will you teach me?"

The dwarf stared at him with his mouth agape.

Confused by his reaction, Cymm stated, "If it can be taught, I can learn it."

The dwarf squinched his face. "Do you even know who Terazhan is? Or believe in his existence?"

"I have heard of Terazhan's Twilight, which was four sunrises ago on my lifeday." The dwarf was not amused. Cymm shifted his weight from one leg to the other, picked at his fingernail, then continued, "After what I have seen with my own eyes, it is hard not to believe."

"Well, that's a start. After this evening, I will have plenty of time for religious lectures." He stroked his chin where a beard should have been. "We will see if my lord's faith is founded."

Confusion racked Cymm's face, and his brows knitted together. "Ahh . . . okay . . . I will be back first thing in the morning to check on Old . . . on Semper, and we can talk more then. I need to get home for dinner. Have a good night."

Hardre shook his head and scratched his chin again. "You as well, young man . . . you as well."

11

Paragon of Learning

Cymm's schedule returned to normal the following day. He was up at the crack of dawn, grabbed a light breakfast, then went outside to do his chores. A few hours later he grabbed a second breakfast before traveling over to the Wither Farm on his horse. Most of the farmers had returned to work. Hardre was down to three patients.

How disappointing. Where is everyone? Does the caring only last for two days after such a significant tragedy?

He entered the house, but low voices made him freeze his position.

". . . could he have known?" Hardre asked.

"I do not pretend to understand the gods," replied Old-Man Semper.

"It was very bizarre. He said the exact words I heard in the Divine Quest. Well, let's see if he even comes back today," the dwarf said.

Semper chuckled. "You obviously don't know Cymm like I do. You best be prepared for training."

Cymm closed the door hard with a distinctive *clunk* and took a couple of loud steps. "Where is everyone?"

He knocked lightly on the doorway to the bedroom before entering. Semper stood next to the bed. "Hey, half-pint."

Cymm's jubilation overflowed as he rushed forward. "Old-Man Semper! You're up."

"Old-Man?" said the dwarf with a disapproving tone.

"Oh, leave him alone!" Semper chastised the dwarf. To Cymm he said, "I am going home today, thanks to you. Hardre claims I need one more dose of healing." He dropped his voice to a loud whisper, pretending to shield his words with a hand by his mouth. "I think he just likes touching me."

The dwarf, already in a foul mood, began grumbling. A mischievous grin eventually took over his visage. "Oh really? Well, last night you were talking in your sleep, 'Hardre, Hardre, please use your big strong hands to heal me!'"

The old man glared in response. "That's not true!"

"Yep, at one point, I heard giggling coming from your room." His friend continued to pile on the retaliation.

"I do not giggle!" Old-Man Semper laughed hysterically, then launched into a hacking attack. His friends froze, waiting, but he recovered quickly without blood on his lips this time.

He rubbed his chest. "Oh, that hurt. Maybe I do need another round of healing." This incited the laughter to begin all over again.

Cymm studied him with newfound respect. *Who is this funny, jovial man standing next to me? Did this near-death experience change him, or did Hardre bring out the best in him?*

He directed his question to the dwarf. "Where will you be staying after today?"

"With Semper, like I usually do when I am in Stallion Rise," replied the dwarf casually.

"Like you usually do?" Cymm thought. "How come I have never seen you before?"

∞∞∞∞

In the middle of Anuberis, the seventh month, and four weeks into training, Cymm arrived a little earlier than usual. He overheard Semper and Hardre talking about the dwarf's missing beard. Eager to learn more, he hid around the corner of the entrance.

". . . they summoned me to stand trial for continuing to teach the beliefs of a *false god*." The priest's voice carried out into the barnyard.

"The City of Delge has changed a lot since we left," responded Semper.

"Well, for rejecting the dwarven gods, the Hearth Council labelled me a *pariah*, shackled and marched me out in front of everyone before shaving my beard off. After all that, they exiled me!" Hardre sounded agitated.

"A pariah? What in the nine hells does that mean?" Semper asked.

The dwarf finished shaving and started cleaning up. "If any dwarf ever finds me with a beard again, they can legally execute me on the spot."

Cymm shuffled his feet before entering, and the conversation halted immediately.

"Shave day?" asked the young man, hoping he might be included in the conversation.

Hardre nodded, then gave his cheeks a brisk slap. "Yep, all done. Ready for your lesson?"

He tried to hide his disappointment, but didn't trust his voice, so he nodded in return. *Was this the reason he was attacked in the barn when they first met?*

Cymm's free time was limited these days, but he didn't mind. He got up early every day to complete his chores before lunch, devoted the entire afternoon to training with his two teachers, and spent the evenings at home with his family.

Anuberis rolled into Oderian which gave way to the month of The Holy One. Cymm had learned a great deal about Terazhan, or "The One True God." Hardre believed Terazhan deserved this title for not abandoning the world of Erogoth. He heard about Melcorac, the first priest of his faith, with his mighty warhammer. The dwarf spent an exorbitant amount of time talking about the holy doctrines surrounding their faith. For example, prayers must occur daily and only to Terazhan; he also learned how to perform those prayers, the good habits and virtues of a priest, and how to bless or sanctify a person or object. However, Hardre emphasized the primary doctrine their faith was based on, "Respect Life and Protect the Innocent," which already aligned with his beliefs. The theology lessons consisted of many philosophical discussions about the definition of life and innocence, and debates occasionally erupted concerning the impact of evil on one's belief. There was also a dark premonition known as The Rending, a prophecy about a cataclysmic event where Terazhan would only be able to protect his followers.

Cymm began sharing his knowledge with the entire village. He was not forceful or disrespectful to anyone about their current beliefs. He simply found convenient ways to make a comparison or to share a parable or to say a prayer. Some of the village still worshipped other gods, but most did not pray to anyone. The young man understood their skepticism what with the scourge of dragons that had plagued the lands for centuries.

After six months of religious training, during the month of Final Harvest, Cymm arrived at Old-Man Semper's barn to find Hardre packed and ready to leave.

He dropped his own satchel, his eyes darting back and forth. "What's going on? Where are you going?"

"I have stayed too long already. Several bounty hunters have passed through Stallion Rise during the past few months," the priest explained.

He examined Old-Man Semper's face, then Hardre's with a wrinkled brow. "Bounty hunters in Stallion Rise? What are you talking about?"

His dwarven friend motioned for him to sit down. "I have been exiled from my homeland for teaching Terazhan's ways. Many dwarves tried to have me executed. Now, they hire mercenaries to carry out vigilante justice. It is only a matter of time before they realize I am here."

Cymm's lips trembled while roaring, "Let them come! This is the safest place for you. We will stand with you."

"Cymm." His first mentor put his hand on his shoulder.

He recoiled from his touch. "What about my training?"

"I have chosen to leave now because there is nothing left to teach you. From this point forward, your relationship with Lord Terazhan is yours to discover," replied Hardre, his voice filled with compassion.

Cymm shook his head in confusion, ignoring the gentle confidence Hardre exuded. "So, I am a priest now? A Cleric of Terazhan?"

"No, you were never destined to be a priest. You are to become a holy warrior, what his Lordship calls a *paladin*. The first paladin this world has ever seen," Hardre said with one fist pumped in the air. "I am told you will begin to see changes immediately, and He will continue your tutelage from here."

The startling news should have rendered him speechless, reeling in thoughts and ideas of what being a paladin meant. Instead, a sadness pulled at his features, and his shoulders slumped. "So, this is it? I will not see you again?"

The old friends gave each other a wink then burst out laughing. "I will be back in two months. I haven't missed Festival in Stallion Rise for the past ten years, and I don't intend to miss this one!" Then a sly smile came across Hardre's face. "Who do you think was going to kick your Uncle Daro's ass for calling him an elf?"

Cymm did not like the joke being played on him. "It was Semper, of course, and you have never been here for Festival."

Old-Man Semper gave Hardre a stern look. "Can we plow one field at a time, please?"

There was an awkward silence while everyone regarded each other until Cymm finally asked, "Where are you heading?" His nerves were still on edge, but he forced himself to breathe deeply.

"Up north to Armak, then to a couple of the Wolf Villages. I will heal many people and shout out '*in the name of Terazhan.*' Then I can come back here to hang low for a little while again," he said with a wink, "and when I do return, we can talk about what you have learned. I can help you interpret anything you have difficulty with."

Later that night, at the dinner table, Cymm explained the day's events to his father who took a moment to comprehend his words. "How will he communicate with you?"

"I'm not completely sure, but Hardre told me there is no talking. Terazhan sends him Visions, and Divine Quests, which I guess are the same thing, but he has to interpret the meaning," he replied.

His father stopped eating entirely engrossed in the conversation. "Interpret? What if you get it wrong?"

"I don't know." He shrugged leaving his shoulders in the "up" position. "Hardre said it is usually obvious what is expected."

"Well . . . you could try healing your mother if you need a little practice," Otec said in a half-serious, half-joking manner.

He stood immediately, inspecting his mother. "Why? What happened?"

Shay sighed, giving everyone a dismissive wave. "Oh, it's nothing. Don't get the kids upset."

"Your mother cut her hand peeling potatoes for dinner," he said anyway.

"Let me see, Mother." Cymm went to her, then reached out his hand, leaving it in the air. His mother peered at him skeptically. She trusted in a different god. He insisted using an expressive hand movement. She begrudgingly unwrapped the cloth hidden under the table, revealing the wound.

"It's not bad," she said. "I'll be fine."

It was a profound cut. The son did not hesitate, exuding confidence that should not have existed. He placed one hand on her palm; the other covered the back of her hand like a sandwich. "Lord Terazhan, please grant your humble follower the power to heal his mother!"

Cymm's hands began to glow.

Shay gulped, trying to pull her hand away. He was too strong and forceful. He gave his mother a reassuring look, and she breathed in deeply. The furrow in her brow disappeared, her shoulders sank, and wonderment appeared. His sister cried out in surprise, then fell silent, staring at the spectacle before her.

Even his father breathed in sharply with wide eyes and mouth agape. This had all been a passing joke to him moments ago.

Cymm could feel something happening. Euphoria washed over him, and energy coursed through his body. A warm sensation passed from Cymm's hands into his mother's. He could hardly describe it, and yet it was the best feeling he'd ever experienced. When the glow dissipated, he removed his hands.

Otec and Bria leaned on the table to get a better view, and Shay began to cry. Her hand was completely healed; not even a scar remained.

Just as Cymm began to relish the excitement—the fact he'd done something so extraordinary—his entire body grew weak. He blinked several times and collapsed to his knees before rolling onto his buttock. The room was silent until his sister startled him by grabbing his hand and hugging his arm. Otec knelt next to his wife, examining her hand. He shook his head in pure disbelief before helping his son to stand and escorting him back to his seat.

"Cymm . . . that was . . . amazing," his father spoke in a subdued voice. "Are you alright?"

He grabbed his cup and drank. "Yes, I am now. The feeling of exhaustion has passed."

"Are you nervous or scared?" asked Bria.

She could read him better than anyone. He thought for a prolonged time, then shook his head in a quick little burst.

His mother tried to dry the tears from her eyes. "How did you know you could do that?"

He searched for an explanation, but nothing came. "I didn't. I just believed I could."

"What did it feel like?" Bria gazed deep into his eyes.

Cymm smiled for the first time since the glow materialized. "Amazing!"

Otec glanced at his son's hands. "It looked different than Hardre's. Did you notice?"

"Yes, the aura was pure white, instead of gold." Cymm scratched the back of his head.

"And . . . when Hardre healed Semper, the glow began inside of the old man spreading throughout his body. This time the glow came from you, from your hands. It was concentrated on your mother's injury."

Otec beamed with pride.

12

After the Dragon Attack

(Present Day – three and a half years
after healing his mother's hand)

Cymm reached out gently hugging the farmer, wondering how he or she could still be alive. He immediately placed both hands on the farmer's face, one on each swollen, puss-filled cheek. He prayed to his god, Terazhan, for healing power, his voice loud and far reaching.

Cymm focused his healing power on the farmer's head, the pure white glow appearing instantly. Hardre had told him long ago the color variation of a priest's aura directly reflected the caster's soul and its pureness. Most considered a golden aura—devout and pious—particularly pleasing to Terazhan. The deity expected his priests to have at least a yellow aura with minimal shards of orange. White, however, was rare and considered immaculate and virtuous. *How does that relate to me?* he had thought at the time. The dwarf had told him only one other had possessed an aura like his, Melcorac "The Holy One." Terazhan's original priest was now enshrined at the Plateau of the Magnificent Sunset, overlooking the Red Sea.

He channeled the healing energy; a warm sensation passed from his hands into the farmer's face. A shudder coursed through Cymm; the exhilaration he was feeling never got old. Before he removed his hands, the healing was already in motion.

Yellowish-green puss ran in rivulets down the farmer's face from both eyes and nostrils, as his body continued to purge itself of the dead blood cells and bacteria. Finally, the huge pustule on his neck and chin burst open, covering Cymm in a vile smelling ooze; then the skin fused, healing itself. The monster before him began to regain human features, and the incessant moaning ceased, allowing Cymm to recognize the partially healed face.

It was his neighbor Sero.

Cymm viewed the surrounding death and destruction. "Sero, how did you survive?"

His fellow villager shook as small tremors ran through his body. "I don-don-don't kn-know." He began to cry again.

"Are there other survivors?"

The injured man shook his head.

"You're healing has begun, but you still have poison coursing through your body. You need rest. We can talk more when you awake. I will try to heal you again in the morning."

He helped Sero to his feet and brought him into his own home to sleep in his parents' bed.

Horses stampeded into the barnyard. Fear radiated from the animals; it was palpable before he exited the building.

Talo sat frozen in his saddle, his gaze shifting from Cymm back to the bodies of his uncle, aunt, and cousin. Tears streamed down his face. He jumped off his horse, stumbled to his cousin, then embraced him as if he hadn't seen him in years. Semper dismounted, slowly shaking his head in disbelief. The old man walked over and joined the embrace.

A distant voice called out, "Cymm? Talo? Are you home?" The trio of mourner's faces twisted at the familiar voice.

"Dad!" yelled Talo when his father came huffing into the barnyard.

"Uncle Daro!" Cymm ran with his cousin to greet him.

"Cymm, we could hear you praying all the way from the rendezvous," he said.

"We?" Talo asked as one of his younger brothers entered the barnyard, and close behind him came the rest of his ten brothers and sisters. His mother, Nové, finally arrived holding little Sara, who had recently celebrated her first lifeyear.

Semper held his greetings. "I need to go check on my household. I trust you can unpack and take care of the stray horses without me." Saying that, he left.

While Talo enjoyed the family reunion, his uncle took him by the shoulder, turned him, and walked toward the house.

"I am so sorry, Cymm. I can't imagine how you feel right now," Uncle Daro started the conversation with watery eyes.

The numb feeling of despair continued, as if he'd somehow tucked every emotion away, deep inside so he could keep moving. "How did you survive? All of you?"

"Your mother saved us, and probably others," Daro said with sadness in his voice.

Cymm froze mid-stride, scowling at his uncle. "How?"

Daro took a deep breath before beginning the story. "Your mother rushed through the door of my farmhouse, 'A dragon's attacking the village; tell everyone to put out the torches.' I knew your mother was not one to jest, so I immediately assigned your cousins to deliver the message to the five closer households, then return to the barn while I rode for the Wither Farm." Uncle Daro took off his hat and leaned against Cymm's house.

"Your aunt took the younger children to the rendezvous point using the grass blankets, and your mother headed for the alarm bell. About halfway to my destination, the alarm bell started ringing and continued for over sixty seconds. I couldn't figure out why she stayed there so long, but on my way back, I saw your mother pressed against the short side of your barn, peeking around the corner. After I made sure all five children were back, I grabbed a grass blanket and ran to check on her."

"She was still hiding in the dark shadows at the corner, and I couldn't tell if she was talking to herself or praying, but as soon as I said a word, she put a finger to her lips and pointed around the corner of the barn. By Melcorac's Hammer, Cymm, the dragon was huge! Bigger than your barn, much bigger," he said, pointing to it, emphasizing the magnitude with his eyes.

"I was intent on charging in to save my brother, but your mother grabbed my arm and asked, 'Where is your family? They need you. Otec and Bria are already dead."' He no longer looked at Cymm; his eyes were welling and glazed over like he was reliving those moments.

His uncle took several seconds to compose himself. Obviously, a part of the story was too painful for him to say aloud. "She finally convinced me there was nothing I could do and to focus on my wife and children. So, I grabbed her hand to take her with me, but her hand was covered in blood. I was so shocked, I let go." He absently wiped his hand on his chest as if Shay's blood were still on it.

"She said, 'Watch over Cymm, and please tell him I love him. I will delay the dragon if I can, so you have time to get your family to safety,' then she walked around the corner into the barnyard to face the beast."

His uncle swallowed hard, studying him intensely. "Cymm, she had a wooden stake impaling her abdomen the entire time. I never saw it until she walked out into the moonlight. She saved my family, then rode to the alarm bell to save the village with that damn thing stuck in her." Tears streamed down his face from unfocused eyes, as he appeared to be reliving that night.

"The grass blankets your mother designed worked. The long stalks of grass woven into them stood up tall when we pulled the blankets tightly around us. We stood in the middle of the field near the rendezvous for a long time. We must have been undetectable from above because the dragons flew right over us in the daylight."

"Dragons? There was more than one?"

"Yes, there were three."

"I should have been here," the young man lamented.

"If you, Talo, and Semper had been here, I am afraid the three of you would be dead right now." Daro held his breath, waiting for a response.

Catching him off guard, Cymm rushed at his uncle who raised his arms to shield himself, and they collided with Cymm holding him tightly. He cried on his uncle's shoulder with body racking sobs. The emotions flooded back violently while the anger inside him continued to build.

Why would Terazhan let this happen?

13

The Dark Arts

A wave of apprehension came over TetraQuerahn as he flew toward Fire Island. His stomach ached, and his lungs would not fully inflate. He was here several months earlier, the last time Ledaedra, the Dragon Queen, summoned all her adult followers. During a speech, the Queen had slaughtered a young blue male in front of the entire army "for his insolence," a pure demonstration of power.

"I want to meet her majesty this time," crowed Ennozarius, tilting her wings from side to side.

"Yeah, that would be nice. Can you arrange that TetraQuerahn?" asked Anekzarius.

Impressing his new paramours was a high priority, but was the risk worth the reward? "You should focus on the purpose of the trip—to have the priests perform the Acceleration Ritual."

Anekzarius raised her eyebrows repeatedly until he smirked. "I thought you were a lieutenant in the army?"

"I am, and you know that. Your attempt to manipulate me was feeble." He glared at one twin sister then the other. "We need to be careful! I am not sure how the Queen will react to our arrangement."

"After we explained it to you, you understood. We will explain it to her also," Ennozarius swooped in close to emphasize her point.

His eyes burned with intensity. "No, you won't!" he said with a raspy voice, "and if you go against my wishes, I will shred you both."

"I have heard she has no less than five consorts at any one time. So why would she care?" asked Anekzarius.

"Do you consider me her equal? I am not. End of discussion." He doubted the twins would pay the price, but he had seen her act unpredictably before. Maybe he should have killed the twins when they arrived at his lair with their indecent proposal. He wanted to, but something about their game amused him. Now, if he could see this through, his offspring would be quite numerous.

"Hello?" Ennozarius said.

Anekzarius bumped the tip of her wing into his. "You still there?"

"Let's just get in and get out. The Mother of Dragons is not to be toyed with. She has held dominion over the seven continents of Erogoth for almost four centuries for good reason." TetraQuerahn sounded like a professor lecturing his students.

"Alright then," Anekzarius said.

"We will follow your lead." Ennozarius flew above him and gently raked his back with her claws.

A shiver went down the large male's back, "We are not eagles, you big tease."

Fire Island came into view in the distance, and TetraQuerahn breathed a sigh of relief; they were not the only ones arriving. He escorted the twins to the ritual chamber—a mammoth cave near the top of the mountain. Many other dragons were waiting to enter the inner sanctum.

Several acolytes rushed around tending to the waiting dragons, trying to keep an orderly process. Two humans in black robes approached the twins with parchment in hand. "The line moves fast, but we need some information to customize the ritual for each drakaina."

"Oh, so formal," came the twins synchronized response before peeking at each other with giggles.

"Alright, please provide your age," said the speaker while his scribe prepared to record the answers.

"One hundred lifeyears, both of us," replied Ennozarius.

Anekzarius lifted her head higher than her sister's. "Yes Enno, but I am older."

"We came out of the same shell. How do you figure?"

"Well, the shell broke on my side first. So, I emerged first, and therefore I am older," she replied with a smug face.

"The shell wouldn't have broken at all if it weren't for your fat head!" Ennozarius rose on her hind legs.

The argument wasn't new to TetraQuerahn. It got ugly fast, but in the end, they promised to never be apart.

Chanting caught his attention, although he did not recognize the language or the accent. *This is a good time to leave.* He strolled down the corridor, the invocations getting louder with each step. He rounded a corner, and the inner chamber opened before him.

A chanting Ledaedran priest wore a scarlet robe with a black hood, and his snout protruded almost eight inches past the cowl. The incantation reached a crescendo, and several human priests and sages hustled to bring forth a sizeable golden vessel.

Three large creatures also participated in the ritual. Each had the body of a snake and the upper torso of a female human. He had never seen a naga before. They remained motionless during the incantation except for a shimmering around the edge of their bodies. TetraQuerahn attempted to inspect them closer when the shimmering ceased, and a ghostly ethereal form sundered from their bodies. The chanting ended and the minister of the ritual lifted the vessel lid, shaped like a dragon with spread wings.

A gasp overpowered both the scrape and clang of the metal cover. An eerie moan reverberated throughout the chamber, sending the naga spirits into a frenzy! They flew to the vessel, entered it, then raced toward the female dragon. The wraiths penetrated the dragon's abdomen, burst from the other side, before rushing back to the vessel. The naga's pace quickened with each iteration of the pattern. They moved so fast that eventually a white ring of mist formed between the dragon and the golden container. Apparitional hands reached out of the mist ring then merged back into it.

So enthralled, TetraQuerahn lost his sense of time; he could not look away. Finally, the spirit naga's pace slowed, breaking the ceremony's hypnotic effect. *It's time to head over to the main camp.* His mind reeled. *All of this to win a war, the Dragon Wars. The Queen is planning a battle thirty years in the future and accelerating the growth of our unhatched wyrmlings. She claims we will double the size of our army; then we will crush the metallic dragons. But at what cost? The Final Conflict, as she calls it, could result in the death of my offspring, the twins, or me!*

He landed near the headquarters ending his ruminations; Ledaedra strategized with her generals—both red and black dragons—and a shadow drake over by her quarters.

"TetraQuerahn, I haven't seen you in a while," said a giant blue dragon catching him off guard.

"I've been busy preparing for the ceremony," he replied with a leer.

The sergeant chortled, "Good for you. I will mark your attendance and inform the Queen. You are free to go."

The stress and tightness in his lungs began to melt away instantly; he couldn't contain his elation. He stretched his wings to take flight.

"TetraQuerahn, the Queen wants to speak with you," yelled the blue dragon trying to get his attention.

He peeked over at The Prismatic Goddess; she had dismissed her generals. His eye twitched as he slowly turned around. The stress and tightness returned with newfound strength. Images of the blue dragon getting ripped apart flooded his thoughts. *Didn't she dismiss the generals right before she eviscerated him?* He groaned but quickened his step. It was not wise to keep the Queen waiting.

"My Queen," he said, bowing his head to the Mother of Dragons. He had never been this close to her. His lungs constricted further. She rose from the elevated stone ledge made of pure black onyx. She stood on two legs, had two arms, and two heads, but the second head erupted from her back like a scorpion's tail between two large leathery wings. The head on her shoulders was that of a red dragon, while the head and long neck protruding from her back were black ether and shadows. Each limb of her body was a different color and melded into a prismatic swirl on her torso.

"TetraQuerahn, I hear you have selected a mate."

14

Resilience

The Reich men rode through the village to every farm, searching for survivors. They avoided the few remaining pockets of yellowish gas in the wind-protected areas. The gas was easy to see and smell.

At the second farm, they found the first survivors, members of the Softtail household. A distraught man sat with his back against a stone well, hitting his head with the side of his fist then pulling his hair. "Why didn't she go to the rendezvous? I told her to meet me there."

"Cymm!" a little boy came running out of the closest barn. "Papa, it's Cymm." The boy turned back to the Reichs. "Are you here to help us?"

Cymm dismounted, kneeling before the boy while his uncle dealt with the man. "Yes, we are!"

"My momma climbed down the well with my baby sister, and the gas got her. Papa says it was so thick it settled in the well." The little boy tried to comprehend the words coming out of his own mouth, but he couldn't, and Cymm was determined to keep it that way.

The little boy pointed to Cymm's neck. "That's Bria's necklace."

Cymm gave the boy's hair a tussle, unconsciously stroking the ogre talisman. "Yes, I am holding it for her."

The search party brought the man and the child back to the Reich Farm, where they could be fed and examined for injuries. They quickly left, heading to the Semper Farm.

Cymm stopped at the gate to the training grounds. "No sign of Semper. How about over there?"

"Nothin'. Let's check the houses," his uncle replied.

Cymm dismounted before the entrance to the barn, unsheathed his sword, and slowly entered. "Anyone in here?" His arm tingled, transforming to an itch before an intense burning sensation replaced it. A pocket of trapped vapors swirled past his arm from the dark shadows.

He ran out of the building to the horse trough, submerged his arm, and vigorously rubbed it. When he removed his arm from the water, a strawberry-sized abscess had formed by his elbow.

"Uncle Daro! Talo!" he yelled.

His cousin entered the training grounds first. "What's the matter?" Seconds later, his uncle came barreling around the corner.

He lifted his arm to reveal the damage. "There is a pocket of gas in the barn; it's still potent, so be careful entering any dark areas."

Uncle Daro helped him to his feet. "No one in the main house, but I found two dead on the porch."

"No one in the second house, but I didn't get to check the third yet," Talo said.

"The lack of dead bodies gives me hope. Maybe they escaped to the rendezvous," replied Cymm.

Uncle Daro nodded in agreement. "Old-Man Semper probably figured that too."

They continued to search well into the evening, finishing the final farm before sundown. So far, only seven survivors had been found, including Sero, but tomorrow they planned to scout the outer perimeter for each household's safe spot.

Later that night, Sero woke up feeling much better, and he ate for the first time in three days. His appearance was still distorted, but he could also talk a little, a good sign of healing. Cymm's current healing power was limited to once per day, but three years ago, Hardre had told him he would eventually be able to cast spells like a priest.

The Reich men left at the break of dawn to continue their search for survivors with the intention of finding their neighbor's rendezvous points. Plainsmen abided by a strict order of loyalty: Household, village, tribe, then clan. This information was never shared outside of the family.

Talo and Cymm knew approximately where to find the Semper rendezvous, based on stories he had shared. However, that information was unnecessary because the cousins could smell bacon frying in the distance. With no one on watch, the Reichs rode into camp without resistance.

Cymm came upon an old woman repairing clothes. "Where is Old-Man Semper?" Before she could answer, Cymm spotted him on the other side of the camp.

"Oh, this should be fun," Daro mumbled.

"Get over it! We need to work together now." He dismounted while examining the camp. "There have to be at least twenty people here!"

"Cymm, what are you doing here?" barked Semper.

"What am I doing *here*? What are you doing *here*? We could smell the bacon at your farm, and you don't have anyone on guard?" Cymm stepped into the old man's personal space. "Were you planning to let us know your family was alright?"

Semper's eyes grew white, matching the color of his clenched fists. Inner turmoil etched his face, but he took a deep breath. "What do you want?"

"I want everyone to come back to the village so we can figure out how many are missing or dead. I want everyone to discuss how we will recover from this, and I want you to help us search for the rest of the rendezvous locations. So far, we've only found seven survivors, not including your household or ours." Cymm answered in a slow rhythmic pace with his hands on his hips.

The old man hesitated, still fighting an internal demon, but the tension finally left his brow. "Alright, give me ten minutes to set everything in motion; then we can be on our way." Semper began giving orders immediately.

Cymm caught his uncle watching him with admiration, even giving him a supportive nod.

Talo yawned, unfazed by the exchange between them. "I can't believe how many of the Semper household survived. Hopefully, the other families did too."

The search party of four left ten minutes later while the Semper household continued to break down camp.

"We have five more rendezvous locations to find," Cymm said.

"I got an idea for one of them," replied Uncle Daro.

Semper rolled his eyes. "Well, I got a couple of ideas."

They persisted until they found all five camps. Later that evening, the village held a mandatory bonfire meeting for the survivors. Tensions were high, and arguments rippled through the small crowd. The heads of Wither, Semper, and Darkmane stepped up on the flat dirt mound to settle the villagers.

"Alright, everyone, settle down!" Old-Man Semper said in his usual, cantankerous way.

The noise level dropped noticeably, but a voice rang out, "This is where I usually stand. Move!" A shoving match began, sending a villager tumbling to the ground. The other pounced on him, punching him in the face.

Semper turned to Darkmane growling, "Take care of your man, or I will."

Zeke reacted immediately, grabbing the man's fist as it came back. "You made your point. Get up."

"*Settle down!*" Old-Man Semper screamed.

Zeke Darkmane returned to the mound. The popping and crackling of the bonfire the only sound as silence fell over the group. "There are currently ninety-one survivors, which means one hundred and twenty-six family members are either dead or missing."

The firelight danced across the face of a mother hugging her child tight to her chest. "So many?"

"Why? Why did this happen?" yelled an old man as he hugged his wife.

Cymm found himself nodding in agreement.

"And hundreds of livestock; how will we rebuild?"

The din rose sharply for several minutes, but the heads did nothing to abate it. After everyone had processed the information at their own speed, a somber veil fell over the meeting, and the silence returned.

Zeke continued slowly, "We need to look for survivors and the dead, so we can verify these numbers, but we also need to move forward."

The head of the Wither household cleared his throat responding to a motion from Zeke. "When the original seven founding fathers of the Armakian Plainsmen built the first tribe, they decided there would never be more than seven villages in a tribe, and each village would have seven households. No more, no less. This tradition has not changed for over a millennium. New heads need to be appointed, and we need to clean up two decimated households to make room for two new ones." The head of Wither lifted his hand palm up toward Old-Man Semper.

"Four heads were killed, including Otec, but only two will be selecting replacements. Reich and Softtail, have you selected your new heads yet?" Semper asked.

Out of the corner of his eye, he spotted Uncle Daro studying him from about twenty feet away. Cymm kept his eyes on the ground, wrestling with this paramount decision. He squinched his face and tilted his head so far that his ear almost touched his shoulder. *I am turning seventeen lifeyears in less than two months. If I choose to be head of household, I will be the youngest ever in the Horse Tribes, but is that what I want?*

While Cymm continued to ponder, another fight broke out. "I can't see! What is happening?"

The eyes of the entire village burrowed into him. He finally met his uncle's gaze, and it was clear that both had made up their minds. Daro nodded to him, supporting him with a half-smile.

Cymm addressed the three leaders. "Daro will be the new head of household for Reich."

Shock spread throughout the crowd, and even his uncle blanched. Semper gave him a chance to recant his statement. "Cymm, are you sure?"

"This is a family matter, not an affair for the village to discuss. Unless my uncle refuses, the decision is final," he replied sharply.

Everyone's attention focused on the potential new head, but he never took his eyes off Cymm. Daro's teeth shone bright, and the corners of his lips curled up in sincere gratitude. "I accept your nomination and will not let you down, Cymm."

The rest of the meeting should have gone smoothly, but the arguments continued.

"Whoever absorbs the two households should get all of their food, livestock, and possessions," said a young man.

"No! It should be divided among the remaining five households. That would be the fair thing to do," replied another.

The argument escalated, dividing the villagers' support between the two men. They were on the verge of a brawl.

"The household absorbing them has more mouths to feed. The others do not."

"Everyone has lost family, food, and livestock. The absorbing process is not an opportunity to gain resources!"

Semper stepped between the two groups. "This is how we resolve our disagreements? Yelling, fighting, and finger-pointing. You should be ashamed of yourselves."

Zeke Darkmane joined him in the middle, putting his hand on Semper's shoulder. Semper shuddered in response, but for appearance's sake, accepted the gesture.

"You appoint leaders to make these decisions in order to avoid such conflicts," said Zeke. "We have already discussed this matter, and after we consult with the two new heads, we will share our decision. Even working together, it will be hard to survive this growing season."

The Softtails picked a new head of household, then absorbed one of the decimated families, and the Darkmane clan absorbed the other.

Talo patted his father on the back. "Congratulations, Dad."

"That hardly sounded sincere. What's going on?"

Talo ran his hand through his hair. "Something doesn't feel right. First, you were conceding; then Cymm just gave it up, without discussion."

"I am standing right here." Cymm shook his head and waved.

An inquisitive expression crossed Daro's face. "So then explain yourself."

"Why would you do that without consulting both of us?" Talo asked.

"Why would I consult either of you?" Cymm yelled.

Talo threw his hands in the air. "Because we're family!"

Daro jumped in quickly, "Cymm, please think before you say something you'll regret."

Cymm took a deep breath with a finger pointed in Talo's face, but his uncle's words bombarded his thoughts. The pent-up heat dissipated slowly. He closed his mouth, whirling around to leave.

His cousin danced in front of him. "Are you joining Semper's household?"

If Talo had hit him in the head with a club, it would have hurt less. With the sting still fresh on his features, he replied, "No! Why would you say such a thing?"

"You can't fool me. Something is up!"

"Your expertise is arrows, not reading minds." Cymm shouted. A tear gradually rolled down his cousin's cheek. "Fine, you want to know why? I will tell you why."

15

Call of the Wild

Lykinnia had been working on her improved invisibility spell for three years. Every modification she made failed to fool Solar. However, she had a good feeling about this one.

She could not shift her physical body to another plane because she was forbidden to leave the Peak of Power, but she could shift all noise, including her breathing.

"Solar is at the altar now," she said to no one in particular. "Time to test my theory."

She left her sleeping abode, immediately cast her improved invisibility spell, then jogged most of the way. She estimated the spell's duration to be only ten minutes, but she could not be certain.

Solar stood statue-like in front of a large scrying window hovering before him. Lykinnia walked up next to him and peered into the magic portal. The handsome young man stood next to a large bonfire.

"Lykinnia."

She groaned, "Seriously?" She glanced up, expecting Solar to be sporting that arrogant grin of his, but he intently stared into the window.

"Lykinnia." The voice sounded strange and distant. *It's coming from the plane I am sending my noise to.* Startled, she ran from the altar, releasing the spell once far enough away. She had sensed the presence of demons, devils, and other creatures before, but they had never tried to communicate with her.

After she had recovered from her fright, she decided to validate her experiment and walked over to the altar.

Solar was still scrying in the open window.

"Hi, Solar. Who are you spying on now?" she said, trying to get a rise out of him.

He immediately closed the portal. "I do not spy Lykinnia. You are not supposed to be at the altar in the evening."

"I saw the portal open. Why can't I peek inside for a couple of seconds? Please?" She cocked her head, pretending to plead.

"No! Not for one second. Shall I call Terazhan?"

"I am leaving." She spun quickly to hide her beautiful smile, already planning how to use her new spell.

16

Divine Quest

The Reich family argument continued to attract the full attention of the village. Talo stood with tears in his eyes waiting for Cymm to continue.

"This is not how I wanted to share this information with you," Cymm said, waving his hand toward everyone listening. "I am going to find the dragons that did this and kill them."

"Alright, the show is over, everybody. Go back to your own business." Uncle Daro began pushing people away.

"I spoke with Sero earlier. He confirmed the dragons flew north when they left. I am guessing they were from Darken Wood. I will start searching there."

Talo was at a loss for words, so he called in reinforcements. "Hey, Old-Man Semper, can you talk some sense into Cymm?"

He had to walk from the other side of the bonfire. "What's going on?"

Talo folded his arms across his chest. "He is leaving and going after the dragons!"

"What? Is this true half-pint?" Semper asked. Daro and Talo nodded in reply.

Cymm replied sharply, "Don't call me that!"

Old-Man Semper shrugged off the rebuke, remaining calm. "There is lots of rebuilding to be done here. Do you really think this is a good time to leave?"

Uncle Daro scratched his head. "Your mother and father would not have liked this. I told you how big the dragons were. They will kill you."

"So, what if I do get killed! Who wants to live in a vile and evil world anyway?" Cymm could feel the arguing solidifying his decision, the anger daring to erupt. "Give the village three days, and they will be over this tragedy and my departure."

A new wave of arguing flared up, continuing for a few more minutes. He ignored their comments until his cousin threw him a curveball.

Talo stroked his chin. "Cymm . . . is it Terazhan's way to seek revenge?"

Cymm's words caught in his throat. He tried a second time to respond, but the same thing happened. His faith, a source that once brought him so much clarity, suddenly abandoned him. Cymm finally clapped his cousin on the shoulder. "That is an excellent question. I will pray and reflect on this starting tonight, until I receive guidance. However, your choice of words is incorrect. I do not seek revenge. I seek justice. This can never happen again to another village."

The argument fizzled. The barrel of rye beer called to them. Cymm used the opportunity to slip away. He was touched by their concern and wasn't upset with them for arguing so vehemently against his departure. Still, this tragedy had changed his entire outlook on the future and eliminated any guilt he had on leaving.

Later that night, in the privacy of his own room, he prayed for assistance concerning the dragons. An intense euphoria and energy surged through his body. He swooned, causing him to almost pass out. The dizziness passed quickly, but he was no longer in his own bedroom.

He was in Bria's room.

While trying to wrap his mind around it, his mother came strolling in.

"Mother!" he said, running to hug her, but she walked right past him.

Shay shook her daughter to wake her. "Bria, time to get up, dear."

"Bria? How can this be?" Cymm's voice cracked, and he staggered to the bed.

"Just five more minutes?" his sister pleaded.

"Your father has already been working out there for a half hour. He needs some help, sweetie," Shay replied before walking out.

"My father? What in the nine hells is going on here?" he said, bending to kiss his sister on the forehead. She sat up and got out of bed at the same time, moving right through him.

Cymm lost his balance and fell forward, sinking into the warm, soft pillows. He recalled Hardre describing something like this to him years ago—a Divine Quest. Maybe this was one, no snap-shot Vision pictures like he usually received.

Bria dressed and proceeded out the bedroom door, sliding her ogre-trophy necklace over her head. He got up and quickly followed her. She grabbed an apple, hugged her mother, then ran out the front door.

Cymm moved a chair, banged on the table, then yelled, but his mom never flinched. He rushed outside to follow his sister. Dawn had not yet arrived, so his father worked by torchlight out near the barn.

Otec had already filled a wagon with cow manure from the barn stalls. It was hitched to a workhorse, sitting twenty feet outside the barn doors. His father leaned against the main entry to the barn wiping sweat from his brow. He waved as his daughter approached.

"Hi Daddy-O," Bria said with a giggle.

Cymm chuckled, recalling the day she invented that name for him many years ago. A small pain began to throb in the back of his head, the result of excessive smiling. He was enjoying this. It felt real. This was how a typical day would have started. Never before had he cared for the repetitive nature of their day-to-day lives, but he longed for it now. The horses were still in the corral and would be let out soon. He would have been—

One of the horses in the corral reared and whinnied. *That's not a good sign.* A frown tugged at the corners of his mouth.

His father grabbed the axe, tossing the pitchfork to Bria. Her small hands barely wrapped around the handle.

A gust of wind raced through the barnyard, blowing out the torch, leaving only a trail of smoke behind.

The horses were blowing, whinnying, and galloping circles in the corral. Cymm's stomach flipped, while his heart beat a rapid drum against his chest. Something was wrong.

"Bria, go get your uncle while I light the torch," his father grumbled.

His sister dropped the pitchfork then ran for Uncle Daro's home on the far side of the barnyard.

Otec strode over to the sconce. "The torch is missing . . ." The surrounding area sharply brightened when a torch reappeared from the sky, landing in the middle of the manure wagon.

His sister had only made it as far as the cart, and now she stood gaping at the torch. Abruptly, she shifted her gaze above his head in shock, causing him to glance up immediately. A huge green reptilian head the size of the wagon appeared out of the dark.

Cymm dove to the side shaking in terror, then rolled back to his feet. A yellowish-green cloud billowed from the dragon's despicable mouth.

"Run, Bria!" he yelled, forgetting this wasn't real. Fear clutched his heart and windpipe.

Her legs didn't move. Her lips quivered, her teeth chattered, and her head scanned from side to side. With tears rolling down her cheeks, she implored, "Cymm, where are you?"

He fell to his knees as if hit by Melcorac's Hammer, and when he hit the ground, the cart exploded. The gases from the dragon's mouth and the manure mixed, allowing the torch to ignite the deadly combination.

Manure and wooden shards flew in every direction. The concussive explosion threw Otec into the barn where he landed hard on the ground. Bria was closer to the epicenter; the explosion hurled her forty feet where she landed on the corral's split-rail fence with a sickening bone-snapping crunch. A split second later, shrapnel from the blast pelted her body. He shuddered with the impact as if being struck himself, intensifying the experience of this nightmare.

Something broke inside him.

His father staggered back to the barn opening, the one he just soared through. He held onto the doorframe for support as a cough racked his body.

His mother, directly behind him, rocked back and forth, wailing. She stared at the broken body of her daughter folded over backward on the fence, oblivious to her own wounds inflicted by the explosion.

Otec struggled toward Bria when a second explosion in the near distance startled him. He lost his balance and fell. Still intent on making it to his daughter, he crawled to the fence so he could pull himself up. Blood trickled between the fingers covering his mouth as another round of coughing took over his body. He paused for a moment to lean against a fence post, unaware of the red fluid leaking from his ears and nose.

Yelling and screaming rose in the background; confusion and chaos were everywhere.

Cymm rose slowly from his knees, almost falling when his legs gave out. "Why Terazhan? Why did they have to suffer like this?"

Otec yelled to his wife, "Tell everyone to put out the torches." She regarded him in a daze, quivering uncontrollably.

Coughing racked his body again. "Shay! Move it. You need to save the village! Put out the torches."

She acted on instinct, heading straight for her brother-in-law's home with the wooden shard sticking out of her back. It was the size of a horsetail, but some inner strength guided her to Uncle Daro's house and inside. The tears continued to soak his face. His mother had always been so strong. He again thought about the cut to her hand.

The door burst open, allowing his mother, uncle, and five of his cousins to pour out. They disappeared between the barns, so he turned his attention back to his father.

Otec had finally made it to Bria's body. He cradled her head in the crook of his arm, scanning the yard. The village alarm bell rang, followed immediately by a woman yelling, "P-p-put out the t-t-torches!"

The alarm bell finally stopped counting the dead, and for the briefest moment—silence. The smell was horrific, a mixture of burnt wood, charred horse flesh, blood, manure, and chlorine. His stomach roiled again, leaving him empty and completely drained. He slowly walked toward his father and sister, intent on kissing his sister goodbye. A sharp pain radiated through his shin as he banged it on the lower rail of the fence.

He stepped through the fence then kissed his sister on the forehead like he always had. He shuddered from the touch of her cold and clammy skin.

The ground trembled, but he ignored it.

He stroked her hair. "I am sorry, Bria, for breaking my promise." He began to sob again. A chilling roar behind him coincided with Bria's medallion hitting his leg, and he jumped in fear. He turned around with his father to find a towering beast in the corral.

He reached over to pat his father's shoulder, but his hand found nothing of substance. "Huh?" Cymm unconsciously moved to the side as the dragon sauntered over, searching his enemy for a weakness.

The dragon's throat rumbled before he demanded, "Light . . . the . . . torches!"

"No," his father said.

"Otec, we need to leave now," his mother called.

He continued to search, but nothing was apparent to him.

"Run Shay!" his father screamed. The dragon laughed like a madman, enjoying the tormenting of his family.

"Now, where were we? Oh yes, lighting the torches!" the behemoth growled fiercely.

"This dragon is obsessed with torches," he said.

"There will be no more torches. Your terror is over!" his mother replied.

He walked back toward the front of the goliath. "You tell him, Mother!" Now standing next to her, he vacillated between pride and sorrow. On the other side of the fence, she showed her wound to his father and the monster.

"It is not too bad. Cymm can help you," his father said, and he took another imaginary gut punch. He reached out to console his mother, but his arms passed through her. A helpless fury built within him, causing him to tremble, culminating in a thunderous roar.

"You should be afraid . . . dragon!" his mother said, as if on cue.

Cymm's eyes unglazed. He picked up a rock and threw it at the monster. "I *will* kill you, dragon!"

". . . watching death come for you!" his mother taunted the dragon.

The giant reptile glowered, spinning its head around behind him.

"Not now," he said at the same time his mother spoke the words. He gawked at her, and he thought she looked his way.

"Before you die, if you get the chance, make sure to ask for the name of your executioner!" His mother was tormenting the dragon. "His name will be Cymm Reich . . ."

His loving visage toward his mother was replaced with a fearsome glare at his enemy. "I will kill you." The Divine Quest ended as the dragon enveloped her with his searing death gas.

17

Loyalty

The Divine Quest sapped his energy, and he slept like a gravedigger after cleaning up from the plague. He awoke well after sunrise, packed his backpack and saddlebags, then ambled over to his aunt and uncle's house for breakfast. He had been moving in slow motion all morning. *How am I going to say goodbye?*

Cymm opened the door hesitantly. "Good morning, Auntie Nové."

"Well, good morning Cymm. Where have you been all morning?" she replied.

He quickly stuffed a slice of berry bread in his mouth, avoiding the question, but she busted him anyway. "You just got out of bed, didn't you? Don't worry. Your secret is safe with me."

"What secret?" Talo asked, entering the room. "Hey Cymm, what's on the scratch list for today?"

He stuffed another slice of bread in his mouth. *This is going to be more challenging than I thought.* "Well, I . . ."

Uncle Daro walked in. "Did I see Cymm heading this way? Oh, there you are. We need to talk about repairing the barn, mending the fence, and tracking down the strays."

Cymm conjured the image of his brave mother to feed his own courage. "Well, Uncle Daro, I have news to share first, since I have the three of you here at the same time." His stomach churned. *Maybe I shouldn't have eaten so much berry bread.* "I witnessed the entire attack on our farm last night." The cold, clammy feel of his sister's body and the smell of burnt hair and flesh lingered in his mind.

"How?" all three of them replied together.

"I prayed for assistance on my decision, and Terazhan showed me everything. The dragon played with them like toys. He wanted the torches lit so he could explode a mixture of gases. Bria was frozen in place from fear, and right before she died, she looked around and called for me to protect her." His voice cracked, and he paused. The emotion of saying everything out loud left him weak and his face damp. He gaged the impact of his words as his uncle shook his head and his aunt mumbled, "Oh dear." Talo hung his head, blubbering.

Cymm pushed on, "What that monster did to my family was despicable, and I won't bother describing how he tormented my mother and father while they slowly died. This world is a horrible place to live, but I can make it better, and it starts with killing these three dragons."

No one tried to talk him out of it this time. Instead, they formed a small huddle, hugging each other with the crowns of their heads together. Everyone's eyes and cheeks were wet.

Nové went back to cooking and baking while his uncle disappeared into the back of the house.

Talo walked out the front door with Cymm, clapping him on the back. "Things won't be the same around here without you."

"I'll miss you too, but I *will* return." Cymm smiled, trying to get his cousin to reciprocate.

Talo peeked up briefly, silently shaking his head. He gave Cymm a rib-crushing bear hug then disappeared back into the house.

As he loaded up his horse, Uncle Daro came over with a small pouch of coins in his hand. "You'll need this for your journey north to get food, shelter—whatever." He put it in one of Cymm's saddlebags, then quickly closed the flap, keeping his hand on it.

"Uncle Daro, you can't afford this with all the repairs to be done." He tried reaching into the saddlebag, but his uncle blocked him with a swat.

"It's not a lot, but I promised your mother I would watch over you. How am I supposed to do that now?" he asked. "If you can't come home soon, at least send word you are alright." His uncle gave him one last hug and left.

As Cymm rode over to Old-Man Semper's farm, he recalled the thousands of times he had made this ride in the past decade. *I may never make this ride again.* He entered the barnyard where he trained with Semper, Talo, and Hardre. A ghost from the past appeared, young Talo nervously hiding behind the barn door while he asked Semper to train them. It all made sense back then. They already played pretend militia, so why not make it official? He wasn't sure if he was about to laugh hysterically or cry.

Am I doing the right thing?

The feeling of nostalgia evaporated when he saw his original mentor walk out of his barn with a hammer in one hand, and a horseshoe in the other. "I thought that sounded like your horse Cymm. A little early for training, isn't it?" The old man retreated into the barn.

He dismounted then followed him inside. An awkward silence persisted until he finally said, "I will be back soon."

Old-Man Semper tossed his hammer and the horseshoe on the workbench. "Ahh, by Melcorac's Hammer, Cymm! What is this really about?"

They sat at the same old wooden table where they had sat so many times before. Cymm clenched his fists declaring, "I don't belong here anymore. I don't belong in this world. This vile, dark, disgusting world."

"Well, what does that say about your parents or me or Talo?" Semper replied with mild indignation, eyes narrowing. "We deserve better."

Cymm slammed his fist on the table, staring him down, and spoke with a low and ferocious voice, "Semper— they killed my family! And now I am going to kill them."

Semper sat silently, pondering Cymm's declaration. "Fine! Give me one hour. Then we go." He stood and started to put his tools away.

"We?" Cymm crinkled his nose.

Semper smirked. "Yeah, *we*. You didn't think Talo and I would let you go by yourself, did you?"

"It would be like a long hunting expedition." Cymm considered it briefly. "Nah. What if something happened to you or Talo? That would be my fault, and I couldn't live with myself. Besides, what if orcs attacked Stallion Rise with all of us gone? Who would protect the village?" As much as he longed for his friends to join, he could not endure more death on his conscience. "This is something I have to do alone."

"And if you die, that will be something I have to live with. I—"

Resignation plastered Cymm's face. "I am already dead inside. My body just doesn't know it yet."

Semper sat back down, biting his lower lip, but Cymm believed he saw understanding and empathy flash across his mentor's face.

Cymm pressed his lips together, putting his hand on Semper's shoulder and leaning in so their foreheads touched, "I will be back, I promise."

"Good Luck, Cymm."

Cymm walked out of Semper's barn, fighting himself with every step. Once he was out of sight, he paused, put both hands behind his head, and took several deep breaths. His biggest fear pressed forward in his mind. *What if this is the last time I see him? What if I don't come back?*

From inside the barn came the unmistakable sound of a backpack hitting the ground and Talo's frustrated voice. "I told you he wouldn't let us go."

18

Dark Deceit

TetraQuerahn shifted uncomfortably. "Yes, my Queen, by order of your mating directive, I am preparing to produce offspring."

Ledaedra returned to lounging on the dark obsidian ledge. "You aren't considering lying to me, are you TetraQuerahn?" Her generals had removed themselves from the immediate area, giving the appearance of privacy.

"Yes, my Queen. I'm a green dragon, after all, but I have calculated my odds of success to be very low." He cringed and waited.

"Are you trying to charm me with your silver tongue?" asked the Queen.

A raspy voice pushed in close off his right shoulder, "More like disgrace his kind!"

He glanced quickly before a green scaled specter dissipated.

Back to his left came chortling from a blue apparition. "It would appear you have been caught in your lothario ways."

The Queen sat upright, batting her double eyelids. "Hmm, a lothario? Is that how you acquired two mates?"

"No, the twins approached me. The mandate has been traumatic for them because they have not been separated since birth. They feared it could be years before they could see each other. Therefore, they made a pact to select one suitor to share. They will be nesting next to each other, so they can see each other every day."

"Lucky you," said a deep, sinister voice directly behind him.

The green scaled apparition reappeared. "Kill him."

TetraQuerahn cowered as he spun a slow circle. In addition to the green and blue, a black apparition surrounded him. By the time he completed the revolution, the Queen's large red snout was in his face, a tremor pulling at her lip revealing more teeth.

"Maybe I should rip your heart out," the Dragon Queen said.

TetraQuerahn gulped. His breathing constricted. He took two tentative steps backward, and thoughts of fleeing raced through his mind.

"Going somewhere?" the Queen asked.

TetraQuerahn shook his head, not trusting his voice.

The apparitions laughed at his expense.

Ledaedra waved her green clawed hand, and the matching apparition disappeared. "You may leave. I expect many fierce and loyal warriors from your offspring."

He fled, leaping into the air after only a few steps.

19

The City of Armak

C ymm moved north avoiding villages and other travelers. Still exhausted from his nightmare-filled sleep the night before, he made camp early, hoping to get right to bed. However, during his evening prayers, Terazhan had other plans.

He received another Divine Quest the moment he knelt to pray. Unlike the first one, he did not experience the swooning or dizziness, and he traveled much further than the room next door.

He was "flying" over the plains heading north, the grass tassels whipping by so fast that they became a blur. He passed over a vast city, most likely Armak, and continued north until he reached the edge of an enormous forest, Darken Wood.

He stood at the edge of the old forest with its large, ancient trees. Familiar grasslands extended to the horizon behind him except for a village that sprang out of the grass a couple hundred yards away. The scent of a pig roasting in the distance accompanied laughter. The comforting experience drew him in that direction.

Cymm entered the community of wooden built homes and recalled the stories his parents had told him. He had never seen anything so bizarre; some were even built from wooden poles and animal furs. This was a Wolf Tribe village.

In the center of the village stood a unique rock formation. He stared at it for a long time, feeling the sun's rays warm his body. For a moment, he angled his face skyward, soaking in the warm glow with his eyes closed. Hot spots emerged on his cheekbones before a chill went through his body as the sun went behind a cloud. *Wait a minute, the sky was clear.* He opened his eyes and tracked an object moving in the sky—a dragon, a green dragon. It was so enormous that the magnitude of his quest sent a second chill deep inside him.

The images around him were losing their sharpness. *It must be ending.* He took one last look at the rock formation before his ethereal body retreated to his campsite. While traveling back, he attempted to commit the rock formation to memory as he had for the face of the dragon.

I am certain Terazhan supports my plan, but what is the importance of that village? Is it a marker, or is the village in grave danger? The Divine Quest ended when I saw the strange rock formation; maybe I should focus on that.

He slowed considerably when the camp and his physical body materialized ahead. Seeing himself lying prone and motionless unnerved him. He merged with himself, then made a crude drawing of the rock formation in the dirt. He practiced it several times before turning in for the night.

He packed up early the next morning and arrived at the City of Armak late in the evening. He had not been to the big city for many years and never by himself. He wandered aimlessly for an hour before he came upon the Broken Horse Inn. The aroma of food wafted into the street, triggering a rumble in his stomach.

Cymm entered the tavern to find only a handful of patrons remained. He grabbed a table, put his backpack on one chair, and sat on the other. He ordered the cheapest food and rented a spot in the cheap common room for the night.

Although the tavern was almost empty, the current patrons created quite a clamor.

One man yelled, "When will these attacks stop?"

"The frequency is increasing again! The Wolf Tribes last month, then the Horse Tribe village two weeks ago," replied a different man.

"That's my village, Stallion Rise," shouted Cymm.

The barkeep said, "Travelers from Bruc were in here earlier. A week ago, five dragons attacked their city. A red and four blacks devastated the city, but they finally killed two of them, and the others broke off the attack. Over one thousand dead!"

Stunned silence filled the room before someone shouted, "I would like to see them try that with Kharad or the City of Mystics!"

Cymm's mood soured, and he ate his meal in silence. He retired to the common room for the evening, more depressed than ever. The shared sleeping quarters were spacious but offered no privacy.

His evening prayers got a little passionate toward the end, "Why don't you do anything? One thousand people died, and you didn't help."

A grizzled old man muttered to another, "Who is he talking to?"

Cymm continued vociferously, "How do you expect anyone to worship you or believe in you if you abandon them like the other gods?"

"Shut yer trap! Or I will shut it for you," yelled a third patron trying to sleep.

"Sorry. This world makes me sick. It's really getting to me," replied Cymm ending his prayers.

Cymm rose with the sun while the city still slept, striding for the front door. The innkeeper entered the bar area wearing the same dress as the night before.

Cymm set his pack down. "Can you give me directions to the Wolf Tribes?"

"Sorry, kid; this isn't the Lazy Wolf Inn," she said.

"Can you give me directions to the Lazy Wolf Inn?"

"It's on the complete opposite side of the city." She pointed in the general direction. "Next to the market. You can't miss it."

He walked into the other tavern as the market began to bustle.

"What can I get cha?" came a voice from behind the bar.

Cymm glanced around, shrugged, then asked, "Can I get something for breakfast?"

A ruckus broke out in the pens and stables next to the inn, catching his attention. Overhearing people shouting for the town guard, he hesitated, then raced out the front door. Upon entering the back building, two wolves were engaged in a brawl, both covered in blood. One wolf pinned the other to the ground, and Cymm instinctively reached for his sword.

"I wouldn't do that if I were you," said one bystander. "Even if the shadow wolf doesn't get you, Lord Barrister or one of his goons will."

Cymm hesitated but didn't remove his hand from his sword. The shadow wolf's handler got him under control and pushed him into a pen. "It was an accident! Please don't call for the guard," he pleaded with the other wolf owner.

"That wolf shouldn't be in the city if you can't control it. Look at what it did to my dire wolf. Call the guard!" the owner of the wounded wolf yelled.

The shadow wolf handler resembled a caged animal. With clinched fists, he took several steps toward the other wolf owner.

Cymm was about to intervene when two town guards walked in. "What's going on in here?" Both wolf owners started talking at once. "Alright! Alright! You first!" the guard said pointing at the shadow wolf owner.

"We both released our wolves at the same time; then my wolf broke free and attacked the dire wolf. Since I arrived first, this orc's ass should have waited for me to clear the area!" explained the shadow wolf owner.

"Who you callin' an orc's ass?" The dire wolf owner lunged at the other, grazing his chin with a fist before being restrained.

"Alright, enough! Your turn," the guard said, releasing his hold on the owner.

"Most of what he said is true, except he went out back to get something. I was already releasing Torc when he came back. So, *he* should have waited for *me* to clear the area." The dire wolf owner reached down to caress his wolf when it whimpered.

Cymm could not believe how much blood it had lost; it would probably bleed out soon.

The owner growled savagely, "If he dies, you will pay for your impatience!"

"City Law is very clear here," said the second guard who showed no emotion. "If the wolf dies, the other wolf will be put to the sword. Also, the owner of the executed wolf will pay twenty gold to the other owner, and pay a city fine of twenty more gold, or spend one month in jail if he can't pay the fines."

Both owners became incoherent as they lamented their losses, wolves, gold, and freedom. Cymm could not tell the order of importance for either of them.

"I can help." His voice intermingled with the background noise, so he yelled, "I can help!"

Everyone stopped talking. He had their attention. He blinked slowly, then cleared his throat, addressing the wolf owner, "I can save your wolf's life." Cymm asked the guards, "Is there a problem if I help?"

The first guard motioned him forward. "Go ahead. If both agree to a settlement, it makes our job easier."

The dire wolf owner already had an eager countenance. "Please save Torc! I will be in your debt."

Cymm knelt beside the beast that was more than half the size of his six-foot-tall at the withers, two-thousand-pound warhorse. Its fangs were too close for comfort, and images of the blood wolf from years before stormed his mind. Nervously, he pulled back his shoulders, saying, "Hold his head tight!"

I hope this works. He swallowed hard. *I've never healed an animal before.*

Placing his hands on the shoulder-neck area of the giant wolf, his booming voice rang out. "In the name of Terazhan, the One True God, I call forth the power to heal!"

The wolf struggled to get away while its owner wrestled it with two arms and two legs, locking it in place. The wound began to glow, then knitted itself together. It breathed in deep, before rising, staring at Cymm intently.

Without warning, the healed wolf let out a baying howl as if it were midnight and all four moons were full. The other wolves in the stable joined in, including the shadow wolf. A shiver jolted down his back. *How eerie, yet beautiful!*

Cymm stood, dusted himself off, then inspected his work from afar. Other than some missing fur, the dire wolf was in good shape, and would eventually make a full recovery. The stable grew uncomfortably silent, and the wolf, along with everyone else, stared at him.

Maybe I shouldn't have done that. He quickly shuffled toward the stable exit, but the dire wolf intercepted him, using its body to block him. Then he began licking Cymm's face repeatedly. Laughter erupted, ending the awkward silence, and the guards forced the crowd to disperse. The sentries spoke to the shadow wolf owner before leaving, applauding the paladin as they passed by.

The shadow wolf owner approached the other, handing him a small bag of coins. "I was told I owed you this." Next, he shook Cymm's hand, and gave him two coins. "Thank you! You saved the day. I am eternally grateful."

Looking at the coins in his palm, his eyebrows lifted. He had never owned a gold coin before. "You are very welcome." The horseman walked toward the exit, pleased with himself, whistling a little tune. However, the dire wolf persisted until Cymm gently pushed past him. The wolf followed him outside.

"Hey, someone made a new friend," said the dire wolf owner. "My name is Torak." He excitedly grabbed Cymm's hand. Torak stood a few inches shorter than Cymm, but he appeared to be a couple years older.

"I am Cymm of the Horse Tribes," he said, shaking his hand.

Torak extended the bag of coins. "This belongs to you."

"You can keep it, but I could use your help finding a specific Wolf Village."

The wolf owner rubbed his hands together eagerly. "Okay! How can I help you?"

The horseman knelt, recreating the rock formation in the dirt with his finger. "I'm looking for a village with this rock grouping at its center, near the main fire pit."

Torak's face lit up. "Tribute Set! It is a sister village to Howling Set, my village, approximately a seven-day walk. We can travel together most of the way if you don't mind going on foot, or I can point you in the general direction."

Cymm knew the original Seven Elders claimed everything revolved around the great city of Armak, so all the village names were determined based on their physical position with respect to the capital city. Those on the city's west side ended with Set, and villages on the east side ended with Rise. *Hmm, is the delay worth the guarantee of finding the village?* he asked himself. *I guess I am not really in a hurry. It could end up saving me time and aggravation.* "Yes. I would like to travel together."

They exited the city gates about an hour later. His warhorse remained skittish around the huge wolf on the first day, but Cymm managed to settle him down with several soft clicks. By the end of the second day, the horse had calmed considerably. The dire wolf liked to roam from side to side but never strayed more than a hundred yards. Torc was rather adept at hunting, catching several prey the first couple of days, including a brace of rabbits and an antelope.

"I rarely feed him anymore," Torak mentioned off-handedly. "He has been self-sufficient since he turned ten months old."

"Well, he is huge! How old is he now?" exclaimed Cymm.

"Not quite a year old yet. Twelve months last week, and dire wolves usually continue to grow well past three and a half years," Torak said, motioning toward Cymm's horse wide-eyed and nodding sideways. "Now Torc is an anomaly for sure, but not the first to get this big."

"That shadow wolf won't mess with Torc once he is full grown!" Cymm proclaimed.

Torak pumped both arms in the air. "Damn straight and wait till he has gone through battle training!"

In the afternoon of the fifth day, the wolfer let out a sharp, loud whistle. "Heads up and be ready." Torc appeared instantly by his side before Cymm could ask, "For what?"

Five men and four wolves emerged from the tall grasses in front of them.

"Hold up!" said a tall, sandy-haired young man about the same age as Torak. "Where do you think you're going?"

"What's the problem?" barked Torak.

"We have no problem with you. You can continue on your way," a second wolfer replied.

"We've been traveling together since Armak. What could you possibly need with my friend?"

The five exchanged glances then looked back at Cymm, rolling their eyes. The wolves flanked them, two on each side. The pair to the right had black fur streaked with brown highlights, and their baritone growls vibrated his bones.

Torak's face transitioned to red. His hands whirled and danced, helping him talk. "What are you accusing him of?"

The first wolfer held his gaze firm on the horseman. "Two nights back, this horseman attacked and killed two wolfers."

Cymm's mouth went agape at the audacity of the accusation. He opened his mouth to assure them they had the wrong man, but Torak shouted in his place, "Well, it wasn't him; I am sure of it!"

"I saw the man myself and chased him here." He pointed to the ground mockingly. "So, I am sure of it."

20

Mother Nature

L ykinnia awoke early, planning to spend the morning with the nymphs. *Well, they really aren't nymphs anymore, but it's a hard habit to break after three and a half years.*

She flash-traveled to their present location and observed them for a while before calling in their language, "Little ones."

The sound of her voice brought them skittering toward her, but they also understood her now because she had been teaching them the Taviian dialectic since the beginning.

Lykinnia took a quick roll call, "Twenty-one? We are missing two friends."

One of the female nymphs and the best communicator, Gillygahpadima, said, "Spiders came last night . . . they get you . . . they get you."

Lykinnia's golden ethereal body flared violently. "Wait here!" She did a broad perimeter sweep, revealing nothing. *No nests, no webs. Maybe they were just wandering through. This has been a very safe area, and we haven't had to move their home base in almost a year.*

Gillygahpadima was the shortest at eighteen inches; some of her kin were already over two feet. All of them had voracious appetites, and ironically, many of them could catch and eat birds.

Lykinnia searched the perimeter again to reassure herself. "It looks safe, my friends. Let's begin today's lesson. How to make a bandolier."

21

Wolf Country

Cymm stared at the scene unfolding in front of him, and the thought of fleeing briefly crossed his mind. Running wouldn't exactly prove his innocence, though.

"As I said, it's not him, and I would pledge my wolf's life on it!" Torak defiantly leaned forward, lifting both hands shoulder height.

All five wolfers went wide-eyed, slack-jawed, and were stunned into silence.

"This man healed my wolf five days ago in Armak; he saved his life. We are leaving now. You can take this up with the Howling Set elders if you have more questions!" He didn't walk around them; he pushed through the middle.

The lead wolfer reached out to grab Torak. "You, uh, I uh—" Torak slapped his hand away. "I will take it up with your elders!" he yelled with red-hot cheeks.

Cymm, still in shock, slowly guided his horse into the path his new friend made.

"This is not over, horseman!" the leader shouted as he passed, but all the wolfers wisely backed away from the horse's rear hooves.

Cymm waited a few minutes, still trying to find his own voice. "Am I in trouble? Should I be worried?"

Torak simply shrugged his shoulders.

"Who were those guys anyway?"

"My guess is they are members of Fang, and they hate the Horse Tribes. They are currently a small group in the Wolf Clan, but their numbers are growing. The worst part is this: They have been known to stage events to sew discord and hatred among the other clans, especially the Horse Clan."

Cymm took a deep breath then sighed. "Just another example of the vileness in this world."

"Huh?"

"Never mind." Cymm shook his head, giving the incident more thought. Why did you pledge his life, and what does that really mean?"

The wolfer's expression changed. "Exactly what you think. If you are found guilty, they won't kill you . . . they'll kill Torc."

Cymm's eyebrows stitched together, and his pulse quickened. "Then why did you do it?"

Torak paused in mental anguish. "You do realize their intent was to kill you, right? No trial, decapitation, your head paraded around for a month in the villages."

Cymm was still hot. "They could have tried!"

"You and your horse against four dire wolves and five wolfers? Good luck!" Torak chortled back.

"I like my chances, and of course you would have helped, right? Or would you have joined your brothers?" He instantly regretted throwing the barb.

The wolfer's face went stricken and he bared his teeth while Torc's hackles went up. "Do you think horsemen are the only Plainsmen with honor? You are innocent. Why would I join them?"

"That's how this world works! Everyone for themselves. Argue, fight, kill, or be killed, then forget about it and move on. Name one good thing in this world!"

Torak hung his head and the tension melted from his shoulders. His head tilted back, locking eyes with Cymm, "You."

The horseman had wound himself up for a rebuttal but blanched at the response. An uncomfortable silence ensued, and they rode like that for a while. Then, realizing he'd lost control of his emotions, he breathed in deeply before saying, "I'm sorry. I'm confused and worried to be honest."

Torak nodded slightly. "I am too, Cymm. You should stay with me and come to Howling Set." He picked up the pace, knowing they were still two days from his village.

Cymm matched his pace. "What's the plan from here?"

"My elders will help us figure out what is going on and what to do next."

∞∞∞∞

Although, the village resembled the one in the Divine Quest, it was very different from his own. The homes were closer together, smaller, and constructed from wood and furs instead of mudstone. Torak's house was quaint and cozy with two sleeping areas, one for him and one for Torc.

Cymm inspected the fifteen feet to the neighbor's house. "So, where is your property line?"

Torak perked a brow at the question. "Property line?"

Cymm observed the house, trying to judge for himself. "Yeah, where should I put my horse. Can I hobble him behind your house?"

"Oh, are you asking about land ownership? No one owns any land. We farm the outskirts together, producing food for the growing season. We don't have to worry about the wildlife eating the crops because the wolves eat the wildlife." Torak laughed at his own joke.

Cymm hesitated, considering the concept. "Very interesting, and I don't see one fence in the entire village, except where you keep the pigs and sheep. That fence would hardly keep a wolf out!"

"The fence is to keep the livestock in, not the wolves out. The wolves know better," the wolfer said, making Cymm laugh. "No, seriously, a wolf would face severe punishment for stealing, just like a wolfer."

Cymm pursed his lips, nodding, but not convinced. He gave his horse a good scratch, one that made his lip curl. "Okay, where is this guy going to sleep?"

Torak waved him on. "Follow me." The wolfer led him to the livestock stable where he made his horse comfortable in a private stall. Torak motioned for him to follow again. "Alright, time to seek council from one of the village elders."

The elder's home was much bigger than Torak's. The rooms were partitioned, reminding him of home. The elder welcomed them into the entry room where they sat at a well-crafted, dark, wood table.

"Elder Batia, this is Cymm from the Horse Tribes. I will now ask him to introduce himself," Torak said in a formal voice with perfect posture. He swept his arm, nodding for Cymm to proceed.

Cymm mimicked his new friend's presentation. "Nice to meet you Elder Batia. I am Cymm Reich of the Reich Household from the village of Stallion Rise, which is about two and a half days ride or seven days walk south of Armak."

"Hello Cymm, I am pleased to meet you," Batia answered. "So Torak, what can I do for you today?"

"I was preparing to leave Armak when a shadow wolf from an eastern tribe attacked my wolf. Torc would have died if not for Cymm. He healed him in front of at least twenty-five witnesses, including two town guards. That was seven days ago. Roughly two days ago, five wolfers confronted us with plans to lynch a horseman. They claim Cymm murdered two people. We are seeking your council." Torak adjusted his posture and waited.

Batia scratched her ear. "You're a healer? Priests are forbidden from carrying a sword."

"I am a paladin of Terazhan or a holy warrior. He gives me the power to heal the wounded and cure the diseased," Cymm replied formally.

Elder Batia nodded, then asked the young wolfer, "Do you think any of them were part of Fang?"

"I did not recognize any of them, but I do not spend much time east of our village. However, I would bet all of them were Fang initiates," replied Torak with fervor.

"Well, if they aren't starting trouble with the hackles from the War Dog Clan, it's with the horsemen. You are welcome to make yourself comfortable in our village. I will discuss your predicament with the other elders. We will try to learn about this murder investigation. Until then, I request that you stay in the village." Batia stood, indicating the meeting was over.

Several days passed, and the month of The Initiate rolled into the month of Harvest.

The sleeping arrangements were cramped in Torak's cozy home. Cymm was assaulted in the middle of each night because Torc would drift into his area and deliver multiple kicks to his back. On the third evening, when the Plainsman rolled over to push him away, the wolf let out a whimper. Then the furry beast rolled on his back with legs flailing in the air, yelping. Cymm could only assume he was chasing rabbits or in the middle of a rematch with the shadow wolf.

Cymm tolerated the growling and running during the late hours, but he could not tolerate the incessant perfuming of the air. The foul smells from horses were bad, but nothing compared to dire wolves. He retched the first few times, but he eventually learned to open the entry flaps to let fresh air in or to take a walk.

The previous night was dreadful; the dire wolf spent most of the day eating giant grasshoppers, the eight-inch-long variety. Apparently, they disagreed with his digestive tract. The vapors were so vile, Cymm staggered out of the home, nearly vomiting. He would keep a close eye on Torc in the future; there would be no more feasting on grasshoppers.

The following morning, the Elder Council summoned the young men to a meeting held by the village campfire for all to hear. Many gathered with interest around the fire pit with red-hot embers. Flames were no longer visible, but a palpable heat persisted.

There were seven elders, like his village; however, this village had a leader. In her late sixties, Tasha had wispy white hair and her decrepit dire wolf followed her every move.

"About a week earlier, someone killed a husband and wife from Endurance Rise while they were hunting in Darken Wood. The following morning, their wolves returned to the village, forcing the elders to send out a search party. The wolves led them straight to the bodies, and they found horse hoof prints throughout the murder scene. They tracked the horseman into the plains and right to you." Elder Tasha pointed to Cymm.

She paused, then added, "Representatives will be arriving from Endurance Rise within a week. A trial will be held after their arrival."

"But I've done nothing wrong! There's no evidence linking me to these murders."

"The other village claims they have sufficient evidence," she replied.

"What is my punishment if I am found guilty?" Cymm tried to keep his voice steady.

"Death," Tasha responded with little emotion.

Torak shot out of his seat. "Actually, Cymm does not suffer the consequences." He drew a wavy line in the dirt with his heel. "I pledged Torc's life."

A collective gasp rose from the onlookers.

"You don't have the right to pledge his life!"

"How could you do that to Torc?"

"You don't even know this horseman!"

He listened until they were done venting, allowing his neighbors to express their frustration. "First of all, I do have the right since he is my wolf and we have passed the bonding ritual. Second, you are correct when you say he is a stranger, but he is innocent of these charges. Third, a shadow wolf from Shadow Rise attacked Torc inside Armak, and he would have died if not for Cymm. Fourth, both of us wolfers could have gone to jail and been forced to pay fines, but this horseman helped us instead of merely watching. He convinced the guards to agree to drop the charges if he could heal him and save his life, which he did." Torak paused at this moment to show everyone the scar still healing and missing fur.

"The kinship Torc feels for Cymm should already be obvious to everyone. Have you ever seen a bonded wolf act this way toward a stranger? When we bond with a wolf, our souls become linked, but Cymm's healing process must be similar. The connection between them is deep." Torak exhaled deeply before sitting down.

No one said a word, creating a long uncomfortable silence. Finally, after almost two minutes, Elder Batia stood. "You presented that evidence in the plains, and they did not believe you. They claim you have been charmed. Can the shadow wolfer be found and brought back to testify? Or maybe the town guard would draft a note with a royal seal?"

"Was there a motive for killing them? Was anything stolen?" asked an elder ignoring Batia's questions.

"Not that we are aware of," replied Tasha.

"This feels like the work of Fang!" another elder said.

"You always blame Fang for everything you can't explain or understand!" yelled a villager.

A second villager joined in. "Yeah, soon you'll be blaming bad weather on Fang."

"If Fang would stop causing trouble with the other two clans, maybe they wouldn't get blamed for anything," responded a third.

"But then they would have no reason to exist!"

"Quiet! Everyone quiet, please. We must focus on action, not on accusations. What can we do to save Torc?" yelled Tasha regaining control of the meeting.

"Shadow Rise is practically a two-week journey each way, and Armak is one week each way. We don't have enough time for either option," replied one villager.

"If we knew the location of the attack, we could confirm it happened, maybe search for clues they missed," said a villager named Wexel.

Tasha replied, "I like it! Head for Endurance Rise immediately with your son and wolves. Come back as soon as you can."

Cymm whispered to Torak, "I could make it to Armak and back in five days on horseback. Maybe I could get the letter with a royal seal from the guards."

Torak eyed him sideways. "Do you really think they are going to let you ride out of here? If they did, what if you come across those wolfers? They would kill you on the spot."

"What if the shaman casts 'eye of the wolf' to see what their wolves saw?" asked a third villager.

"They already tried that, and the wolves did not see anything," replied Tasha.

"How about having an elven druid from Vallen speak with the trees or the forest animals?"

Tasha shook her head slowly. "That will take too long, but do not lose heart. There were many good ideas, and we will fight for more time. In the meantime, please stop by an elder's home with any other ideas. Thank you." She left, her ancient wolf hobbling along beside her.

22

Guilty until Proven Guilty

F ive days later, the contingent from Endurance Rise arrived at Howling Set. They kept to themselves, settling into a large home reserved for guests, awaiting the next day's trial.

Late in the morning of the following day, an elder found Torak and Cymm lounging in the wolfer's home. "Alright, you two, the elders request your presence."

The wait had been unnerving; a quick glance of unspoken words passed between them. They made their way to the village center, collecting Torc on their way.

"I am a little nervous," Cymm revealed in a low whisper. *Nervous? More like terrified. How did it get to this point? How could someone tell an outright lie and change his life or end it? Just another example of a world without honor. If this trial goes sideways, should I submit to their false justice?* "Have you ever been to one of these before?"

Torak's face paled. "I have witnessed several trials, but never one for murder. I feel like I'm going to throw up."

Given his complexion, Cymm believed it. Guilt devoured the paladin's stomach. "I'm sorry this is happening; I caused this problem."

"This is *not* your fault! No matter what happens, I will bear you no ill will. Fang is another story," the wolfer barked slamming his fist into his palm.

They entered the village center to a large chattering crowd of over one hundred villagers buzzing like a swarm of bees. Every seat was taken, save two, but more people continued to arrive. The new friends silently entered the throng, joining the elders in the middle. Cymm held his head high and his chin jutted out.

Elder Tasha engaged them with a warm smile. "Thank you for joining us."

The trial began within the hour in front of a crowd that had doubled in size.

"I am Elder Tasha, the lead elder of Howling Set. I will preside over the trial."

"I am Elder Batia of Howling Set. I am a member of the jury."

Introductions continued with the elders from both sides explaining their role in the hearing.

"I am Torak, and this is Torc, and we reside in Howling Set. I am the lead witness. Torc has pledged his life in support of Cymm."

Whispers and murmurs erupted from the crowd.

"Silence! Or you will be asked to leave," Tasha demanded, rolling her hand to continue.

"I am Stefo from Endurance Rise. I am the lead witness accusing the horseman."

"I am Cymm Reich from Stallion Rise, and I will defend myself." He desperately tried to keep unease from reaching his voice.

One of the elders from Endurance Rise spoke again, "A week ago, a husband and wife were murdered by this man in Darken Wood while hunting." The elder pointed at Cymm.

Noise erupted from the crowd again. Cymm's neck craned around nervously trying to interpret their feelings. People were standing and leaving. "What is going on?" he whispered to Torak,

"That's it for today."

Cymm remained seated. *How bizarre, nothing like a Horse Tribe trial.*

The delay turned out to be advantageous for Cymm because Wexel returned late that evening with essential information.

Wexel paced back and forth waiting to begin. "A wolfer from Endurance Rise took me where the attack occurred. It was approximately five miles from the village and a few hundred yards into the forest. The killer attacked the man from behind, then cut the woman down while she tried to draw her sword, according to the guide."

Wexel paced anxiously. "We followed the depressions left by the attacker's horse toward the plains. A mix of wolf, human, and horse prints slowed our progress. Once the tracks broke out of the forest into the tall grass, they disappeared. We meticulously searched, finding only human and wolf prints, before giving up a mile into the plains. So, we returned to the murder site to continue searching."

"My son had a great idea— 'Let's see where the horseman came from,'—and we searched for hoof prints in the opposite direction. After tracking them for half a mile, they abruptly ended, as if the horse could fly."

One of the elders noticed Cymm shaking his head. "Do you have something to say?"

"Horses don't fly! They are heavy, leaving clear, easy-to-track prints. Someone is playing games."

No one argued his point, and the meeting concluded a few minutes later.

The real trial began in the morning with a larger crowd. Elder Tasha rose. "The representatives from Endurance Rise will go first, presenting their case and evidence. Then Howling Set will go next. Each village will have the opportunity to refute the other's statements."

Cymm learned a lot that morning about some wolfers' feelings toward his kinsmen. Endurance Rise spent four hours citing the history of grievances against the Horse Clan, which had nothing to do with him. They broke for lunch and reconvened two hours later. The list of grievances continued for another hour, rolling into an hour-long explanation about how the Wolf Clan has tried to repair the relationship with the Horse Clan.

Finally, they got to the real issue, stating the same claim and evidence, with no surprises until the very end. The elder from Endurance Rise held his hand up. "This was found near the dead bodies. It is the only other physical evidence we have; it must have been dropped by the perpetrator in his haste to get away."

Cymm's heart pounded, his mind raced, and he glared at Stefo with blazing eyes. The elder held Bria's necklace aloft. He wanted to reach for his neck, to validate its absence, but he didn't dare.

"Stefo, can you describe the horseman you saw fleeing from the murder?" asked the elder still holding his sister's ogre trophy at arm's length.

He pointed at Cymm with a wide, enigmatic grin. "It is easy. He is standing right there. It appears he wants to say something or perhaps claim his necklace."

Elder Tasha replied, "That is not how we do things here. Finish your charges."

The elder from Endurance Rise replied, "Actually, we are done, let him speak."

The paladin clenched his teeth, ignoring the theft of the medallion, trying to concentrate on his defense. "I thought you told the elders you never saw the horseman, only the horse's hoof prints and a trail through the tall grass?"

"No, we saw you from afar, but we couldn't catch up to you," Stefo answered calmly.

He schemed for a split second, trying to set a trap. "So, I was riding my horse away from you? Trying to get away, right?"

His adversary didn't blink. "Yes, that's correct."

Cymm snickered and puffed out his chest. "Then how did you get a good look at the horseman if you couldn't catch up and his back was to you?"

Stefo hesitated, his cheeks warming rapidly. "No, but—"

"Maybe you were chasing a centaur?"

The crowd erupted with laughter at the mention of a beloved Plainsmen's fairy tale.

"It was not a centaur!" Red with embarrassment, Stefo tentatively peeked at his elders for support.

Cymm ignored his response, tilting his head mockingly. "When you confronted me, I was walking my horse, heading toward you."

"That doesn't mean anything! You came across Torak, cast a spell on him, jumped off your horse, and pretended to be best friends for the past week." His smug attitude returned. "You do cast spells from what I have heard, correct?"

Cymm exhaled slowly. "I do not cast spells. I am a healer," he said with hands out to his sides, palms up.

"So, you cast healing spells, but no other spells? That explains everything," his adversary chuckled.

Cymm was flustered, and while he struggled to gather himself, Elder Tasha said, "We have new information to share. Wexel, can you please tell everyone what you found?"

Wexel reiterated his findings, precisely as he'd described the night before. Grunts and muffled speech ensued.

"There were five wolfers and four wolves tracking the horseman. Of course, we stepped all over the tracks. I am surprised you found any. As for the tracks leading into the site of the murders, they didn't disappear. Did you find a creek or stream nearby?" Stefo's silver tongue paused, and he raised his eyebrows.

Cymm stared hard. Had he been briefed on this information already?

Wexel's eyes rolled to the side as he recalled the details of the area. He glanced at his son. "Yes, not real close, mind you. We searched up and down—"

"Well, there you go! He used the stream to hide his tracks. You didn't look far enough," Stefo said with both hands in the air as if he had just won.

Cymm finally got control of himself, recalling his next line of questioning. He took a deep breath while pulling himself upright. "Wexel, do you remember the shape and size of the horse prints? If so, can you please draw one in the dirt and ash?"

Some people grumbled, straining to view the image while others huffed at the waste of time.

Cymm asked him, "Are you sure this is correct?" Wexel nodded, and his son concurred. Cymm turned to Stefo. "Do you agree with the drawing?"

The wolfer paused, his elders leaning forward. "Of course! Basic horse prints, not from a centaur," he added quickly with a flourish.

"I agree these are basic hoof prints from a riding horse, but I have a warhorse, which wears enormous horseshoes." Cymm adjusted the drawing on the ground. "Like this; we can bring the horse over to examine if—"

Stefo exploded with anger, "How many lies will we tolerate? He knew we tracked his horse's prints, so now he has added bigger horseshoes to appear innocent!"

Although most of the crowd was from Howling Set, to Cymm's dismay it appeared less than half of the gathering supported him.

"Torak wouldn't lie!"

"None of the horsemen respect us!"

"Torc's life is at risk. We need better proof!"

"He should have never pledged Torc's life!"

Most of the crowd searched for answers, pointing fingers, shoving, yelling.

"That is not true! I did not . . ." Cymm began, but a fist landed among the crowd as the agitation grew. Why wasn't the truth enough?

Torak placed a hand on his shoulder. "I have the answer!" He repeated this several times, but his voice blended with the chaos of the debate.

The wolfer grabbed Torc's scruff. "Help me!"

Torc issued a loud baying howl, and instantly hundreds of wolves joined in. Cymm's skin crawled, leaving little goosebumps behind.

The crowd instantly fell silent. A strange excitement filled Torak's voice. "We need to summon the shaman! He can cast the eye of the wolf!"

Both lead elders said at the same time, "That has already been done."

"Not on Torc. He has witnessed everything from the moment he was healed until we were confronted on the plains. It will be obvious at least five days passed, and Cymm accompanied us the entire time!" Torak danced happily in place.

Elder Tasha cried immediately, "Send for the shaman!"

23

Second Nature

L ykinnia had not visited her creature friends for a couple of days because Solar had been monopolizing the altar. She approached the platform early on the third morning to find him already there.

"You will have to find somewhere else to pray today," Solar said, without bothering to look over his shoulder.

She stormed away, stomping her feet, her words making an unintelligible noise. Returning after midnight, she had cast her new invisibility spell on her way to the altar.

Solar was still there.

What can be so interesting? she thought, intending to find out. She stepped onto the platform, not making a sound. She positioned herself behind him so she could peer into the window.

"Why are you bothering this boy?" she said aloud, sending her voice to the other plane. The young man's anxious expression showed he wrestled with an internal demon. She empathized with him; he seemed lonely, even though another young man and a giant wolf slept next to him.

He shifted his position, trying to get comfortable, then reached over to rub the wolf's ribcage. She stared into his eyes, her eyelashes fluttering, then she sighed deeply as something stirred inside her.

Solar peered down at his arm, slowly rubbing a spot near the joint; his hand narrowly missed her face. Realization came to her at last as she exhaled on his elbow again.

"Lykinnia?" he asked as she rapidly backed up and hopped off the platform to the ground three feet below. She ducked below the level of the platform, anticipating his next move.

Solar crouched, twisting his torso to the right, then quickly stood while untwisting. A radiant burst of energy pulsed from his body in a spherical shape. "Hmm. Lykinnia, you're playing with fire."

The familiar sound of the scrying window dismissal proceeded his departing footsteps. Peaking over the platform, she saw Solar step through an open portal, *vrrrummp*. It imploded and disappeared.

She returned to sit on the edge of the platform, waiting, occasionally peeking over at the space where he disappeared. After three minutes, the fabric of space unfolded.

She giggled. Solar's head popped out of the small rift, scanning in all directions.

She rose, positioned herself at the altar, waiting for him to leave. "Nice try, buddy."

"Lykinnia," said the voice from the other plane.

She immediately ended her invisibility spell when Solar's head disappeared, then she flash-traveled back to Darken Wood.

Her golden ethereal form hovered in the usual meeting area, the only illumination. No movement, no sound, but that was expected. They should be sleeping.

Crack. A stick snapped to her left.

"That's odd." She went to investigate, her breath catching in her throat. The light from her body had startled a giant spider. One of her nymphs lay paralyzed in front of it, half-covered in webs.

24

Eye of the Wolf

The shaman entered the village early the following morning, rolling past Torak and Cymm. He rode in a two-wheeled cart pulled by a set of wolves. Cymm's mouth fell open; his appearance didn't align with his expectations. He figured the shaman would be wearing a headdress made of antlers or thick robes of furs and skins, but neither was true. He also didn't have a bird perched on his shoulder or feathers in his hair. In fact, the only thing setting him apart from the other wolfers was the staff he carried.

Word of the shaman's arrival spread quickly, and a crowd materialized at the village center.

While following the crowd, Torak explained, "The Wolf Clan consists of four tribes and four shamans, one per tribe. Each shaman selects a successor to begin training at the age of eighteen. This one took the mantel from his mother only five years ago."

The chaotic din grew louder, forcing Cymm to lean closer to hear him. ". . . since our binding ceremony six weeks ago."

The newcomer drew a larger crowd than yesterday, and people were arguing over spots to sit on the ground. An intense energy permeated the air. His heart began to race, feeding off the crowd's emotions. *Why is everyone so excited?*

The shaman beckoned Torak to come forward with his bound companion. They joined him in the center near the firepit containing red hot coals.

Waving his arms and chanting, the shaman summoned the fire elementals, enraging the coals until flames blazed as tall as his horse.

The crowd went silent.

Arcs of flame shot higher, circling each other before wrapping themselves into a ring of fire. The orange band had a diameter of six feet, a thickness of eight inches, and hovered above the firepit, chasing its tail like a wolf.

The wolfer shuffled his feet, picking at his fingernails. Torc sat next to his master, scratching his neck. The shaman reached out, placing his hands on top of their heads. Both human and wolf went motionless, as if paralyzed. Their eyes blazed red, then beams of light shot from their eyes toward the fire ring.

Cymm recoiled from the sudden discharge of energy, using his forearm to shield his eyes. He tentatively peered over his arm to find an image coalescing into a three-dimensional hologram inside the ring. His arm dropped, and so did his lower jaw. He pushed to the edge of his seat, leaning in, staring, unblinking, refusing to miss a second of the augmented reality.

The ominous muzzle of a shadow wolf lunged forward, followed by a loud whimper and fur flying everywhere. More growling, more whimpering. Cymm observed the fight with the shadow wolf again, but from Torc's perspective. The image rotated ninety degrees when Torc fell to the ground, the shadow wolf towering above him. Torak appeared out of nowhere, delivering a flying knee to the wolf's head before pushing him away.

Torak took a defensive position between the combatants, but an unsteady image of his attacker still appeared through his companion's leg.

The eye of the wolf swirled; people raced to new positions as time sped up. Cymm approached Torak as he knelt next to the wounded animal.

"I can save your wolf's life," the horseman yelled.

"Go ahead; if both agree to a settlement, it makes our job easier," a guard replied.

The young wolfer implored, "Please save Torc! I will be in your debt."

Cymm knelt beside the beast, "Hold his head tight!"

The crowd laughed when Cymm's eyes went wide next to the dire wolf; then a brilliant white light washed out Torc's vision. When it subsided, the wolf ran next to Cymm through the woods, approaching a river.

Many of the villagers gasped, and others cried out in anger.

"He can't cross twice. Can he?"

"This is madness!"

"How did they get to the River of Binding?"

Before they reached the river, Torc stopped running, bringing Cymm to a halt. The wolf peered back the way he came, toward his bound partner in the distance. He locked eyes briefly with Cymm before running back to Torak.

"Good boy!"

"Torc's a good wolf."

"This is still madness!"

In a flash of white light, the image changed, and once again the wolf lay on the stable floor with Cymm kneeling over him. Yet again the scene swirled, people moving insanely fast, until they were leaving the gates of Armak. They walked at a moderately fast pace for the passage of five sunrises until Stefo's gang approached.

The shaman slowly released his control over the bound pair, and the image in the ring instantly disappeared. Finally, their eyes returned to normal when the ring of fire retreated into the red-hot embers from whence it came.

The crowd whispered in satisfied tones. Cymm stared into the empty air above the fire, still entranced by the experience. *Wow, so vivid and accurate, except I never ran in the woods with Torc.* While the eye of the wolf still enthralled him, the silence evaporated.

"I told you Torak wouldn't lie."

"He still shouldn't have pledged Torc's life."

"How did they get to the River of Binding?"

"The horseman must be a shaman for his tribe and tried to steal Torc!"

"Oh, shut up, idiot!"

"You should be ashamed of yourself, Stefo!"

The elders from both villages raised their hands.

"Silence!" Elder Tasha yelled, waiting for the remaining arguments to end. "The trial is over, and by unanimous decision, Cymm is not guilty. Torc's pledge has ended."

The villagers disbanded faster than they arrived. The lead elder from Endurance Rise came over to shake Cymm's hand, apologizing for the mistaken identity. Several other elders from their envoy followed suit, but Stefo held back.

When Cymm was finally alone, Stefo sauntered over and shook his hand heartily like they were old friends. His hand tightened around Cymm's, his eyes narrowing under his furrowed brows. "As long as you stay in the north, this isn't over. Time to run back to your little farm down south."

Stefo tried to leave, but Cymm crushed his hand. His shoulders leaned forward, eyes fixated on him, delivering his next words with serious intention. "When I am done with my business in the north, I will come looking for you to take back what you stole." Cymm motioned with his chin toward the ogre nose ring now hanging around Stefo's neck.

"Take it now," whispered Stefo. "Give my elders a reason to call for a mistrial." After a few moments, he forcefully withdrew his hand with a low growl, then returned to his group with a prideful grin.

Cymm shook his head, still reeling from the shock and anger. The exchange left his fists clenched at his side. *What else can this world throw at me? I am sick of this.*

"Everything all right?" asked Torak.

"That orc's ass just threatened me!"

"What?" said the wolfer in disbelief.

Cymm pinched the bridge of his nose to relieve the tension building between his eyes. "He said I better leave the north, or else."

Torak put his hand on Cymm's shoulder. "Hey, what did you think of the eye of the wolf? Pretty cool, huh?"

Cymm smirked at the diversion, "It was very cool. Was the image three-dimensional for everyone from all angles?"

The wolfer nodded up and down enthusiastically. "The best part is he used my memories to fill in the gaps including the dire wolf's green color blindness."

"Look at these guys." The young wolfer motioned toward the visiting group as they left his village. "I guess they don't mind that Stefo wasted several days of their lives."

Cymm rolled his eyes. "Well, it was an honest mistake."

Torak shook his head and punched him in the shoulder. "I usually try to stay out of other's business, but I must ask you, what is your purpose in the north? Tribute Set is your destination, but to what end?"

"It is a long story. Let's grab some lunch. I will tell you while we eat," the horseman said.

Torak replied, "Sounds good." Torc jumped around more excited than before.

Cymm pointed at the dire wolf. "No grasshoppers for you!"

The dire wolf stopped jumping around, moaning with displeasure. *Did he understand me?* The dire wolf walked away with his head down, tail between his legs. The two young men pointed at him and burst out laughing.

The village held a small celebration in honor of the bound pair. Cymm planned to attend and be on his way in the morning, but not before Torak offered to accompany him to Tribute Set.

It took them most of the day to get there, but as the late afternoon turned to evening, Tribute Set appeared above the grasses in the distance.

"So, you don't need to enter Tribute Set, only the woods north of the village, right?"

Cymm sat astride his warhorse. "As far as I can tell, that is correct."

They skirted the village until they reached the edge of the forest.

Torak patted the massive warhorse. "Cymm, Darken Wood has many dangerous creatures besides dragons. Be careful."

The paladin dismounted. They gripped hands and embraced. "I will visit you and Torc on my way back home." He gave the dire wolf a hearty tussle of his ears, mounted his horse, and rode west along the fringe of the forest.

He identified the entry point into the forest from his Divine Quest, then urged his horse inside. A few hours remained before sunset to begin searching, but fifty feet in, the gray shadows turned to black ones. After a few hundred feet, he pulled back on the lead. "Slow, my friend. No need for a hoof injury."

Click Click. His horse stopped. Cymm dismounted after only twenty minutes, leading his steed on foot until his own feet were barely discernible from the shadows. He stumbled for a second time and decided to make camp.

He ate a cold jerky dinner, placed his back against a big broad tree trunk, and five minutes later was sound asleep.

25

Survival

"Little ones, awaken." Lykinnia's shrill voice echoed throughout the dark night. The brightness of her body increased with her fury, and the spider could not stand against her onslaught of light. It cowered, trying to shield it eyes, then skittered away, leaving its paralyzed victim behind.

Two of the larger nymphs, or tavii, as she had decided to call them, appeared next to her, wearing brown leather bandoliers. Tucked into slots on the shoulder belts were several sharp weapons, which they drew immediately to cut the webs from their friend.

She quickly searched the perimeter, finding several spiders in the vicinity.

"Little ones! We must leave. Hurry!" She flew through the area, resembling a lightning bug more than a girl. She hoped the flashing would not only scare the spiders but wake any remaining insect friends.

She returned to the meeting area to find a battle in progress between two spiders and ten nymphs. Another nymph lay motionless on the forest floor next to a spider.

Lykinnia raced to join the skirmish. "Shield your eyes!" Her next flash went supernova, temporarily blinding one of the spiders, and causing the other to flee in fear. A host of insects descended on the remaining arachnid. They brutally cut it, bit it, and heaved on its legs. Overwhelmed, the spider collapsed. The tavii were relentless until they had dismembered it, and its insides oozed over the ground.

Lykinnia sighed in relief when Gillygahpadima finally joined them. "How many should there be?"

Still half asleep, the insect answered, "Sixteen."

"We've lost five more in the last few days?" She counted those present. "Sixteen. There are more spiders nearby. We must carry our wounded friends and leave now."

26

A Noise in the Dark

A modicum of light filtered down through the canopy to awaken Cymm the following morning. He had lost all sense of time in the forest, but with the charcoal light, he assumed it was a couple hours after the break of dawn. Torak's fellow villagers had donated two weeks of food rations, which he would need to supplement with hunting.

The forest was easy to traverse because no underbrush existed. The tree trunks varied in size, but most were massive. Infrequently, he came across a tree fallen from age, wind, or disease, allowing the sunlight to flood the forest floor. In this rare oasis, saplings and other growth fought to gain height and control the sunlight, creating a dense patch of brush and a meal for his horse.

After three days of using a weaving search pattern, he still had found nothing. In the early morning of the fourth day, Cymm woke suddenly with the hair on the back of his neck standing up. He unsheathed his sword with shaky hands, trying to remain calm. His campfire had gone out long ago, but there were still a few tiny embers.

A twig snapped.

He slowly stood with his back against the tree.

"Cymm?" the mysterious visitor whispered his name from nearby.

He froze. *How do they know my name?*

"Cymm, we have to go!"

He let out a deep breath; his shoulders sagged. "Torak? What are you doing here?"

The bound pair stepped around the tree. "No time to talk! Get on your horse and ride east. We have to get out of here." Wolf and wolfer immediately ran in the direction he had indicated, expecting him to follow.

Cymm rushed to gather his belongings, and within a few moments he mounted his horse heading east. The leaves on the trees defiantly and efficiently filtered the daylight, ensuring near darkness. Shadows danced and taunted him beyond thirty feet. His friend's head twitched from side to side, scanning, maybe listening. Cymm, silenced by the furtive movements, pushed his horse to a slow trot to close the gap. A high-pitched chatter, still far off to the south, made the hair on his neck snap to attention while a low-pitched clicking reverberated throughout the forest.

The sound penetrated Cymm's skull; his head ached. Poor Torc shook his ears, whimpering. Torak waved of his arm, then pointed to a rocky knoll up ahead. They climbed the backside, then hid between the rocks at the top. He had secured his horse to the closest tree before soothing him with clicks and ear scratches. As the light in the forest increased, so did visibility. The wolfer scanned the forest floor from the rocky knoll. Cymm did likewise to no avail.

"What is it? What is making that awful noise?" Cymm whispered.

Torak pointed into the distance; the entire floor undulated. The horseman blinked and leaned in closer, trying to make sense of the anomaly. Torc issued a low growl, glancing at his partner for reassurance. They locked eyes for several tense seconds, then the dire wolf fell silent. Cymm had witnessed this "exchange" before. *Did the binding allow them to understand each other?*

Tens of thousands of two-foot-long ants, streamed through the forest, heading northwest. The men remained where they were, observing the ants swarm by. Running amongst the stragglers were scores of gnolls, vicious humanoid creatures. Each had the head of a hyena and a foul temper. The pursuers pinned the ant's head to the ground with a pitchfork, and a second gnoll ripped the body clean off, stripped the legs, and threw the remains into a large wooden cart. The hunters had at least thirty carts and many were packed to the brim.

The young men watched quietly until the hunting party moved out of sight. They retreated down the hill, heading northeast, away from the chaos. Cymm mentally withdrew for a few minutes but could hold it no longer. The words slipped out of his mouth in a rush. "What in the nine hells are you doing here?"

Torak snorted happily. "Torc and I aren't going to let you find the dragons by yourself." His smile faded quickly when Cymm's face contorted in anger.

"Why doesn't anyone support me? I can defeat the dragons by myself!"

"No, you can't! In fact, the three of us will probably fail, but I'm still willing to help you knowing we may die," the wolfer confessed.

He staggered backward and sat on a rock, not expecting the answer he received. He opened his mouth to respond, raised his hand with the pointer finger extended, but the words escaped him. Deep down, he also had his doubts from the beginning, but memories of his strong mother, dependable father, and sweet, innocent sister kept him going.

Torak's words rocked him to his core.

The wolfer stiffened with regret. "Cymm . . . I am sorry. I didn't mean to—"

"Yes, you did, and maybe you're right," he said drumming his fingers on his chin. "You are a good friend to speak honestly."

"Well then, here is some more honesty. Either we travel together to find the dragons—"

Cymm perked a brow. "Or?"

"Or Torc and I continue to track you," said the wolfer, catching him off guard again.

What would I have done if Talo and Semper had followed me? Can I live with myself if they die? A devious look appeared on Cymm's face. "Fine, have it your way. But I hear green dragons love to eat wolves and wolfers!"

Torc moaned and rubbed his head against his partner's shoulder.

∞∞∞∞

After five days in Darken Wood, he prayed frequently for help to find the dragon's lair, but each time he received the same Vision of the rock formation. After two weeks in the forest, he drew the rock formation in the dirt again, and Torak confirmed it was Tribute Set.

"It's been four weeks. What in the nine hells are we scouting for?" asked the wolfer.

"I have no idea. Have you ever seen a dragon's lair before?"

"No, but maybe your god has!" the chords in the Torak's neck were straining.

"It could be a hole in the ground, a cave, a hidden grotto, or a pile of rocks. Who knows!" Cymm's frustration spilled into the discussion, but his anger resided with Terazhan's directions.

"I didn't realize this was going to be a year-long expedition," the wolfer continued to rant.

Cymm pointed southeast. "For you, it doesn't have to be! Start walking. You'll be home in two weeks."

Torak's laughter echoed through the still air.

"What's so funny?" asked the paladin with eyebrows knitted.

"First of all, you are not getting rid of me so easily, and second—" He walked over to Cymm, spun him entirely around, lifted his arm, and extended his pointer finger. "That's the direction of my home! If I left now, you would end up in the Mighty Forest north of here and wouldn't know it."

"Yeah, right!" Cymm gave him an intentionally fake smile before scanning the canopy.

They widened the search area for two more weeks, and still nothing. Finally, with their food almost depleted and hunting unreliable, they made the difficult decision to head back to the plains.

It took several days to break out of the woods, then another to get back to Tribute Set. Cymm tried to calculate how much time had passed since he left Stallion Rise—at least two months. That meant the month of Rhomerian was waning, and he had celebrated his seventeenth lifeday while searching in Darken Wood.

His horse moaned and snorted while grazing in the plains, causing Cymm to suddenly laugh. *When I get home, I will gorge myself on berry bread,* he thought, rubbing the horse's shoulder.

"Is something amusing you?" asked Torak.

"Oh, daydreaming about food is all. Which reminds me, we need to buy some for my horse."

He left his steed outside the village to graze, drawing an approving nod from Torak, both hoping to draw less attention.

Acquiring food was much cheaper than the Plainsmen thought. They bought or traded for several stacks of jerky, dozens of sausage links, and a few loaves of nut bread. As they packed the food in sacks, Cymm observed the village center.

Next to the fire pit, he saw the rock formation. He recalled the Vision that infiltrated his mind constantly, and although they were similar, they were not the same! He circled the rocks, changing his perspective while the pit in his stomach grew. *This is why I kept receiving the same Vision from Terazhan when I prayed.*

Torak asked, "What's wrong? This isn't what you were looking for?"

"No, these are different!" Cymm replied.

The shaman walked out of his home—drawn by the noise—with curiosity on his face. "Is there a problem?"

"Shaman do other villages have a rock formation like this?" the young wolfer asked.

"Rock formation? Do you mean the Binding Stones? The same Binding Stones that bound you and Torc together," the shaman replied in disgust. "How disappointing?"

Torak tried to crawl inside himself, and his furry friend was there in a flash to console him. The wolfer turned to leave with Cymm on his heels.

"What happened? Are there other Binding Stones?" he asked.

"Yes. Every tribe has a shaman, and every shaman's village has Binding Stones. I am sorry, Cymm. I didn't realize those boulders were the Binding Stones. I have only seen my own ritual, and the excitement and nerves blocked some of the details."

He waved his hands. "Okay . . . so how many Stones are we talking about, and where are they?"

"There are three more; one is west of here, and the other two are south and east. Since the dragons flew north, it must be Binding Set, which is four and a half days west." Torak was talking to himself as much as to Cymm.

After exiting the village, the paladin let out a loud, sharp whistle, and his warhorse came running. "Let's be on our way then."

The wolfer gave his usual sideways glare. "Two days till Anuberis; maybe I will be home before the end of that month."

"Not likely, dragon bait." Cymm chuckled while waiting for his reply.

So consumed with their bantering back and forth, they never saw the character lurking in the shadows of the closest house. Watching them, waiting, biding his time.

27

Stefo

After the trial, it was a long, two-day journey back to Endurance Rise for Stefo. The elders he traveled with saw no need for chastisement, but he worried about what awaited him when he arrived home.

He knew his father, Brato, would hold him to a "higher" standard.

Stefo entered his home, greeted his father, quickly unpacked, and moved for the door.

"Where do you think you are going?" Brato asked.

"To hang out with my friends. Why?" When the young man spun around to face him, his father struck him hard in the chest, stealing the breath from his lungs. He collapsed to his knees; confident he knew what would come next. His father beat him with a large blackjack, an experience he had become familiar with. He curled in a ball, envisioning the day when *he* would hold the blackjack.

His father was proud of the weapon he had designed. It was a long, thin leather bag containing iron sling stones and sand, stitched closed with a four-inch grip. Stefo had been hit with it often but never in the face, so the bruising wouldn't show.

Brato stood over his prone body, breathing heavily. "Next time I send you out with a task, you better not return until it's finished!"

Stefo had just turned eighteen a few months earlier, but the beatings began so long ago, he wasn't sure when they started. However, he did know the increase in frequency and severity coincided with his father losing his bound wolf, Jalko.

That was almost four years ago in the City of Armak. An argument preceded a fight, and Jalko ran away. His father blamed the wolf's departure on the horseman he fought, claimed he cast a spell to confuse Jalko, causing him to flee. Brato still searches for him, even issued a standing reward for his safe return.

Stefo's stomach churned; he knew his father beat Jalko too. The wolf's freedom gave him hope that one day he would be free as well, so he hoped he never found him.

After losing his bound wolf, his father became very creative. Not only did he invent the blackjack, but he also initiated the group called Fang.

Is it over? thought Stefo emerging from his daydream, his father's footsteps receding. He sighed, *Until the next time. Why can't I be strong like Jalko? Leave and never return.*

He lay on the floor, still struggling to breathe. *How many times did the blackjack hit me?* He had blocked out most of it, again.

"Are you listening to me, boy?" Brato said stridently from a chair across the room.

Stefo remained curled in a fetal position on the floor. "Yes, I am listening."

"Tomorrow, you will put a team together to head back to Howling Set. I want you to kill the horseman and bring back his body. We will use it to stage another attack to prove his guilt after all. Am I clear?"

"Yes, sir," Stefo mumbled while pain coursed through his body. He crawled to his room and climbed into bed.

It was a restless night, pain shooting through his body with every movement. He struggled to get out of bed in the morning, but knew he had no choice. Healing would have to occur on the road, so he rounded up seven other Fang members, all his friends, and left the village by lunchtime.

The gang proceeded directly to Howling Set. Stefo entered the village well after midnight on the third night. He slunk from home to home undetected, entering his destination like a shadow. He stood over his target, imagining his father's face.

How can you feel so safe in your little home? He reached down, grabbed a pillow, and put it over the man's mouth. The sleeper's eyes shot open in a panic, he issued a muffled scream, then grabbed for his attacker's wrists.

"Fang bites swift and hard," he whispered into the man's ear, and he immediately stopped struggling. Stefo removed the pillow, throwing it to the side.

"You scared the fur off my neck!" cried the elder from Howling Set, the same elder that told him about Wexel's report during the trial. "How dare you enter my home at night!"

"Brato wants the horseman's head, and you will help me get him out of the village and away from Torak," Stefo made himself at home in the man's chair, grabbing an apple from the table and taking a snappy bite.

"I can help you with one of them. The horseman left the village the day after the trial heading for Tribute Set, but Torak and Torc went with him. I am not sure where they were heading after that." The Fang informant sat on the edge of his bed now.

"Thank you! Fang bites swift and hard," Stefo said.

"And never misses the mark," replied the elder.

28

The Clearing

They had already traveled four days and expected to arrive at Binding Set in the next few hours.

Torak had been unusually silent for the past hour. "This is not my tribe. To walk into their village, we are going to have to trade again."

"Alright, what do we have to trade?" He scanned his horse for ideas.

"Not much. Furs and skins would be the best. Do you have more coins?"

"Hunting to trade will delay our progress," Cymm replied, pulling out the pouch on his belt and shaking it. "I still have a few coins."

When the village was a few hundred yards away, he dismounted and walked his horse. Torak glanced at him quickly and nodded. "You have learned a great deal about how the wolfers perceived your clan."

"Doesn't hurt to be cautious. I plan to leave him outside the village when we enter." Cymm rubbed and scratched the horse's withers.

"Even with all these wolves romping around?" Torak had a devious smile as he pointed to the closest ones.

The paladin puffed his chest out with pride. "If the wolves know not to attack pigs and sheep, then let's hope they are smart enough not to mess with a two-thousand-pound warhorse. These iron-shod hooves pack quite a punch."

Torc took the lead into the village. A crowd gathered around the visitors but grew more prominent when the trading began.

The young men were able to purchase scores of arrows, as well as additional food. They traded some of the sausages they bought in Tribute Set for spices. Cymm had many offers for the leather jerkin he wore, but he politely declined.

Most importantly, the paladin noticed the Binding Stones were identical to the picture in his mind. "Yes!" he yelled, pumping both fists in the air.

"You must have gotten a good deal for the sausage," Torak teased.

He pretended to scowl at the wolfer. "We got it right this time. Let's wrap up and head for Darken Wood."

"You really aren't mad at me for getting it wrong the first time? You are a rare friend!"

Although the Divine Quest occurred many weeks earlier, Cymm confidently strode to the edge of the forest, contemplating whether to enter. Since it was late in the day, the amount of light in the forest would diminish quickly. They decided to camp at the edge of the plains and enjoy a mini feast with an early morning start.

"Torak, you have been a loyal and trusted friend, and I will ask you to keep your word to me," Cymm said, starting a long-overdue conversation.

"What promise did I make?" he asked with his face squinched.

"When we find the dragon's lair, both of you will remain a safe distance behind with my horse while I enter alone. In return, I will give you, my word. If the situation is hopeless, I will try to return so we can figure out how to defeat them together." He had accidentally mimicked Old-Man Semper's crotchety demeanor, and the thought filled him with a sense of longing. He yearned for home, but things would never be the same and he had no intention of turning back.

The bound pair gazed at each other for a long moment, then Torak replied, "I never agreed to—"

Cymm interrupted, "Wait, what was that?"

Torak shrugged. "What was what?"

"The staring communicating thing I see you two always doing."

Torak gave Cymm a non-committal look with a crinkled face. "As I was saying, I never agreed to that, but I will if you intend to honor your commitment."

"Agreed," Cymm said, offering his hand to seal the deal.

Torak shook his hand, but when he turned around, Torc peeked up at him.

Cymm yelled inside his own mind, *"They did it again!"*

The following morning, they rose shortly after sunrise. By the time they ate and broke camp, sunlight filtered into the forest.

"That was the best night's sleep I have had in months," Cymm pronounced practically bouncing. "We are definitely in the correct place now. In my morning prayers, I received a new Vision!"

Torak stretched his arms above his head and yawned. "Well, don't hold back."

"I saw a huge pile of trees, at least fifty feet high, with a large crude opening. The pile was elevated on a natural dirt hill, situated in the middle of a forest clearing." He gestured wildly with his eyes and hands, extenuating each word.

"Where is all this energy coming from? You just can't wait to get killed by a dragon, can you?" Torak massaged the remaining sleep from his eyes.

Cymm shrugged. "To expedite my killing and your devouring, I am also eliminating the winding search pattern. Instead, we are taking a straight-line path to the north." He pointed northward, then glanced over at Torak with pride.

Torak rolled his eyes. "It won't be so easy when we are in the middle of the forest."

For the first three days, the area teamed with wildlife, deer, elk, boar, and wolves. They had no problem hunting for food, keeping their reserves for later. However, by the fourth day, the large game had disappeared, and by the morning of the fifth, the forest grew eerily silent. An ominous feeling grew inside Cymm, causing him to check frequently on his friend's position. The feeling escalated as they crept silently through the forest for more than an hour.

A large clearing appeared up ahead.

They pushed forward to the next hillock. Cymm dismounted, hobbled his horse, then taught Torak how to take the device off.

Torak slapped him on the back. "Don't take any unnecessary risks! I bet we can get forty or fifty wolfers and be back in a month. Many of them will do it for the treasure."

"I have no interest in the gold, and I do not make promises lightly!" he replied shaking Torak's hand firmly. He patted Torc's head, rubbed his horse's flank, and departed quickly.

Mid-day approached as Cymm stood at the edge of the extensive clearing. His heartbeat quickened, and a lump had grown in his throat preventing him from swallowing the saliva accumulating in his mouth. The clearing was devoid of trees, but a strange vegetation thrived with jagged thorns, vines, and twisted undergrowth.

Across the clearing, a mountain of freshly uprooted trees waited, identical to his Vision. He took his first couple of steps, along with a deep breath, all the while thinking about his family facing these beasts alone. The thoughts emboldened him to continue.

As he cautiously walked toward the pile of trees, a vine no thicker than his thumb crawled toward him. A shiver went down his spine. He quickly unsheathed his sword and hacked it into pieces. With each step more vines slithered toward him like snakes, tearing at his clothes and skin with their sharp thorns. His path, a meandering skunk walk, helped him avoid most of the clearing's strange, new growth.

After cutting through several bushes, he eventually made it to the center of the clearing, suffering only a few minor scratches. It would be a nightmare to walk through this clearing once this aggressive undergrowth had taken over. Fortunately, he would be long gone. After a short walk clockwise around the tree mound, he found the entrance. The hole continued out of sight. It didn't go into the pile of trees; it went down into the earth. He plastered himself against a giant tree trunk and root ball, his heartbeat racing out of control.

He had reached his destination.

"Calm down, Cymm," he told himself. "This is for your family!"

He silently drew his sword and a deep breath, then he slipped around the edge and down into the tunnel.

29

Forged Mettle

S tefo and his hitmen had already been tracking Cymm for over four weeks. They had been close once before, but a gnoll hunting party had wiped out miles of his tracks. Now they were closer, only one day behind, and he could predict Cymm's weaving pattern.

It was early afternoon, and Stefo had everyone spread out, with the wolves running vast arcs, looking, sniffing, and tracking. Laret, his best friend since they were five lifeyears and second in command, walked next to him.

"I hope we close the gap today," Laret said.

Stefo raised his eyebrows twice. "Yeah, I would like to find them tonight, sleeping by their little campfire. Tie them up, roll them into the flames, and watch them cook like elk meat."

Laret cringed. "There's something wrong with you. How about we just kill them?"

Everyone ran toward Stefo instinctually when a wolf yelped in significant pain. Safety and strength in the pack was the first lesson in combat training.

An eleven-foot-tall shape materialized from behind an enormous tree, chasing the injured wolf and wolfer.

Stefo could tell they weren't going to make it. "Hold your position!" The remaining men flanked him, their wolves forming a line in front of them.

Laret yelled encouragement, "Don't stop! Keep running." When the wolf stumbled, its companion hurtled over its hindquarters to intercept the monster.

The wolves charged to help their friend, and the men followed, leaving behind the best defensible terrain. Before help could arrive, the hill giant swung his club, clobbering the human so hard he flew twenty feet into a tree and died; then the giant lumbered toward the wolf.

The other six dire wolves descended upon the enemy ferociously shredding its legs. Three arrows hit the giant in the neck and chest. No longer able to stand, the monster crashed to the ground, grasping for the wounded wolf.

Stefo commanded, "Hold your arrows! Do not hit the wolves!"

A low grunt came from behind, reminding him how foolish he had been to charge. Stefo dove to the side, barely avoiding a crushing blow, but Janek, another childhood friend, crumpled under the force of a club.

Janek's soul partner flashed into a defensive position, standing over him, growling savagely at the new hill giant. Stefo stared at the demonstration of loyalty, yearning for his own wolf yet again. He had tried twice already, once at sixteen and again a few months ago, but he could not get a wolf to bind with him.

The giant's club descended toward Janek and his wolf, but the rest of the wolves arrived a moment later, pounding the giant like an avalanche. A dire wolf in mid-leap encountered the incoming club, cracking its skull. It fell dead at the enemy's feet.

Meanwhile, a third hill giant took two long strides, collapsing their flank. It struck two men a glancing blow, sending them to the ground. The other men bombarded it with arrows.

Stefo rolled to his feet, discarding his broken bow to the side, and drew his long sword. He shifted his weight to launch into a sprint when something grabbed his leg. Peering back, he found a bloody, horrific view. The original giant crawled toward him with half of its face ripped off, including one ear, exposing bone where its eyebrow should have been.

The giant yanked him forcefully off his feet with a sickening *crunch* then a *pop* in his knee. Excruciating pain flooded his mind. His face scraped along the ground as the monster dragged him closer. Stefo rolled from his belly to his back and forcefully sat up, driving his sword into his enemy's eye socket.

The battle still raged behind him, so he quickly withdrew the sword from the dead giant. He rolled to his stomach and rushed to stand up, but his leg would not support him. As soon as his knee buckled, his vision blurred from the pain. He plummeted to the ground, striking his head on a rock below.

Get up! he yelled at himself. *Brato has beaten you ten times worse! Get up!*

30

Rest and Recovery

Two weeks had passed since that brutal fight in which they lost three wolves and three wolfers. Everyone in the party had been injured, and they hobbled into the village of Tribute Set to find a place to rest and heal.

Stefo couldn't believe his luck when he saw Cymm and Torak enter the village. He didn't care what they were searching for in the woods or how the Binding Stones were involved. While eavesdropping, he discovered where they were heading.

Laret walked up behind him. "Was that who I think it was?"

"You bet your wolf's ears." Stefo's eyes were gleaming. "Did the horse give it away? Tell the boys to pack up. We leave in the morning."

∞∞∞∞∞

Seven days later, Stefo and his four-man kill squad, Laret, Janek, and the brothers Tomek and Basten, approached a clearing in the forest. None of them had ever seen anything so massive in Darken Wood.

"Here we go, boys. That clearing up ahead must have been his destination," he said.

Tomek was on his knees inspecting prints. "We are close, less than one hour behind."

"If we pick up the pace, maybe we can head home today." Janek rubbed his sore shoulder, the one that took the impact when the giant clobbered him.

"It's already been a month and a half. What's another day?" Laret scoffed. The shaman at Tribute Set had given him the opportunity to bind with the fourth surviving wolf, but the loss of his own still lingered like a festering wound.

"Janek's right; let's get this over with," said their leader, picking up the pace. "Remember, this is a kill order for the horseman. If Torak gets in the way, kill him too."

"Speak of the devil," Janek said, pointing over Stefo's right shoulder.

As they rounded a hillock, Torak, Torc, and a horse came into view. Torak tried to step up into the stirrup, but the horse whinnied and sidestepped, causing him to fall.

"Whoa! What do we have here?" Laret pointed and snickered at Torak lying on his back with his feet in the air. "Looks like a turtle!"

"Take the horse down. The horseman must be around here somewhere," ordered Stefo.

One wolfer notched an arrow, but the horse had galloped out of range before he could let it fly.

Torc issued a menacing growl, placing himself in front of his companion.

"Torak, I am going to give you a one-time opportunity to join Fang." Stefo and crew walked casually toward him.

"I thought there was no such thing as Fang," Torak countered, slapping Torc on his hindquarters to get his attention.

"We both know that's not true. Stop delaying and make a—" Stefo stopped abruptly as Torc took off running in the same direction as the horse. "Get the horse and wolf; I will deal with him."

Torak used the diversion to sprint away from the clearing, leaving everything behind. Laret quickly pulled back on his bowstring while the other wolfers sent their wolves to pursue the animals that got away. Torak's attempt to outrun an arrow failed, and it embedded in his hamstring. He fell to the ground like a rock, writhing in pain.

Laret notched an arrow to fire from close range. "He doesn't want to join us."

Stefo shoved his bow off target. "Hold on. Maybe he needs some encouragement."

A fight broke out in the distance between horse and wolf. A mix of grunts, painfilled horse screams, and wolf yelps drifted through the air. Before that fight concluded, a three-wolf battle began in a different direction with snapping, snarling, and barking. The chaotic sounds echoed through the forest like a long-forgotten nightmare.

Stefo lost interest in Torak. "Tie him up!" He drifted toward the sounds of battle, torn about which to listen to.

A few minutes later, the noise abruptly ended, and each wolf owner recalled their partner. Janek's agitated wolf returned alone.

Stefo pointed at the wolf. "What's wrong with him?"

Janek held a finger up still staring at his companion. "Hurry! There's a wolf in trouble!"

Everyone but Laret took off running, following Janek's wolf. He led the way around the clearing, staying in the woods, then popped out right in front of a trapped wolf.

Basten rushed forward. "Come on; help him!" The wolf struggled with a thorny vine wrapped around its hind leg, pulling it toward the main stalk. Stefo jumped to its aid, severing the vine while Basten carefully unwound the separated piece from the wolf's leg. The thorns were embedded deep in the muscle.

Their leader scanned the area. "Where is the dire wolf?"

"Torc ran further into the clearing," replied Janek.

His face twisted in anger. "Then let's go."

"But the vines are attacking . . ." Tomek instantly fell silent from the glare he received.

"So, you are scared to go after the wolf. Unbelievable!" Stefo rolled his eyes, walking toward the center of the clearing by himself. As soon as the closest vine sensed his presence, it attacked him, draining him of the confidence he possessed seconds before. He cut it to pieces in a frenzy but then quickly retreated to the group. He patted Tomek on the back while putting an arm around Janek's shoulders. "Okay, maybe we need a plan to get across the clearing!"

When they returned, Torak was still unconscious. The third wolf had returned limping, its mouth covered in blood.

They tied Torak to a tree right outside the clearing. Stefo took the lead and stepped into the clearing again with two wolfers off each shoulder. He had created a safe pocket in the middle for the wolves to walk or limp in.

31

Death to Dragons!

lthough the sun had achieved its zenith in the sky, the daylight barely penetrated the crisscrossed and weaved trunks creating the canopy over the dragon's lair. With his sword in hand, Cymm crept down the fifty-foot-long tunnel until it opened into a large cathedral chamber. His nerves were on overload, so he hesitated at the entrance. Sweat beaded on his forehead, his stomach churned, and a slight tremor commandeered his hands. He placed a fist on his chest to ease the building pressure, then closed his eyes for a moment.

He thought of them . . . his family. All the good times they had, the life he loved, the life he had lost. He recalled his favorite fishing hole, and the first time Bria put bait on her own hook. The shake in his hands subsided.

He peered in from the tunnel opening, surveying the chamber with dilated eyes. The enormous cavity measured at least two hundred feet in diameter and thirty feet high. A pile of gold and treasure materialized far off to the left.

Cymm held his breath listening for movement, but somehow the silence terrified him more. He mustered the courage to step inside, traversing the perimeter of the chamber counterclockwise. He made it a quarter of the way around the circular room when he encountered a giant bird's nest with four-foot-high sidewalls made of branches, rocks, and grass.

A creaking noise broke the silence from inside the nest. The sound continued, steadily filling the void, so he slowly peered over the edge. Three very young dragons, each almost four feet in length, sprawled within.

Any remaining fear dissipated in a snap. Neither the youth nor innocence of the creatures eased his hatred. He clenched his teeth and gripped his sword handle so tightly his knuckles turned white. Through the haze in his brain, he thought, *they killed my family, and now they are starting a family of their own!*

He climbed into the nest and stood over the sleepy hatchlings with two hands on the hilt of his down-turned sword. His body trembled in anger; two tectonic plates competed for top position within him. His eyes stared off into the distance; he could not think straight. Images of his parents' dead bodies streamed through his mind, along with the crow pecking at his sister's eye socket.

Why do I feel so hot? Why are my muscles trembling?

The image of his sister appeared in his mind right before the wagon exploded.

NO! He forced it out of his mind. *"Cymm, where are you?"*

"I was too late," he uttered to himself.

He raised the sword, taking several deep breaths, but he stopped himself as they stirred peacefully in their sleep. *These wyrmlings did not kill my parents or sister.*

When he regained complete control of his emotions, he took several steps back and leaned heavily against the nest wall, blinking rapidly until the tears and his hazy vision disappeared. Before he could pray for guidance, voices streamed down the tunnel.

32

Trapped

Stefo hacked the vines as if in a trance, with a wild look on his green ichor-covered face. The men whispered behind his back, barely audible over the blood thundering in his ears.

"I think he is losing his mind," said Tomek.

"Maybe, but his plan is working," Janek replied.

Tomek examined his body, "I haven't been scratched yet. Maybe the insane aggressive approach is the way to go."

You haven't seen me insanely aggressive yet, Stefo thought.

They had to circumvent many depressions in the ground, the result of uprooting the trees. Finally, they reached the center of the clearing next to the gigantic mound of trees, where a twenty-foot safe zone existed, protection from the vines and undergrowth.

"What could have caused all this damage?" Laret shielded his eyes from the sun as he scanned the entire clearing.

Suddenly Janek's wolf issued a low growl, and his partner rushed over. "Footprints, this way," he said with a wave of his arm. The group followed him only a short distance.

Stefo grinned with pleasure when a gap appeared in the tree trunks, revealing a tunnel.

"This is where the road ends for the horseman. Same formation, but wolves take the lead," he half-whispered.

Five men and three wolves quietly crept down the tunnel. When they reached the bottom, Stefo evaluated his surroundings. With the absence of a second entrance, his confidence grew; his quarry had nowhere to run. "We know you're in here, horseman! Show yourself!" From the center of the tunnel with his hands on his hips, he barked out more orders. "Janek, Laret to the left, and Tomek, Basten to the right."

Laret called out almost immediately from the left, "Stefo, there's a lot of treasure over here, thousands of gold coins!"

The Fang leader sniggered to himself. "We found your stash, horseman! Not only are we going to kill you, but we're going to be rich also!"

Stefo paced the width of the tunnel several times before the wolfers on the right reported in. "There is something over here . . . maybe a giant bird's nest."

"Bird's nest? Do the wolves smell the horseman or not? Is he hiding in the nest?" Stefo laughed at his own joke.

"Hold on. We're checking."

"What? I asked if he was in the nest." Stefo strained to see into the dark.

"Yes, one second."

This comment tempted him to leave his post. Visions of treasure and a nest that could hide a full-grown man romped through his mind. *That's what the horseman wants. Me to leave the only exit unattended.*

He cleared his throat and yelled, "Hey, are you two stuffing coins in your backpacks?"

Laret called out from the other side of the chamber, "No, but you should see how big this nest is!"

The wolves were running in circles, sniffing everywhere, hunting for the horseman.

Stefo yelled, "He must be in the nest!"

"The horseman isn't in the nest! Only three giant lizards. Maybe they are his pets," reported Tomek.

The Fang leader glanced back quickly to make sure the horseman wasn't running up the tunnel, "Janek, come back and guard the exit!"

Stefo studied the gold pile, muttering to himself, "How did he get all this? Something is not adding up." He rushed over to the nest.

"By Melcorac's Hammer, what are you doing?" the leader asked.

Laret executed the last creature in the nest, then circled back to double-tap each one. He mumbled spitefully, "My wolf is dead. Now his pets are dead."

"Warpaint!" bellowed Basten, enthusiastically drawing horizontal lines on both cheeks.

Tomek reached down to grab a handful of blood. "Yeah, warpaint! They don't need it anymore." In addition to painting his face, he drew symbols on his arms and leather armor.

"Hey Stefo, where do you think he went?" asked Janek from the passageway.

Stefo climbed into the nest, kneeling to examine the bodies. "Stop goofing around!" A chill ran down his back, his face draining of color. How could he fix a mistake like this? "Oh, Ledaedra, forgive us."

Tomek stared into his eyes. "What's wrong?"

"Run!" the leader yelled, vaulting from the nest. "We are in a dragon's lair!" Despite the terror coursing through his veins, he still believed he could survive this.

The ground trembled slightly; the dirt falling from the ceiling showered the Fang members as they fled. Wolves and humans sprinted toward the exit, amidst the hollering.

"Move quicker!"

"Get out of the way!"

The light streaming down the tunnel suddenly disappeared.

An agonizing scream echoed down the shaft, stopping everyone in their tracks.

Stefo's eyes rolled from side to side as he listened intently. *Was that Janek?* He had been guarding the exit.

The labored breathing of Janek's injured wolf surged into the room moments before he did, followed by a rumbling sound. Stefo dove to the side as a vast head burst into the chamber with a deafening roar. The monster swiped the hindquarters of the retreating wolf, causing it to stumble, and the serpent's twenty-foot-long neck shot forth. Ribs crunched before the wolf emitted a final yelp.

Stefo threw himself against the dirt wall near the tunnel opening. His elbow mere inches from the dragon's right haunch, but the bulk of its body remained in the shaft, blocking his escape.

Fear took over. It consumed him, controlling his every thought. Stefo trembled until his neck and back cramped. He was four lifeyears again, lying in bed, frozen in fear, listening to a scrapping noise outside his window. The Bogman had come to get him. His mind fought an internal battle between fight and flight, trying to determine his best chance for survival. The struggle droned on.

This was Dragon Fear.

The monster had trapped everyone in the lair except Janek, but he was pretty sure what happened to him. Stefo tried to unsheathe his sword silently, but it rattled against the scabbard.

With no light coming down the tunnel, the few rays that managed to filter through the mesh of tightly stacked trees, stood in stark contrast to the darkness. These beams of sunlight interweaved throughout the chamber, glinting off the dragon's scaly, green body.

Stefo raised his sword, mustering his strength to swing, but the adrenaline dissipated as quickly as it built. *If I swing, the dragon will know I am here.*

In the meantime, the two remaining dire wolves attacked the dragon's front legs, Basten and Tomek fired arrows, and Laret charged with his bloody sword.

One arrow bounced off her thick hide, then a second ripped through the sail on the top of her head and neck. The dire wolves' ferocious growls were accompanied by slashes from their claws and bites that shredded flesh from the dragon's front legs. Blood flowed from several deep gashes.

Pressed up tight against the dirt wall, Stefo watched in amazement as the wolves danced circles around each other.

The dragon lunged at a retreating wolf only to get a face full of claws from the other. The dragon released a beastly roar.

None of Laret's attacks had scratched the dragon's hide, but this time he swung like he was chopping wood, delivering a six-inch cut on its left shoulder.

The fear subsided in Stefo. *Maybe we can win this battle!* His sword began to rise.

The dragon bit down on Laret's torso, sinking its teeth into his chest. The wolfer's head, shoulders, and one arm were entirely in the giant lizard's mouth. Laret was resilient, though, and swung his sword one-handed up toward the monster's face, creating a small cut below its eye.

The enraged dragon lifted and shook him savagely, side to side, until his body separated in two pieces with a shower of blood and gore. A drop of blood splattered against the back of Stefo's raised sword hand. He examined it in a stupor. His eyes furtively moved to the dragon in time to witness the upper torso of his best friend cast aside like a ragdoll, landing with a grotesque smack.

Regret and guilt clawed their way to the top of his mind, but self-preservation reigned supreme. His sword hand slowly lowered.

Basten and Tomek rained arrows down on the monster, but only one had penetrated her thick hide. They dropped the bows, drew their swords, and Tomek scowled at Stefo. "Hey, what are you doing?"

The ground shook, and dirt fell from the ceiling, distracting the brothers. The dragon leapt further into the chamber, pouncing on a dire wolf, pinning it to the ground. It savagely tore at the wolf's midsection with razor-sharp teeth.

The other wolf attacked her neck ferociously while Basten and Tomek hacked at her head, trying to get her off the wolf.

The wolf whimpered and squirmed before letting out a final yelp.

Stefo took one last glance at the battle, then quietly but quickly slipped around the corner and into the tunnel.

33

Escape

L eaving Anekzarius behind, TetraQuerahn lifted off the ground; he enjoyed spending time with her. He soared through the air, the breeze rippling his head sail as he banked hard to the left.

A dragon roared below; it was Ennozarius.

In his haste to return, he landed heavily outside the lair, stumbled, and almost collapsed. He hurried into the dark tunnel, his eyes shifting instantly to infra-vision. Halfway down the shaft a bright red humanoid figure materialized against the sidewall, hiding in a niche.

"Move or die!" the monstrosity said in a baritone voice.

He hesitated a moment to give the thing a head start, then stormed down the tunnel trying to crush it. As TetraQuerahn entered the chamber, the human dove to the side, and the dragon's rampage immediately thrust him into the action.

TetraQuerahn evaluated the situation, finding the dire wolf to be the biggest threat. He caught the wolf by surprise and clamped onto his hindquarters with his jaws. The wolf let out a loud yelp. While whimpering, it dug its claws into the dirt floor trying to find purchase, but Ennozarius grabbed the dire wolf by its front half, and the two dragons ripped it in half.

Done with the wolf, Ennozarius pushed past two men swinging swords and strode toward the nest. "What is that metallic smell?" Her head came back around sniffing. "Do you have blood on you? Dragon's blood?"

She didn't wait for a response, rearing up she brought the full power and weight of her body down on the shoulders of one of the men. The force snapped his spine and legs, killing him instantly.

"To-To-Tomek!" the surviving one screamed, horror-stricken.

Ennozarius hastened to the nest. TetraQuerahn rounded up the two remaining humans, prodding them with his nose back toward the center of the chamber.

"Steffffffffo, why di-di-didn't you help?" asked one of the human creatures.

"TetraQuerahn, our hatchlings are dead!" Ennozarius screamed. "Kill them!"

His claws eviscerated the talkative one, shredding his leather armor like paper. The human fell to his knees, watching six feet of his intestines uncoil from his gut onto the dirt floor. TetraQuerahn fixated on the human attempting to put them back where they belonged; he quickly shifted his focus to the eyes. *There it is*. He loved to watch the light blink out.

He turned toward the one called Stefo.

"Wait!" the human cried, "W-w-we didn't kill them. Cymm d-d-did! This is his." He held up a large circular copper ring tied to a leather thong hanging from his neck. "We f-f-found it in the n-n-nest."

"Oh? Enno, this one had nothing to do with it," he said with mock sincerity.

"Kill him!" Ennozarius roared.

TetraQuerahn took a moment to consider the scene. "Hmm. He didn't have blood on him, and he has proof someone else did it. I would hate to kill an innocent. Maybe if he does us a favor, we could let him go?"

Enno issued a low growl, creeping toward the human.

"Anything, I will do—do anything!" The one called Stefo took two hesitant steps away from Ennozarius toward TetraQuerahn, eyeing her cautiously.

A sly smile stretched across TetraQuerahn's face. "Do you have a torch?"

"A torch? You want me to l-l-light a torch . . . okay, yeah, I have a torch," Stefo said, fumbling through his backpack. Then he ran to get two more packs. "Right here, here it is . . . a torch!"

"Light it!" the male dragon said.

Click, Click, Click. The human shuddered so strongly he couldn't get the flint to spark. *Click, Click, whoosh*! Finally, the torch sprang to life, and he held it aloft.

TetraQuerahn sighed. His thoughts drifted back to fond memories of things exploding. With newfound energy he said, "Put the torch out with your hand."

"Huh?" Stefo's nose crinkled.

"You said 'anything' and without the gloves." The dragon waited patiently.

The human's gaze shifted to Ennozarius then back to the male dragon. In a flurry of movement, Stefo secured the torch with his thighs, ripped both gloves off, and smothered the torch with his hands. His eyes grew; a look of anguish pillaged his strength before he fell to his knees, but he never cried out.

TetraQuerahn enjoyed the sizzling of his skin, but not as much as the smokey, tangy aroma of burnt flesh. "Impressive! Follow me outside, and I will let you go."

"You will not let him go!" Ennozarius fumed, closing the distance to the human.

"You better run before I change my mind, or she eats you." TetraQuerahn chuckled when the human's eyes widened again; then he sprinted up the tunnel.

"TetraQuerahn! TetraQuerahn! Fine, I will kill him myself." He stepped in front of her to block her path, moving slowly up the passage.

The goliath fixed Ennozarius with a frosty glare back over his shoulder. "If you touch him, you will die." He brought his gaze back to the front, observing Stefo pause to look and listen before entering the clearing.

34

Awestruck

Cymm observed the battle with a mix of horror and amazement from thirty feet above the chamber floor. Swift thinking and climbing had saved him from the chaos he witnessed. Standing on the edge of the nest, even at his height, he could barely pull himself into the network of tree trunks above. He took care not to shift; any micromovement could send dirt and stones raining down, revealing his location.

When Stefo, with Bria's necklace, and both dragons were finally leaving, he shifted to get the blood flowing to his numb legs, but his mounting frustration distracted him, and he slipped.

His fingers dug into the contours of the bark, while his legs dangled above the nest, clearly visible from the tunnel. The argument between the dragons paused and he held his breath, waiting.

Finally, the altercation resumed, and he exhaled, listening to the dragons depart the lair. He managed to haul himself back up.

Tears pooled in his eyes while he considered the daunting task before him. *Can I do this?* The savage, one-sided battle he'd witnessed between Fang and the dragons indicated otherwise. The anger brewing deep in his bowels erupted, overshadowing his self-doubt.

He prayed to Lord Terazhan, and a wave of peace coursed through his body, but he ignored it. "Why would you support my decision to come north when you knew I had no chance of succeeding!" The paladin exclaimed louder than he should have, "Show me how to defeat them!" He curled his fingers into a tight fist, and the pressure turned his knuckles white. "Answer me! Or I swear, I . . . I . . . will never pray to you again!"

Tears streamed down his face, blurring his surroundings, then his vision suddenly cleared. He stood in the nest next to the dead dragons.

What the . . . Am I hallucinating? he thought until he saw himself climb down into the nest. An intense euphoria coursed through his body while the room began to shimmer.

This is a Divine Quest.

His twin laid the hatchlings side by side, selected the largest dragon, cut its head off, put it in a bag, and sprinted for the exit. The room blurred, making him very lightheaded. He blinked and instantaneously found himself back where he started thirty feet above the floor.

Did he answer me? Cymm shimmied down the tree trunk and dropped into the nest. Focused on every detail, he sprang into action.

He grabbed the torch from the middle of the chamber, but with one quick glance, the largest hatchling was obvious. It took a few swings before he severed the head, then wrapped it in his cloak. He rolled over the rim of the nest, threw the torch to the ground, and raced for the exit. Treasure glittered in the distance. *Maybe next time.* He pumped his arms faster, avoiding the bodies, blood, and gore. He paused at the entrance to look and listen before he entered the clearing.

35

A Promise Kept

When Stefo got to the end of the tunnel, he peered around both corners. He held his hands down by his sides, still in a partially cupped orientation, fearful if he opened them the charred skin would crack. The two dragons were arguing behind him, so he bolted for the path his team had cleared through the vines and brush.

He instinctively crouched when a swoop sounded from above. Burning pain seared his chest and back. Inspecting his body, he found large talons piercing him.

Above him, the belly of the flying goliath blocked his view. Below him, the ground dropped away at a furious pace.

Stefo groaned, punching the dragon claws in frustration. An agonizing pain flashed every time his fist struck. "No!" He shifted, moaning in pain. "I thought you were going to let me go?"

The dragon chuckled in a sinister manner. "Yes, I am going to let you go."

The grip on Stefo's shoulder released, and a rocky outcropping, almost two hundred feet below, rushed up to meet him. The fear of impending death escaped his lips as incoherent babbling.

The other dragon swooped in and banked a loop around him, cackling wildly.

With his dying breath, he cursed his father.

36

Death's Door

After scanning both directions, Cymm quickly escaped to the left, leaping over the body of a Fang member. He retreated the way he came until he found a path ten feet wide straight to the woods line. Pieces of plant and chlorophyll littered the ground.

This must be where Stefo crossed.

Cymm ran through the clear path to the forest, not once needing to use his sword. After safely returning to Darken Wood, he paused to watch the two dragons flying in the distance, beyond the tree mound.

A low growl emanated from behind him, and he rotated slowly to confront his enemy. A wolf limped toward him, stained dark crimson from snout to tail, particularly its muzzle. Cymm retreated slowly as he unsheathed his sword. The creature faltered with a whimper—it was Torc.

Cymm rushed forward to help rip out the thorny vine wrapped around his front leg and still sucking his blood.

"Oh, my friend, what in the nine hells happened to you? You must have chewed through more than one vine to be here." The paladin reached out to heal him. "Terazhan, please provide me the power to—" Torc licked his face, then backed away. He tried several times to heal the wolf, but he could not get within arm's length. "I am trying to heal you. Do you understand?"

The wolf stared him down until they locked eyes, then the animal pushed an image into his mind. It was a dark scene with Fang wolfers attacking Torak, Torc, and his horse. Guilt rocked him, for it was the same location he'd left them before entering the clearing.

Cymm acted on instinct, running to save his friend. "I will not forgive myself if anything happens to either of you!" he yelled over his shoulder to Torc. The wolf headed in the opposite direction. He threw his hands up in exasperation and followed with a loud huff.

Fifty feet away, on the opposite side of a huge tree, slumped Torak. His cold and lifeless body lay hog-tied to the tree. Horror filled him; he had seen dead bodies before, but this was different. Refusing to give up, he wet his own ear before placing it near the wolfer's mouth. A cool sensation tickled the small hairs where he moistened the ear.

"He's alive!" he exclaimed to Torc.

The wolf panted excitedly, licking both men repeatedly. Reacting so quickly he startled the dire wolf, he shouted, "I call upon the Mighty Lord Terazhan to grant me the power to heal!" His booming voice echoed throughout the forest. Thoughts of the dragons crossed his mind. Cringing, he trailed off to a whisper.

The wolfer's heartbeat and breathing grew stronger, more rhythmic. Cymm untied then rolled him over, revealing an arrow stuck in the back of his leg. Removing it would have to wait until morning. Now, Torak needed to rest.

Cymm pointed at Torc, "Stay here and guard him. I need to find out what happened to my horse." He turned around to find his horse limping into view.

He jumped up and ran over to greet the horse. "Hey bud, did you hear me praying? We need to move in case anyone else heard me." His hand froze in mid-stroke.

"Oh Terazhan, how—" Deep claw marks ran down both sides of the equine's hindquarters, so deep the skin and flesh folded over. Bite marks straddled his windpipe; scratches covered his ribs, and the cuts on his abdomen could have disemboweled the horse if they ran deeper. "You are lucky to be alive."

"Lord Terazhan, I realize I am demanding today, but my horse cannot travel and will probably die if I do not heal him. If we do not leave this place, all of us will die from Stefo and his new dragon friends." He didn't feel any different and had no idea if Terazhan cared. He added, "I will promise you a new devout worshipper if you grant me a second heal this day!"

37

A Natural Feeling

I t had been almost seven weeks since Lykinnia assisted the young tavii to flee from the marauding spiders in the middle of the night. Since then, she had been visiting nightly, patrolling while they slept. Unfortunately, her efforts had not prevented the loss of four more nymphs.

Besides night watch, she also spent a lot of time zooming around searching for new safe zones. The spiders in this region were plentiful and typically nocturnal, so she had them traveling during the day, sleeping and defending at night.

Lykinnia headed to the altar much earlier today, just before sunset, hoping Solar had already vacated the area. However, Terazhan had joined him at the altar, both staring intensely into the scrying window.

The young lady cast her invisibility spell and snuck up behind them. A thought immediately crossed her mind, *I bet they are spying . . . yep, I knew it.*

"He has indeed become more demanding," Solar said. "The cost to you is pretty steep."

Terazhan replied, "It will pay off tenfold, or maybe one hundred."

Solar faced him. "But you will have to—"

"Of course," was all his divine majesty said.

Lykinnia yawned; her eyes drooped. "Please leave!" she yelled into the vortex. "Maybe I should breathe on Solar's elbow again." She giggled mischievously.

She pursed her lips, but the mood changed abruptly.

"This will drain you too much; I don't think . . ." Solar argued vehemently. Lykinnia had never seen him so animated.

"Already done."

Lykinnia peered into the scrying window between the two tall males, witnessing the young man's hands glowing brightly. She drew in a sharp breath, "That's not possible! How—"

His hands radiated a beautiful, pure white aura. He caressed his horse and healed its deep wounds. *He must love animals like I do*, she thought.

"Lykinnia!" said the voice from the void.

She sighed, completely losing her focus for the first time in her life. "What?" she said dreamily as the horse rested its muzzle on the young man's shoulder.

"I need your help!"

Lykinnia gasped in shock and instantly closed the portal, but in her haste, she accidentally terminated the invisibility spell. Terazhan and Solar slowly scowled at her standing between them before their eyes darted toward each other.

38

The Surgeon

Cymm needed to save Bria, but Stefo had ahold of his sister's arm. He dragged her into the dragon's lair, taunting her. "Do you want to see what your brother did?"

She whimpered in response.

Cymm tried to lift his arms, but he could not move.

She reached for him, "You promised to protect me!"

Cymm woke in a panic, screaming, "Bria!" The cold and clammy feeling of her dead body came racing back.

Torak stoked the fire, already awake. "Same dream again?"

The horseman looked down, breathing heavily.

Torc came running over to bathe his injured friend's face. He even gave Cymm a few licks, breaking the awkward silence.

"I assume you have a plan for this?" he asked, pointing at the arrow shaft still stuck in his leg from yesterday.

Cymm examined it. "First of all, welcome back to the land of the lucid. Second, the arrow will be taken care of this morning. We might have to push it through."

Torak wore an exaggerated visage of fear. "We? I won't be pushing anything. It's all up to you, my friend."

Cymm enjoyed seeing his friend return to normal, but he feared this next step might set his recovery back a few days. The Plainsman's arrow wound experience was limited to horses, and even then, he was a novice. The arrow would not spin, push, or pull, so he concluded the arrowhead had pierced and lodged in the femur. To make matters worse, the head continued to loosen from the shaft as the adhesive and sinew dissolved in the blood and other fluids. He would have to cut a large slit in his leg to remove the arrowhead.

A memory of his father came rushing back. He had used a buckle and strap from a saddlebag to dislodge an arrow stuck in a horse's scapula.

With a deep sigh, he began cutting the stitching on one of his saddlebag straps. His hands were shaking; a single thought permeated his mind: *What if he dies before I can remove the arrow and heal him?*

"I'm not sure about this," he admitted.

"That's not what I want to hear, Cymm." Torak shook his head while petting Torc.

After sharpening and cleaning his dagger, the paladin swallowed uncomfortably. "Should I tie you down? This is going to be painful, and there isn't anything I can do to help."

Torak choked in response, taking a second to find his voice. "It might be good to tie me in place, but I will also connect with Torc, which will numb the pain a little, but still be quick!"

Cymm gathered the rest of the supplies. "I will be as fast as possible. I will also gag you. We don't need every creature in a ten-mile radius hearing you scream. Let's get this over with."

"You have the bedside manner of an executioner. Tell me something positive. Did you kill any of the dragons? I see you have blood on you, but you don't appear to be injured." Torak's eyes lit up hopefully.

"I have a combination of wolf, horse, human, and dragon blood on me," Cymm answered cryptically. "I'll tell you the entire story when we are done here."

He cut the leg two inches in each direction, extending the current hole a tad short of five inches. The wolfer had already linked his mind to Torc's before they started, but the pain overpowered the connection. Torak bit down hard on the gag and released an agonizing, muffled scream before he lost consciousness. The wolf pawed him to no avail, so he switched to circling the camp on patrol.

Cymm cinched a belt above and below the injury to flatten the tissue and prevent the opening from tearing. A lot of blood leaked out, but not as much as he'd anticipated. He fought through a second bout of dry heaves, relieved that he'd skipped breakfast.

Quickly, he slid the arrow shaft through the hole of the rectangular buckle. He pushed the clasp down using two fingers on one side, the dagger on the other. Once it traveled over the back of the arrowhead, he spun the buckle ninety degrees locking the shorter width into place with the triangular-shaped arrowhead.

Cymm grabbed the leather strap attached to the buckle and pulled. Nothing!

He repositioned himself, kneeling on Torak's leg, with one knee on each side of the wound. He then wrapped the leather strap around one hand and grabbed it with the other. Pushing down hard with his knees and pulling up with both hands, he created much more force. He heaved, muscles straining, the leather strap creaking, followed by a loud snap. Cymm went flying backward, landing on his back and rump.

"Ahh, by the bones of Tiamat! I broke it!" Cymm held up the strap to inspect it. The arrowhead remained wedged inside the buckle, and now it hung at the end of the intact strap. Relief flooded his body. "Terazhan's blessing on you, father! Your trick worked."

His celebration ended abruptly. He threw the buckle aside, placed his hands directly over the bloody wound, and prayed in a thundering voice to Terazhan for the power to heal his friend.

The beautiful, pure, white aura sprang forth, penetrating deep into the leg. When the light faded, Cymm removed his hands to reveal a deep purple scar. The wound had been sealed, but not entirely healed. Additional injuries also lingered from the Fang beating he'd endured.

Cymm cleaned up and prepared to move their camp to the southeast. He hoisted Torak and draped him over the horse again. "We must keep moving. There's a chance Stefo or the dragons are trying to find us," he explained to his unconscious friend.

After an hour, the band of walking wounded stopped. Cymm contemplated making camp but decided to rest for only a few hours.

The paladin found a comfortable spot to pray. "Terazhan, thank you for healing my horse. I am confused about the dragon head. How is that going to help me defeat the large dragons?" He stared at the large burlap bag in front of him containing the balled-up cloak with the head inside. "Terazhan, I have relied on your guidance, trusting in the path forward, but this does not make sense."

In response, a Vision forced its way into Cymm's mind; enormous towers guarded a mountain pass.

Maybe Torak can help me identify them when he awakens.

Prayers and a tense morning were over. So, he sat down to eat a cold lunch with his back against the tree. He contemplated the Vision he just received and promptly fell asleep.

39

Coming to a Head

Ennozarius gave TetraQuerahn the silent treatment for two days until she could take it no longer. "Where were you while our hatchlings were being slaughtered?"

He did not respond immediately; he even considered slashing her with his talons to ensure she never verbally assaulted him again. Instead, he growled in response, "You know where I was."

"With my sister Anekzarius, right?"

He hissed the words, "Yes, which is exactly the deal we all agreed to. Wasn't it?"

"Do not twist the story to fit your needs! You could have gone to visit her after I returned from hunting! You should have been here to protect them!"

"We will have more hatchlings before long," he said slyly trying to coil his neck around hers.

She gave him a scowl, stopping him in his tracks. "I still cannot find TetraQuezar's head; I have looked everywhere!"

Confusion blanketed him. "What? What are you talking about?

"Your son!" Ennozarius screamed. "Your largest son, TetraQuezar, had his head cut off, and I can't find it!"

"You said none of the thieves escaped, so it must be here. Is any of the gold or treasure missing?" TetraQuerahn inquired.

"No, not one coin. I counted it twice."

"See, it must be here. Tear the nest apart." He left to find Anekzarius.

40

The Negotiator

The following day, Cymm healed Torak again. The color of his complexion was returning along with his strength.

"You should have seen this battle. It was brutal." Cymm poked at the fire while eating a cold breakfast. "The two dragons killed four men and three dire wolves effortlessly. They would have killed Stefo, except he told them I killed the baby dragons."

"Why didn't you kill them?" asked Torak.

Cymm blinked, slowly shaking his head. "They didn't kill my family."

"Fair enough. How did you get out?"

Cymm explained the Divine Quest in detail—how he forced it to occur, the beheading of the baby dragon, and his sprint out the front door.

The wolfer's eyes lit up like a child asking to hold his father's sword. "Can I see the dragon's head?"

He unwrapped the large-cantaloupe-sized head with two-inch horns sprouted from the brow. Its tongue lolled out to the side, and a sail was present but not very prominent. Its skin was emerald green with an iridescent glitter, like fish scales.

He wrapped the head again, deep in thought. "What am I supposed to do with this thing?"

Torak shrugged, pinched his nose, but still gagged. "I have no idea, but it reeks! You should definitely throw some preserving berries in that bag."

"Good idea. I will when we get back to the plains."

They broke camp, and Torak mounted the horse on his own. While Cymm led the horse, he described the encounter in more detail, including the mind-numbing fear he had entering the lair and the amount of treasure he left behind. Torak nodded in response, listening intently.

The paladin's face brightened. "I received a new Vision this morning. I believe it was of the High Towers protecting the pass through the mountains."

"I have never been there. Hey, do you remember Wexel? He is well traveled. Maybe he could help you validate what you saw." They set their course for Torak's home.

They strolled into Howling Set twelve days after Cymm had entered the dragon's lair. Torak escorted him to Wexel's home, knocked on the open doorway, and left.

"You're not staying?" asked Cymm.

"I need to report Stefo's treachery to the elders. I'll catch up with you later."

Cymm rotated back to find Wexel standing in the doorway.

"Welcome back, Cymm. Come in."

The paladin bowed his head in respect as he entered. "I hear you have traveled across the realm. I am hoping you can help confirm my next destination."

Wexel sat, pointing to another chair. "Where you headed?"

"The High Towers. Can you describe them to me?"

"Yes." Wexel shifted, getting comfortable, deeply considering the question. "They are in the Knife-Edge Mountain range, which probably doesn't help since that range is over twenty-five hundred miles long. Are you able to find the Knife-Edge?"

Cymm tilted his head and raised one eyebrow. "The whole eastern border of the Realm of Legerdemain."

"Just checking. There are three passes through the entire mountain chain. High Tower Pass is one of them. The High Towers of Sethanon are in Legerdemain and the High Towers of Delagor are in the Realm of Dragon's Bane, protecting the eastern entrance."

Wexel opened his mouth to continue, but Cymm interrupted. "Other than location, how do you tell them apart?"

The wolfer chuckled. "You don't. They are identical from all angles; the only difference is the location and terrain around them. Do you need directions to get there?"

"Yes, please." Cymm leaned forward.

"There is a road fifteen miles east of Endurance Rise going north into Darken Wood. Forty to fifty miles into the forest, the road splits north to the Elven cities and east to High Tower Pass. Stay on the road for a couple of days. You can't miss them. Is that it?" Wexel asked.

"Yes, thank you. I have heard so many stories growing up about the epic battles involving the towers. I can't wait to finally see them." He left with a spring in his step.

Cymm and Torak arrived back at his home almost at the same time.

"I am going to push on my friend," Cymm said in a melancholy tone.

"It is getting late. You should spend the night." Torak had a mood to match.

"I assume you are staying here."

"Yeah, someone needs to deal with Fang before it gets worse. I plan to investigate the source of the problem." The wolfer's eyes were glassy as he stared off into the distance.

They spent the night celebrating and storytelling, but Cymm rose early the next morning. He rode east, the direction Wexel had given him to reach the road, giving Endurance Rise a wide berth. When he reached the road, he encountered traveling merchants, which he traded several skins for a heavy riding cloak with a hood to replace the one currently soaked in dragon's blood.

In the evening of his third day, he came across the junction in the road that Wexel had mentioned. *It must have been a while since the wolfer traveled this way.* A tavern, inn, cartwright, and wheelwright had established a small hamlet called Sleepy Willow. He rode past several gigantic willow trees, but many more existed behind the buildings near the small lake on the northeast side of the junction.

He didn't have much money, but his hunger and the need for a good night's sleep were controlling his thoughts.

The dilemma weighed on him as he entered the inn and greeted the bartender. "Good evening."

"Hello, I will be right with you." The bartender continued to the corner of the bar where a dwarf hunched over his drink.

Cymm had a seat at the other end of the bar, trying to ignore the conversation between the barkeep and the dwarf.

"I had hoped that was my ticket to High Tower Pass." The dwarf quaffed the rest of his beer.

"You are doing the right thing. Traveling through the pass without an escort is dangerous." The barkeep motioned toward his empty tankard. "Another?"

"I'm traveling that way. I can escort you," Cymm replied, with his head held high and his shoulders rolled back.

The dwarf covered his mouth, amused by Cymm's *joke*. "I'm seeking a hardened warrior, not a young man."

"Well, fortunately for you, I am both," Cymm said.

The dwarf rolled his eyes to the barkeep. "Okay, kid, let's see what you got."

"Not in here; take it outside!" the man behind the bar yelled.

Cymm led the way out the door, turning quickly with his sword drawn.

"Whoa! What are you doing?" The dwarf threw his hands in the air as he backed up.

Cymm dragged himself upright, trying not to let the confusion show. "Sparring. You said . . ."

The dwarf dropped his hands to his hips and stared unblinking. "If I were good with this sword, I wouldn't need you. So, prove you're worth hiring."

Cymm notched an arrow and held it in place with his left hand, squeezing firmly so the shaft of the arrow pressed against the shelf on the bow. He drew his dagger with his right hand and threw it twenty-five feet, piercing the trunk of a large tree. Then, immediately he fed the bow to his other hand, aimed, and released the arrow, which stuck within one inch of the dagger a split second later.

Cymm loved performing this feat. It was one he had practiced thousands of times back at his father's barn, since Old-Man Semper wouldn't allow it during training. He smiled, imagining the scolding he would be getting now. *Are we training for the circus or to protect our village?*

"Wow! Are you as good with the sword?" asked the dwarf.

Cymm gave him a friendly smile in reply. "Yes, I can handle myself. So, what do you say, Master Dwarf? Am I hired?"

"Dwarf? Dwarf!" He clenched his fists, steam billowing out of his ears. "How dare you call me a dwarf!"

Cymm's face turned red. "I . . . well, you—" He scratched his head. "See . . . well Hardre said . . ." He examined him again, a long white beard, a full head of hair, three foot nine inches tall, with chocolate brown skin and violet eyes. *He looks like a dwarf to me.*

The short humanoid waved him off in frustration before retreating into the bar.

The Plainsman retrieved his dagger and arrow with his head down. *So much for that opportunity.* He peeked in his coin pouch at the dwindling remains. *Maybe if I apologize? I think halflings are short.*

Cymm walked back into the bar, approaching him sheepishly with slumped shoulders. "I'm sorry if I offended you, but I have no idea how I did." His better judgment told him to leave out the halfling comment.

"Leave me alone!"

Disappointed, Cymm returned to the opposite side of the bar and ordered the cheapest food on the menu. He couldn't afford to rent a room for the night, so he nursed his ale until his food came, finished eating, then stood to leave.

"Hey, elf," yelled the short man at the bar.

Cymm surveyed the bar room again; they were the only two in the tavern. His eyes came to rest on the short man now gaping at him. "Me? I'm not an elf."

The other man took a long pull from his tankard. "Well, I'm not a dwarf. I've already been waiting for days, and you're my only option. Do you still want the job or not?"

Cymm beamed. "Are you trying to sweet-talk me?" The little guy's lips thinned, while he glowered at him. The plainsman quickly asked, "Where are you heading?"

"To the dwarven mines at the source of the Silver River."

"Do you live there?" the paladin asked.

"No! Dwarves live there," the little guy sighed, taking several deep breaths. "I'm a gnome from the Kharnal Mountains in the Realm of Tranquility. My name is Dontono."

"I have never met a gnome. My name is Cymm Reich from Stallion Rise in the Armak Plains. Where is the Realm of Tranquility?"

"It is past the Realm of Dragon's Bane," the gnome replied.

"How much are you offering?"

"Twenty gold—"

"Twenty gold!" Cymm yelled.

"No, you misheard me. I said twelve gold."

"No, you didn't. However, I will take twelve at the end if you give me five now," he countered.

"Deal! We leave at first light, so don't get all drunk tonight!" cautioned the gnome, handing over five gold pieces.

"You don't need to worry about me." Cymm returned to his side of the bar with a new swagger in his step. He placed the five gold coins on the bar in front of him so he could admire them. He drummed lightly on the counter when the bartender arrived.

"I guess I *will* be needing a room for tonight," he said cheerily.

The bartender quirked a brow. "You ain't the sort to dishonor a deal, are you?"

"No, never. Why?" asked Cymm.

"The going rate for the deal you just made is thirty gold. Keep that in mind if someone asks you to escort them back here."

Cymm slowly looked over at the gnome who paused in the middle of a drink and gave him a sly wink.

41

Still Missing

TetraQuerahn had spent the past two weeks with Anekzarius, giving Ennozarius time to mourn. He decided it was time to check on her. When he got to the entrance, he paused to listen as her lamenting drifted up the tunnel. Begrudgingly, he entered with the intention of helping his consort.

Ennozarius, stressed and exhausted, trembled. "I still can't find the head. I searched everywhere, including the trees covering the lair."

The large male lay down next to her, thinking. "Hmm . . ." He recalled the conversation with the last thief alive. *"Wait! We didn't kill them! Cymm did."*

"Enno, what did that last thief say? 'Cymm did it.' Right?" he asked.

"What? Oh, yeah, I believe so," she replied in a daze.

"At the time, I assumed Cymm was one of the idiots with dragon's blood on him, but now I am not so sure." He continued to play with the puzzle in his mind.

Ennozarius stopped her whimpering, lifted her head with perked up ears, hope etched on her face.

"He also said 'We didn't kill them' —*we*. Why would he have said 'We'? He should have said 'I' unless someone else was here or had already left!" Anger swelled inside TetraQuerahn, boiling to the surface.

"Does the name Cymm mean anything to you?" she asked.

"No! What am I missing? Do you recall anything else when you first entered the lair?" he asked.

"Well . . . no one else escaped. I meticulously blocked the tunnel, ignoring the wolves ravaging my front legs, and I didn't launch myself into the lair until I heard you land." Ennozarius emerged from the dark place in her mind, distracted by the questioning.

"What about the human I found in the tunnel trying to escape?" questioned the large male.

She replied, "He stood at my flank the entire time, waiting for me to move. I knew you would take care of him. Hmm, I remembered something. While hunting for the hatchlings, I did not eat, so I returned to the lair ravenous. With a heightened sense of smell, the stench of human and wolf overwhelmed me, but I also picked up the faint scent of horse. And I love to eat horse!"

"Horse! Did you figure out where the smell came from? Maybe they left a horse tied up outside the clearing. I will go check now," TetraQuerahn said.

"No, I haven't eaten in weeks. I will check for the horse!" Ennozarius said with vigor as her spirits returned.

42

Xylona

Cymm and Dontono got a late start in the morning, traveling in silence for three hours while the gnome worked off his hangover.

Cymm finally asked, "Hey Dontono, what horrors are you expecting on this road?"

"Anything really. This road is not patrolled by elves, humans, or dwarves. The tavern owner warned me not to travel without an escort," he answered candidly.

They covered roughly thirty miles the first day, passing many travelers with guards. The wagon could not be taken off road, so they made camp at the edge.

The second day's travel began at sunrise with a significant increase in conversing. Dontono was a traveling salesman, an inventor who made his way around the realms hocking his inventions. It had been a three-year journey, but only this final leg remained between him and his home.

"Cymm, have you ever been to the City of Mystics?" the inventor asked.

"No, I have not, but I've heard of it," Cymm replied honestly.

The gnome shook his head with a huff. "Heard of it? Of course, you have! It's the capital city of your realm. It's the safest place to be now with literally thousands of mages living and training at the Towers of Wizardry. A thousand dragons couldn't take that city over."

"Hmm, really?" the paladin said skeptically.

"Anyway, in the middle of the city is an enormous colosseum where weekly battles are held. While there, I saw three warriors take on an ettin. The dim-witted, two-headed giant had a massive club. The beast killed two warriors before succumbing to its injuries, and the surviving warrior won three hundred gold pieces!" Dontono completed his tale with a flourish.

"Three hundred!" the Plainsman exclaimed. "Why would anyone need that much gold?"

The gnome chuckled, rolling his eyes.

In the late afternoon on the fourth day of traveling, they came upon the intersection of High Tower Way and the Great North Road.

A short road veered off to the right just before the crossing, continuing south for one hundred feet to a small town.

Dontono didn't pause. He directed his steed straight for the fifteen-foot-high wooden stockade fence surrounding the town.

Dontono proclaimed, "Thank the gods! It appears we will eat and sleep well tonight."

Cymm responded, "There is only one God that matters! Terazhan, the rest have all but abandoned us. Have you not been listening to anything I said these past four days?"

The gnome held his hands up in mock surrender. "Okay, kid, if you say so. It's merely a saying."

The paladin nodded to acknowledge the apology. "I'm not interested in spending coins this night. Maybe we should make a quick stop for supplies and continue on."

The gnome fixed him with an angry glare. "Nonsense! I will pay for your room, and you will help me unload and carry my belongings inside. Deal?"

"Yeah," he reluctantly agreed.

"Oh, but you're on your own for food and entertainment." The inventor showed his teeth, the corners of his lips curling up significantly.

Cymm shook his head as the definition of "entertainment" formed in his mind. *He'll be up late tonight drinking, and it will be another late start.*

They rode past a giant statue of a female elven warrior on their way to the gate.

Cymm examined the statue. "What's the plaque say?"

"Xylona," replied Dontono.

"Is that the name of the warrior or the town?"

Before Dontono could respond, a guard replied gruffly, "Both. Gates close at dark."

Four guards stood stoically at the entrance, two on the ground and one in each of the twenty-foot towers supporting the gates. They entered the town to find a stable to the left and an inn with a tavern straight ahead.

The gnome puckered his lower lip and tapped his chin. "Catchy name, Bed of the Beholder."

Cymm stared in disbelief. He had been hoodwinked again. "Have you been here before? Or is it a coincidence that all the guest rooms are on the second floor, and I am unloading your wagon?"

The gnome shrugged with a sparkle in his eye.

Cymm rested against the railing outside the doors of their side-by-side rooms. The balustrade protected a balcony overlooking the bar and common area. He had finished unloading the wagon into Dontono's room and wiped the sweat from his brow. Cymm scanned the patrons below with mild interest before he realized the gnome was among them.

"How did he . . ." Cymm turned to find the doors closed, then walked downstairs to the Axe & Hammer Tavern. He took a seat next to his employer.

The inn and tavern were owned by a large, extended family of mountains dwarves, like his dear friend Hardre. The owners were bustling around, catering to a large crowd. The dwarven bartender called out to Cymm, "What can I get cha?"

A devious grin pulled at the corners of his mouth. "I'll take an ale."

"Make that two," the gnome said polishing off his first tankard.

As soon as the bartender disappeared, Cymm asked the gnome, "Are you two related?"

"You better watch it, kid!" the gnome said, trying not to smile.

Cymm's brows stitched together, and he folded his arms. "I am hardly a kid."

"How old are you?"

"Seventeen."

"I am two hundred and twenty-one lifeyears." He paused, taking a drink to emphasize the magnitude. "So, *kid*, what are you going to have for dinner?"

Cymm decided to explore the town while he considered his options for dinner. It should have been an easy decision, cold jerky, or a hot meal from the bar, but his funds had been almost depleted before landing this mercenary gig. His horse finished off the last of the feed yesterday with nothing on the side of the road for grazing the past two days. So, he was concerned the money from this job might have to last the rest of the journey to cover his horse's needs and his own.

He found a small market in the process of closing for the day. He purchased a sack of apples and a couple bags of oats for his horse. As he walked back to the inn, a shiny suit of armor caught his eye; like a magnet, it drew him closer. The plate armor on display was magnificent. He ran his finger down each crease, across each joint, daydreaming about how he would appear dressed like a Knight of Kharad. Only, he would have the holy symbol of Terazhan, a warhammer parrying a sword over an ornate intercross, emblazoned on his chest.

By the time Cymm made it back to the Bed of the Beholder, he was famished. He took a seat downstairs at a table away from the crowd gathered around Dontono. The gnome had brought one of his gadgets downstairs to demonstrate to the owner. A group had formed around him as if he were a street performer.

His product included a large wire basket supported eighteen inches above the table by a smooth spiral metal slide.

The slide ended in a small catch tray attached to a swinging pendulum.

"No, it's supposed to crack the egg in the bowl, discard the shell, then grab another egg and repeat." Dontono ran his brown hands through his thick, white hair.

"Maybe you need to fill the basket," a helpful patron offered after noticing the wire basket could easily hold a couple dozen eggs.

It failed again.

The gnome pressed the heel of his palm into his forehead. "Ahhh, it has always worked before! It must be the slightly smaller eggs. Maybe I can adjust the catch tray or the counterbalance."

"Bahh, this thing ain't never gunna work!" a dwarven patron jeered.

"It probly ain't never workt!" said another, laughing hysterically.

Cymm observed Dontono manhandle his device, muttering to himself. He continued to work on his invention, finally claiming, "I got it! Now it's going to work." His violet eyes twinkled.

The inventor put two eggs in the basket before rotating the device to his left. The eggs came out of the basket, gliding perfectly down the slide again. Then the pendulum swung back, scooping the first egg with the catch tray on the first try. The pendulum swung around, releasing the egg straight at one of the dwarves with a big mouth, hitting him right in the nose. The egg cracked, dripping all over his beard.

A shocked silence filled the room until the second egg went airborne, hitting the other dwarf in the forehead. The crowd erupted with laughter, pointing at the two dwarves covered in egg.

"I guess it does work!" a patron yelled.

"Hey, I will buy two of those egg slingers!" another added, joining in on the fun.

The laughter around the room riled the two dwarves who had been hit by the eggs. Their tomato-red faces contrasted comically with the dripping, yellow yoke. Both stared daggers at the gnome.

The owner stepped in, "Alright, enough of this! Pack this thing up and get it out of here."

As the gnome disassembled the machine and cleaned up the mess, several members of the dispersing crowd promised him free drinks. He took his invention back up to his room, not noticing the two dwarves following him. Cymm bound up the stairs after them, but they were already beating the egg yolk out of him.

"Alright. You taught him a lesson. He's had enough," Cymm said gruffly.

"What do you care?" a dwarf asked, punching the gnome again.

"I'm his father," he replied sarcastically.

Both dwarves hesitated, examining him, then each other, then back to him, and burst into laughter. One dwarf pushed the gnome to the floor; the other one kicked him for good measure before they walked back downstairs, still laughing.

"His father! That's a good one!"

"Did you see how big that guy was?" the other asked.

Cymm helped Dontono to his feet, and the gnome leaned heavily on him. "If you ask me if I am related to those two, I will bite you!"

The Plainsman assisted him into his room before retrieving the scattered parts of his invention. While Cymm picked up the pieces, the crowd below hollered at the two dwarves.

"Hey, long beards; are you going to buy one of those egg-slingers?"

"If you buy two, you could take turns shooting them at each other!"

"Come on guys. Leave 'em alone. Stop egging them on!"

The crowd went crazy over the last line. The two dwarves stood and marched out the front door to find another tavern.

Cymm returned to the room with the unbroken pieces to the thankful moaning of the gnome. "Dontono, why did you intentionally shoot those eggs at them?"

"Me? Didn't you see what they were doing? They were harassing me the entire time I was trying to make a sale," he replied angrily, clutching his chest and gut from the pain. His face had already started to swell.

Cymm's judgment began to melt away as he recalled a promise he had made. "Tell you what, my friend, if you can list three things I told you about Terazhan, I will make your pain go away."

Dontono laughed then cast him a skeptical gaze. "What? Are you some kind of priest or something?"

"Three things, in the next minute, starting now!" he said sternly, taking a step back and crossing his arms over his chest.

The gnome didn't hesitate another second, and he quickly rattled off five.

"I guess you were listening." Cymm placed his hands on the gnome's chest. "Lord Terazhan, I call upon your power to help heal this newly converted disciple of yours!"

"Disciple?" Dontono started to protest but fell silent when the pure, white light burst forth, forcing him to shield his eyes. The light persisted for a few seconds before the gnome breathed a sigh of relief.

43

No More Horsing Around

etraQuerahn had not visited Ennozarius in six days. After his last visit, she had seemed better, so he hoped her improvement continued. He stormed down the tunnel into the lair, surprising her.

"Enno, I got it! I figured it out!" he exclaimed, trying to catch his breath.

Ennozarius drifted in and out of sleep, sprawled on the treasure pile. "Figured what out?"

"The horse aroma! Do you remember the horse farm where we were blowing up the manure piles a few months ago?"

Enno tried to recall the details of that night, how they met TetraQuerahn and why, but she drifted back to sleep.

He tried again, more forcefully. "Enno! This is important. Do you recall the farm?"

Her eyes were thin slits when she replied, "Where is my sister? How come she doesn't visit me anymore?"

"She thinks you blame her for the death of our hatchlings," the male answered bluntly.

Her eyes glazed over and closed again. "Did you know we were born from the same egg, and dragon eggs weren't intended to hold more than one hatchling?"

He fumed. "Yes, you both have told me a dozen times. The farm, Enno."

"It is not my sister's fault; it is your fault. Twin dragons have a hard enough time surviving inside the egg. We shouldn't be fighting each other now," Ennozarius said.

Ughh, here we go again, he thought and began tuning her out. *Unhatched dragons kill each other, or grow too fast and crack the shell prematurely, or starve due to lack of nourishment.*

". . . and Anekzarius and I beat the odds . . ."

"Ennozarius! The farm!"

"Yeah, I remember it," she replied fully awake. "Why?"

"I never mentioned this before, but one of the female farmers told me Cymm Reich would come and kill me for what I did to them. The human that lit the torch said, 'Cymm did it.'" TetraQuerahn bounced and pranced as if he were a little wyrmling.

Ennozarius shook her head slowly. "Not likely. I saw blood on the one human's sword and on the clothes of two others."

"It can't be a coincidence. Maybe he helped with the executions." TetraQuerahn stomped one foot for emphasis.

"Maybe, but how could he have found us?"

"Good question. I am not sure I could find his village again," he replied honestly.

"Go if you must, but I need to talk to my sister." Ennozarius laid her head down.

He could tell her mind was still processing the new information.

TetraQuerahn flew high over the Plains of Armak, trying to retrace his flight path from several months ago. He spent many hours circling, attempting to find the farm or at least the village, but nothing jumped out at him.

His frustration had reached a climax when he saw three travelers on the road below. The mighty dragon swooped down landing in front of them. He reveled in the fear stemming from both human and horse, so he leisurely settled into place.

"If you run, I will kill you!" the behemoth said in the common tongue. "I am looking for someone called Cymm Reich." No one responded. "If you do not answer, I will kill you."

The riders fought to control the horses while his patience grew razor thin. "This is the part of the conversation where you participate. Quickly!"

"Is he f-f-from the Ra-Ra-Reich Farm?" replied one of the travelers finally.

"Maybe. Where would I find the Reich Farm?" the green goliath said skeptically.

"In Stal-Stallion Rise, two da-da-days directly south of Armak." The traveler's teeth chattered as he spoke.

"Thank you," he spoke directly to the man answering him, then instantly turned to the man on his right, eviscerating both horse and traveler.

The remaining two horses reared, but both men froze. Finally, the talkative traveler yelled, "Why? Wa-wa-we answered—"

"I was very clear. I said, if you do not answer, I will kill you." He rose on his hind legs, and five pinkish-red spheres of energy shot forth from his talons, burrowing into the other silent man's torso. The shock slowly drained from his face before he slipped from the horse's back, hitting the ground hard. The male dragon casually spread his wings, taking flight over the remaining traveler.

Late afternoon had arrived, and TetraQuerahn circled high over four villages, uncertain which was Stallion Rise. He still did not recognize anything; maybe it looked different in the daylight, or the farmers had already repaired the damaged buildings. He prepared to land at a random farm when a partially damaged barn stood out. He swooped in for a little reconnaissance, and his memory kicked in—this was where the woman confronted him.

He took a destructive tour of the village, ripping a barn apart using brute strength. At a different farm, he snapped most of the fence posts, then chased the horses out of the corral. Finally, he ripped the entire roof off the home at the far side of the village.

He circled back, landing heavily in the barnyard, close to where the wagon of manure exploded. He further damaged the barn with one swoosh of his tail.

The village bell rang; people were screaming, "Put out the torches!"

TetraQuerahn threw his head back, roaring to the heavens. He had found the farm.

44

Control Your Own Destiny

Cymm sat in the common room, impatiently tapping his foot; the gnome had not appeared yet. After waiting for over an hour, Dontono finally plodded down the stairs.

"By Melcorac's Hammer, did you come back downstairs last night for another beating?" Cymm asked in exasperation.

Dontono waggled his finger, emphasizing each word. "You better watch your tongue with me! You're not my father."

Cymm grinned. "I was last night!"

Dontono opened his mouth, but Cymm jumped up and walked away. "I will get the horses and wagon. You can start carrying your stuff down the stairs."

The silence as they departed Xylona lasted longer than when they left the hamlet of Sleepy Willow. However, by midday, the gnome's mood had changed and the funk he exuded burned off like the mist.

"Cymm, can you tell me more about Terazhan?"

The paladin's face lit up. "Well, did you experience positive feelings or emotional well-being when I healed you last night?"

"Come to think of it, a feeling of peace completely replaced the pain! Like I was at home in my workshop tinkering on my latest invention," the traveling salesman replied with satisfaction.

"What you felt was Terazhan, and he would like it considerably if you prayed to him to thank him for healing you. He tries to protect all good beings and cares what happens in this world. Each race may have their own beliefs and gods, but most of those are false gods; the others abandoned us when the dragons came," he finished his sermon. Cymm rubbed his horse's flank. "Hey Dontono, tell me more about the City of Mystics."

The gnome tilted his head, gawking at him. "Have you heard any stories about the sewer system?"

"No," Cymm replied.

"Well, the population is over thirty-five thousand, including the slums, and at any given time, there might be another couple thousand travelers passing through," the violet-eyed gnome began. "So, you can imagine how much waste is generated daily. The sewers get flushed regularly by letting water in from the River of Spells. All of the excrement is pushed to a holding cistern located under the slums."

He chuckled, then continued, "Some of the lower-level mages get assigned to this substation and are responsible for dehydrating the mixture. The sewer workers shovel the "mud" into large two-foot-wide, three-foot-long, and one-foot-high molds." Dontono paused to take a drink from his waterskin.

Cymm shook his head in silence, wondering where this could possibly be going.

The gnome rubbed the back of his neck while checking the position of the sun. "The filled molds are transported to the main processing station where additional mages cast mud to stone spells, creating large blocks that can be easily transported. The emperor for the City of Mystics had the "brown stone" hauled to the docks and exported to many nations on different continents, selling it for a premium due to the rarity and the color variation!"

"No. You're making this up! That is not true," Cymm argued but laughed at the absurdity of it all.

"It is completely true. Moreover, the best part is several years later, his secret came out when red dragons attacked Hagarth in a legendary strike. The flying reptiles melted the stone with their fire breath, causing the palace to smell like an outhouse for many months! The two cities were on the brink of war for over a year. Now, everyone calls it *shitbrick* instead of brown stone."

They both laughed hysterically. The next several days passed quickly with similar storytelling. The terrain began to change, and the road rolled through the foothills of the Knife-Edge Mountains.

On the fifth day from Xylona, they stopped to rest. Cymm found a secluded spot to pray and was about to conclude his session to Terazhan. "I'm almost to the towers, and not sure what to do when I get . . ." Before he finished his sentence, his next Divine Quest began, sending him to the towers.

They stretched high above his head, guarding the entrance to a pass through the mountains. He flew into the gateway straight to the other side, where the second set of towers stood. He continued flying over the ground for many miles until he came to an ancient tree on the side of the road. The tree had fallen apart from multiple lightning strikes. Large decaying pieces were strewn around it. He left the road to the south, flying straight toward the mountains, where he found a small meandering path going up into the foothills. The trail ended at a village, and the Divine Quest paused before ending.

"No!" Cymm resisted the return to his body, the pressure in his head mounting. "I will not be led around on a leash. I gave you a new believer; now how will I defeat the dragons?" he snapped.

An unbearable force assailed him. Massive pressure pushed against the inside of his skull in opposite directions. He grabbed his head with both hands hoping to hold it together. The more he resisted, the more everything around him elongated. Objects became particles then micro-particles, before he fell into the gap between the last two recognizable somethings.

He plummeted into nothing. The agony continued as the strange black environment flowed around him like water. It enveloped him slowly and methodically. It was neither wet nor suffocating, yet it burned. He teetered on the precipice of surrender to make the pain stop when a loud, popping noise occurred.

He struggled to keep his balance, feeling as if he'd been thrown or pushed forcefully. Then, instantly he appeared back in the village.

45

Liar by Nature

Lykinnia had spent the past three weeks in detention, confined to her tiny abode. Usually, she did not mind. She'd use the time to read, study, and do research, but these were not normal times.

Her initial punishment had been one week, but two more were added after several attempts to escape. Two of Solar's friends were assigned to guard her door constantly, so she finally conceded and did her time.

"Free at last!" she yelled, bursting out of her front door, almost hitting Solar.

With no sympathy, Solar said, "Next time you teleport behind me at the altar, you will be confined for two months."

Lykinnia had lied to Solar and Terazhan. She explained that a miscalculation in the coordinates of a teleportation spell had caused her to end up at the altar. Of course, they didn't believe it was an accident.

The young lady headed straight for the altar, glancing back over her shoulder to make sure he couldn't hear. "There won't be a next time because you won't catch me." They had no idea she stood behind them invisible for a while, which bolstered her confidence. She would have gotten away with it if that silly boy hadn't broken her concentration.

She replayed the image of him caring for his injured horse. When her heart began racing, she shook her head to clear the distracting thoughts. The voice from the void concerned her more than Solar. She needed to address the issue immediately or cease using her new invisibility spell.

"I hope you guys are okay," she said, referring to her taviian friends. She had never left them alone for one week, let alone three. Stepping up to the altar, she placed her hands on it and instantly flash-travelled to the Lower Darken Wood region.

When she arrived, her stomach rolled with pain at the gruesome sight. Carcasses littered the area. Fortunately, all were spider corpses, with the legs ripped off the bodies. Gore and black ichor coated the forest floor, the leaves of nearby plants, and the enormous tree trunks.

"Hello, my friends, are you here?" she asked tentatively in the high, shrill language.

Gillygahpadima appeared almost instantly, materializing out of the small grove of remaining plant life after the previous battles.

Without a greeting, the agitated insect asked, "Where have you been?"

Lykinnia pushed her hurt feelings aside. "I am so sorry. I could not come. What happened here?"

"Spiders came every night. There are only eleven of us left." The insect hovered very close to her ethereal face; the color changes of her body were quite visible, including some tinges of red. The knot in Lykinnia's stomach intensified. So many had died. She needed a new plan.

What remained of her little colony gathered from their hiding places high above in the tree branches and others from the shrubs below.

With a cracking voice she said, "I am sorry I abandoned you the past few weeks, but it was not my decision, and I tried to join you. We need to leave immediately. I will scout ahead to find a haven, but the new plan is for you to come and live with me until you are fully grown."

Now I need to figure out how to get them to the Peak of Power safely.

46

Sidetracked

The Divine Quest continued for Cymm, and he floated further into the village. To his relief, the searing pain in every fiber of his body had dissipated.

He wound through the small dwarven village before coming to a home. He skirted around the outside of the house and entered a forge in the backyard. A human patted a dwarf on the back; the human was him. Both were laughing, examining a giant sword in front of them.

Cymm enjoyed watching the camaraderie until a portal opened and ripped him through, back to his body. When he opened his eyes, Dontono stood directly in front of him.

"You alright?" the gnome asked.

He composed himself before responding, "I'm fine. What's the problem?"

"The problem is I have been standing here for two hours watching your eyes twitch under your eyelids!" explained Dontono, "Are you sure you're alright?"

"Two hours? Are you sure?" he asked but noticed the sun had shifted significantly in the sky.

"Yeah, now what is going on?" his employer asked.

"I was praying to Terazhan and got lost in the moment, I guess."

"Hmm, let's get moving," Dontono said skeptically. "We will need to travel later into the evening to make up the time we lost."

The road continued due east, rolling over the hills for the next three days. The dragon head was now many weeks old. The additional bag did not help; the stench permeated the area, growing worse each day.

Dontono sniffed the air, then his armpit. "What in the nine hells is that smell. Is it me?"

Cymm didn't want to explain the rotting head. *How would I even begin to? I still don't understand it myself.* "Hey, look at the Knife-Edge Mountains on the horizon."

"Did anyone pass us by today?" asked the inventor, clearly misdirected.

"Hmmm, I don't remember anyone," he replied deep in thought.

"Yeah, me either. Kind of strange based on the traffic we have been seeing." Dontono called a halt; then he began setting up his wagon for the night.

They got an early start the following morning under clear skies, but a few hours later, the Plainsman noticed smoke rising in the distance.

"We haven't seen a traveler in a day and a half, and I don't like the smoke up ahead. What do you think?" The salesman outwardly appeared worried, with his face pinched.

"Yeah, something's not right. Once we get closer, I will scout ahead to see what is going on," Cymm volunteered.

Dontono fell silent for a moment. "That sounds like a good idea."

Two hours later, they came upon two injured elves on the side of the road. The elves were hesitant to talk but issued a warning. "I wouldn't go any further. Bandits are waylaying travelers and stealing their goods!" Then they moved further down the road away from them.

"Maybe we should head back to Xylona and wait for a raid party to clear them out?" the gnome said, wringing his hands.

"That could be weeks; I can't wait," he replied.

Dontono considered his words for a moment. "We could go back to the Great North Road and turn south to the next pass?"

With one clenched fist in front of him, he struggled to keep the passion from his voice. "My path leads through the High Tower Pass, my friend. I cannot veer from this destination!"

They sat quietly for a while before agreeing to part ways on friendly terms. Cymm received a partial payment of two more gold pieces.

Dontono offered the two injured elves a ride back to Xylona and rode out of sight. When the inventor disappeared over the next hill, he continued toward the mountains again, concerned with what lay ahead.

Maybe I could go around the ambush. He left the road traveling due south for a mile before continuing east. As he crested his second rolling hill, in the valley below were six injured and dirty humans, a man, two women, and three children. The man had a severe life-threatening gut wound.

The children began crying, and the women stepped in front to protect them. The man held his wound with one hand and a sword in the other.

The paladin sighed and walked his horse slowly down the hill but not directly toward them. At the bottom of the hill fifty feet away, he dismounted and called over to them, "I am not your enemy! Were you attacked on the High Tower Way?"

The man breathed in deeply. "Yeah, what's it to ya?"

Cymm nodded, respecting their cautiousness. "My destination is the pass and I'm trying to avoid whatever attacked you. Is that possible?"

"Yeah, but there are two waylay stations a couple miles apart from each other, so I would stay off the road for five miles before you cut back toward it," the man offered.

"Thank you." His eyes veered to the man's belly. "Mind if I examine your wound?"

The man gave him a once-over. "You don't look like a cleric?"

"Nah, I am not a priest, but I can help you. Have you ever heard of Terazhan?" He walked closer to the man with his hands raised. "Please put away your sword."

The man hesitated.

Cymm pressed on. "If I wanted to kill you, I would still be on my horse!"

The enormous beast knickered as if on cue, and the man sheathed his sword.

"Sit back like you were and relax. I need to touch your wound." The man did as instructed, while Cymm began his prayer to Terazhan. Pure white light sprang forth leaving those watching with wide eyes and open mouths. He removed his hands from the completely healed gut wound.

A little girl broke free from the women, running to the man. "Daddy, Daddy! Are you going to live now?"

The dark thing in his mind loosened its grip for the first time since he began this journey. Engrossed in his thoughts, he jumped when something grabbed his ring finger. The hopeful face of a little boy met his seeking gaze.

"Pweese save my daddy too!" exclaimed the child, pleading with his eyes.

The towering Plainsman lowered himself to engage the little boy, but one of the women swooped in and carried him back to the group. Cymm scanned the surrounding area to no avail.

The man he healed stood and extended his hand to Cymm. "Thank you, friend, but I have no way to repay you."

"Remember this, Terazhan is a merciful god." He pointed at the little boy who grabbed his hand. "Where is this boy's father?"

The man shrugged. "We aren't sure. He could be dead or in the slave cages."

Horror swept through Cymm, and his jaw dropped. "Slave cages?"

"Yes, the gnolls have built many cages on wheels and are raiding caravans to fill them. They transport their prisoners back through the High Tower Pass to their homeland for trade, food, and sport. My wife could be among them." He paused with tears in his eyes. "Please forgive my manners. I am Zecarius of the Stormcaller Clan."

"I am Cymm Reich of the Armakian Horse Clan and the First Paladin of Terazhan," he replied, puffing out his chest. "How many gnolls were there?"

"I would estimate fifty. There were many cages, and most were already full. Why?" asked Zecarius.

Cymm scratched his chin, tracking the clouds in the sky. "I can't let them take slaves, but I can't fight that many either."

"You have my sword! What's the plan?" Zecarius exclaimed.

"And Katara's!" said one of the women. He searched her over, eying the short swords strapped to her waist.

"Even with three, we still don't stand a chance against fifty, but I have an idea."

47

Courage Runs Deep

When TetraQuerahn landed heavily in the barnyard, he sent a slight tremor in all directions. The house in front of him shook; the hanging pots inside rocked into each other.

He inhaled for another roar when the door opened slowly, and out walked a human toward the damaged barn.

TetraQuerahn chuckled. *Bravery runs deep in this family, and probably stupidity too? Why would you willingly walk toward me?* "Is this the Reich Farm?" the behemoth inquired.

"Yes, are you l-l-looking for a h-h-horse to ride?" the human forced a smile, trembling, waiting for his response.

"Entertaining. I am *looking* for Cymm Reich. Does he live here?" the gargantuan serpent craned his neck forward to evaluate the human's response. Being a master at lying, he had become quite adept at separating fact from fiction.

"He did until four months ago wh-when a dragon like you killed him." The human's eyes were furtive, its voice cracking mid-sentence.

"I see. How are you related to Cymm?" he asked, approaching the problem from a new direction.

"I am Daro, and he is my nephew, my brother's son. Why?" The human's fear was already dissipating.

The right corner of the dragon's mouth curled so much it almost touched his eye socket. "Is or was?"

"Huh?"

"I distinctly recall killing two old people, and a young girl at this farm, but not a younger man or boy." TetraQuerahn methodically dissected the questionable story.

"That is correct. He was snatched from his horse's back by a dragon and dropped to his death," Daro said with his eyes rolling up to the left.

The green monstrosity closed the distance between them instantly, lowering his head so their noses were less than a foot apart. "You are lying!"

"Why would I tell you the truth? Why do you seek him?" Daro's shoulders slumped.

Hmm, this one no longer fears me. "The thief has something of mine."

"Cymm is no thief!" The head of Reich Household leaned forward, pointing his finger.

"If you tell me where he is, I will not kill you," TetraQuerahn grumbled, shifting his weight from side to side.

"He went north to kill you. He is probably waiting for you now in your lair!"

"He better be; if not, when I return, I will kill everyone in this village!" The dragon's eyes sparkled, and he breathed in deep.

"You said you would not kill me." Daro stumbled backward in confusion.

"Ahh, I see; when you lie, it is noble, but when I lie it is evil." The dragon resumed drawing in a deep breath.

Daro did not attempt to run; resignation crept across his face. "I hope he already killed your two friends."

"Enno!" TetraQuerahn's voice rose an octave in terror; then he immediately took wing right over the pathetic human, knocking him to the side in his failed attempt to snatch him.

He disappeared into the sky.

48

Rescue?

They waited until dark to leave. Cymm tied his horse to a tree while clicking to him softly, offering several ear scratches. He told the woman staying behind to release the horse if trouble comes a-knockin'.

They snuck back toward the road until the sound of strange voices made them freeze. The glow of several campfires came into view over the crest of the next hill. After crawling to the top, they remained flat on their bellies, counting the gnolls and cages capable of holding seven prisoners each. Cymm estimated seventy-five of the enemy and over thirty wagon pens, half of which were already full.

The gnolls, or hundar as Katara called them, had minimal guards posted, probably because they were patrolling the roads to find more travelers. Meanwhile, the rest of the creatures were around the campfires hooting, howling, arguing, and eating.

He motioned for Zecarius and Katara to follow him before sliding backward down the hill. He circled around the next hill to examine the cages from afar; none had any doors. To construct the cages, hundar used thick wooden poles with the bark still on them and grass rope. Breaking or cutting the poles would be difficult, but a sharp blade would easily cut the rope.

A refinement of his plan materialized in his mind, and he quickly shared it with the other two before withdrawing to wait.

Shortly after midnight, the enemy changed guards, and the rest prepared to sleep. Within ten minutes, the activity within the camp diminished. The three separated, making their rounds to each cage. They cut the bottom two corners, creating "doors" out of the entire back wall. The rear section could now swing up like a hinge, allowing the prisoners to escape. Some of the prisoners were waking as the rescuers began cutting the ropes, but they were instructed to wait for the signal. The escape plan required everyone to flee simultaneously. The mass chaos would confuse the captors, improving their chance of survival.

As Cymm approached the ninth cage, he heard a shuffle behind him. He whirled to find a gnoll guard bearing down on him. The paladin raised his hands to catch his enemy's arm with the descending khopesh, but it stopped mid-swing. A sword blade emerged from his enemy's chest, missing his shoulder by mere inches. The body slumped forward, falling to the ground, and Katara appeared behind it wearing a wicked grin. She gave a wink before running to the next enclosure.

They opened twenty-two cages containing over one hundred prisoners, but it still didn't feel like enough. Cymm's desire to free them all had logic battling instinct, but the entire gnoll raiding party slept around the remaining cages. He struggled to give the signal, not ready to give up on the other captives. Zecarius appeared carrying an arm full of weapons.

"Oh, this changes everything," the Plainsman whispered with a gleam in his eye.

"There are more where these came from," Zecarius murmured.

"Katara and I will start distributing them. You go get the rest."

Zecarius disappeared before he finished talking. Cymm began questioning the prisoners, but many could not fight due to age, fear, or injury. Still others were weak from lack of food and sleep. This left him with thirty fighters to cover their escape.

Ting . . . Ting . . . Clang . . . The paladin cringed, trying to locate the origin of the sound. Zecarius had dropped a sword. The rescuers froze in place listening. A low growl, followed by grunts and whoops, erupted from the main area.

"Hyenas, everyone out of the cages! Let's go!" Cymm ordered. "Retreat to the first hill."

Prisoners were jumping or falling out of the cages in a panic. The banging of the make-shift doors echoed throughout the quiet night. The enemy camp began to stir. Gnolls ran around in confusion, trying to discern the cause of the noise.

The hyenas, however, had no such problem, and they charged the fleeing prisoners.

One enormous human prisoner and a dwarf were taking over the defense with a new plan.

"Rally to me!" cried the large human stepping forward to protect a fleeing child. He cut down a hyena, killing it with one blow.

Cymm frantically directed the fleeing prisoners toward their temporary camp where he left his horse. After the last of the escaping prisoners passed, he returned to help those standing their ground. Eight hyenas were already dead with minimal casualties to the prisoners, but the entire pack of gnolls was descending on them.

Where is Katara? "We need to fall back!" Cymm demanded.

Zecarius had already rallied to the big man but locked eyes when he recognized his voice.

Several other prisoners responded immediately. "No, hold the line!"

Cymm opened his mouth to speak but seethed instead. *Who is in charge here?* he asked himself as he moved into the line. *Old-Man Semper would be fuming right now! Skirmish, run, regroup, repeat. That's what we need to do.*

His thoughts were bashed from his mind as the first wave of gnolls hit the defensive line. The vicious assault was borderline insane, and all six hundar died upon impact, along with four prisoners. Several other prisoners were knocked to the ground in the frenzy. Before Cymm had time to breathe, the next wave of twenty attacked, and those lying on the ground scrambled to their feet. The enemy surged more intelligently, but still aggressively. A blur of swords, blood, and death ensued. The battle trudged on slowly and arduously. The captors moved to flank the prisoners.

The large human immediately adjusted the formation. "Form a circle!"

A thirst for battle replaced Cymm's fear, and he cried aloud, "For Terazhan, the One True God! Help us!" A globe of shimmering white light materialized out of the air encompassing the paladin and most of the prisoners. The enemy recoiled in fear while the escapees took advantage, cutting down six more gnolls and injuring several others.

The paladin's aura enhanced the entire group's visibility and appeared to hinder the enemy's attacks as much as it helped his allies. A boisterous cheer rose from the prisoners, a rallying cry of strength and courage. The remaining gnolls were invigorated when twenty-five more joined the attack with roughly as many close behind.

Nine prisoners were down, but twice as many gnolls and all the hyenas were already dead. The remaining enemy, well over fifty, were now surrounding them two or three rows deep. The large human, dwarf, and two elves were dropping hundar with every swing, but the rest were struggling. *We will all be dead in the next ten minutes at this rate.* Cymm pushed on, trying not to let the sounds of battle alter his determination.

Two more prisoners fell dead next to him, and he closed the gap to stand shoulder to shoulder with Zecarius. In the bleakness, he marveled at the benefit of this formation, and the simplicity of protecting each other's backs.

A raucous battle cry blared from behind the enemy. Katara had brought thirty more fighters from the neglected cages. The chaos of the new attack left some of the gnolls fumbling with surprise, and the prisoners made them pay again.

The "Big Man's" sword arced in, killing his tenth gnoll, according to Zecarius.

The dwarf standing next to him announced, "Another fine display on how to die. Who's next?" as his opponent crumpled before him. He continued to taunt the enemy, delivering the promised results.

Only fifteen escapees from the original group remained, but the arrival of Katara's support uplifted their spirit and increased morale significantly.

The two groups of prisoners formed a slaughterhouse, butchering the monsters caught between them. The hundar tried to regroup, but the tide of battle had quickly swung in the prisoners' favor. They pressed the remaining twenty-five gnolls, breaking their courage, and many in the back row ran screaming for the pass.

Zecarius yelled, "They are escaping to get reinforcements from the other group. Stop them!"

The Big Man belayed that order. "Hold the line!" Even a bellicose dwarf arriving with Katara heeded the command from the big guy.

Five more fled, and the prisoners fell upon the remaining ten like a storm wave crashing on the shore. As soon as the last gnoll fell, the magical aura surrounding the paladin dissipated into the ether. Several prisoners stared at him in awe. Cymm found himself glancing down at his body, trying to grasp the meaning.

Zecarius's arms were flailing. "There are at least fifty more in the camp they are running toward, and it is only two miles away!"

The Big Man came over, clapped Cymm and Zecarius on the back and shoulder, offering his sincere gratitude. The

Plainsman stood six foot three, but this man towered over him, approaching seven feet tall.

"How in the nine hells did they ever capture you?" asked Cymm, meaning every word.

"Went to bed drunk, woke up in a cart, not very smart!" he laughed at his own bad rhyme. "Maybe I'll become a bard when I make it home. Okay, people! You have less than thirty minutes before the gnolls return in full force. Gather what you need and run. Most of us are heading south to get the children to safety, but the choice is yours. You can also head west for the town of Xylona."

Cymm, Zecarius, and Katara followed the Big Man south to find a large, anxious group of prisoners gathering at the rendezvous.

Zecarius's daughter hysterically yelled at a man standing next to his horse. The paladin approached slowly. *What is going on?* The man threw her to the ground and untethered his horse. Cymm rushed over and picked her up while the thief encouraged the horse to step on her.

"I am sorry! I tried to stop him. I am so sorry. I tried to protect your horse." The little girl sobbed.

"Don't you worry, little one; my horse knows his master." He eyed the man on his horse with a calm disposition. "I suggest you get down before you get hurt."

"Oh, shut up or I'll trample you with your own horse!" the man yelled with a sneer. "What is that horrendous smell?"

Everyone stopped what they were doing, intrigued by the spectacle. The horseman issued several loud clicks and a sharp whistle. His horse immediately laid down and rolled on its side, pinning the man's leg to the ground.

The thief screamed in pain while pulling a dagger, then cocked his arm back, intending to stab the horse. Cymm charged the man, but Zecarius beat him there, kicking the man in the head before disarming him. He picked up the dagger and placed it against the trapped man's throat.

"Wait!" Cymm's eyes darted through the crowd. "Will anyone speak for this man?" No one said a word; he sighed heavily. "Then he is accused of thievery and—"

"No gratitude for being rescued and the audacity to try and trample my daughter!" Zecarius showed no mercy and slit his throat from ear to ear.

Despite all the gore he'd seen over the last few weeks including the rotting dragon head he carried, Cymm cringed at the sight. Two whistles and a click filled the air, and the horse sprang back to his feet. He put the girl down, and she ran to her father.

"Not quite what I had in mind. Taking a finger would have sufficed," the paladin said.

"We saved his life, and he plans to pay us back by stealing your horse and killing my girl? He got what he deserved!"

Zecarius grabbed Cymm's arm before he could leave. "Come with us. There will be safety in numbers!"

"My destination is on the other side of High Tower Pass," he replied, pointing toward the mountains.

He squeezed Cymm's arm tighter. "That is madness! All of the hundar will be going through there also!"

"Yes, but first, they will come looking for you. While they are heading this way, I will ride hard for the pass. I will be okay." The paladin exuded confidence.

"My sister will be extremely disappointed! She has taken a liking to you." They both eyed Katara while she tended to her niece.

Cymm blushed and hesitated, briefly questioning his decision. *What would life be like with a strong warrior like Katara by my side? Would we live in a city, the plains, or somewhere exotic, and how many children would we have?* For a moment, he let himself dive deep into the fanciful daydream. He'd never considered it before, and the more he imagined it, the more he yearned for it.

His fantasy abruptly turned dark. His mind shifted from her cradling a new baby to her broken body lying on the ground, a green dragon's talon pinning her down and blood dripping from its teeth. He shook his head, snapping out of it, and forcefully withdrew his arm from Zecarius.

"She is brave and beautiful, but I must continue my quest." He hurried over to say goodbye to both aunt and niece. He hugged Katara a moment too long before complimenting her again on her exploits in battle.

Cymm knelt in front of the little girl. "What's the matter, little one? Did he hurt you?"

"My name is Tanya! And I am not little or hurt," the girl replied with tears still in her eyes.

He eyed her with a gentle stare of confusion. "Then why do you cry?"

"I want to be like you! Why can't you come with us and teach me?" Tanya said, fixing him with puppy-dog eyes.

She caught him totally off guard. He had never thought about the possibility of a second paladin. He would have to consider this and pray. *No reason I can't teach her about Terazhan, though.* "I will make you a promise; in a few years, when you turn fourteen lifeyears, come find me at Stallion Rise, and we will talk about this again."

Half of the prisoners had already left, and the rest were about to follow. There wasn't much time. Zecarius came over to collect his daughter. "We must leave now! Thank you again Cymm. May our paths cross again someday."

"Cymm Reich of Stallion Rise," Tanya muttered, as if trying to burn his name into her memory. "I will see you next year if my father allows it! I turn fourteen in the month of Rhomerian." Her eyes remained trained on him as her father pulled her along behind.

"We share the same lifemonth," he said aloud. *How can she be thirteen?*

Katara pouted, rubbed his shoulder, punched him hard in the same spot, then ran to catch up with her brother.

"Hey!" he yelled, rubbing his arm, "Teach your niece to use a sword."

"Give your horse a bath! He stinks," she replied with a smirk.

He quickly mounted his horse to leave when he saw the little boy who grabbed his hand being carried by his father. With a big smile on his face, he waved to Cymm yelling, "Tank you!" The man also waved, then ran to catch up with the other escapees.

Cymm added a couple extra miles off road, as Zecarius had suggested, before merging back onto High Tower Way as dawn broke. He surveyed a clear road in both directions, then picked up the pace in case gnolls were heading back this way.

The mountains were getting close, and the towers on each side of the road were beginning to materialize. He had not slept at all last night, nor would he sleep until the other side of the pass, no matter how long it took.

He used the time to analyze everything transpiring in the last twenty-four hours, especially the almost failed rescue mission. *If everyone had retreated, like I said, it would have been a massacre. Those new defensive positions we formed minimized the number of gnolls that could attack, allowing us to protect each other's flanks and back. Thank Terazhan for the "Big Man's" impressive leadership! I want to learn to lead a group of strangers against incredible odds like that.*

He planned to seek out the "Big Man," or people like him in the future, to gain knowledge on warfare tactics. Unfortunately, being isolated in his village had not facilitated the learning he found necessary. Semper had taught him a lot, but he had learned as much from Torak, the "Big Man," and Katara.

His mind drifted to Katara. *Why did she punch me in the arm?* He rubbed his shoulder. *She's not like any girl I have ever met. Not really a girl, more like a woman of nineteen or twenty. Nothing like Syra, the only girlfriend I've ever had.*

Girls are so confusing, even little girls! How can Tanya be thirteen lifeyears? She looks ten or maybe eleven! How can she know she is ready to commit herself to Terazhan?

Cymm paused, laughing at the absurdity of his thinking. *I committed myself to Semper for militia training at ten lifeyears, and to Hardre for paladin training at thirteen. In fact, I healed my mother's hand at the age of thirteen.*

Watch out, Erogoth! Tanya Stormcaller is coming. This thought made him happy, but the feeling drained away as he entered the shadow of the towers. He had arrived.

It was midday, and the Towers of Sethanon loomed above him as he entered the pass unchallenged. *Where are all the guards? Why are the gates wide open? No wonder the gnolls got through so easily! No one is protecting the Realm of Legerdemain.*

The walls climbed out of sight on both sides. He craned his neck upward seeking the top, but before he found it, his stomach lurched. He nudged his horse to pick up the pace, drawing a deep breath to control his anxiety.

Click Click . . . Click Click, he attempted to sooth his horse, "I am nervous too, buddy. I have never seen anything like this. Let's get it over with. By the way, Katara was right; this dragon head is making you smell."

The path varied from ten feet wide to fifty feet wide with an occasional crevasse breaking off to the side. An ambush from above did not concern him as much as the sporadically falling rocks.

"If you see a rock crashing toward us, run!" He rubbed the horse's flank.

His mind drifted back to the battle against the gnolls. *What was that sphere of white light? It brightened the night, gave courage to those around me, but is it also a shield? Did it demoralize my foes? They did run at the end. Either way, it is an extraordinary new paladin power if I can make it occur again.*

The shadows were growing long in the mountain pass when he noticed towers looming ahead. When he got closer to the High Towers of Delagor, he understood why Wexel couldn't help him. They were identical to the ones he'd passed earlier.

He slowed his horse from a canter to a trot and eventually to a walk as he drew closer. These gates were also open, and still no guards. He walked through the gates unobstructed. No sounds, bodies—living or dead—or signs of blood. Only complete desolation. A chill went down his spine. *This is not right!* However, he did not have time or interest to investigate, so he encouraged his trusty steed into a trot, then back to a canter.

He had entered the infamous Death Valley; more blood had been spilled here than anywhere in the world, and he did not intend to let his horse graze this close to the gates.

49

Applying Pressure

Cymm slowed the pace to a walk again when dusk arrived, but he didn't stop until well after midnight. He tried to give his horse plenty of time for a cool down; they had covered many miles in the past twenty-four hours. He guided the horse off the road to the north toward the mountains to find a stream for drinking and a sheltered alcove for a fire.

The horseman rubbed and brushed his four-legged friend, cleaned his hooves, massaged him, then wrapped him in a couple of blankets. He also gave him extra apples; he had earned them. Tomorrow would be an easy day with lots of grazing.

He prayed before going to bed, receiving a duplicate Vision of the dead tree. It caught him by surprise because it had been many days since his last one. While pondering this, he had a greater revelation: *Maybe it's because I veered off course.* Fifty-three hours without sleep limited his reflection, and slumber overtook him faster than ever before.

In the morning, he woke to the sun already in the sky. He had no intention to hurry today, so he took his time eating and saddling his horse. The Plainsman walked for the first hour instead of riding, his horse following without a lead rope. He needed to get back to the main road to find the ancient tree, but he trekked southeast, figuring the tree was still many miles away.

As he walked, he took in the scenery. "Death Valley, what a horrible name for such a beautiful place!" Mountain ranges surrounded him on three sides. The Rainbow Mountains spanned his entire view to the south, and the Knife-Edge Mountains covered the north and west.

The legends claimed this valley soaked up more blood than anywhere in the world, especially near the Towers of Delagor. Before the towers were built, many battles had been fought on this land over the centuries. Inevitably, hordes of orcs, gnolls, goblins, ogres, or hill giants funneled here to conquer the continent, which was why humans, elves, and dwarves built the towers together where they did. They kept Legerdemain safe from these marauding and plundering creatures; unfortunately, they did nothing to help with the dragon plague.

For centuries, the flying menace has been attacking and killing throughout Legerdemain, the only apparent motive being to wreak havoc. However, according to Dontono, dragons had never attacked the City of Mystics. He said, "Dragons don't fear much, but they do fear wizards, especially large groups of wizards. The City of Mystics has thousands of mages. It is the mecca for wizardry, providing training for people worldwide, even ogres! Many years ago, the dragons mounted an attack against the capital city in Toragan, learning a valuable lesson. Many high-level wizards thwarted it. They repeatedly cast spells turning the dragon's wings to stone, and if the crash didn't kill them, the warriors on the ground did."

Cymm made it back to the road by midafternoon; then traveled until late morning on the third day. The skeleton of a once magnificent tree loomed ahead, but now large pieces, which had broken off from lightning, wind, and decay, lay scattered around the rotting trunk.

He traveled south the rest of the day, the mountains drawing closer, but still so far away. After making camp, he prayed, only to be tugged into another Divine Quest.

His ethereal form separated from his material body, traveling south to the Rainbow Mountains. He again saw the meandering path up into the foothills, but this time he forced landmarks into memory. He moved to the same large hut in the middle of the village and swung around to the back before finally coming to a stop.

He stood there observing a dwarf banging a hammer on steel, standing in the middle of a blacksmith workshop, complete with a forge, bellows, anvils, and the rest of the works.

A voice called from the front of the house, "Warhez are you out back?"

Cymm gawked at his doppelganger approaching the workshop. He scrambled to get out of the way, but not fast enough, and he walked right through him. He cringed during the experience, hoping it would never happen again.

After recovering, he whirled around to see Twin Cymm pat Warhez on the back as the dwarf pointed at the sword in front of him. His twin picked up the sword, examined it, checked the balance, made a few lighthearted swings, then celebrated with the dwarf.

The weapon so enamored him, a whistle escaped his lips. *What a spectacular sword!* Exquisite designs were etched into the blade's metal with fine detail. The blade stretched a foot longer than his own, didn't taper until the tip, and the hilt extended long enough to grasp with two hands. It had two four-inch catch blades at the base of the blade above an empty oval socket and the cross-guard. It was not a claymore or a two-handed great sword; it was a bastard sword.

The workshop shimmered and started to fade before his material body called. When he opened his eyes, the moon Phoenix had shifted in the sky. He guessed an hour had passed.

He began pacing back and forth, gazing at the moon. *What if my material body were in danger? Would I snap out of the trance? Would my ethereal form receive a signal?* His faith in Terazhan wavered. *Can or will he protect me? If not, how do I refuse a Divine Quest?*

The following day, in the afternoon, Cymm arrived at the foothills of the Rainbow Mountains. The terrain transformed drastically from flat to rolling, making it difficult to find the meandering path. He retreated to the plain to scan from a distance, and he located it two hours later. He rode for another hour before arriving at the edge of the village. He dismounted, standing next to a sign he couldn't decipher— there were no words, only a symbol.

Cymm walked his horse into the village straight to the dwarf's home, emulating the Divine Quest. A putrid, sour smell drifted through the hamlet, overpowering the rotting dragon head, but he could not determine the source.

What a desolate place. Maybe everyone has abandoned the village. He called out toward the hut, "Warhez are you about?"

The door creaked open, revealing a dwarf covered in open-sore wounds. "You have doomed yourself human!"

More dwarves came out of their homes, surrounding him. They were also covered in open sores, including the children, and a new wave of stench overpowered him.

At least they won't notice the bag I carry, he thought, trying to breathe through his mouth.

They formed a dense semicircle around him at a distance, staring.

Warhez continued, "Didn't you see the sign! Now you must live out your remaining days or years here with us."

Cymm asked in confusion, "What sign? What do you mean?"

"This village is plagued by a flesh-eating disease from Bardonril, The Maker. There was a sign before you entered saying to stay out, but now you're infected!" he replied.

"My Lord Terazhan protects me from all disease. I can help. I'll cure each of you of this plague." The paladin peered around, expecting to see excitement or relief.

A village dwarf pointed at another dwarf in the throng. "That's what he said a month ago. Now, look at him! If a priest can't do it, what makes you think you can?"

Cymm eyed the infected priest. "Whom do you worship?"

"Dennari, the telluric mother goddess," the dwarf replied proudly.

"She may be powerful, but she is no god!" he proclaimed with hands in the air, upsetting many dwarves, who began protesting. "Witness the power of Terazhan!" Cymm approached Warhez. He slowly reached out toward the unmoving dwarf, resting his hands on his head, and thumbs on his forehead.

Cymm chanted a prayer while his hands grew in luminosity to a brilliant, beautiful white. Many gasped, leaning closer. Warhez attempted to push his hands away, but by the time he succeeded, every sore had disappeared.

The dwarves surged forward.

"I'm next!"

"No. Heal me!"

"I will give you an ingot of gold to heal me!"

"Please heal my children. I will do anything!"

Cymm worried the dwarves may crush and injure each other.

He towered over them, his face turning red. His arms came up and he screamed, *"Stop before someone gets hurt!"*

Many of them cowered, but all recoiled. He estimated at least two hundred dwarves surrounded him, yet he still made the following commitment. "I will not leave until everyone is cured!"

The dwarves began to cheer and applaud.

"I can only heal one person a day," he reminded them, putting a damper on the festivities.

Warhez shook his hand with rounded shoulders and eyes filled with sadness. "I wish I had believed you. My daughter needed your help more than I did. She is about to die."

Terazhan must have known this, Cymm thought. *This is the bargaining chip to have the dwarf craft the sword for me.* However, deep in his heart, he hated the idea of taking advantage of this poor father grieving his daughter's imminent death.

The pride on Cymm's face vanished as he shared in Warhez's sorrow. He walked his horse toward a tree off to the side of the house, and the crowd of dwarves parted instantly.

"Is he leaving?" one whispered, then two more said the same.

"He looks sad. What happened?"

"What did you say, Warhez?" yelled a dwarf.

"He better not leave because of you!" cried another.

Cymm didn't respond; his mind whirled while he contemplated his next move. *It's risky, but the reward should be worth it for everyone, including Terazhan. Besides, I don't want the dwarf to make the sword for me; I want him to want to make it for me.*

He tied his horse to the tree and returned to the group. Everyone waited silently. "I told you I can only heal one of you each day, but I have decided to try to heal a few more."

An instant frenzy began.

"Me!" said ten dwarves.

"Pick me!" twenty others said.

Dwarves were pushing and shoving.

"Stop!" his voice boomed like thunder again, and they did. "If this happens again, I am leaving. Do you understand?"

The dwarves moaned and groaned their agreement. Some shook a neighbor's hand or wrapped an arm around a friend's shoulder.

After a minute of observation, Cymm stroked his chin. "I need everyone's help, or this will never work. You have seen the power of Lord Terazhan. You all must pray to him to give me the power to do it again. He will choose the recipients."

The dwarves raced to be the first on their knees, the first to pray, maybe hoping it would help them get selected.

Cymm clenched his fists and rolled his shoulders, trying to relieve the tension. How could he or his god allow these dwarves to continue to suffer? He began pacing back and forth while praying. "Lord Terazhan, the great healer and merciful god, I call upon you to remove this scourge upon these good people. They—" His voice cracked, and he groaned in pain. His arms shot out straight to the side, and his head rocked back, gazing skyward. Two golden bolts of lightning descended from above and struck Cymm, one in each eye.

He screeched in agony.

50

It's in her Nature

Lykinnia remained diligent the past five days and visited her taviian friends daily. She had found a huge oasis of greenery, and they had been there ever since. She continued to search for the next home base, but for now, this place had proven to be very safe, with all eleven still alive.

She ended her reconnaissance when the pain in her head began, allowing the flash-travel process to whisk her back to her body.

With both hands planted on the altar, her eyelids flitted open to the voices of Solar and Terazhan in the distance.

She stepped off the platform with a curt wave. "Kind of early today, aren't you?" She hurried past them, back to her abode.

Phew, that was close! Why is Solar so early today? Hmm, and why is Terazhan with him? Most peculiar. Let's find out. She giggled and blinked out of sight before heading back to the altar.

She assumed her favorite position between the two nine-foot-tall beings.

Of course, still spying on Cymm with his pure white aura. What are we doing today, young man? She had stopped talking into the void because the voice unsettled her.

Diseased hill dwarves were swarming Cymm, immediately following a successful heal with his special aura. She barely noticed his hazel eyes and strong chiseled jawline this time. Placing her hand to her mouth, she faked a yawn, and turned to leave.

Cymm called out to the dwarves, "You all must pray to Terazhan . . ." The god and Solar were quite agitated.

Oh, this should be good, she mused, turning back around.

"You cannot do this!" Solar's arms uncharacteristically flailed about.

She saw Terazhan give him a scowl that should have put him in his place.

"You are not strong enough—" Solar pleaded.

"How dare you!" replied the god.

Lightning repeatedly struck around Terazhan and the altar, forcing Solar to leave the platform and Lykinnia to dive for cover. She came out from under the altar when she felt safe, resuming her position.

The air snapped and crackled; her hair began to float. Cymm's agonizing cry drew her attention; he writhed in pain.

What is going on? She took two weary steps back, and golden lightning bolts struck Cymm and Terazhan simultaneously.

A deafening clap resounded, and the shock wave knocked her backward. She stumbled and clambered to get away, only to fall off the back of the platform, her head slamming into the ground.

She gaped from her back as Terazhan thrashed in pain, shrinking in size. Her vision grew fuzzy and faded to black.

51

Was it Worth it?

ymm's body blazed with a golden aura, contorting in fits and starts, racked in pain while he grew three feet taller. His eyes filled with golden tears that streamed down his face. His voice dropped three octaves to a deep baritone. "Do not despair. Your salvation is at hand!"

Golden lightning bolts shot forth from his body, striking every dwarf present. Once struck, a tremor went through the dwarf's body. They lost consciousness and fell to the ground. Nine-foot-tall Cymm walked through the village striking more dwarves with lightning, including those that could not walk to him. After falling to the ground, the stricken regained consciousness completely healed. The excitement in the village continued to accelerate, escalating to passionate fervor as dwarves ran home to bring their sick loved ones forward to receive Terazhan's blessing.

The towering avatar toured the village for ten minutes, returning to the front of Warhez's hut, where the dwarf emerged from his house holding the frail, almost lifeless body of a young girl. Lesions completely covered her; one of the sores on the side of her thigh had eaten so much flesh her femur could be seen.

Warhez lifted her as if offering her up for sacrifice with a sorrow-riddled face. However, Cymm had begun to shrink, and no lightning bolt was forthcoming. The dwarf knelt before him with his child still in his hands. He implored with a primal growl, "Please save my daughter!"

The shrinking avatar looked down with robotic movement, the golden liquid still pooling in his eyes. He knelt, resembling an automaton more than a human, and placed one hand on the dwarven girl's leg and one on her head. The power surged from Cymm, streaks of his aura mixing with the golden halo surrounding him. Shocks of pure white contrasted heavily with the gold in his eyes. The hundreds of radians interleaved, allowing him a tiny window of observation.

Dwarves crowded in, fighting for a clear line of sight. The little girl's body went rigid, and she cried out in pain. Warhez's mouth hung agape, his eyes asking the avatar for guidance.

The hole in the young girl's leg filled with white lattice-structured cells, weaving a pattern back and forth until it filled the void completely. At the same time, dozens of other sores on her face, hands, and arms simply disappeared.

Eradication of the disease was complete; Terazhan had saved the village.

Warhez's face went from awe to blubbering and weeping. While still on his knees, he gazed to the sky, shouting, "Thank you, Terazhan the Almighty Healer!"

Warhez's wife, who had remained at the door to their home, called out, "Warhez Ironfist?"

The dwarf could not respond, so he stood with his daughter still in his hands, slowly nodding his head. His wife ran over with wet eyes to snatch the girl from his arms, kissing and hugging her tightly as if she feared it was all a dream.

The rest of the village chanted, "Ter—a—zhan," softly at first, but building to a crescendo nearly two minutes after it began, continuing for nearly five minutes.

Cymm had returned to his normal size. Still on his knees, he tottered and swayed, trying to regain control of himself. He heaved out a staggered breath, desperate to comprehend what his god had done, unsure he'd ever be willing to do it again.

The dwarf leaned in to stabilize him, giving him a hug with the strength of a bear. Cymm passed out in his arms.

∞∞∞∞

Cymm's thoughts were hazy as he sat comfortably in Warhez's house, drinking an incredibly fine ale.

"I wish I had something else to offer at the moment," the dwarf said, fluffing another pillow for Cymm.

"This is good." Cymm took another gulp enjoying the flavor. "How long was I out?"

"A couple of hours, long enough for the villagers to plan a huge celebration for tomorrow, where you are the guest of honor."

Cymm finished his beer and stood when he recognized the late hour.

The dwarf jumped up, knocking over a footstool in the process. "What do you need, my friend?"

"I need to take care of my horse and make sure he is comfortable," he replied, walking out the door.

Warhez followed him. "Is there anything I can do to help? Bring water, or food, or even build a stable?"

He shook his head in empathy. *What would I have done if someone saved my sister or parents from dying?* "Yes, water would be very helpful. Thanks." Other dwarves had already brought the horse a wagonload of fine-grained grasses from their stone mill. Cymm had noticed the mill when he entered the village, hoping they baked bread or cakes.

Exhausted, he finally came to terms with the massive amount of power channeled through his body. Although, he wondered, *Could I have stopped him from entering my body? I didn't consent to be an avatar, but I guess I insisted on healing more dwarves.* He recalled the strange feeling of not controlling his own body or seeing more than shadows through the golden liquid filling his eyes.

His ears, however, never ceased functioning. Warhez's voice had wavered when he asked Terazhan to heal his daughter. The ensuing gasp, the catch when he inhaled, the dwarf struggling to breathe. *What a memorable moment!* He'd healed others, but not like this. The happy crying, the rejoicing, made his heart swell and his eyes fill with tears.

Warhez returned with two buckets of water.

"Thank you. I will join you inside shortly." But he never made it back inside, nor did he pray. He did not recall curling up in the pile of grass or his horse nudging him as he ate from the grass around him.

In the morning, he woke to an audience. Several dwarves who crowded around him were now yelling at each other for waking him.

The blacksmith came out of his hut, confused by the commotion. "What's going on?"

"How could you let him sleep in a pile of grass?"

"Why did you let him sleep outside?"

Cymm sprang to his feet, hurrying over to Warhez. He put his arm on the dwarf's shoulder, which satisfied most of the dissidents.

The dwarven gratitude was endless. Their despair-filled lives had changed so drastically and so quickly. All this attention made him uneasy, but he had to balance his discomfort with insulting their hospitality and generosity.

Two new dwarves approached him with a basket of warm bread and a basket of fresh fruit. He took one of each and insisted they give the rest to those with nothing to eat.

He followed the dwarven blacksmith around to the back of his hut. Warhez began whistling while he cleaned up his workshop, which had fallen into disarray.

Cymm steeled his nerves. "I have a big favor to ask of you, but first I must tell a story."

The paladin's serious demeanor caused the blacksmith to stop whistling. He found two stools, dusted them off, and placed them a few feet apart. They both took a seat.

Cymm shared his trials and tribulations from the beginning. He started with his arrival home from the hunting trip to find his family massacred, his village in shambles. The dwarf shook his head with misty eyes. He continued the story as he traveled north to kill the wyrm responsible. The false murder charges from the Wolf Clan stirred a growl from Warhez. Next, he reenacted creeping down the tunnel to the dragon's lair. Then he disclosed the uncontrollable fear swelling inside him during the entire encounter.

Warhez nodded in approval. "You are a brave lad, and three less green dragons in this world provides a safer place for my daughter."

Cymm proudly shared the rescue mission of the people in the gnoll slave cages before entering his village. "Warhez, my entire journey has led me to this point; specifically, to you!"

The dwarf's focus shifted from the floor to him in bewilderment. "How can this be? Have we met before?"

"No, we have not. You have seen the raw power of my Lord; he sent me to find you. By providing images in my mind, he guided me to your village and to you." He paused to let this information resonate.

"When you first entered our village, I wondered how you knew my name. You and Terazhan saved us. I can never repay what you did for my daughter, Cymm!" He started to get choked up. "I will always be in your debt."

The paladin smiled, hoping this request would be as easy as it appeared. "Well, the reason Terazhan sent me to find you is for your blacksmithing skills. He has shown me an image of you crafting a magnificent sword, made from a metal I have never seen."

"The metal you saw in this *image* was mithril, and it is very valuable because of its strength and beauty," the dwarf replied.

"Warhez, I do not have much in terms of wealth, but maybe we can figure—"

The dwarf sprang from his seat, the stool toppling behind him. "You will not pay one copper coin my friend!"

Cymm recoiled from the irate dwarf.

"I told you I could never repay what you have done for my family and this village. I will make you the finest weapon this world has ever seen!" The blacksmith extended his hand to help the paladin stand, then continued cleaning his workshop with renewed vigor.

52

Master Weaponsmith

During the celebration, Cymm heard many stories about Warhez's affinity for parties; however, last night he'd left the gathering first. The dwarf rose early, and the paladin found him tinkering in his workshop alone. Ten minutes later they were joined by several other dwarves before heading out for the mithril mine an hour away.

For the next two days, Warhez had his team of dwarves smelting the mithril ore to remove the mineral from the rock; then they took two more days to remove the impurities from the ore. The furnace blazed hot for several days, but the captain repeatedly reprimanded his team for letting the temperature fall below three thousand degrees. His assistants were responsible for adding a sawdust mixture to the furnace to enrage the fire while pumping the bellows to feed it air. When the molten mithril belched, they poured it into ingot molds for future use.

While the smelting process occurred, Warhez also constructed the mold for the sword. For two weeks, they recreated and rebuilt the mold until it aligned perfectly with the Vision Cymm received every time he prayed. The finalized mold now had the proper blade length, four-inch catch blades, and a large socket in the hilt. The blacksmith used interchangeable and connectable mold sections for the blade, but the oval socket, catch blades, and hilt needed to be designed and built from scratch.

Terazhan's Twilight had come and gone before the mold was finished. With a collective sigh, the dwarven assistants pulled up a stool or hopped up on a workbench, and Warhez disappeared.

Cymm peered around; an undeniable wave of excitement rippled through the air. He sat on a workbench, joining them. He wasn't invited, but then again, neither were the others.

Warhez reappeared to hoots and whoops.

One of the dwarves eagerly licked his lips as he held his hat to his chest. "Warhez, that better be the good stuff!"

"'Tis, of course 'tis!" called another.

Warhez lifted his eyebrows multiple times in succession before slamming the small keg from his shoulder down on a workbench. *Thunck!*

"Ahh, it must be the really good stuff." The assistant stomped both feet on the floor.

Warhez produced a mithril tap and spun it around his finger before hammering it home. The others whistled and clapped. The master smith produced six tankards from a lower shelf, setting them out next to the keg. "Alright boys, this is the really good stuff, aged for over twenty years." Warhez cranked the spigot on the tap and poured the first. "Cymm, come on up. You get the first taste."

"Oh yes . . . that makes sense," a dwarf said.

"Yes, come on, Cymm," added another.

"Go on Cymm!" two more said.

Cymm cleared his throat uncomfortably. "But I didn't do anything. No mining, no smelting, and I barely helped with the mold."

Warhez delivered the tankard, setting it on the bench next to him. "This forge would normally run seven days a week, all day long, before the plague came to our village. Do you want to guess the last time we lit this forge?"

Cymm surveyed the dwarves around him; they stared back with wide eyes full of hope and promise. He cleared his throat again, "I-I don't know."

"It has been over a year. We closed it up, vowing never to relight it. We made that promise under the assumption of death. You have brought us life and hope. So, when you say you did nothing, I say you are the only reason this forge was relit." The dwarves cheered.

Cymm hoisted the tankard, quaffing a mouthful while his companions waited anxiously for his reaction.

A dry, mild heat assaulted his senses, warming his body. His mind drifted back to sunny summer days fishing with Bria. The warmth continued to pulse through him; he took a deep breath, and the air intensified the tantalizing taste that awakened his salivary glands.

Cymm nodded in appreciation, stroking the tankard with renewed interest. *So that's what all this fuss is about.*

The other tankards were poured quickly, and the party began. A lyre appeared out of nowhere, accompanied by several bawdy dwarven songs. Cymm did not recognize most of the words, but he got the gist from the crude actions he observed.

The paladin knew this exceptional occasion was a once-in-a-lifetime experience.

Later that evening, while praying, a Divine Quest replaced the Vision of the sword. Twin Cymm and Warhez worked together to remove the horns from the dragon's head. His twin crushed both horns into a fine powder on a workbench before wrapping and storing the head. After the blacksmith melted the bars of mithril in the crucible, he added the dust while the dwarf stirred it in with a ladle.

All night, Cymm tossed and turned as images of the sword burrowed into his mind. The following morning during breakfast, he explained what he saw to an upset blacksmith.

"Are you sure the horn powder wasn't used as a reducing agent or a coagulant?" Warhez tapped his foot while tugging his beard.

Cymm threw both his hands in the air. "I don't even know what that means. I saw you placing the bars of pure mithril into the crucible and melting them."

"Yes!" The dwarf stood. "That eliminates the reducing agent, which means we don't have to start all over. So, what happened when you added the powder? Did it get absorbed easily, or did it clump together, creating a floating skin on top of the molten metal?" Warhez asked masterfully.

"It was absorbed; not a trace could be seen," Cymm replied without hesitation.

The dwarf sat back slowly while drumming his fingers on his own forehead, then quickly rose. "Let's get ready to pour!"

It took most of the morning to get the furnace back up to the proper temperature so the ingots of mithril would melt. In the meantime, Cymm had the pleasure of dissecting the decaying dragon head. The once green and vibrant skin had become dull, floating loosely over the rotting flesh beneath it. Unfortunately, the preserving berries had been added too late, and the rancid smell burned his nasal cavity. He almost vomited several times, but he could not plug his nose. He needed to hold the dagger in one hand and the tongs Warhez provided in the other. Eventually, with significant effort, he pried the horns loose, separating them from the skull. He immediately rewrapped the remains to reduce the awful smell, replicating the steps in the Divine Quest.

Warhez provided a grinding stone and Cymm went to work on the horns. Once they were ground into a fine powder, the dwarf placed the powder into a covered bowl to keep the wind from scattering it.

The blacksmith's crew kept pumping the bellows and adding fuel to the furnace along with the sawdust concoction that made the fire roar.

By midafternoon, the master weaponsmith determined the ore was ready. Warhez stirred the molten metal wearing thick leather gloves while Cymm added the dragon horn powder precisely as he'd seen in the Divine Quest. Finally, after a half hour of simmering, mixing, and pumping the bellows, the smith announced it was time.

Everyone got into their required positions, the workshop suddenly buzzing with excitement. Two dwarves were on each side of the crucible, holding the long-extended handles, while two others grabbed buckets filled with water. Warhez stood next to the mold, holding the pouring ladle. With no further delay, the dwarves worked in tandem, filling the mold halfway.

"Stop! Stop! By Bardonril's beard!" the smith cursed in frustration. "The dragon horn did not fuse with the metal." He thought for a few minutes. "I want the furnace two hundred degrees hotter this time." Shock and angst manifested on each crew member's face. They did not say a word but cast sideways glances around.

While they increased the temperature, the blacksmith emptied the mold into an ingot cast, then cleaned and reapplied the mask to the sword mold.

The sun had dipped below the horizon, and they were now working by torchlight. Finally, they were ready to pour again. The molten metal flowed like water this time, filling the entire sword mold. Warhez smiled, pleased with himself, setting it aside to cool. He established a schedule to maintain the furnace overnight at a lower temperature. The dwarf planned to reheat and pound the blade in the morning.

By morning, the blade still exuded heat, but it had cooled enough to remove from the cast. Warhez separated one section of the mold at a time until the blade popped out. Everyone noticed the glimmer in the smith's eyes—even the dwarves busy with the fire craned their necks for a peek.

With the blade successfully removed, he grabbed the tang and his hammer in his thick leather gloves and swaggered over to the furnace. He stuck the sword in the coals, heating six inches of the tip until it glowed red hot. He placed the blade on his anvil and struck his first blow, shattering it in three pieces.

The words coming out of his mouth were both obscene and loud. He carried on for so long that his wife appeared. "Warhez! Your daughter can hear your vulgar mouth inside the house!"

Warhez's head shrank into his shoulders like a turtle, and he sheepishly sought support from Cymm, his eyes begging forgiveness.

To emphasize her point, she said, "And besides, what would Terazhan think?"

The paladin did not offer sympathy, but after she left, he whispered, "Don't worry. I curse on occasion too." After validating she had left, they burst out laughing.

The smith put the broken pieces back in the crucible and let them return to molten metal. "Get it back up to three thousand two hundred; then before the pour, we will push it three hundred more degrees and hope that does it."

None of the dwarves moved, except their heads shook slowly from side to side. One dwarf finally spoke his mind, "The furnace won't survive. It will sunder." The other dwarves nodded in agreement.

Warhez leaned against a workbench and spoke in a subdued tone, "Yes, possibly, but it should only be for a few minutes. I am willing to take the risk, even if it means building a new furnace."

"Then we need excess water on hand," another dwarf said.

"And we should evacuate this side of the village," a third added.

"And—" began the original dwarf.

"I agree; put everything in motion," Warhez said.

By midday, they were ready to go. The master weaponsmith added the extra ingot with the dragon horn powder to the crucible, rebuilt the mold, masked it, and stirred the molten mixture many times. He gave the word, and the dwarves began driving the temperature three hundred additional degrees.

The furnace roared and creaked, filling the air with a palpable tension. To manage the blaze, the dwarves used extended pokers, but they warped, then melted. The raging sound of the fire was frightening, like a red dragon spewing fire as it dove from the sky.

Whoosh, whoosh. The bellows were working double time, the intensity of the heat drenching everyone in sweat.

The furnace groaned. "Okay, let's pour."

While swinging the crucible away from the furnace toward the pouring ladle, one dwarf's beard began smoking. He quickly dunked his head in a bucket. Another dwarf replaced him, helping to position the crucible properly. They tilted it while Warhez worked the ladle, evenly distributing the mithril in the mold, completing the third pour.

The entire group piled out of the workshop, chests heaving to breathe the fresh cool air; two collapsed on the ground to rest. The furnace had survived.

When they returned, Warhez removed the blade from the mold, then placed the tip into the furnace. Glowing red hot, he set it on the anvil and struck it with the hammer. *Clang!* He beamed from ear to ear. *Clang . . . ting, ting, clang.* Everyone cheered and clapped.

"Cymm, this is going to take a while. You should sit down or come back in a few hours." The dwarf returned to heating and hammering with his tongue hanging out to the side.

Cymm returned three hours later to find a tired but excited dwarf.

Warhez pointed at the sword in front of him. "Now, I still have many days of work ahead of me, but here is what we have so far."

Cymm picked up the sword by the tang to examine it. He made a few lighthearted swings without the hilt. "It's light," he said, then swung it again with wide eyes. "This is amazing!"

For over a week, the dwarves worked the bellows while Warhez pounded the mithril blade into shape. Every night he went to bed with his arms aching from the jarring impact, and each day Cymm's admiration of Warhez's skill grew.

The master weaponsmith projected another week of work to temper the blade, finish the hilt, assemble the sword, and sharpen the edge. The blacksmith built a hilt capable of receiving the impressive ten-inch-long tang on the sword. The pommel or counterweight for the blade could now be determined to keep the weapon in perfect balance. He also put a double edge on the catch blades and reinforced the oval socket to ensure there were no weak points. Finally, he tempered the blade to perfection, making it strong enough to cleave through iron.

53

The Speaking Stump

The dwarves planned another celebration for tonight because the paladin planned to leave in the morning. Everyone attended, including the children, and Warhez seized the opportunity to speak first from the stump.

"My daughter, Almira, was born on the eighth day of Breeze." The proud papa puffed his chest out. "I can remember the first time she talked; she said 'Mama,' and the first time she walked, holding my pinkie. I have a fond memory of the first time she picked up my blacksmith hammer and the first time she made me breakfast."

The story appeared to be a long one, and Cymm expected everyone to groan, but instead, they cheered, warming his heart immensely.

". . . seven lifeyears and inflicted with The Maker's Disease! What kind of life is that? She fought for a full year, fourteen months, and even though she is a fighter, I am not sure how much longer she would have lasted." A tear rolled down his cheek and into his beard while his lower lip quivered.

"The hole in the side of her leg was so deep you could see her bone and so wide my hand could not cover it! Her future was bleak until Cymm showed up, and we hid in our houses hoping he would go away. Now the light of my forge can dance, run, sing, and make me breakfast again," he proclaimed with his arms raised, and everyone laughed.

"I have decided my next task will be in the name of Terazhan! I will build a shrine where all are welcome to pray or give thanks to the One True God, who saw our suffering and saved us." Every dwarf cheered, whistled, or banged their tankard in response.

A few others went, but within the hour, Warhez jumped back on the speaking stump.

"I know, I know. I already had a turn, but I didn't get a turn at the last party," he said with a smirk, to the delight of most dwarves.

"This sword is the greatest accomplishment of my life. I have no doubt Cymm will wield it with honor and pride." He motioned toward the paladin. "Can you please show it to everyone?"

Cymm did as requested, walking around the gathering, showcasing the magnificent weapon. While he made his rounds, Warhez went into detail, describing each step of the process, from mining to refining and from pouring to tempering. Dwarves cheered and banged on the table again.

"Over the past few weeks, I have gotten to know Cymm very well, and I call him friend." More raucous cheers and banging occurred. "I am assuming most of you would like to do the same—especially since he saved all of you and your loved ones. We have never had or allowed anyone but a dwarf to stand on the speaking stump, but I call on Cymm to come and share a story with us." Warhez stepped down and motioned for him to approach.

The human hesitated, waiting. There were no objections, but then again, he didn't hear much support either.

54

Insanity is Contagious

TetraQuerahn returned from Stallion Rise several weeks earlier to find everything in order. Both Ennozarius and Anekzarius were safe, reporting no signs of intruders.

The powerful male dragon told Ennozarius, "I found the farm; they told me this fool came north looking for us, and he would never leave until we were dead."

Her eyes fumed, regarding him with an irrational energy. "Did you raze the village?"

"I did not have time—"

"You better be teasing me! They admitted—"

"You dare to question me!" he roared, the sail on his head unfurling. "I rushed home to make sure *you* and your sister were safe!"

It had been more than two months since the death of their hatchlings, and TetraQuerahn had personally witnessed the long road to Ennozarius's recovery.

"Fine, I am safe. Now go back and kill everything!"

"That is an option, but it will mean leaving you and your sister alone for two more days, an opportunity he may be waiting for. A risk I am not willing to take. I plan to greet him when he arrives," he answered firmly.

The female dragon screeched, slamming her tail into the wall of tree trunks; a curtain of dirt and dust showered them. "Fine, I will go. Tell me how to find it."

"You were against me going in the first place. What has changed?"

She screeched, banging her long neck this time into the tree trunks. "At first, I was pretty sure the bodies were intact until after you dropped the human from the sky, but I wasn't positive. While you were gone, another detail about that day came to mind. The torch." She glared at him accusatorily.

TetraQuerahn's confusion did not stop him from responding kindly, "What torch?"

"The torch you made the human light inside the lair. When we went outside, it was sitting here." She stomped her foot on the floor. "And when I returned, it was over here."

TetraQuerahn cocked his head, processing the information, considering the possibilities. "Hmm, are you sure?"

"I knew you were going to say that!"

It was true. He questioned her sanity and judgment, considering both to be severely impaired. However, the next day, he began scouting the area for intruders.

55

Salvation

ymm continued to stand awkwardly in front of everyone. Meantime, the uncertain dwarves swiveled their heads around. One by one, beginning with Warhez, they began chanting "Ter – a – zhan." Cymm walked toward the speaking stump slowly, trying to think about what he would say.

The dwarf interrupted his self-reflection and told him confidentially, "As long as it is true and from your heart, they will love it."

He didn't need to stand on the stump since he towered over the dwarves, but he wanted to be part of the tradition. It measured four feet in diameter and two feet high, further exacerbating the height disparity with his new friends.

A buzz went through the crowd; many rudely whispered or pointed at him. Some motioned to his new height while others imitated lightning bolts hitting them. Dwarves banged their tankards, calling for silence.

A flicker of doubt pulled at his insides, and his mouth dried up. He swallowed until he found his voice again.

"I recently met a young girl of thirteen lifeyears who told me she wanted to be a paladin like me, committing her life to Terazhan. At first, I thought it was ridiculous at her age, but then I remembered at the age of thirteen, I made my commitment. My religious studies began with a dwarf named Hardre Ironcore, a mountain dwarf from the city of Delge." Shock pulled at the crowd, and many glanced at their neighbor for confirmation that they heard him accurately. "That is correct. I learned about Terazhan from a dwarf. He is not a human or a dwarven god; he is a god of all people. He has been with us for millennia, and yet many people are unaware of him and fewer worship him." He stepped down from the speaking stump.

Warhez yelled, "What in the nine hells was that? It doesn't count! Get back up there and tell us something about you, the salvation of our village."

Cymm frowned in response, scowling at the dwarf, but the smith's words sent a shiver through his body. The paladin scratched his head vigorously. "What did you say?"

"Everyone thinks you are the salvation of our village. Tell them something about you!"

He stepped up on the stump with a changed attitude and a purpose. "Where I come from, the Plains of Armak, gathering enough food for livestock and people is essential for the survival of each family and the tribe. This occurs mostly in two hectic months—Harvest, the fifth month, and Final Harvest, the twelfth month. Festival, the fourteenth month, however, is a time for celebration and family bonding."

More tankard banging and cheering rang through the night, bringing him comfort and a feeling of belonging. His mind reeled with childhood memories—the love he had for his family and all the little things he'd taken for granted, believing he'd always have them.

"It is commonplace for families to travel for weeks if they can make arrangements for someone to feed and water their livestock. When I was fourteen, my father decided we would go to Hot Springs to celebrate Festival. It was a day and a half ride, and both Reich families went, all seventeen of us." He half smiled, trying to keep the tears from welling in his eyes.

"There were games and competitions in the morning, mostly related to horse riding, then swimming in the afternoon." The dwarves groaned. He paused, looking around uncertainly, but Warhez reassured him to keep going with a nod of his head and a flick of his wrist.

"My cousin Talo won the bowmen competition from the ground and from horseback, setting a record for the most points ever scored from the ground," Cymm proclaimed to banging and cheering.

"In the afternoon of our second day there, many kids were swimming in the cold-water lake." Again, more groans. Cymm paused, but slowly continued, ". . . while the adults were drinking and relaxing in the hot springs. My cousin and I were left in charge of the other eleven Reich children, and we made sure they stayed close to shore."

"After only ten minutes, screams and chaos erupted as children scrambled for shore! Talo and I quickly got our brothers and sisters out of the water amidst the mass exodus. I peered out across the water to find several children struggling to get to shore, fifty or sixty feet out. Then a little girl went under, flailing against the water." Cymm paused and took a drink.

"That's why I never go in the water," a dwarf yelled, seconded by several others.

"Or a bathtub!" Another dwarf pinched his nose, drawing many jeering laughs and raspberry sounds.

Cymm shook his head but pressed on. "So, I grabbed my sword before running into the water to help. I am not a very good swimmer, so I pulled kids toward me in the shallower water, then forced them toward the shore. When I pulled the last boy's arm, he yelled at me, 'Stop! I am holding my sister's hand.' I immediately went under water to find a brave little girl holding her brother's hand with a giant snake coiled around her hips and legs."

"I rushed forward, grabbing her torso under her arms, and stood up forcefully, pushing with my feet against the coils of the snake's body wrapped around her, and she sprung free! I literally threw her several feet toward shore, and the brother never let go of her hand." *See, he was a good brother; he was there for his sister. Cymm, where are you?* rang out in his head.

He stumbled over his next words, and hesitated, while trying to compose himself as the wave of panic ran its course. The dwarves exchanged many looks of concern.

Cymm shook his head vigorously, which finally cleared his mind. "I yelled at the boy 'Get out of here,' but the snake didn't go after the brother and sister. As they scrambled away,

I felt its fangs sink into my shoulder." Cymm pointed to his left shoulder as many children snuggled closer to a parent.

"Don't worry, little ones. I am here. I made it." A few chuckles rang through the crowd. "But I no longer had a sword; I dropped it to free the girl. So, I grabbed a snake coil with my right hand, hooked part of its body with my left arm, and started hauling the snake toward land. At forty feet from shore, the first arrow came sailing in, and Talo hit it with a second moments later. The snake released my shoulder, striking at my neck while coiling around me. I told my cousin to give me his sword, and he rushed into the water with two other boys. The four of us hauled the snake toward shore while it bit my leg. About ten feet from shore, it reared back to strike my face, and I decapitated it."

"Parents were streaming into the area at this point to find their children. Many of them were thanking or congratulating me, but here is why I'm sharing this story. The little girl, weak from almost drowning, found the strength to stand when I came to check on her. She pushed past her family, hugging me intensely. She whispered, 'You are my salvation.' Salvation is how I feel about Terazhan; he has given my life purpose. From that day forward, I have attempted to bring the feeling of salvation to as many people as I can, even at the expense of my own life!"

Cymm stepped down, and everyone cheered noisily and banged their tankards until they saw the master smith walking toward the speaking stump again.

"Warhez, give someone else a chance!" someone yelled.

Warhez's wife ran up to intercept him, whispering in his ear, but he gently moved her to the side saying, "This is very important!"

He stood on the stump, waiting for the crowd to settle. "The last time I was up here, I said Cymm would wield the sword with honor and make our village proud. However, what does he say when someone asks him about the sword or if he tells the story about how he cured a couple hundred dwarves of a horrible disease? It was a dwarven village in the Rainbow Mountains? Our village needs a name, and I propose we call ourselves *Salvation*."

Warhez retired from the stump for the night, and his vote passed unanimously. Cymm stayed a little later than the previous party but called it a night after the children went to bed.

He received a new Vision that evening of a mountain towering over the mountains around it. He finished packing, then turned in for the night. He woke long before anyone else but delayed his departure until Warhez finally stumbled outside.

Cymm approached. "Good morning my friend. Are you familiar with a huge mountain in the Knife-Edge Mountains?"

The dwarf rubbed his eyes. "You are referring to the Peak of Power. It is south of the dwarven city of Delge, and it is the source for the great River of Spells. Why do you ask?"

"Well, it is my next destination, but I need to figure out how to get there."

"There is a path through the Rainbow Mountains going down into Delf Wood, a back way to the Peak of Power, but your horse would never make it. He can stay here until you return," the dwarf said.

"Nah, I can't leave my horse," the Plainsman replied immediately.

"Then you have two options, through High Tower Pass and south on the Great North Road, or head east around the Rainbow Mountains, then south until you hit a road, west through the High Pass of Rell, then north on the Great North Road," Warhez rattled this off like a realm-to-realm messenger.

"By Melcorac's hammer! How do you know all this?" exclaimed Cymm.

He chuckled richly. "I haven't lived here my entire life, and I've been to Delge a few times to give demonstrations on blacksmithing."

"Which way would you recommend?"

The dwarf shrugged. "Legerdemain is usually safer to travel through, but you could encounter the other half of the gnoll party on your way back to Xylona."

Cymm clasped hands, then embraced Warhez. "Thank you again for this magnificent sword."

"Thank you for saving my family and my village."

By now, everyone had formed a receiving line, and he rode out of the village.

He paused for several minutes when he got to the bottom of the last hill, officially entering Death Valley again. He peered left toward the Towers, then right to go around the Rainbow Mountains. Finally, he headed back the way he came.

56

Nature's Trail

Lykinnia approached the altar in the early morning rubbing the back of her head subconsciously. It had been a month since she flew off the platform, striking her head on the ground, and it was a good thing she didn't need assistance because no one came to help her.

Well, that was not completely true, and her skin crawled to think about it. When she regained consciousness, a hovering hand stroked her hair. Still in a daze, Lykinnia leaned into the feminine hand. She enjoyed the gentle, caressing touch, which evoked memories of her childhood before her mother died.

Her eyes popped open to find a disembodied arm from the elbow down, floating in the air above her head. The priestess let out a muffled scream from behind her own hand. Her invisibility persisted, so she quickly dismissed the spell that should have ended hours earlier.

The voice from the void discovered her awareness too late, "Lykin—" She lay back on the ground shaking, and the arm was sucked back into the closing void. After Lykinnia had composed and healed herself, she stumbled home that night to fall into bed.

Although a month had passed, she still couldn't shake the feeling. A shutter coursed through her body as she stepped up to the altar. *The lightning bolts struck Terazhan right here before he shrank to my height. And they struck Cymm. This must be related to his aura.*

She had always loved the color of her own aura. It was beautiful and perfect—so she thought until she saw Cymm's. *How could he have a more righteous aura than mine?*

Lykinnia placed her hands on the altar, willing her spirit to flash-travel back to the Lower Darken Wood. She gathered the nymphs when she arrived. Her ability to find safe havens the past month had resulted in no deaths, leaving all eleven still with her.

"We are getting close! Only a few more weeks of travel, and you will be with me." The insects buzzed with excitement. "But the next part of the journey will be difficult. I cannot find anywhere for you to hide or rest for the next couple of days. When you aren't resting briefly in the treetops, you will keep marching toward the next sanctuary." Lykinnia knew the dangers that lay ahead, and a knot grew in her stomach as she led them toward their next refuge.

57

Entomophobia

ymm exited High Tower Pass early in the afternoon on the fourth day after leaving Salvation. He had no intention of returning to Xylona. Instead, he followed the mountains rolling through the foothills for a few days. Eventually, he would try to intersect with the Great North Road.

He spent six days heading south by southwest as he stuck close to the Knife-Edge Mountains before Darken Wood swallowed the foothills and they came together.

The month of The Holy One had arrived, and six weeks had passed since he parted with Katara, Zecarius, and

Tanya. They had also traveled this way, and after two close calls with hill giants, he hoped they were all right.

The odor of the decaying dragon head continued to intensify, assaulting his sense of smell. It was a constant reminder of the death and destruction his village had experienced. Only a strong breeze provided relief now, and a few vultures had locked on to his position, escorting him south until he entered the Darken Wood.

He made camp just fifty yards into the forest. After eating a cold dinner, he prayed, during which he whisked away to the Peak of Power, over the tops of trees, straight to the mountain.

Upon his arrival, he noticed two things immediately, a large pool of water reflecting an iridescent light and a giant altar made of pure white stone on a platform overlooking the pool. Twin Cymm stood before the altar with his new sword in one hand and the decaying dragon head in the other; then he pierced the head with the sword—

The Divine Quest ended abruptly, and he flash-traveled back to his body at an insane speed. He became nauseous and a little dizzy before strange lights began flashing in his eyes. The speed slowed drastically as he descended through the canopy of treetops toward his body, but the flashing lights continued. The urge to puke suddenly disappeared, when a giant spider came into view ten feet above his prone body. It tried to maneuver past a pulsing amber haze that hovered around his head.

Cymm passed the arachnid, went through the amber aura, and merged with his material body. He quickly rolled to the side, but the sudden movement made his stomach lurch, and a splitting headache replaced the dizziness. He vomited on the ground and struggled to his feet.

He unsheathed his old sword, listing from side to side as if he were on the deck of a ship in rough waters. Four spiders skittered toward him in the failing light, but the amber glow flashed in his eyes again. Temporarily blinded, Cymm pointed the sword in front of him like a spear, afraid to blindly swing for fear of losing his balance.

A beautiful face appeared in the flashing lights before they dissipated, and his vision returned. Two spiders merged with two others as his eyes came into focus, and he no longer saw double. With his sword pointed down, he backed away slowly; his stomach was still queasy. Both enemies were about to launch themselves at him when his warhorse and another horse came out of nowhere. The horses reared, making loud blowing noises, before descending on the spiders and crushing them. Blinking several times, the Plainsman closed his eyes, trying to make sense of the inconsistency. His stomach heaved; he suppressed the urge to vomit, but a gut-wrenching dry heave ensued. When the episode passed, the dizziness disappeared, and so did the image of a second horse.

His stomach still churned, but he had his vision and balance back, no longer seeing quadruple. He inspected the two-foot-diameter dead spider in shock. *How could it have gotten so large?* He leaned against his horse, petting him, but his steed seemed skittish. Cymm scanned the area; another spider silently descended toward the ground. He sliced the arachnid in half still using the old sword. His gaze shifted frantically as several more approached. He grabbed his backpack, then jogged back to the edge of the forest leading his horse.

About thirty feet outside the woods, he turned to confront whatever chased him. Dozens of red, glowing eyes dotted the woods line glaring at him from the confines of the forest. Cymm hastily mounted his horse heading north, parallel with the forest's edge. The speed of the arachnids was frightening; they hurtled toward him with relentless determination. Most stayed tucked among the trees, but a few crept past the safety of the woods. One enormous spider, with a bulbous abdomen three foot in diameter, outpaced them all, gaining on him.

The warhorse needed no encouragement. It whinnied loud before surging into a gallop, but the spiders kept pursuing until he veered away from the forest, going deeper into hill giant territory. Confident he was no longer being followed, he circled back, making camp at the edge of the mountains, a few hundred yards from the forest.

He slept intermittently throughout the night with glowing red eyes haunting his dreams. In one such dream, he stood paralyzed as a spider wrapped his sister in a cocoon only twenty yards away. It moved slowly at first, the momentum picking up with each spin of her body. Her terrified eyes locked on his with each rotation; her arms reached out toward him. He couldn't reach her; he couldn't help her; he couldn't save her. She struggled to breathe.

"Bria!"

He startled himself awake, sweating despite the chill in the night air. His breathing came fast and deep. He surveyed the vicinity, groaned, rolled over, and settled back in. After struggling to fall back asleep, he forced himself to recall the face he imagined when the spider attacked. While focused on its beauty and calmness, slumber finally overtook him.

He woke at sunrise feeling exhausted, scarfed down a cold breakfast, and entered Darken Wood again. After an hour, he slowed to a fast trot, remaining sharp and leery. *What else is lurking among these trees?* His eyes continued to scan the surroundings for enemies.

Since he had no idea how to protect himself while he slept, he rode through the night with a torch and changed his course to intersect with the Great North Road. It was a long night, but dawn finally came. As the daylight filtered through the canopy of leaves, he took a break, letting his horse rest for a couple of hours. Although the frequency of spider webs had reduced significantly, they had not disappeared.

In the early afternoon, Cymm came upon an intricate web laced between two trees. A sizable insect struggled in its sticky fibers, but its efforts proved futile. He traced the filaments into the shadows above; a spider had sensed the vibrations and descended to evaluate its catch.

A shrill sound sprang from the insect. *Looks like he'll be eating good today.* He urged his horse closer, squinting at a giant praying mantis almost eighteen inches long. A smaller variety of these creatures was plentiful in the plains around his village, and he liked them very much. When the spider drew within two feet of the insect, Cymm moved into position, still astride his mount. He took a full swing and sliced the spider in half.

He quickly examined the tree branches above but found no more arachnids. When he attempted to cut the praying mantis free, it emitted a shrill noise again. He stopped immediately, expecting a spider behind him. False alarm. The sharp noise repeated, piercing his eardrums as soon as he returned to cutting the web. He reached for his ears. "I am not going to hurt you."

The Plainsman continued to saw through each strand with his sword, cutting a circle around the praying mantis. It fell four feet to the ground where it struggled to get loose from the web but only entangled itself further. He sheathed his sword, dismounted, and grabbed the poor thing. Determined to keep moving, he mounted and picked at the web while the horse walked. The praying mantis didn't squirm or make noise until Cymm unsheathed his dagger, at which point it screeched in fear. He gently cut the web in a couple of safe locations, which allowed him to successfully peel off the entire web.

The praying mantis used all six legs to force his hand open, then flew away.

"You're welcome!" Cymm called to the fleeing insect, chuckling to himself.

About ten minutes later, he noticed a vast amount of sunlight pouring into the forest ahead. A huge tree had fallen, uprooting two others on its way down. New green life covered the forest floor, flourishing in the bath of unimpeded sunlight.

The Plainsman took a break to eat and kept a sharp eye out for trouble. While his horse grazed, he enjoyed his jerky and strolled around the oasis of greenery. It took a few minutes to walk the perimeter, longer than he expected. He returned to find the praying mantis he'd rescued hovering twenty feet from his horse. It had a large bundle of lengthy sticks tied and slung over its shoulder.

"Whoa! You tied a knot?" the paladin asked.

As he approached, the mantis flew to the opposite side of his horse, issuing three piercing shrieks. The horseman had no intention of leaving until his horse had time to eat. In the meantime, he pretended to retrieve something from his saddlebag. The insect seemed equally intrigued by him. Now much closer, he could tell the sticks in the bundle were three feet long, and each "stick" had multiple joints. That's when it hit him. They were legs from a spider.

The insect charged him so quickly that he couldn't react before it zipped past his head. Cymm spun to follow its trajectory. It intercepted another praying mantis flying directly at his back with a dagger in each tarsus.

The second creature to arrive wore a leather bandolier which crisscrossed its thorax and held several more dagger-like objects.

While shrill, high-pitched noises emanated from both creatures, a third arrived to join the tussle. They appeared to communicate with a combination of high-pitched noise and motion.

He left his sword sheathed with his hand on the hilt to avoid spooking the creatures. However, they frequently pointed at him, which he found quite disturbing. Finally, all three insects landed on the ground, and the first untied the spider legs to share with the others. It retied the remaining legs into a smaller bundle, and the insects ate voraciously.

The Plainsman watched with fascination as they went to work on the approximately two-inch-diameter spider legs. Typically hidden from view, their mandibles expanded from behind triangular faces. They easily cut through the spider legs' chitin-like shells.

His warhorse had moved thirty feet away from the commotion, showing complete indifference toward the creatures. Cymm kept a nervous eye on them; he found their aggressive behavior and constant furtive movements unsettling. Two short antennae protruded from their forehead between large, red, bulbous eyes that constantly twitched, and their heads snapped from side to side. Moreover, the dozens of sharp spines covering their front legs were intimidating.

Nevertheless, the original praying mantis had returned the favor, berating its friend for trying to attack him. Each calmed considerably after eating the spider legs. He grinned to himself as they held their front legs up near their head. *Maybe they are praying to Terazhan.*

"Time to go," he mumbled, leading his horse out of the thicket before jumping in the saddle. He glared at the insects, then headed west to intersect with the Great North Road.

A faint crunch brought the paladin's head around abruptly; the bugs were following him at a distance. He spun around in the saddle, riding backward to observe them. Now four creatures were wrestling over the remaining bundle of spider legs. Cymm considered firing a couple of arrows to scare them away but decided not to. He didn't have a reason to hurt them . . . yet.

Before he spun back, facing forward, two more slightly larger praying mantises joined the group, but these two found flying difficult. They flew for twenty to thirty seconds before falling to the ground, then skittered and jumped into the air to fly again. Cymm couldn't tell if they were injured, or if their girth impeded full flight. The two larger insects wore fully stocked crisscross bandoliers. He sighed heavily. A threat seemed to loom around every corner, and he grew tired of always being on the defense.

He considered his options. *I can outrun them but galloping through the forest isn't very safe. Or I can deal with the issue now.* He pulled his horse around to face them.

58

On Patrol

etraQuerahn had been flying patrol missions for the past ten days, all to no avail, but on the tenth day, he spotted intruders. No ordinary intruders either; they were hill giants, a green dragon's archenemy. There were six giants, two large males, a female, and three adolescents sneaking about, trying to enter the cave.

The dragon had the element of surprise. He swooped in low, intending to spew one big blast of his breath weapon. Instead, he snatched a hill giant child, and raced back up into the sky. He delivered the first two to Anekzarius to hold hostage, returning for the third.

He dove with his claws extended, as a spear whizzed past his head and embedded in his rear leg. He craned his neck around to inspect the damage to his thigh, then brutally ripped it free with his mouth, grinding it to pieces between his teeth. With blood dripping from his knee, he snatched the third child roughly and soared back into the sky.

He would enjoy killing the remaining three.

He delivered the last child, banked around, and landed. The hill giants approached in a straight line. *So predictable.* He gave them a moment to get closer. A flying boulder hit him in the neck. He shook it off, releasing a large cloud of chlorine gas. The female anticipated his breath weapon, sprinting to the side to avoid taking damage. The males were engulfed in the gas as they charged; their skin immediately erupted in puss-filled boils. TetraQuerahn stormed through the fog, eviscerating them both.

He sauntered over to where the female hill giant hid behind a pile of boulders. "Follow me, or I will kill your children."

She jumped up. "No . . . No kill. I come."

A few hours later, TetraQuerahn and the two female dragons were in the clearing working together. They leveraged their innate ability to develop, nurture, and twist the undergrowth as only a green dragon can, to prevent more intruders in the future. Poisoning vines and enchanting bushes. When they were finished, the clearing was no longer recognizable and no longer a clearing at all.

59

The Crossroads

Cymm sat astride his warhorse, staring at the six praying-mantis-like insects. They stared back in defiance, unmoving. His patience grew thin; his horse stomped the ground ready to charge, until a two-foot-long wasp buzzed down between them. As soon as the mantis pack saw it, excitement filled the air, and they gave chase immediately. The paladin led his horse around with a tug on the lead and slipped away.

Early evening had come, and Cymm had not seen a spider web in many hours. His horse stumbled again over a fallen branch, confirming they shouldn't attempt another all-night travel session. Cymm resigned himself to making camp but vacillated over starting a fire. Not for heat, but to keep the creatures at bay. Of course, it could also be a beacon, drawing unnecessary attention. Finally, he built a small fire; at least he'd be able to see his attackers.

He vowed to never eat cold, hard jerky again, while chewing on a thick piece and tending the fire. Normally, he would have prayed after eating, but he procrastinated, fearing he might receive another Divine Quest. If he did and another mob of spiders attacked, it wouldn't matter if he returned on time with nowhere to run. When he finally prayed, he only received a Vision of the pure white altar perched over the iridescent pool reminding him to start heading south.

His jittery nerves kept him awake. Every small gust of wind or rustle of a leaf forced him to wonder if something lurked in the darkness. Eventually, his mind gave in to slumber, but not without his sword lying on his chest.

He awakened abruptly to the crackling of the fire. His eyes snapped open, reflexively clenching the handle of his sword tightly. The roaring fire did not startle him as much as the monstrous blue beetle hovering over the flames. He sat up quickly, moving the sword into position, prepared to swing before he realized the beetle was upside down and motionless.

"What in the nine hells . . ." Several strange clicks came from behind the five-foot-long roasting beetle. He cautiously peered over it, discovering the mantis six-pack he had left behind. With sword in hand, he rose to his full height, letting the fire light dance across his face. He caught the insects by surprise, and they recoiled.

One praying mantis finally approached him, while the others took a defensive position. The closest insect hovered at eye level, out of reach, and stared him down. This action bewildered him, but not as much as when the mantis crossed its arms over its chest, performing a very human-like action. The mantis stared at his sword cocked back, ready to strike, before locking eyes with him again.

The paladin hated how silly he felt, even more, how rude he was being. These creatures had done nothing wrong, at least not yet. He slowly sheathed his sword.

As if on cue, the chitin shell of the beetle lost integrity, splitting open with a resounding *crack*. The pack of insects cheered, instantly forgetting about him, shifting their focus to removing the beetle from the flames. One of the larger praying mantises pulled a sharp rock from its bandolier, cleaving the carapace the rest of the way. They set it aside to cool, and Cymm sat on the ground with his back against a tree. His horse, once again, had failed to provide a signal of danger.

Maybe I should trust his instincts. If they desired my death, they had their chance while I slept. Still, he fought against sleep until he couldn't hold his eyes open any longer.

He woke in the early morning to dim light weaving its way into the forest. Across the burned-out campfire, he found the bug crew sleeping around the remnants of the beetle shell. As soon as he moved, they roused, ready to travel.

He broke camp and mounted his horse while the insects fell in line behind him. "I am not looking for travel companions." They paid him no mind, following him until late in the evening when they arrived at the Great North Road. Cymm made camp a few hundred yards back to avoid travelers, and the insects hunkered down by the fire again.

The following morning, the paladin stoked the embers while the original mantis joined him. He rubbed his hands together close to the coals, almost losing his balance when the insect mimicked him. Cymm went to gather sticks, with the same mantis following him. It rubbed its tarsus together, held them out, then pointed at the branches in his arms. The Plainsman dropped the wood he carried. "Yes, Fire!" He also completed the sequence of hand movements.

Communication remained limited, but as they traveled south on the Great North Road, they developed hand signals to allow for essential communication: sleep, eat, big, small, fire, hunt, camp, stay, come, see, yes, and no. When the insects killed another giant beetle, the original mantis rushed over to him. To his delight, the insect put two words together at the same time using four tarsi, "Big" and "Fire."

During their trek south, the decaying dragon head attracted the attention of large flies the size of an apple. They buzzed Cymm and his horse but would eventually land on the reeking bag. When a fly began circling, he would spin around in the saddle to watch the inevitable show. A mantis friend would land on the horse's hindquarters, locking its prey with its gaze before beginning a rhythmic dance. The insect's booty swayed back and forth, hypnotizing the fly, and allowing the hunter to pounce. Their lightning speed and grasping technique were amazing. He had viewed the performance countless times by the afternoon of the eighth day, when they arrived at the Crossroads, a place he had been before.

Dwarven law required Hardre to return to the city of Delge every five years during the month of First Twilight to re-evaluate his "Pariah" status. Less than two years earlier, Cymm, Talo, and Old-Man Semper accompanied the dwarf to the Crossroads on his way to report to Delge for his assessment. Cymm was fifteen lifeyears at the time, and anxious for his friend.

They were all anxious that day when they arrived at the Crossroads for Hardre's second re-evaluation. The dwarf knew to surrender himself to the guards at the small outpost in the northeast section, and the Stallion Risers left to hunt in the plains for a few days. They returned hours before the guards appeared escorting their friend back to the outpost. Cymm noticed that a few dwarven tradesmen complimented the retinue from Delge.

"Heads up; we got company," Old-Man Semper whispered.

"The tradesmen?" asked Talo.

"Definitely bounty hunters. Stop at Copper Rise to shake them?" asked Cymm.

The old man nodded.

A couple of hours later, they entered the town of Copper Rise, turned around, and waited inside the gate. When the three dwarven tradesmen passed through the gates, the Plainsmen left town, scowling at them as they ambled by on their ponies. They continued down the road a couple miles until they came upon tall grass on both sides. To set the ambush for the dwarves, Cymm and Old-Man Semper went to one side, Talo and Hardre to the other. As expected, fifteen minutes later, the dwarves crested a small rise in the distance.

Semper barked out orders, "Talo, kill shot to the one in the lead. Hardre, take the one on your side of the road; Cymm and I got the other."

"Got it!" replied Talo.

Hardre hefted his hammer with a grunt.

Cymm shook his head vehemently. "No! I will not support an assassination from the shadows. They must have a chance to explain themselves."

When the dwarves entered the section of the road with the tall grass, the paladin stepped out on his warhorse, blocking the road. "Where are you heading?"

"What's it to you?" said the lead dwarf.

"We saw you enter Copper Rise. Is there a reason you left so quickly?" He continued his investigation.

"We decided to continue on our way since it was still early in the day," the same dwarf answered.

Cymm took a deep breath, sighing deeply. "Very well. You are tradesmen by appearance. Can I see your wares?"

The lead dwarf sneered at him smugly. "How about I show you my axe? Where's the dwarf, whelp?"

The young leader slowly nocked an arrow to his bow, then pulled the string back. "Turn back to Delge, or you will be dealt with."

"Okay, you want to see my axe," the dwarf yelled, urging his pony to charge.

Cymm shouted, "Release!" Three arrows hit the arrogant dwarf simultaneously, one puncturing his eye. The injured vigilante slid off his pony and hit the ground hard.

The paladin notched another arrow with slow confidence. "Here's a new deal. Get off your ponies and walk back to Copper Rise or Delge. That is the best offer you will receive."

The dwarves dismounted slowly. "What about our friend?"

Cymm gritted his teeth. "You have bad taste in friends. You can carry, drag, bury, or leave him. I don't care!"

They chose to take his body with them, but after they got a few hundred yards down the road, they strip-searched him and rolled his body to the side.

"There is no honor among thieves!" Old-Man Semper scowled at the retreating figures.

Cymm longed for those days again, for his home, friends, and berry bread.

His reminiscing ended abruptly as three dwarven guards emerged from the brush on the side of the road. He had arrived at the Crossroads.

"Hail traveler!" exclaimed one of the dwarven sentries. "Are you in route to the great city of Delge?"

"No, just passing through to the south," he answered, sharing no details.

"Whoa, watch out!" Another dwarf pushed past the warhorse followed by two others, all retrieving the battle axe slung across their backs.

"No! They are with me," Cymm bellowed. The dwarf gazed back in confusion. "We are traveling together. They are my . . . pets."

"Fine, move along. Keep those things close, or they will be slain."

Cymm motioned to the mantis "Come" and "Big," hoping it knew that meant *come fast*.

A few hours later, when he felt he had traveled past any additional dwarven sentries in the woods, he left the road to the southeast, toward the mountains and the River of Spells.

The mantises fanned out to hunt. He could only assume for another beetle.

60

Destination

After three full days of travel, the insect pack still followed with no sense of straying. He didn't understand their persistence; the only logical conclusion he came up with was fire. They had developed a few more hand signals, but full conversations would never be possible at this rate.

The paladin withdrew from his daydream at the sound of rushing water. He spurred his horse ahead until the forest opened in front of him. His breath caught in his throat. A shiny platinum river rumbled past him to the southwest—the River of Spells. He had heard the river's color changed eight times, depending upon the direction it flowed. All four compass points and the four points in between.

He knelt by the edge of the river with cupped hands and plunged them into the water. The platinum water swirled around them obscuring his view, but as soon as he lifted his hands, the trapped liquid turned crystal clear.

"Terazhan, be blessed! This is miraculous. I wonder if it is safe to drink." He did it again, playing in the water. The insects peered around his backside, and one even perched on his back. Their buzzing increased with each passing second. The paladin could tell they were happy, or the mantis equivalent, but had no clue why.

They traveled upriver for an hour watching the sun drop in the sky. The river emerged from a valley up ahead, and deep in the same valley rose a solitary peak much higher than the mountain range around it.

It took a day and a half to arrive at the base of the Peak of Power where several immense boulders lay partially submerged in a large pool of water. This was not his destination. He craned his neck back, admiring the showers of water cascading down the mountainside. Past the four waterfalls, he could almost see the top where he hoped to find the altar. A mile back, he had noticed a switchback trail climbing the left side of the mountain peak, and he found the trailhead easily. Surprisingly, the praying mantises took the lead.

The path inclined sharply, but it provided sound footing for his horse. It took an hour before they came to the first change in direction, another hour until they arrived at the second. The insects buzzed with excitement, and every so often, the original mantis would turn back, signaling, "Come . .

. come." In all, six progressively shorter switchbacks covered a total of ten to twelve miles to reach the top.

The trail leveled off to a partial plateau. Half of the peak had been cleaved to create a flat level surface, but the other half still rose to its full glory. The Pool of Age covered the western most portion of the plateau; a thick wall of rock held the water in place. This same wall created the first of the waterfalls he witnessed, a cascade of several hundred feet. Prominently displayed was a pure white altar which rested on a stone ledge three feet above the water.

Although early evening began, the sun still blazed bright in the sky at this altitude above the treetops. Walking toward the altar, he came to an abrupt halt; the praying mantises had vanished. For weeks, they had followed him like puppy dogs, now disappearing without a trace. He scratched his head but continued toward his destination.

He knelt before the massive altar to pray, the surface rising above his head. A sense of peace rushed through his body, so raw, pure, and very powerful.

The sound of footsteps crunching on small stones resounded behind him followed by a deep voice. "It has been a long journey Cymm Reich. Are you ready for the next step?"

"Yes, my Lord. Is it really you?"

"It is. Cymm, rise and complete the Rights of Melding. You have seen it in your mind's eye; you know what to do. However, you will need this to complete the process." Terazhan arced his hand through the air toward the altar. A bolt of lightning descended from the sky blasting a shard of stone from the corner; it tumbled between the paladin's knees.

"I have many questions, Lord!" His mind kept reeling, and try as he might, nothing came to mind. Somehow, he commanded his legs to stand; then he placed the shard on the altar. He twisted around to face him, sheepishly staring at his boots.

"That is expected, but we don't have much time. What is on your mind?" asked Terazhan.

Think, think, think. Okay, deep breaths. His heart rate settled, and his mind cleared.

"Why do you allow so much pain and suffering to occur? My family didn't have to die. The thousand citizens of Bruc didn't have to die." He cleared his throat uncomfortably, gazing up into the god's eyes before continuing. "We have done some good, but it's not enough!"

Terazhan smiled, but it didn't reach his eyes; nor did it set Cymm at ease. On the contrary, an eerie feeling overtook him. Had he taken the bait? Not seen the trap? Why did he feel like the praying mantis caught in the spider's web?

"At a younger age, I fancied a maiden and kept a watchful eye on her. One day she traveled with her family by ship to another city, and a storm overtook the vessel. An enormous waterspout formed, and I took action to protect her by pushing it in a slightly different direction. Unfortunately, while I guided the ship to safer waters, the waterspout hit land, killing five hundred people," Terazhan replied.

"The wind I generated to propel the ship gained momentum, and halfway around the world, a tsunami formed, devastating the coastline. More than a thousand fisherman died. The ocean turned over, killing fish for hundreds of miles, and the surviving fisherman couldn't catch fish for months. A few thousand more died of starvation during the upcoming growing season." Terazhan paused for a long time, watching him.

Cymm's defiant posture and countenance melted away; when he finally understood the lesson, he sighed deeply. "Then all is lost?"

"No!" Terazhan's voice boomed. "I am convinced a more surgical method will work, and you are my surgeon! A paladin will be able to succeed in helping individuals where divine attempts would fail." Cymm smiled, slowly nodding in appreciation.

"On the last Divine Quest, when I returned from here, a mob of spiders attacked me."

"I wondered why you left so quickly."

"I didn't leave. I didn't realize there was a threat until I arrived back at my body. You must have sent me back." Terazhan wore a puzzled expression, confusing Cymm even more.

"Hmm, interesting. Well, I am working on a time dilation technique, which will bring you back to your body within seconds of departure, regardless of how long you have been gone. In the meantime, I will scan the area more closely before letting you travel. Let's begin," the One True God replied, anxious to start the Rights of Melding.

"One last question, please."

"Continue then," the god said.

"Hardre once told me I would be able to cast spells like a priest eventually, but that was four years ago. Did he misinform me?"

"Hmmm," Terazhan pondered the question, "A fair request; you have achieved sufficient skill and demonstrated your piety. Once you leave this mountain, I will begin sharing images of the available spells that you will be able to use once per day. As your knowledge and power grow, you will gain access to more powerful enchantments and gain the ability to cast multiple spells each day."

The news elated him. "Thank you, my Lord."

"The ceremony must begin while the sun is in the sky. Perform it precisely as I showed you." Terazhan withdrew from the altar.

The paladin concentrated on the Divine Quest, replaying it in his mind for the thirty-third time, focusing on the tiny details. When he finally started the Rights of Melding, the sun had dropped low in the sky. Ominous black and gray clouds rolled in from nowhere, and portions of his chanting were erased as lightning struck and thunder boomed around him.

He walked down to the pool's edge, scooped water to cleanse his hands, filled his empty water skin, then used it to purify and cleanse the altar's surface. He performed all these acts while he continued to chant.

Next, he removed the dragon head from the bags; the acrid smell assaulted his nose before he cast the first bag aside. This disgusting, decaying head reminded him of the day he returned to his village and the horrific stench of hundreds of dead people and animals. The head had become a symbol of death and despair, weighing heavily on his heart and mind.

He hoped to be rid of this burden he'd carried for so long.

He unwrapped it, blocked his nose with his shoulder, but still dry heaved twice. His fingers sunk into the bloated, rotting head, disturbing several maggots feasting on facial flesh.

The thunderheads zapped each other with heat lightning above him while forked bolts continued to rain down around the altar. The paladin removed the newly crafted mithril sword from its sheath, impaling the dragon head through the eye socket up to the cross-guard. As it entered the brain cavity, it made a wet slurping sound before it easily pierced the back of the skull.

He held the sword above his head with two hands on the hilt and the point toward the heavens. His chanting reverberated off the unbroken mountain top to rival the thunder as the final phase of the ceremony began.

The green leathery skin on the dragon's head rippled as if alive, and large veins appeared to pulse beneath it. Tremors ran through the reptilian skin before it brutally ripped free of its host intact, sounding like the sickening mixture of leaves crunching and mud squishing. It swirled around the sword, creating a dichotomy of light and dark as the lightning struck. The edges tore and tattered until it shredded itself into thousands of bright emerald particles still racing around the weapon. Eventually, the particles gravitated together to form an ethereal, green ball hovering and throbbing in the air.

The Shard of Power fractured from the altar rose to meet the green sphere. The two collided in a cascade of emerald sparks, a new shower occurring with every pulse. Finally, the remaining mixture settled into the empty gem socket of the sword and coalesced into a large, brilliant emerald.

The dragon skull and decaying flesh blazed with an eerie, green light. A massive pulse bulged the grotesque visage before it exploded. Hundreds of bone fragments and rotten meat pelted the paladin and sword alike.

Cymm ceased chanting. The Rights of Melding were complete. He collapsed to one knee, holding the altar for support, then lowered the sword to the ground. Physically and mentally drained, he slowly lay in front of the altar. His vision faded in and out.

61

The Priestess

Cymm woke the following morning feeling rejuvenated. A beautiful young lady stared down at him silently. The booming voice of an old man jarred him fully awake. *"Good morning, young man. It's about time you woke up."*

He sat up, then rubbed the sleep from his eyes. Gawking back at the gorgeous girl in priestess robes, he wondered, *Do I know you?*

"Maybe you should say hello!" the old man's voice thundered.

The Plainsman held his head in pain; it felt like he had a hangover. Looking over his shoulder he replied, "I will." His nose crinkled as he tried to locate the old man.

"Are you talking to me?" the priestess asked. "Or shall I leave?"

"I was talking to the old guy . . ." he sputtered.

She giggled, twirling her robes. "Do I look like an *old* guy?"

Her sweet and intoxicating laugh immediately made him nervous, like he was about to meet the King of Armak.

"Yes . . ." he stammered, shook his head, then quickly uttered his next words. "I mean, no. I mean, I am Cymm Reich. What do your friends call you?"

"I am known as Lykinnia, but I really don't have any friends, except . . ." Two enormous creatures landed, shaking the earth.

"You have no friends?" said one of the beasts.

"Maybe she sees the future, brother?" said the other.

"Maybe the future and the past?" replied the first.

"Very funny!" Lykinnia crossed her arms over her chest, pretending to pout. "I meant friends like this." She motioned toward Cymm. "Not friends like that." Her hand swirled in a circle in the direction of the brutes.

A low grumble issued from the giant, ten-foot-long monster with the body of a lion, the face of a man, and large wings of an eagle. He stomped off toward the altar to inspect the damage.

"Oh, Kamac, I still love you!" she said with a giggle. Both beasts gave her a scornful glare before wandering off, but the Plainsman stared blissfully. "Cymm, forgive my manners. I am not used to having company or an intelligent conversation."

"I can still hear you!" said one of the beasts in a huff.

"My lady, how can I help you?" Cymm said, using the altar to help him stand.

"You have already been of great service to me," she teased.

"Then we have met before?" He waited to claim a mental victory.

"How about we talk over breakfast instead of here at the altar?"

His confusion lingered, but his hunger for something other than dried jerky overpowered his need for answers. He visually scanned the perimeter until he located his horse, then nodded enthusiastically.

The paladin shamelessly admired her pure white priestess robes. His smirk disappeared, instantly replaced with the red of embarrassment. Bone fragments and rotten flesh covered his body, adding to his smell. He had not bathed for the past month.

"Lykinnia, before or after breakfast, I would like to bathe and wash my clothes. Would that be possible? Maybe in the pool?" He motioned toward the one by the altar.

"Oh no, not in the Pool of Age! There are cold and warm water springs you may use after breakfast," she responded amicably, turning to lead the way.

Cymm brushed off dragon head remnants behind her back as they walked. She offered him a pitcher of water to wash his hands when they arrived at a stone table. He fidgeted under her scrutiny, examining his filthy armor, clothing, and body. Her robes were spotless; everything about her was pristine, orderly, and well-groomed. Why did he have to meet her like this?

He bit into a large, juicy strawberry; the flavor exploded in his mouth. The sweet mixed with the tangy, lighting his salivary glands on fire. He quickly grabbed two more, popping them in his mouth.

Splat! A large chunk of dragon matter fell from his hair onto his plate.

The paladin blanched at the disgusting thing, losing his appetite immediately. *I must appear equally repulsive.* With a scarlet red face, he addressed his hostess, "I think it's time for that bath."

The shock on her face morphed into a laugh, which he found exhilarating.

Carrying a priest's robe in her hands, she led him away from the table, in the opposite direction of the altar.

"Is that for me?" he asked.

"Yes, I thought you might like something clean to wear after you bathe," she replied with twinkling eyes.

"Thank you. I can carry it." Cymm reached out to grab the robe.

She inspected him up and down. "Or not."

He quickly withdrew his hand. "Yeah, good call."

He spent a couple of hours bathing, cleaning his clothes, and getting dressed. Approaching the stone table, he noticed Lykinnia wiggling the fingers of her waving hand. A bright amber glow manifested into bowls of fruit, bread, and cheese.

His eyebrows raised in excitement. "We do know each other! You were the amber creature who saved me from the spiders," Cymm said confidently.

Before she could comment, the six missing praying mantises appeared at the head of the table.

Cymm waved to them excitedly. "Oh, there you are! Lykinnia. These are—"

"Yes, thank you very much for escorting my friends to me," she said.

He gaped at her, stuttering in confusion. "What? Friends? How?"

"This is the service you performed for me. The one I mentioned this morning. They would have never made it through the dwarven kingdom without you, especially at this young age. Plus, the fire seemed to keep the spiders at bay." She listened to the buzzing and shrill chirping from one of the smaller ones. "Oh yes, and Gillygahpadima wanted to thank you personally for rescuing her from the spider's web."

He shook his head and smoothed his hair. "You understand them?"

"I can currently speak fifty-six languages fluently, and Taviian is one of them." She sat up straight and adjusted her robes.

He leaned forward, putting his chin on both hands with elbows on the table. "What else can you tell me about them?"

"Well, they are a new species I recently discovered, called tavii. When they finish growing in a few years, they will be as tall as you!" Lykinnia exclaimed, clasping her hands together.

Cymm stared with his mouth open wide. "You gotta be kidding me."

"Very true, and they will be fierce fighters with unwavering loyalty. I have already found a location perfect for them to thrive and multiply."

With a gesture, the priestess offered to pour him more juice. "By the way, they call you the Spider Slayer because

Gillygahpadima saw you cleave a spider in half with one swing. Spiders are their natural enemy."

"Speaking of spiders, was that you who rescued me?"

Lykinnia held one long slender finger to her lips, giving him an almost imperceptible nod. He danced quietly in his seat, congratulating himself for solving the mystery, then quickly glanced around. *Why the secrecy?*

They finished eating in comfortable silence. Making eyes at each other and smirking, she even raised one eyebrow. He laughed so hard and unexpectedly that he choked on his food.

After lunch, they walked through the orchard on the east side to stretch their legs and continue talking. Lykinnia picked an apple from the tree. "Do you mind if I give this to your horse?"

"Not at all," he said, also picking an apple to bring back.

On the far side of the orchard, Cymm saw three doorways built into the side of the mountain. Above them rose the remaining mountain peak that had not been sundered.

He pointed. "Lykinnia, where do those doors lead?"

"Lord Terazhan lives in the far right, and the door on the far left is mine, but I usually sleep under the stars." She scanned the sky with a delicate smile.

"Me too!" His body warmed and his head buzzed with inebriation, but he drank juice and was completely sober.

She played with her hair and batted her eyelashes.

Not helping! Definitely, not helping! "Lord Terazhan confirmed I will receive priest spells shortly. Can you explain some of the lower-level spells to help my learning?"

Kamac came swooping in, landing heavily between the rows of trees in the orchard. "What are you still doing here?"

Lykinnia reacted quickly. "Kamac! Is that how we treat guests?"

The sphinx grumbled, "I didn't mean it that way! I thought he had pressing matters."

The priest and paladin finished their walk through the orchard before going their separate ways for most of the afternoon. They agreed to reconvene for dinner at dusk.

He took the opportunity to pray and wash his clothes. He had considered burning everything except for his leather armor, but he had nothing to replace them. Later that evening, he arrived to find the table already set, including a bounty.

"Lykinnia, what would you be doing at this moment if I weren't here?" asked Cymm.

She peeked at him over the top of her goblet of wine. "Hmm, well, I would probably be reading, studying, researching, or maybe all three. Why do you ask?"

"When I began this journey, I insisted on travelling alone, probably to wallow in my misery, but it's a lonely way to travel. How about you? Do you ever get lonely up here?"

"I was not kidding before; I do not have many friends, but I do have my clerical studies. I also spend my free time learning arcane magic, like a wizard," she said excitedly.

He laughed, "Of course you do! Because ninety-two languages and the responsibilities of a high-level priestess are not enough to keep you busy."

"Cymm Reich of Stallion Rise! I said *fifty-six languages*." Lykinnia giggled and wagged her finger at him. "Why have you come to the Peak of Power? What will you use the sword for?"

He shared the story of his quest with her, starting with the return from the hunting trip until he arrived at the Peak of Power. A need for privacy rushed through him when he teared up over his sister, but the calm and reassuring demeanor of his hostess allowed him to continue.

". . . and I wasn't there for her when she needed me, but if I can kill the dragon that murdered her, maybe I can find some peace," he concluded his story.

The priestess gazed into his eyes, shredding his soul, making him squirm. "Revenge can devour one's soul, leaving one changed. They seek to fill a void but end up empty. Maybe you will find peace by remembering the good times you had with your family; cherish those memories. Still vanquish your enemy, but do not focus on the evil, or it will consume you."

How can I not focus on the evil? He lost interest in the conversation. She continued to talk, but two thoughts pushed forward in his mind, the cold and clammy feel of his sister's skin and the torture his parents endured before they died. Time sped up in his mind; he could not control it—an avalanche of futile resistance. Weak and helpless, the buzzing energy gained momentum, becoming a thundering collapse of—

"Cymm, are you alright?"

He breathed in sharply, and his vision came back into focus. "Oh, yes. Goodnight Lykinnia, I will be leaving in the morning to finish my quest."

Lykinnia's mouth dropped open, but no words escaped, and she blinked twice before closing it.

He left to find a comfortable spot near the Pool of Age, where he fell fast asleep.

In the morning, they accidentally met at the altar to pray. After saying their separate prayers, Lykinnia invited him to sit down for a quick breakfast together.

"Is something on your mind?" Cymm asked.

"Yesterday was the most fun I've had in a long time, but I fear my words last night offended you," she replied with her head down. "Do you really have to leave today?" With her hands behind her back, she twirled slightly.

Cymm considered this for a moment. *Why not rest one more day?* He took another moment to look at her . . . to really look at her. She was so beautiful, intelligent, and easy to talk to. Something about her felt like home, yet at the same time, she presented an entirely new world to explore. About to concede, a thought forcefully pushed forward, *why not stay two days, or one week, or . . .*

He laid his hand gently on her shoulder "I will make you a promise. As soon as I kill the dragons, I will return to tell you all about it."

Her head popped up. "You better!"

62

Lykinnia

The priestess watched until he passed out of sight.

A voice in her head said, *"Lykinnia."*

"Yes, Terazhan?" she replied mentally.

"Do not address me that way!"

She stood up a little straighter. *"Yes, Father."*

"How long do humans live?"

She could tell he was not pleased. *"Oh Father, he is merely a friend."*

"Do you think I am a fool? I do not want you to get hurt or spend your life alone."

She huffed. *"I am already alone! Isn't he a good man?"*

"He is a great man, but he is a man, and again—"

"Yes . . . I know how long humans live, but there are ways—"

"No! That is not an option!" Terazhan exerted his will, forcing her to her knees. She struggled for a minute, then shielded her mind before staggering to her feet defiantly.

"Father . . . I seem to recall you did it for Mother . . . did you not?"

"She was a high elf," he said solemnly, *"and they can live two thousand years, not one hundred. More importantly, you are too young to sacrifice any of your life force."*

She was already working on improving the life transference process as one of her many secret research projects in tandem with her investigation on how to resurrect someone who had been dead for hundreds of years. Both were needed to restore her mother.

"Father, he travels alone to face three dragons; the chance of him succeeding and keeping his promise to return here is unlikely."

"Again, with the games, do all children believe their parents are fools? If he is triumphant, he will return, and you will release him from the charm or spell you have over him."

"Father! I would never do such a thing. Sometimes you treat me like I am five hundred lifeyears. Are you aware my millennial lifeday approaches quickly?"

"Lykinnia . . . send him on his way. He has work to do and many good deeds to complete." Terazhan severed the link and departed.

63

Dragon Sin

Cymm rode his faithful steed down the mountain trail, leaving Lykinnia, the Pool of Age, and the Altar of One behind. His thoughts quickly turned to the mission: three enormous dragons. *How can I complete such a task? One of these beasts alone could kill a hundred warriors.*

"*I will help you,*" came the booming old man's voice from yesterday. "*We will figure it out.*"

A smile pulled at his lips. Turning he exclaimed, "Kamac! Did you come to apologize?" but the sphinx-like creature did not present itself. "Kamac? Are we playing games now?"

"Kamac? The flying beast?" asked the same voice.

A chill went down his spine when he identified a slight difference in the voices. He immediately drew his new sword. His adrenaline surged; his heartbeat pounded in his ears, hindering his attempt to listen for movement.

An eerie green mist swirled around the gem on his drawn sword catching his eye for the first time since the ceremony. *There will be time later*, he thought as he admired the mixture of beauty and power. His horse casually grazed as they rode along the path.

He took a deep breath, commanding, "Reveal yourself, enough of this game!"

"Fool! Don't be an orc's ass! I am right here in front of you . . . in your hand. I am trying to introduce myself. I have decided my name will be DragonSin."

The voice is in my head? He ran his fingers through his hair. *Lykinnia couldn't hear it yesterday, and my horse can't hear it now. It kind of makes sense. Or I am going mad.* He rambled on, unable to wrap his mind around this strange occurrence.

"Well, hello DragonSin, my name is Cymm. Nice to meet you," the sword said sarcastically, attempting to mimic Cymm's voice. The paladin ignored it, and both fell silent for the remainder of the descent.

Once they were in the valley and alongside the river, the sword tried to engage him again. *"Cymm, are we there yet?"* The paladin remained silent and stoic.

By early evening, they were exiting the valley and entering Lower Darken Wood. The sword tried yet again, *"Hey Cymm, what's for dinner?"*

He'd had enough. He dismounted his horse, unbelted his scabbard, and lay the sword on a fallen tree. When he walked away, the sword switched to verbal speech. "I wouldn't do that if I were you; I sense evil nearby."

The new voice startled his horse which whinnied in fear and bolted further down the trail a couple hundred yards.

"Sorry, Cymm, I would have continued with telepathy, but we must be much closer for that to work," it said.

He turned back to the sword, grunting in frustration. He knelt, praying for guidance. Peace and tranquility immediately coursed through his body; he breathed in deeply and exhaled. An image of a great battle coalesced in his mind. He held the sword high above his head with his boot on the head of a fallen enemy. The Vision ended. *Hmm, subtle.*

His horse brayed as Cymm strapped the sword diagonally across his back. Three humanoid creatures were harassing his friend. One attempted to pull the horse off the path with his bridle while the other two pushed the horse's flanks. Cymm whistled in three short bursts; his horse reared in response with hooves flailing, almost connecting with an orc face. The orc fell to the ground, then rolled to its knees, drawing its sword.

Meanwhile, the sword sang an awful tune emanating from behind Cymm's right eye. He winced in pain, his eyesight blurred, and he cried out, "Sing out loud or not at all!" At fifty feet away, the singing stopped abruptly. Cymm's vision sharpened into focus, and he froze, staring in a stupor. The orc with the sword flew backward twenty feet as if struck by Melcorac's Hammer, but it never landed. A broken tree branch protruded from its chest, and it hung there dead, six feet off the ground.

The other two orcs craned their necks to observe their cohort. Terror flashed across their faces; then they ran off into the woods screaming.

"What are you waiting for? They are getting away!" DragonSin exclaimed irately. *"Get on your horse. We can ride them down. Cymm!"*

He snapped out of his paralysis, running toward his horse again. "What's wrong? Did they steal something? What did you see?" but the sword didn't reply.

The paladin jumped on his horse, lunging off the trail in a flash. The orcs did not stand a chance of outrunning a horse, and they weren't smart enough to split up or to head toward the thicker woods. Once he closed to fifty feet away, they fell to their knees, holding their heads, writhing in agony. By the time Cymm dismounted, they were dead. Their bloodshot eyes stared vacantly, and blood ran freely from their noses and ears.

He checked the orc's pockets, pouches, and bags. "What did you see them take, or what did they do?"

"It is not what they did; it is what they are . . . evil, and so they must die," it said.

"What? It's not that simple," Cymm said. "They—

"It . . . is . . . that . . . simple!" DragonSin said. *"What if Lykinnia strolled down this path? They would have attacked her, or robbed her, or worse!"*

"She can take care of herself . . . she would have—"

"You are missing the point. They are evil; will always be evil. A dormant wickedness lying in wait for an innocent person to hurt. Unless someone eliminates the threat. We are the someone." DragonSin paused its lecture, but Cymm refused to respond.

"If a mosquito lands on your arm, what do you do?" the sword asked.

Cymm replied without pausing, "I smack it!"

"*Exactly. You don't wait to see if it is going to bite. You know it is going to try to suck your blood. So why must we wait for evil to be done before we can act? How many—*"

"Not so fast! Evil is not black and white; you can't say the absence of good is evil, and the absence of evil is good." The chords in Cymm's neck tightened; his breathing was labored.

"*Why not?*"

"Because many people span the spectrum, committing both good and evil acts!"

"*Agreed. They fall in a different category, but that does not change the truth of what you said. The absence of good is evil.*" The sword emphasized the last two words.

Cymm was still querulous. "You sensed evil in the area . . . how does that work? How can you be certain they were evil or had evil intentions?"

"*It is hard to explain but imagine it this way. When you see the color green, do you know it is green? Do you confuse it with blue? What if you saw another shade of green? Would you recognize the color? It is that clear to me,*" DragonSin explained in a calm voice.

The Plainsman pondered this for a while, getting back on his horse. They were back on the main path before DragonSin continued. "*Cymm, I have examined your soul. I know how you felt when you saved the little girl from drowning, when you saved the terrified farmer from being smashed by the ogre's club, and when you freed all those prisoners from the gnoll cages. You are a good, honorable man, but you need to decide now. If we aren't aligned, then there is no we.*"

He contemplated the sword's argument. *It makes a good point, but isn't it possible for evil to become good or vice versa? What if someone does an evil deed in order to do good?*

"I can hear everything you are thinking." The sword sounded amused.

"Explain this to me, sword! A few years ago, I came across three dwarves trying to murder my friend; they were assassins. I gave them a choice to turn back from the evil path they were pursuing; one did not, and we killed him. The other two turned back, so we let them live. Tell me, if we came upon those two dwarves right now, what would happen?" he asked, still refusing to communicate telepathically.

"The short and simple answer is they would be killed, or you would die trying to kill them. However, let us say only one of them is evil; the other is following because he is scared that the evil one will hurt or kill him. In this case, one would die; the other would have the chance to flee," the sword answered honestly.

Cymm focused on the evil one, "But he hasn't done anything!"

"Don't be naïve! How many people had he assassinated before he tried to kill your friend? Now that you let him go, how many more people has he assassinated since then? Why do you believe only your eyes can judge evil deeds?" asked the sword.

His face twisted, contorting in outrage. "I never said that! What gives you the right to be the judge and executioner on the decision of evil?"

"Because I plan to root out the purest of evil, the complete absence of good." The sword continued to grind on his will.

"But what is your definition of evil?"

The sword paused for the first time. *"The enjoyment of killing, hurting, maiming, or any other cruelty to another. It is intentional, wicked, immoral, and from the mind of a sentient being. Therefore, an earthquake is not evil, and a rainbow is not good. They are not sentient things which cannot be assigned these qualities."*

"There are still exceptions . . ."

"Maybe. Let's take the same two assassins and pretend they are standing in front of us again. I tell you the one on the left has murdered ten people, and he killed someone a week ago. The person on the right has also killed ten people but has not committed murder in over a year. Which one do you consider worse? What if I also tell you both of their hearts are pure black, evil to the core?" The sword continued to push its case.

"You evaluate each potential victim to that level of detail?" Cymm asked leerily.

"No. I go into much more detail than that. Do you remember what I told you about your past? One of those events goes back ten years. I can probably evaluate someone's entire life in a matter of seconds." The sword paused. *"Oh, and one more thing, I love to kill dragons. Especially green dragons!"* The sword emphasized the last part.

Cymm considered the discussion, turning it over in his mind several times. *Is intent enough to kill for?* he asked himself. *Should I have killed the other two assassins? My family would have never died if someone had killed the green dragons years ago because they were evil.* He squeezed the leather grip on the handle of the sword so tightly it stretched and groaned. *Bria didn't deserve to die! I will be the surgeon that removes the cancer from this world!*

"Hi DragonSin, my name is Cymm. Nice to meet you," Cymm said with passion, and to his surprise, the sword laughed. A haunting sound but it qualified as a laugh. *"So, DragonSin, how far can you throw a green dragon?"*

64

Copper Rise

For the past four days, Cymm had been receiving Visions of spells he could now use, which aligned perfectly with what Lykinnia had explained.

Earlier this evening, he entered the small town of Copper Rise, booking a room at an inn. In the middle of the night, the town bell clanged, jarring him awake after only a few hours of sleep. He sat up quickly, trying to ascertain what had awoken him. The screams emanating from outside grasped his throat like an invisible hand, clenching tighter with each breath. Half asleep, he shuffled over to open the window as the scent of smoke drifted in. A haze had settled over the town; several stores were already blazing while others were being ransacked. Many townsfolk were injured, a few lay dead in the streets.

He pulled on his boots, grabbed his chest armor, and strapped DragonSin on while running downstairs. He threw the front door open; a quick survey of the town guard revealed a scattered and scared bunch. "Rally to me to save the town!" He emulated the Big Man, setting a defensive line.

He then cried out, "For Terazhan, the One True God!" A globe of pure white light burst forth surrounding him. The paladin shone like a beacon, drawing the town guard to his side as he killed another gnoll.

DragonSin pulled the closest gnoll toward Cymm, causing it to lose its balance. The paladin cleaved it from neck to chest, but there were still dozens left to deal with. The sentient artifact currently crushed the mind of three more hundar, as the Stormcallers dubbed them.

The paladin visually inspected both flanks, catching several glances from town guards. Their eyes now glowed with intensity, confident and stalwart, a complete transformation from ten minutes ago. They advanced on his command, slowly taking back sections of the town. When more than half of the gnolls lay dead in the plaza, the raiding party's confidence disintegrated, and they ran for the gate, hooting and howling.

The townsfolk cheered, raising their makeshift weapons in celebration. However, before the hundar could get out, the gate swung closed, trapping them inside. The gnolls growled like cornered savage dogs ready to fight to the death.

The gate and the raiders were less than fifty feet away. Cymm charged, honoring his agreement with the sword. DragonSin had already dropped three new enemies to their knees, making them thrash in pain. He continued to charge, hoping the town guard would follow. Halfway to the gnoll pack, the paladin fell to the ground, a crossbow bolt stuck in his leg. The hundar howled, recovering the will to fight, running to finish him off.

He quickly rose to a knee, pulling the bolt from his thigh. The damage wasn't severe, but there was a concerning brownish-green paste with a faint, flowery scent smeared on the shaft. The remaining gnolls were almost upon him. He forced himself to stand. *Poison could not act this fast, could it?*

Arrows *whizzed* and *zinged* all around him. Four of the enemy fell dead. The town militia archers had arrived.

The town guard rushed forward to form a line next to him, intercepting the remaining raiders. The hundar howled and whimpered in fear as their ranks continued to decrease. The paladin decapitated another enemy while standing on the back of the gnoll he just killed. DragonSin dropped three more to their knees. The town guard and militia finished the remaining raiders. With a cheer, everyone swarmed the new town hero as his spherical aura disappeared.

After healing himself, he set about healing the injured with the town clerics from the local temple. Cymm rocked back in surprise when he learned they were disciples of Terazhan. The paladin got an opportunity to try his first spell when he came upon an injured woman. The aura from a priest's healing spell originated from the "patient" in a more substantial form like Hardre's. Entirely different from the healing power of a paladin. The priests whispered to each other about his white aura, staring in awe.

One priest asked, "Are you a priest or a warrior?"

"Neither or both," Cymm answered. "I am a paladin of Terazhan, a holy warrior."

"The color of your aura is quite impressive," exclaimed a second priest.

"Yes, it is magnificent to witness such a thing!" proclaimed a third.

He squirmed under their adoration, unsure how to respond. He nodded his head, then returned to his room at the inn.

The following morning, after eating a hearty, complimentary breakfast, his journey continued. The poison dripping from the crossbow bolt that struck him consumed his thoughts. *I am surprised the wound did not reopen, or fester, or at least get angry and swollen.*

"You are immune to the effects of poison as long as I am in your possession," DragonSin said, reading his thoughts.

"I am immune to poison and still immune to disease granted by Lord Terazhan?" questioned Cymm.

"The benefit I provide you does not impact any other benefits you receive," the sword answered.

A mini crowd had gathered, to yell and cheer, as he rode his horse out the gate. Within a year, much to his chagrin, the town erected a statue of him in the market square. Cymm's foot rested on the body of a dead gnoll with his sword held high.

65

Cold Reception

Eight days after leaving Copper Rise, Cymm trotted into Stallion Rise, expecting a warm reception. It was now the middle of Gathering, six months after leaving his home. The village wallowed in disarray, with damaged buildings and broken fence posts unaddressed. He entered the Reich Farm barnyard without fanfare and unnoticed. A knot seized in his belly and wouldn't let go.

"Uncle Daro! Talo! Where is everyone?" He walked his horse over to the corral, noticing recent and significant damage to his father's barn. He stood at the wooden rail where his family died, tracing the heart with his finger.

"Cymm!"

"Aunt Nové! Where is everyone?" he said, concern etched upon his face.

His aunt ran to hug him with tears in her eyes. "We thought you were dead! It has been so long. Come inside. I will send for Daro and Talo."

Once inside, he came to a halt, inhaling deeply. The berry bread he'd been longing for called to him. While devouring his third slice of bread, his uncle and cousin stormed into the kitchen through the front door. They fell upon him like giant blankets about to smother him. Their eyes were wide, and their grins were big. The three of them leaned the crowns of their heads together, rejoicing.

They sat at the kitchen table, and Cymm endured small talk while he waited for the real conversation to begin. Uncle Daro raised his eyebrows to Aunt Nové, and she replied in kind.

Ten minutes later, a horse galloped into the barnyard, whinnying loudly as the rider brought the animal to an abrupt halt. The paladin jumped to his feet, drawing his sword. The chair flew backward with such force that it hit the wall.

"Whoa Cymm!" cried Talo. "Relax!"

Daro opened the door, and in strode Old-Man Semper straight to Cymm, embracing him whole-heartedly. His cousin joined in again for a brief three-way hug.

Before Old-Man Semper could admonish Talo, Cymm advised him quietly, "What are you doing?"

Old-Man Semper gave Cymm a stern look. "Leave your cousin alone."

Did he seriously take Talo's side over mine? He did not like this feeling.

Talo registered no sign of noticing. "Cymm are you alright? It must have been tough out there by yourself. I should have gone with you!"

"Yeah, we both should have," the old man added, smiling at Talo for support. "Whoa! Nice sword!"

Everyone's eyes shifted to the unsheathed sword with the tip dug into the floor. The eerie green mist swirled slowly around the gem in the hilt, the mithril blade reflecting like a mirror. "I am alright, simply being cautious."

Daro took the lead. "Alright, sit down. We have a lot to talk about."

Semper added, "I sent for the other heads. They should be here shortly."

His uncle began, "The green dragon returned and damaged more buildings, including Otec's barn. He then landed in the barnyard demanding to know if this was the Reich Farm and your whereabouts!"

Cymm placed both elbows on the table, burying his face in his hands. *Stefo must have told him.*

"The dragon called you a thief. He claims you took something belonging to him. Is it the sword he wants back?" his uncle asked, nodding toward it.

"No." Cymm paused, twisting his face. "Well, kind of. I went into the lair and found three dragons."

Aunt Nové gasped, "Oh my, three at the same time?"

"Yes," he chuckled, "but not the three that attacked our village. They were very young hatchlings. I don't think I have ever been so angry as at that moment. My face burned red hot, my hands were shaking, and my vision was blurry. They killed my family, and now they were starting a family of their own. It's a long story, but I didn't kill them, although I wanted to. I did decapitate one and I took the head with me."

Talo's mouth went agape. "Oh no! Is that why he is looking for you?"

Nové greeted the other heads of household quietly at the door, filling them in quickly.

"Partially. My Lord Terazhan instructed me to sever the head of the largest dragon and take it with me."

"By the nine hells! You killed one of the beasts?" exclaimed the head of the Softtail household, the last village leader to arrive. They paused to get everyone caught up.

Zeke Darkmane asked what others were thinking, "Do you still have the head?"

"No. I used it to create this sword." He laid it on the table. "I have traveled hundreds of miles, maybe a thousand, to create this sword. I have journeyed into the Realm of Dragon's Bane and fought many battles, all with one goal in mind. The creation of this sword."

Some of the household heads sighed, others groaned, and Wither hit himself in the forehead several times with the palm of his hand.

"Then we are doomed!" Zeke Darkmane finally said.

"Hold up!" Old-Man Semper yelled at everyone in the room. "Let's hear him out. So, what is your plan?"

"I am heading back to the dragon's lair; it will take me approximately nine days to get there by horse. With this sword, Lord Terazhan claims I can defeat them."

The room erupted into chaos with everyone trying to speak at once.

"Well, can you defeat them?" Old-Man Semper asked, his voice rising above the rest.

"How do you make a sword from a head?" asked the Softtail leader.

"What if he returns?"

"Can you unmake the sword?"

"What if you anger the dragons even more?"

"I am not waiting around for death to come!"

Daro slammed his fist on the table, "Quiet!" After several moments of silence, a horse nickered outside. "This will not solve the problem! We will work together like we always do, even if we decide in the end to pursue our own paths." No one else said a word. "We will take turns speaking and rotate through by seniority. Semper, you have the floor."

For the next two hours, they discussed, argued, shared ideas, and guessed what the dragon's response would be to the many scenarios. The most challenging constraint was the month of Final Harvest, only six weeks away. All seven households agreed not to abandon the village or the crops until they finished the harvest. Therefore, they placed someone on guard at the town bell twenty-four hours a day. Each household's responsibility covered one day of the week.

Most households would replenish their rendezvous locations, and Daro gave each family one of the grass rugs that Shay invented, showing them how to make and use them. Some planned to camp at their safe haven. Others sent family members to another village, and the rest stayed put, ready to flee.

They also agreed that Cymm should leave in the morning and not delay at Stallion Rise.

Everyone left except for Semper. Aunt Nové set the table around the four men. They would have a late dinner tonight.

"Would you like to stay for dinner?" she asked Semper.

"Thank you, but I should be getting back to my own table," he replied respectfully.

"Cymm, there is no easy way to say this. Hardre is dead," Semper stated bluntly.

And at first, he didn't believe him, but his mentor's solemn face struck him violently.

His muscles tightened. The sensation started in his fingers and toes, a paralyzing feeling, working its way toward his core. When it passed through his stomach, a wave of pain followed, as if he had eaten rotten food. By the time it reached his chest, he could barely breathe. He tried sucking in air, but the tightening continued from his chest to the back of his neck and into the base of his skull. "What? How?"

"Vigilantes or assassins. They snuck into my house late at night, killing him while he slept," Semper replied.

Small tremors riddled Cymm body. "He was here? In Stallion Rise?"

DragonSin reminded him of a conversation they had when they first met, *"Cymm, it could have been the two dwarves you let go."*

The cruel thought tormented him. He was so distraught that he replied aloud instead of in his mind, "My thoughts exactly. I will hunt them down and . . ." His mistake became evident when he saw the concern on everyone's face. Talo's eyes were wide and filled with fear. ". . . I will find those responsible," he said, trying to cover for himself.

"Last thing I promise." Semper breathed in deep and exhaled, fighting back emotions. "They beheaded him and took it with them."

A single tear rolled down the paladin's cheek. *How ironic.* "I'll deal with them next."

"Cymm, you can't fight the entire world or fix every wrongdoing," his Uncle Daro said.

"Watch me!" he rebuked him sternly, then excused himself, needing some fresh air.

Semper shuffled outside after him. "I'm sorry I put all that on you, but I thought you deserved to know."

"I'm glad you did. I will stop by in the morning before I leave."

Semper face drained of emotion; he nodded before departed quietly.

66

Armak City Law

Two and a half days later, Cymm arrived at the City of Armak late in the afternoon to find a line outside the gates. The guards were interrogating everyone who entered the city. It intrigued Cymm, as several people in front of him were denied entry and directed to the north side of the city wall.

"Are you a refugee from Raist or Bruc?" The guard repeated the same question.

Cymm narrowed his eyes. "No, why does it matter?"

"Both cities have been devastated by dragon attacks recently, and we have special accommodations and work for anyone from those cities. Are you from this realm?"

"Yes, I am from Stallion Rise. Why can't everyone enter the city?"

"We have had too many people sleeping in the streets. If you're caught sleeping in the streets, you'll be arrested," the guard said sternly. "By the way, I am sorry for your losses as well." The guard motioned him toward the city, moving on to the next person in line.

He couldn't figure out why the guard's condolences meant so much to him, but they did. His spirits lifted as he headed directly to the Broken Horse Inn for dinner and a place to sleep.

The inn's tavern was packed, and despite the solemn news the guard shared, the crowd was in good spirits and boisterous. Several patrons called out to Lord Barrister, First Sword to the King of Armak. The paladin settled into the last seat at the bar, placing his order for stew, bread, ale, and a room.

He settled into a relaxing position when a strange vibration tore through his body startling him. It reminded him of striking a rock with a hammer. He spun around, expecting to find the source.

"Cymm, unsheathe me," DragonSin said.

"What? I can't do that. I will break the City Law!" he replied.

"A significant evil is among us. Unsheathe me and exclaim 'Dispel magic,'" the sword persisted.

The paladin hesitated, then stood, drawing his sword. "Dispel Magic!"

Many patrons gasped in shock, shielding their eyes as a moderately bright aura shot forth from the sword.

Two assassins blinked into view immediately behind Lord Barrister and the lieutenant on his right. The killers remained motionless, waiting for some unknown signal. A paste-like poison glinted off their drawn daggers. When they realized their magical invisibility had dissipated, they exploded into motion. One assassin attempted to plunge his dagger into the back of Barrister anyway while the other dashed for the door.

Several people warned Lord Barrister, and he spun in the nick of time to identify the cause of the commotion. He fell backward in distress toward the side of his chair trying to escape his assailant. He successfully deflected the dagger with his forearm. At the same time, the other three men at the table immediately pounced on the assassin, subduing him.

The other fleeing assassin stumbled and fell, thrashing on the floor for almost two minutes before lying still, compliments of DragonSin. Patrons inspected the body with blood leaking from every orifice, laughing at the idiot who poisoned himself.

Lord Barrister forced his way over to him. "Sheath your sword now and come with me."

"I did it to prevent your murder," Cymm said locking eyes, but with a subdued voice.

"The ends do not justify the means," he whispered in return.

The four King's guards led the assassin and Cymm outside like criminals.

"He saved your life Barrister!" said one of the patrons.

"His sword is clean, no bloodshed!" another said.

Cymm could not believe these strangers were supporting him.

Most of the bar emptied into the street, following Lord Barrister.

"You have no honor if you arrest this man!"

"Should he have let you die?"

"Word will spread, Barrister."

"How about you, Grom? He saved your life too. Have you no honor?"

Lord Barrister turned toward the angry mob with blood running from the gash in his forearm and dripping from his elbow. His eyes grew large while he scanned the crowd. "Good people of Armak, please return to your affairs, and do not delay me any further."

Several pebbles pelted the officer, not causing damage, but sending a clear message.

"Arrest the next person to throw something or say anything!" he instructed his lieutenant.

Lord Barrister wobbled and almost fell, but Cymm reached out to stabilize him. The officer examined his forearm in disbelief. "The poison moves . . ." Barrister's voice changed from normal to a whisper, ". . . the poison . . . it rages through my body." He keeled over, falling to the street.

"Cymm, you can save him," the sword said.

"How?" he replied in disbelief.

"Actually, it will take both of us. I can cure the poison, and you can heal the wound," DragonSin responded indifferently.

Cymm drew his sword once again. The bystanders gasped, shouting their displeasure at the paladin. He laid the blade directly on the wound and shook off the guard's hand grasping his shoulder. Another guard reached for his arm on the other side, but he persevered until it happened. Dark green and black ink burst from the wound as if squirted from an overripe fruit. It swirled in the air as it vaporized into a mist before being absorbed by the sword's emerald.

The guards unintentionally released their grip on him, unsure how to proceed. He returned the sword to its scabbard. The paladin placed both hands on the open wound. He chanted aloud, his voice booming out to Terazhan. When he removed his hands, Lord Barrister's arm was healed. The First Sword to the King had been saved.

During the chaos, the assassin in custody had slipped away. The guards were in an uproar.

"DragonSin, can you tell which way he went?" the paladin asked.

"The assassin is currently being dealt with," the sword replied.

"No, do not kill him! He needs to stand trial in front of the city; then he will die." He attempted unsuccessfully to force his will. *The assassin must be in range.* He ran to the closest alley and found him writhing in pain. *"Stop this!"*

"I cannot take the chance," the sentient weapon said.

The paladin yanked him to his feet, then rushed him out into the main street, throwing him at the feet of Lord Barrister. "I found him in the alley trying to escape."

Lord Barrister replied, "Who are you?"

"I am Cymm Reich of the Armakian Horse Tribes and First Paladin of Terazhan, the One True God."

"You are free to go, and you have my eternal thanks." Lord Barrister extended his hand to shake Cymm's to the elation of the crowd.

The paladin retired for the night, planning to strategize with DragonSin about the upcoming battle. The following morning, he stopped by the apothecary to discuss a transaction.

67

The Dragon's Lair

A three-day journey from Armak to the edge of Darken Wood lay ahead, followed by two and a half more days to reach the clearing.

He found it effortlessly the second time, but now a foul stench permeated the air. The vegetation no longer appeared sparse and young. Somehow in a matter of months, razor-sharp, thorny bushes and thick vines that slithered like snakes, had inhabited the entire area.

The Plainsman dumped the remaining apples from the sack Lykinnia gave him, opened a bag of oats, and released his horse, hoping he would be here for him if he returned. After a quick prayer, he entered the tangled jungle of brush. A vine coiled around his ankle. He halted, quaffing the potion he had purchased in Armak, an idea DragonSin had recommended based on the description of his first visit.

The vine immediately uncoiled, wriggling away from him. The rest of the undergrowth also heeded his command. Some of the areas were so thick he had to hack his way through, but within a half hour, he stood on the edge of a small clearing. He finished hacking through the final wall of vegetation and entered the micro clearing around the mountain of trees. Standing off to the side, he braced himself for his return to the dragon's lair.

While he collected himself and caught his breath, DragonSin said, *"I cannot scan the entire lair, but I only sense the presence of one evil being."*

"If there is only one dragon, this is what we were hoping for," he told the sword.

He crept toward the opening, taking a deep breath. A clattering noise emanated from the tunnel, so he hurried back to his hiding spot. A substantial humanoid emerged carrying bones and other refuse and threw it at the wall of thorns.

"If it isn't gnolls, it's hill giants! How many evil creatures are in this realm?" He clenched his fists and jaw.

"Cymm, this giant is not evil," DragonSin corrected him.

The paladin concentrated hard, *"I cannot sense anything!"*

"Patience, there is nothing to sense. In time, a minor version of my power will be yours."

"We cannot wait any longer. What if another one returns? Wait a second; if the hill giant isn't evil, maybe it is being held against its will."

The hill giant fell backward on its butt, sobbing. The giant had several long, deep scratches on its arms, legs, and back, giving him an idea of how to advance the plan he developed with DragonSin.

He stepped out of hiding, "Hello, are you okay?"

"Leave lone slave," the hill giant said.

"I am not a slave, and those are some nasty cuts. Did the dragons do that to you?"

The hill giant frowned. "No, dorns do dis." The giant motioned to the deep scratches all over its body.

A cruel voice from the tunnel hissed, "Traga? Are you still here? You aren't trying to escape again, are you?"

"Come quickly! I can help you escape," Cymm whispered with rapid hand motions.

"Come back now, or I will go get the head of one of your children," the cruel voice taunted.

"Leave lone . . . go!" Traga gestured him away before hurrying back into the lair.

The paladin sighed, hanging his head at the setback, then looked up and started climbing.

"What are you doing?" asked the sword.

"Trying to get you within fifty feet of the dragon!" replied the paladin forcefully.

"Okay. That's a start, but you will need to attack."

The green dragon's voice carried through the mountain of trees. "Traga, you need to make sure everything is clean, and rebuild the nest for the new eggs I am about to lay."

"Yes, Boss-Lady," the hill giant replied.

"If you disobey me again, I will feed your oldest child to my hatchlings. *And you will watch*!" the dragon hissed. "It is not easy for a mother to see her offspring dead. Is that what you want?"

"No . . . no kill, no eat, Traga no bad!" Traga ambled up the tunnel making the same clattering noise as before.

"I am in range. I will start slowly at first, then surge the power. You need to get in there and finish the job," DragonSin said.

Ugghhhh, the dragon issued a loud painful groan.

Cymm reveling at the sound, continued to work his way down into the mountain.

"What . . . took you . . . so long?" The dragon's raspy voice confirmed her pain.

"You no look good," Traga said.

"I am . . . fine!" raged the dragon.

Through the gaps in the stack of trees, the paladin caught glimpses of green scales and its neck sail.

"What . . . are you . . . gawking at?" The large reptile winced, breathing hard.

Who is the dragon talking to? Cymm shifted his head until he found a gap in the trees to assess the situation. His movement caused small stones to fall to the floor and a faint cloud of dust in the air.

"Who were you . . . talking to . . . outside?"

The prisoner gazed up at him and she began to tremble.

Oh, Ledaedra's bones! he cursed; his time was short.

"Tell me . . . now . . . or . . . your children . . ."

He hurried into a more advantageous position, creating a curtain of dirt and stone. His eyes locked on Traga's for a moment; neither one moved.

"Traga talking him," the giantess said tentatively, pointing toward his hiding position. The giant lizard extended her neck upward, scanning the ceiling with hate-filled eyes.

Any sense of fear had faded, being replaced with raw determination. Cymm launched himself at the dragon below.

With the sword pointed down, leading the way, DragonSin sang the same awful tune as before.

"For my family," he whispered as the sword's long blade pierced the dragon's left eye. The paladin's feet landed on its brow and snout. He drove the blade all the way to the cross-guard; he clutched the handle firmly when the wyrm began to flail in agony.

His sweaty palms and the sheer ferocity of its thrashing made him leap for the nest twenty feet below. Leaving the sword embedded, he crashed into the nest, but rolled out, slamming into the wall, bruising his shin, knee, and shoulder. The pain in his hip and the wetness slowly soaking his pants had him very concerned.

The monster continued to roar and shriek while a green essence swirled around the beast and the sword. The skin of the dragon rippled and singed black in scattered small patches.

Traga charged him wielding a large bone club above her head. He fumbled for his dagger, but she bore down on him before he could draw it. She lunged at him, grabbed him, and dove for the nest. The monster's head pounded the floor where he lay a moment before.

"You save Traga. Traga save you," she said breaking into a broad smile.

Cymm eyed her with confusion, and a wrinkled nose. He rolled to his knees, never taking his eye off the dragon, watching for movement. He breathed a sigh of relief, realizing the wetness on his hip was the shattered remains of the potion.

"We get Traga children?" the giant asked with wide eyes. "Dey in other dragon home. Come I show you," Traga said.

"Other? There are two lairs?" the paladin scratched his head.

"Yes, two boss-lady dragons and one big boss," Traga said on the way to the tunnel.

He limped over to the dragon whose tongue hung out between its teeth. He pulled the sword free from the dead body. *"DragonSin, scan the area for evil."*

"No evil detected," the sword reported.

When he exited the lair, the giant had already climbed the mountain of trees. The pain in his hip had gradually subsided, and he forced himself to climb.

She pointed north toward a cave in the cliff. "Right der . . . dey took Traga home."

"Alright, the other two dragons are in that cave?" he asked.

"No. Big Boss hunting; no eat long time. You name Cymm?"

He lost his balance, nearly falling off the heap of trees, or at least through it. "How do you know me?"

Traga bounced with glee, rubbing her hands together fast and forcefully. "Ugh, ugh. Dey say Cymm come kill bosses; big laugh."

The paladin clenched a fist in front of his face in anger. *No one believes I can do this.* "Not so funny now, is it?"

"Yes . . . very funny. Traga funny!"

Cymm shook his head. "That's not quite, ahh, never mind. Let's go, get your home back, and find your kids."

Traga gave her liberator a huge bear hug, lifting him off his feet. The pressure was so intense that he moaned. She immediately decreased the squeeze. "You Traga best friend!"

They gathered their belongings from the lair and lingered by the dead creature.

The giantess asked, "What 'bout gold?"

"I will come back for it," he said.

"What 'bout dragon?"

"I will come back for the head. Why?"

"Green dragon good eats. Traga come back body," she replied with hands on her hips and a proud shake of her head.

Cymm laughed, and Traga's cheeks jiggled. "Dat not funny. What in boss-lady mind when died? Guess? No? . . . You sword! Now dat funny." The giantess held her belly and roared with laughter.

68

The Cave

Dusk quickly approached as they exited the first dragon lair, heading toward the second.

"Did you notice the undergrowth?" asked the sword.

He kicked at the warped, wilting, and decaying vegetation.

"Traga no scratch!" the giantess said gleefully but gazed toward the sky nervously.

"Is the dragon returning soon?" he asked.

"Soon?" She raised both shoulders and hands in response.

Two of the four moons were shining in the sky, assisting them in their trek to the foot of the cliff where they stopped to rest.

They had closed to a couple hundred yards away from the cave, but a new wall of thorns blocked their path. Cymm's mood turned sour, and he argued with DragonSin about how to proceed.

Traga paced back and forth. "What wait for? Kill dragon boss-lady, get Traga kids."

"Be patient. I'm trying to figure out how to get through the thorn wall without having to hack each vine and bush," snapped Cymm.

"Not go drew, go over! Dat why Traga gets moves over der. Traga scape climb cliff. No use secret entrance; it blocked."

He scanned the cliff. Climbing the ridge would not be easy for someone his size. However, she was especially equipped for this climb being nearly ten feet tall with knuckles dragging on the ground as she walked.

"Traga, show me the secret entrance."

She motioned to the other side of the cave. "It way over der."

Halfway to the other side, the moonlight glinted off a distant object to his left. He approached it warily, not realizing how far away it was. As he got closer, the faint odor of death grew, filling his nostrils. He stood over the object which reflected the moonlight. Cymm smiled. Bria's ogre talisman hung around the neck of a corpse. It had beckoned him, like a beacon.

"From dead no take!" Traga said shaking her head.

"This is mine. He stole it from me," he replied in a primal voice making the giantess cower away from him.

He bent over the body staring at Bria's necklace. His tears dripped freely, sounding like rain as they hit Stefo's hardened leather armor. He carefully removed it and polished it on his sleeve. Placing it around his neck, he stroked it and whispered, "I got one already Bria."

As they approached the cliff, voices in an unrecognizable language caught his attention.

"Cymm, I sense evil ahead," DragonSin said telepathically.

"Could it be the dragon?" he replied.

"Not likely, although I do sense two evil beings."

Suddenly, the giantess let out a squeal before running into the dark shadows of the cliff. Cymm followed at a slower pace, stopping when two immense humanoids appeared in front of him. Pushing eleven feet tall, they towered over Traga, especially the one she hugged.

A wave of nausea coursed through his body; they were evil. His immediately elation was replaced by a nervous lump in his throat. *"Sin, please wait a minute . . . not now,"* he pleaded.

"Do you have so little faith in me? The dragon must die first. It's like the assassin I let live until he tried to escape; then I even let you turn him in, right?"

"You and I have different memories of the assassin being handed over for trial, but basically, you are correct."

Cymm returned his attention to the giants. ". . . brother Teevor, and Bak. Dey no talk Common," she said. "Traga say you save Traga and kill Boss-Lady."

He nodded at the two new giants. "Hello."

They stared back without responding.

The tallest giant, her brother Teevor, said something he didn't understand, while motioning to him. Bak laughed in response. The insinuation of jealousy was obvious, even before the giant stepped toward him.

Traga intercepted her brother, yelling at him in their own language. She made a slashing motion at his private area with her hand, and he immediately stepped back in line.

She told Cymm, "Traga say no fight, or Traga kick stones."

To break the tension, the paladin said, "I will check the secret entrance to see if I can get through."

He walked around the giants to enter the small cave, which narrowed quickly. He found it hard to believe Traga could fit in here. About fifty feet in, the tunnel made a sharp turn to the right before winding another two hundred feet to a dead end. Boulders and a stalagmite had been shoved into the opening from the cave.

"I can probably crawl through the opening near the roof, but there will be no quick exit," Cymm said to the sword.

"I can forcefully push one of the rocks free."

"Yeah, let's wait on that."

By the time the Plainsman returned, the two giant males had already scaled the cliff's face above the thorns.

"Traga, what is going on?" asked Cymm. "Are they attacking the dragon by themselves?"

"Dey say no need you."

He shook his head in frustration. "I thought we would rescue your children first, through the secret entrance. When they were safe, we could deal with the beast."

Dawn approached when he reentered the secret passage, and Traga left to join her brother. The paladin waited in the dark, listening. The eerie green light of the sword did not illuminate much, but he covered it, so the glow did not reveal his position.

While he waited for "a sign," DragonSin said, *"I sense the presence of two evil beings in the cave."*

"Two?" replied Cymm, *"Maybe the giants? Or two dragons?"*

"I cannot tell, and they are too far away to attack," it answered.

Cymm became impatient. *"I need to find out what is going on."* He crawled through the small opening near the ceiling. The faintest light began to creep into the cave, causing dark shadows to appear. Rhythmic breathing, interweaved with snoring, filled the cavern. A splash of daylight finally illuminated the cave and exposed a nest with four eggs. Four adolescent giants shifted in slumber, but he could not see the dragon.

The giantess yelled from the entrance, "Hey Boss-Lady, we talk now!"

"Cymm, two of Traga's children are evil," DragonSin conveyed.

"I can sense evil on the largest," he replied excitedly.

"Yes, pure evil is the strongest, but so is the second biggest," the sword claimed.

He shook his head in concern for Traga. *"Let's deal with the dragon first."*

The two largest children, identical except for their size, wore the exact same bearskin tunic and breeches. After whispering to each other, the second largest yelled back to his mother, but Cymm could not make out the words.

Traga replied, but no one moved.

The youngest hill giant, wearing only a loincloth, started to cry. Traga came clomping down the tunnel, calling to him. She screeched to a halt when she entered the main cave. As soon as the youngest saw his mother, he ran to her, but Traga cautiously kept her distance, pointing and yelling at the largest child.

A flurry of activity occurred all at once. Cymm dropped to the floor, approaching slowly, concerned with Traga's strange reaction. The second largest child backhanded his smaller brother who stood next to him. The violent hit sent him staggering into the wall, where he crumpled to the ground. Also, the shape of the largest giant shimmered and grew quickly, transforming into a full-sized green dragon. Cymm blinked several times to verify that his eyes hadn't failed him.

Everyone froze, except the dragon, who unleashed her breath weapon without hesitation.

Traga forcefully pushed her youngest child, now standing next to her, out of danger. He skidded across the floor, unravelling his loincloth. The giantess had left herself completely exposed to the deadly fog.

Her real eldest son in the bearskin tunic flew across the room, striking his mother in the back and sending her sprawling to the floor. She landed out of the serpent's toxic cloud of chlorine near her butt-naked child. She shrieked in pain from the small blisters already forming on her right arm.

Her eldest son took the full impact of the vapors, and open sores and pustules appeared all over his body. He hit the stone floor convulsing.

Traga rolled over, scowling. "Why hit me?"

The deadly gas expanded, momentum sending it up the short tunnel. Teevor stood in shock, watching it about to engulf him. A rock soared from the floor near Cymm, striking Teevor in the chest. With the trance broken, he bolted up the tunnel, diving to the side when he exited.

Traga accepted a helping hand up, a comical sight until the mother's expression changed to horror. "Cymm, save son! He save Traga, help!" He stopped convulsing.

He shook his head slowly, sorrow rendering his voice a shaky whisper. "I am sorry; it is too late." Internally, he admonished the sword. *"Really! You couldn't wait to kill him?"*

"This way she can mourn her son as a hero, instead of hating you for slaying him."

The dragon charged up the tunnel, chasing the hill giant, its sworn enemy, while DragonSin pulled two large stones off the stack that blocked the secret entrance.

"Get your other two children and head for the secret tunnel before the gas spreads." Cymm hesitated, motioning for Traga to hurry. He then yelled, "For Terazhan, the One True God!" and raced up the tunnel to join the battle. The sphere of pure white light popped into view, dimming as he ran through the dispersing haze.

A loud *thud* caught his attention, followed by bone cracking and crunching. Up ahead at the mouth of the cave, an immense boulder rolled off the dragon's left wing.

She roared in pain, craning her neck around, to search for her attacker. Her wing hung limp and useless, dragging on the ground.

She unloaded a new, powerful blast of chlorine gas directly at her assailant from above. The giant's agonizing moans and hollers repeated until the monster clamped on to and slammed the giant thirty feet down to the ground.

The paladin didn't see Bac go down, but Teevor wildly attacked the dragon's right flank, sinking his huge, spiked club into its shoulder.

Cymm dodged the giant lizard's tale as it raced toward him. He extended DragonSin out while running past the dragon's left rear leg and was astounded by the gash he opened on his enemy's thigh, almost the length of the sword. The skin shriveled away from the wound as if burned, and the muscle smoked and sizzled.

The dragon screeched in pain, a terrifying sound which made Cymm's skin prickle. However, her attention never left Teevor. She snapped her razor-sharp-teeth-filled jaws at his large frame. She then lunged at him, her claws knocking him on his back and opening two parallel gashes across his chest. The dragon reared to pounce on Teevor.

The paladin growled as he ran along her flank—his window of opportunity closing. Slipping under her broken left wing between the front and back legs, he positioned himself perfectly to receive her descending bulk. The sword tore through the beast's hide, muscle, and ribs, entering her evil heart.

Teevor lay on his back, glaring at the dragon with a mixture of fear and hatred. Even though Cymm just saved him, the giant glanced at him the same way.

While twisting and torquing the sword, he uttered to himself. "For my family."

The sword interrupted his thoughts, *"Push me deeper!"*

The dragon swatted Cymm with its left arm. He flew backward, losing his grip on the sword and landed hard on his back, knocking the wind out of him. Gasping for breath, he struggled to sit up. His sphere of protection still engulfed him but didn't lessen the blow.

The monster's skin changed color from light to dark green in large swathes. Her vibrant green skin now mottled with splotches of charred black.

The paladin rushed forward to retrieve the sword and successfully grabbed the handle, but it would not budge. The catch blades were so far into the beast that they lodged between two ribs.

Teevor had also regained his footing and smacked the dragon with his club.

DragonSin began to sing with excitement as it continued to drain the enemy's life force. The dragon inhaled sharply, and then choked.

"Get out now! Her heart is collapsing from the stress," the sword warned.

"No! I will be exposed without you." Cymm glanced at Teevor.

The dragon's long neck and head plummeted to the ground, but miraculously the upper body did not.

"Make it quick." The sword no longer sang. *"I can't hold the torso up for much longer."*

The magical sphere fizzled and disappeared while Cymm worked the sword back and forth, finally sliding the blade out as if it were in a sheath.

"You need to get out now!" exclaimed DragonSin.

He backed up several steps, then ducked under the broken wing as the body came crashing down.

Teevor hurried over to Bac's lifeless body. The giant bellowed and hammered his friend's chest before slumping over him.

The paladin—the recipient of a seething glare—took a seat away from the giant on the other side of the cave opening.

A noise rumbled out of the cave, and both men lunged to their feet as another green dragon came crawling over the top of the dead one. Cymm fumbled to unsheathe DragonSin while Teevor hoisted his club, shaking his head in defeat.

"How could we have missed something so big in the cave?" he asked the sword.

"Traga big-boss lady now!" the beast said.

Teevor dropped his club, erupting into hysterical laughter with his hands on his knees.

When Cymm recognized Traga's voice, he said, "This is not funny. The other dragon could come back at any time."

"Traga big fight now! But no stank breath." She swatted and bit the air.

"How did you change shape?" he asked.

"Magic dust, now Traga dragon," she growled and hissed.

Simultaneously, a strident, more terrifying roar echoed in the distance. Heads snapped in the direction of the first lair.

Traga craned her long serpent neck around, placing her head next to Cymm's. She continued to stare in the direction of the roar. "Uh oh . . . you in trouble!"

Most of the thorn bushes and crawling vines surrounding them were shriveling or returning to normal.

The paladin paced while combing his fingers through his hair. "Traga, get your kids and run!"

"No, he catch us!"

He stared at her big green face. "Okay, grab the dragon's tail and drag it back into the cave quickly. Teevor, hide Bak's body, then join us."

"You no Big Boss!" replied Teevor in Common, as he started dragging Bak by the legs.

You don't speak Common, huh? I guess I will need to deal with you next.

Cymm and DragonSin rolled a boulder away from the entrance, up against the cliff. He looked back quickly at the mountain of trees to find a dark shape approaching. His stomach knotted in nervous excitement.

The hunted dragon approached.

The dragon that took everything from him.

The paladin stroked the medallion around his neck; his eyes smoldered. *Time to atone for your sin, dragon.*

He ran down the tunnel to find Traga. "He's coming!"

69

Someone is Going to Pay

TetraQuerahn landed outside of the lair he shared with Ennozarius. He had a peace offering for her.

She is going to like this. Maybe we will start working on the next brood of hatchlings tonight. He had brought her a strawberry roan from the Golden Lake region. To TetraQuerahn, all horse meat tasted the same, but that was not the point. Enno would not agree. She had commented many times about how long it had been since she had . . .

What is that smell? He rushed down the tunnel. Ennozarius's body lay contorted and unmoving on the ground. She had been murdered. "Enno!" he roared in agony.

His tail turned heavy as iron, and each muscle tightened into tiny knots, starting at the tip, and running right up his back. A chilling sensation locked the bulky muscles in his legs, and he began to hyperventilate. Guilt riddled his emotions, powerful and consuming. He wasn't there when his hatchlings needed him, and now he had failed her.

He nuzzled his head against hers. "I should have been here to protect you."

A wave of nausea tore through his stomach like a sword. His head and neck lurched like a snake striking, and he expelled half of the horse meat he had recently eaten. The pain in his stomach subsided, so he returned to caressing her. "I will avenge you; your death will not go . . . Anny?"

The pain in his stomach returned tenfold. Fear and anger replaced the mourning that froze his muscles. A surge of power erupted from his core, releasing him from the bonds of mental captivity. He imagined himself bursting out of an ice cage.

"Anekzarius!" He issued a deafening roar, so loud Ledaedra herself would have heeded his warning. He raced up the tunnel, launching himself into the air.

"Death is coming for you," a distant voice whispered in his mind.

"No, death is coming for whoever killed Enno!" he replied with a growl.

He slammed down on the blood-soaked ground. "This is not possible!"

He belted a savage roar skyward. The scent of hill giant hung in the air with the overpowering smell of dragon blood.

A muffled growl came from the cave.

"Anekzarius? Let her be okay," he said, rushing down the tunnel.

70

The Line between Good and Evil

The large male's head appeared in the tunnel moments later. The giantess in dragon form had blood dripping from her fangs and claws. She stood over the motionless, dead body.

The goliath growled at Traga menacingly. With fear in her eyes, she took several steps back, away from the corpse. Then he came forward, rubbing his head against the dead dragon's. He glanced up at the pseudo-dragon with small tremors running through his snout.

"Why?" he asked with his head low and appearing ready to pounce.

Traga did not reply. Instead, she traipsed in, sniffing the air all around him. He rocked back—about to strike—but she coiled her neck around his.

Cymm and DragonSin remained hidden in the back of the cave by the secret entrance, and Teevor behind the nest.

The mammoth dragon rejected the courting and banged his head and neck against hers. "You smell like a hill giant."

"Dem tasty," Traga replied, flicking her tongue.

A thick hill giant accent saturated her voice, and Cymm hung his head; the ruse was over.

"Liar!" he roared. "You didn't eat the slaves. You are a slave and a burglar that found my magic dust."

Cymm crept forward until DragonSin could attack, hiding behind a stalagmite.

The goliath shook his head from side to side, scratching at his ear as if an insect had crawled into the canal. While distracted, Traga bit deep into his neck, moaning as the dragon blood danced across her tongue. She bit deeper, ripping flesh from his neck. The male roared in pain, whirling to face the counterfeit dragon. His talons raked deep gashes across her chest.

A slight whimper escaped her lips. Cymm prepared to cast a spell while Teevor hoisted a boulder and propped his club at his feet.

The paladin nodded in satisfaction when the dragon shook his head violently. DragonSin dispensed more pain.

Traga dug her claws into the dragon's back, and the monstrous wyrm flailed to get away. He bit her neck viciously, causing her to cry out in agony, and Teevor went into a rage. The hill giant hurled the large rock at the dragon's back and charged with a battle cry. Cymm jumped into the fray, releasing a light spell directly in the serpent's face; his nose shone like a lighthouse.

The dragon howled in surprise. "Do you know who I am, you little worm? I am TetraQuerahn, a lieutenant in the Dragon Queen's Army." The colossal head shifted futilely attempting to peer around the blinding light. TetraQuerahn stumbled into the pretend drake's body. He lashed out viciously with his rear foot, opening several gashes in Traga's belly, revealing her entrails. She collapsed to the ground with a thud.

She was going to get kicked again if he didn't do something. Cymm charged TetraQuerahn's right flank yelling, "For Terazhan, the One True God!"

The pure white orb engulfed him.

Teevor, still belting out a war cry, sunk the spikes of his club into the dragon's backside. The partially blind dragon targeted the sound and pain, connecting solidly with his whipping tail. The giant slammed into the wall.

"Transform back!" the paladin yelled as he stepped over Traga's neck, lunging at his nemesis. He slashed the dragon's rib cage, ripping his chest open, exposing ribs, several of which were now protruding from the laceration.

He swung back in Cymm's direction, "Yes, transform back so I can see which miserable wretch you are!" The behemoth shook his head again.

Happiness swelled within the paladin. *"You are a beast!"* he said to the sword.

"No, the beast is in front of you, and he is far from dead. Now, wipe that dumb smirk off your face and attack!" the sword stammered, as if under great stress.

Traga transformed to herself, recovering slightly after her body and wounds shrank to normal size. She struggled to her feet with a whimper, staggering with her first step.

Cymm pushed her toward the secret exit. "Get out of here!"

TetraQuerahn ears perked up and he lunged for the fleeing hill giant. Still hampered by the light spell, he missed her wildly, but his front right leg clipped Cymm, sending him sprawling.

Teevor recuperated from his battering against the wall, and his club hit the dragon's left flank with a solid swing. The giantess continued to limp toward the exit holding her stomach with both hands while the paladin gingerly got back to his feet, rolling his neck in a circle.

The light spell on the dragon dissipated, but his paladin aura continued to illuminate the area. The dragon's teeth shone brightly as his lips curled like a vicious dog about to attack.

71

There's a Line?

TetraQuerahn attempted to summon a spell for the third time but struggled with the proper sequence and annunciation of the words. The blinding light disappeared, but the searing pain still existed in his head. The escaping female hill giant drew his immediately attention.

He galloped forward two steps while breathing in deeply. The human sprinted toward him from the right with a white sphere of energy surrounding him. "I will deal with you next."

When his front talons struck the floor, pain exploded in his arm. A moment before he exhaled, the human's mighty swing had arced in, severing his arm at the elbow. It smoked and sizzled as if on fire.

The emerald monstrosity reared, roaring in pain. He hit his head on a stalactite so hard that a two-foot section broke off and plummeted toward the human's head. TetraQuerahn waited in anticipation for the crushing blow, but the giant chunk of rock changed direction abruptly, zipping off at a right angle to strike the wall. The dragon bellowed in anger, but it had lost some bluster.

Several smaller pieces of rock rained down upon the human, cutting him. The human's head tilted back, and their eyes met. The orbs contained only hatred and malicious intent. For the first time ever, the dragon feared for his life.

TetraQuerahn continued to focus on the pain in his arm and the miserable wretch attacking him, so he could not say when the headache disappeared. With the realization, came the release of his first spell. Five spheres of pinkish-red energy two inches in diameter shot forth from the dragon's remaining arm. He directed each of them, and two slammed into the hill giant's chest, and three more raced toward the human.

The human panicked and froze, but with some effort, he raised a sword yelling, "Dispel Magic!" Two energy balls zipped by the sword and burned right through his leather armor into his shoulder and chest. He cried out, struggling to keep his sword up, stumbling backward. The emerald in the sword absorbed the third ball with a shower of sparks.

"A magic sword? That will look nice in my treasure trove," he said, taunting the man, hoping he would make a fatal mistake.

The agonizing pain blazed back to life inside his head, like a large worm burrowing deep within his brain. He considered banging his head on the ceiling again to clear his mind, but he had a better idea.

TetraQuerahn rotated, trying to put both enemies in front of him. The hill giant rushed in, sinking his spiked club into his left shoulder while the human stepped under the dragon's left arm and sliced a deep gash in his armpit. He bellowed in pain yet again, but his plan had worked; he had positioned them perfectly. Toxic chlorine gas billowed forth as he unleashed his mighty breath weapon, engulfing his enemies.

The battle was over.

72

Yes... There's a Line

ymm saw the terror in the hill giant's eyes before the dense yellowish-green fog filled the cave, blinding all of them. The hill giant's steps pounded the stone as he ran up the tunnel, then ceased abruptly. A body collapsed to the floor, gasping, choking.

The reek of the rotting, decapitated dragon head did not compare to the vile and disgusting aroma of the dragon's breath. The acrid, malodorous scent made his mouth and eyes water, but otherwise the paladin remained unaffected. He used the thick, yellowish-green gas to cover his next attack.

He immediately spun around and came racing out of the cloud with his sword held high, bringing it down in a two-handed overhead chop on the immense reptile's left flank. The power in the swing was so massive it opened a four-foot-vertical laceration between two of his enemy's ribs. *Pop!* A gust of wind and viscera assaulted Cymm, pelting his face and body. He had punctured his left lung, which burst like an overripe gourd thrown against a rock.

The dragon wheezed, struggling to breathe. "Wait, please. I can help you, powerful master!"

The paladin hesitated, out of breath, chest heaving from exertion. *Master?*

"Do not be fooled by his sly tongue. We are close. End this now!" yelled the sentient artifact in his mind.

Suddenly, he recalled something his mother had said to the dragon. A smug smile pulled at his lips while his magical aura evaporated. "Shouldn't you be asking my name?"

"Alright. I will play your game. Who might you be?" gasped the dragon.

"I am Cymm Reich, First Paladin of Lord Terazhan. I will be your executioner."

"Cymm Reich? You don't look like a horse farmer, you murderous thief!" hissed TetraQuerahn, his head inching closer.

"You murdered my family and many others in my village," the Plainsman hissed back with a voice so full of hatred he didn't recognize it. "I would say we are almost equal, although I heard you threatened everyone again. What was it? Death to all if I did not return the head I 'stole'?" Cymm held the sword between them, mockingly saying, "In essence, I have returned the head!"

"I see you are enjoying this," TetraQuerahn growled. "It reminds me of my conversation with your mother before she died and how much I enjoyed it."

The dragon's cruelty toward his parents made him grit his teeth. *Although am I any different? Even if he deserves it, tormenting him makes me just like him. Maybe Lykinnia was right. I should concentrate on the positive memories.*

"Cymm, focus!" came the mental blast from DragonSin.

"It was unfortunate your mother and sister had to die . . ." The devious beast twisted the dagger causing him emotional pain. The paladin flinched; the words were more damaging than any physical wound the dragon had delivered so far.

Cymm felt the piercing gaze of the beast scrutinize his reaction.

The anger in the sword's voice could not be measured and it implored him, *"You are playing with fire. He is not to be toyed with. Kill him now!"*

The dragon slithered his neck down slowly, positioning himself to attack, but Cymm still delayed his swing.

TetraQuerahn's loathsome tongue continued to wag, "Your mother was strong and brave."

Again, the beast's gaze bore through his skin, examining his soul.

"No! I need to know why." Cymm finally acknowledged the sword.

"Because he is evil, excessively evil. We had an agreement!"

"Your sister was so young and innocent."

The dragon's words caused him to flinch again, and he saw the dragon smirk. The Plainsman steeled himself, preparing for his sister's final moments to replay uncontrollably in his mind. The terror on her tear-soaked face as she scanned side to side, asking for him.

"Cymm, where are you?" Her voice and those words had haunted him while awake and asleep for many months.

"Why?" he asked the dragon with tears starting to well in his eyes.

The dragon lifted his head in confusion, giving up some of his advantageous position in the process. "Huh?"

Tears rolled down his cheek, and he did not care. "Why kill? Why destroy? Why torture? I searched the entire village and did not find one bite mark. You didn't eat anything!"

"Why?" TetraQuerahn chuckled. "This is the reason you held your attack. Foolish human, you should have moved on with your life."

"I couldn't. I still can't. I should have been there to protect her!"

The dragon reared back in shock, but swiftly realization replaced the look in his eyes; then his brows knit together, and he lowered his head again. He snarled as he spoke, "It has been you in my mind all of this time, causing the pain and confusion and now stealing my memories!"

TetraQuerahn lunged in a berserker-like frenzy with his mouth wide open and teeth bared. His canines approached a foot in length and were razor sharp.

DragonSin yelled, *"Cymm!"*

The paladin dodged to his right, spun ninety degrees to his left, and swung his sword down in a two-handed chop severing most of the dragon's neck. The monster collapsed, dead before he hit the floor. Cymm swung again to finish the decapitation.

A white gas or smoke lazily wafted toward the ceiling from the chasm between the dead beast's head and neck. His left eye twitched several times while he tried to determine whether his sanity had left him. The smoke had formed an image of his sister, and she hovered in the gap, smiling at him. He shook his head slowly in confusion. His hallucination continued as other apparitions, including his parents, rose from the dragon's neck cavity. All of them dissipated when they hit the stalactites above, but Bria lingered.

She put both hands over her heart and extended them toward him.

"I am right here, Bria," he whispered, caressing the talisman around his neck before falling to his knees in tears.

73

Lykinnia's Research

L ykinnia could hear the cheer erupt from the altar, a half-mile away at her abode. Terazhan, Solar, and a few others had entrenched themselves there for the past two days, forbidding her to join them or pray.

They must be watching Cymm again. She considered participating, but the voice, and now the hand from the void, still unnerved her. She had not used her improved invisibility spell since, but curiosity and fear battled within her.

"What could they possibly be cheering about?" As soon as she said it, she knew. "Cymm is fighting the dragons!"

She left her books open on the table and ran for the altar with the words to her spell dancing on her lips.

The past two days had not been a total loss. Lykinnia had finally discovered the solution to a problem she had worked on for the past two years. Although her father would not teach her how to perform the life transference process, she had already figured that part out on her own. She had struggled with how to do it safely without impact to her own life span. *If only Terazhan had known this, he would not have had to sacrifice such a significant portion of his life force for Mother.* Her mother should have lived well beyond the normal span of her race, but she had died. Her father had told her that her mother's research on a complex spell had been her demise.

Like mother, like daughter, I guess. The thought brought her comfort as she exposed herself to the void once again.

At least a century ago, she had developed an advanced clerical spell of resurrection. All she needed was her mother's body, or a hair, or a fingernail. Excitement had overwhelmed both her and her father as they opened the middle door between their quarters. Her dad was . . . happy, but as they searched, joy turned to panic and fear, which morphed into sadness. Her mother's entire abode had been incinerated; nothing but ash remained. Her father left with shoulders slumped, saying, "Lykinnia, your mother is dead."

She would not accept this. Her current research explored a non-corporeal version of resurrection, which still eluded her. However, when she figured it out, she needed to be prepared to extend her mother's life because her father's transference would not be viable. She knew he would do it again, and if he used the same process, it would probably kill him.

Her millennial lifeday was of paramount importance because it was perilous to perform the process before then. Her research had revealed the transfer needed to be done in small increments when both life forces synchronized sinusoidally, which minimized the oscillations on the influx of energy. Recovery of the transferred life force during synchronization occurred automatically because the transfer contained mostly burn-off from the normal aging process. If she performed it correctly and at the right time, she could safely extend someone's life with minimal impact to her own longevity.

She pulled up short of the crowded platform, positioning herself to weave through them.

"How did that happen?" Terazhan asked with one hand on the back of his head.

Solar closed the scrying window. A somber mood settled over the group.

Did Cymm get injured or killed? Was the battle already over? Her concern grew with each passing second.

"That was not how I expected it to end." Solar crossed his arms over his chest, shaking his head.

A feeling of dread filled Lykinnia. *Get control of yourself! You just met him.*

"My guess is the boy's power is no longer a secret. Someone else was meddling," said a figure she had never met.

Silence and head nods followed.

"See what you can find out. The boy will be heading this way shortly," Terazhan replied.

Lykinnia breathed a sigh of relief.

"Yes, to visit your daughter, I hear," a stranger said with a raised eyebrow.

Terazhan glowered at Solar with displeasure. The winged man cringed, then disappeared into a vortex of his own making.

Lykinnia flushed, her heartbeat accelerating. A feeling of happiness rushed through her; she became light-headed, and her skin prickled. The euphoria lingered as she proceeded toward her quarters, skipping with excitement while performing calculations in her head. *I guess my new process could be used on my mother and Cymm, and when my stubborn father discovers it had little impact on my life, maybe he will stop treating me like a child!*

She materialized in front of the research books she had left open on the table.

"So, my life force and Cymm's synchronize only twice a year, one of which is the day after my millennial lifeday. Sometimes Melandri can be so obvious," she said, referencing the Goddess of Fate.

74

Aftermath

C ymm wasn't sure how much time had passed when the giantess yelled into the cave, "Hey Big Boss . . . you need Traga help?" She received no answer. "Hey, Traga no enter. Come out!"

Cymm rose to his feet, staggered out of the cave, and collapsed before the blood-soaked giantess. She picked him up gently as if he were one of her children, bringing him over to her sons.

"You save Traga again, and Traga children. You Traga best friend!" she said.

"I heard you yell for the Big Boss?" he said with a chuckle, his emotions beginning to regulate. "Were you talking to the dragon?"

"You, bone brain. Anyone kill three dragons Big Boss!" Traga's voice rose an octave, and her arms were flailing. Glimpses of her entrails poked into the deep gashes. "I am sorry Traga . . . but Teevor didn't survive. The toxic gas killed him."

She fell to her knees with tears in her eyes, pulling at her straggly hair. "Traga hate dragons!" Even on her knees, she was taller than him.

He forced himself to sit up and hugged her big belly. She pulled him in close, still sobbing. When she closed her eyes, he began to pray. He quietly called forth the healing power of Terazhan; his hands and her belly glowed with beautiful pure white light. Although her abdomen wounds were entirely gone, lacerations still covered her chest and neck.

Her eyes widened in astonishment. "You god?"

"No, but a mighty god helps me. Terazhan. I will teach you how to pray to him. Sorry if the light startled you, but I don't want you to die," he replied softly.

"Traga no die! Traga strong like you," she exclaimed. "Big feast comin'. Invite ten lots giants. Three dragons feed two ten lots."

He assumed she couldn't count, but "ten lots" meant there could be dozens or hundreds of giants in this clearing in the next two weeks. "We need to move my share of the treasure to the other dragon's lair to avoid conflict between me and your guests." He left the rest unsaid.

She shook her head in agreement. "Traga no need much. Why you need much?"

"I don't need much either, but many people suffered at the hands of these evil creatures. I plan to use the gold to help them." He patted her shoulder. "Will you and your children be safe here?"

"Yes, some giants eat, no leave. New clan!" Traga happily informed him while holding her arms out wide.

"I am going to take the dragon heads back to Armak. Is any magic powder left?"

Her smile disappeared. She showed him the storage location for the pouch, but reluctantly gave it up. The pouch was closer to a small sack and contained a lot of dust.

"How about I fill a small pouch, and you can keep the rest?" Cymm offered.

"Yes . . . Yes . . . Boss-Lady Traga come party many times!"

During the next two days, Cymm retrieved his horse and transported the dragon heads to Armak in the form of a roc. A few months ago, Dontono told him a story about these enormous birds capable of carrying an entire elephant away. Using the magic dust, he polymorphed both human and horse into a roc. After delivering the final head, he transformed back and rode into the city as if he had done all this before.

The paladin bought dozens of different sized sacks, a few chests, six draft horses, and a small wagon. He intended to transport every last coin back to the city, along with the scrolls, the ring, the gems, the book, and the two wands.

Before he left the city, he paid a courier handsomely to write and deliver a message to Stallion Rise. "Give this note only to Daro Reich or Old-Man Semper. Make sure they can read it. If not, read it to them."

The note read as follows:

I have successfully defeated the dragons! All three are dead, and their heads currently watch over the gates of Armak. I will be home soon with food, supplies, tools, and building materials to share amongst the village. If Tanya Stormcaller arrives before me, allow her and her family to stay in my home.

Cymm Reich

Cymm rode for Howling Set. Although it was a little out of the way, he wanted to share the good news with his friend. Four horses pulled the wagon; the other two were rotated daily. The warhorse led the caravan, and they arrived three days later. Both wolf and wolfer rushed to greet him as he dismounted.

"Cymm, it has been over three months! I worried for you. Torc and I were about to start searching," Torak exclaimed, shaking his hand heartily.

"All is well, my friend. Torc, you are huge!" Cymm ruffled his scruff. "I have killed all three dragons."

"What! How?"

He wrapped his arm around his friend's shoulders. "I will share my story with you while we ride. I need your help to pack up *our* treasure."

"Our?"

"That's right. You and Torc are about to be rich. There is a lot to carry," whispered the paladin.

"Thank you Cymm, but I live a simple life."

"You could use it to eliminate Fang or buy livestock for your village," he replied with a shrug.

"I will help you because I have missed your company, not for the treasure. I can be ready to leave in an hour."

Once they were out of sight of the village, Cymm said, "Please ride one of the horses. We need to get there quickly. The entire clearing is about to be swarmed by hill giants."

Torak climbed into a saddle. "Hill giants? Maybe you should start at the beginning."

Cymm shared the entire story as Torc frolicked through the grasslands. They arrived at the clearing early in the morning on the fourth day, coincidentally Terazhan's Twilight.

The paladin went ahead to scout the clearing. The scent of smoke and roasting meat drifted past him with the wind. His stomach rumbled. *Wow! That actually smells pretty good.* He finished scanning the area before returning to the group. Humans, horses, wolf, and wagon entered the clearing and stopped at the entrance to the lair. Although the draft horses were finally comfortable around the wolf, they would not enter.

Ten feet into the tunnel, the sword startled him, *"There is evil in the lair."*

He left the warhorse and unsheathed his sword, motioning for Torak to be quiet. He crept down the tunnel and found two hill giants packing gold into sacks.

"What are you doing in here? Didn't Traga tell you this area was off limits?" Cymm's brow furrowed, and his nostrils flared.

"You no tell me do!" said one of the hill giants, reaching for his club. Before he could grab it, he flew backward with his arms and legs trailing, as if hit in the torso by a huge, invisible club. He slammed into the wall of trees, collapsing to the dirt floor.

Cymm charged the other one, but DragonSin yelled, *"Wait! This one is not evil."*

The paladin stopped in mid-swing, confused. *"Is it possible there are more like Traga?"* "Torak, don't attack this one unless he attacks first."

"Head hurt. No brain, bad!" yelled the evil hill giant, smacking himself in the head.

Cymm killed him with two swings, although the sword did not cut hill giants as well as dragons. The other giant dropped his club immediately, shifting nervously between feet.

"Do you know Traga?" Cymm asked with his sword at the ready.

"Yes, Traga friend!" the hill giant said.

"I am Cymm, the one that killed the three dragons. Tell Traga I am cleaning up, and if any other hill giants come over here, I will have to kill them. Do not tell anyone else."

"Yes, Big Boss!"

"Take your club and go."

"Thanks, Big Boss!" The hill giant ran up the tunnel.

Cymm visually inventoried the treasure. When he located the book, he breathed a sigh of relief. His friend hadn't moved and stood gawking at him.

"What?" he asked.

Torak raised both hands with fingers spread wide. "What? What in the nine hells was that?"

"I only kill those with evil in their hearts," he said as if it should be obvious.

"Not that! You threw a hill giant fifteen feet and slew him as if he were a gnoll. Then you dominated another, commanded him to deliver a message, and he called you Big

Boss." Torak's arms flailed while he paced. His friend was hysterical.

"I told you this sword makes me formidable, which is how I killed the dragons. We need to keep moving! I am not sure how long the hill giants will listen to Traga, and there could be more than one hundred over there," he replied.

"One hundred! We will talk later; get moving," the wolfer said seriously.

The horseman secured the book first and most of the magic items, then helped bag the coins. Most of the coins went in the wagon; they double bagged them and hung them from the horses when they ran out of space. They kept the pace slow and the distance reasonable to avoid stressing the horses and arrived back at Howling Set five days later.

"One thousand gold coins is more than I will spend in two lifetimes. Thank you," Torak said with a big smile.

"Torak, you could use more gold to buy mercenaries to weed out Fang," he tried to convince the wolfer once again to take more coins.

"This needs to be handled more tactfully, and besides, I have already identified the leader of Fang."

Cymm leaned forward. "You have?"

"I think it is Brato, Stefo's father," Torak replied in a hushed tone.

The paladin stood. "Let's go to Endurance Rise now. If he has evil in his heart, it will be obvious, and I will slay him on the spot."

"A horseman, killing their leader? Surely, by now, you realize how absurd that idea is."

Cymm slowly sat down. "But I want to help, and I don't want you to get hurt."

"It is a risk I am willing to take. I need to catch him in the act so I can prove how despicable he is. I know he killed the husband and wife, then accused you."

"Please be careful! When I am done in the south, I will come back to help you weed out every Fang member. My sword can help me determine their intentions and past deeds," the paladin shared passionately.

"You may not see it or believe me, but you have changed a lot in three months."

Cymm considered his words. "Is that good or bad?"

The wolfer did not respond immediately. "You accomplished an impossible task. One where everyone thought you would fail, including you."

Cymm opened his mouth to argue but then hung his head.

"Instead of celebrating and returning to your life, you are in search of more risk and opportunities to avenge wrong-doings. You are probably planning a trip to Delge to—"

"How do you know?" The paladin felt uncomfortable and shifted side to side.

"You said Hardre was assassinated. It wasn't hard to figure out."

"Torak, this is my *new* life."

He spent the night with his friends and left in the morning.

75

Homecoming

Cymm arrived in the city of Armak four days later and went straight to the Temple of Terazhan.

"These coins are to be used to build a temple in the City of Mystics. This direction came straight from our Lord."

"Terazhan's Will be done!" the three priests chanted in unison. They helped the paladin unload the sacks and bags of roughly twenty thousand gold and silver coins. He still had a couple thousand coins, gems, and many items he believed to be magical.

He stabled the draft horses, paid the apothecary back, and rode to the King's Court to discuss an important matter. With a large donation, his request to erect a monument outside the gates using the three dragon heads received approval. An elven emissary from the northern city of Elmsway had the next audience with the king.

Cymm slowed his departure.

The elven representative addressed the king with a bow. "Your highness, it is nice to see you again. A fortnight ago, the great city of Elmsway was attacked by two black dragons who suffered significant damage. My Lord asks . . ." A royal guard ushered Cymm out of the courtroom, and the voice trailed off.

He waited outside fifteen minutes for the elf to leave. The ambassador exited through the same door, fuming, and muttering to himself.

"Hello, Master Elf. Can I ask about your city?" Cymm asked confidently. The elf hesitated for a moment but then ignored him and kept walking. He persisted. "My village was attacked by three green dragons many months ago, and we are still trying to rebuild."

"Did the king also tell you the coffers are bare?" empathized the elf.

"No, I am funding the rebuild myself, and I would like to help your city," he said, waving for the elf to follow him. The emissary hesitated again. "My horse is right here."

"DragonSin, is he telling the truth? Will he return to Elmsway with the pledge I give him?" Cymm telepathically communicated.

Cymm reached into a saddlebag slowly as the elf came close.

The sword was silent for a while. *"Elves live much longer than humans. Give me a few more seconds to explore his mind. He tells the truth. He is loyal to the Lord of Elmsway."*

Cymm opened a small bag, poured several large emeralds into his own hand, then studied the elf's eyes. They were wide with shock, as Cymm placed the entire bag into the elf's shaky hands. The ambassador's mouth hung open, and he stared back with his hands still extended.

The paladin attempted to push the bag toward him. "They are real. I estimate the entire bag is worth more than five thousand gold pieces."

"Thank you! I do not doubt they are real and worth three times as much. Who shall I tell my Lord gave this generous gift?" asked the elf with a bow.

"I am Cymm Reich, first Paladin of Terazhan, but the gift is by the grace of my Lord." He mounted his horse.

"We have a Temple of Terazhan in Elmsway. You should visit one day, Cymm Reich First Paladin of Terazhan." The elf bowed again.

He went directly to the Artisan's District for the next item of business and found two artists willing to work together on the dragon monument. They received half payment up front; the rest would be paid by the priests upon completion.

Cymm spent the night in the temple, rising shortly after sunrise. He arrived at the market as it opened, creating quite the buzz. First, he hired six farmers with large wooden wagons and two mercenaries to travel to Stallion Rise. Next, he loaded up the wagons, including his own, with calves, chicks, and lambs, as well as bushels of fruit and vegetables. Then, he bought tools, wooden posts, poles, and the caravan rolled south before midday.

Cymm still had four hundred gold coins left, a small pouch of diamonds, a small bag of rubies, and items he believed were magical, much more than he needed. He was excited to go home, but he couldn't wait to reunite with Lykinnia to share his adventures.

They arrived in Stallion Rise late in the morning during the month of Sendarian. It had taken four days to travel from Armak, and again no one greeted Cymm as he entered the village. Only two weeks remained until Final Harvest began, but the long days had already begun. The wagons stopped at the center of town, near the alarm bell, where his henchmen began unloading.

Finally, Old-Man Semper came riding up hard, dismounted, and embraced him. "Everyone has heard the good news, but they are hard at work."

Cymm gave him a big hug. "Help me figure out how to divide this fairly. If we need more, I will figure out a way to get it delivered."

His former mentor put his arm around his shoulder, marveling at the massive amount of goods he brought. "You did good half-pint. You did good."

Daro and Talo reigned their horses in twenty minutes later, and a rowdy, emotional reunion commenced. The two heads divided everything fairly, not evenly, based on what each household lost and needed.

Talo pulled Cymm aside to share some good news. "I am to be married during the month of Festival."

"Congratulations! That is only a couple of months away. I have an early wedding gift for you. I want you to live in my house, make it your home, and raise your family. You can add on as more children come." A tear trickled down his cousin's face.

"We could live together . . . like family," replied Talo.

"Talo, my brother, I will not be here long." He sheepishly waited for his reaction.

His cousin's face contorted with anger. "You've barely been home an hour! Why?"

"I have an important date with a woman," he said with a wink.

Talo pursed his lips and rolled his eyes. "Yes, I heard the letter. Tanya Stormcaller."

Cymm's face shifted in slight repulse. "No . . . no . . . no! What is wrong with you? Tanya is only thirteen lifeyears! She is coming to Stallion Rise to train to be a paladin. So please provide her and her family with food and shelter until I return."

"Oh, then who are you going to meet?"

"Lykinnia." He told the story about their first meeting and how she had asked him to come back after killing the dragons.

"You will be back for the wedding, though, right?" asked Talo.

"Of course, and I plan to help with Harvest for a few weeks also," Cymm promised.

They stayed up late talking, restoring their bond, but early the next morning Cymm hit the road. He pushed the pace, so he could get to the Peak of Power in eight or nine days.

76

Crush

Cymm had not seen Lykinnia for almost two months. During their first meeting, he had discovered she loved to read, so he was both nervous and excited to present her with the ancient tome from the dragon's hoard.

When he arrived at the Pool of Age, he found her already at the altar. He rushed to the platform with the book in hand. "I have returned as promised," he proclaimed enthusiastically.

"Shhh, I am praying," she replied.

"No, you're not. You only pray in the morning." He pushed up next to her and set his gift on the altar. *How can I have such powerful feelings for her after such a short period of time?*

Lykinnia blushed. "I have been watching you climb the windy trail below. What is this?" She motioned toward the book.

"I brought you a present," he said with a flourish.

"Oh, it's an old magic-user's spell book," she said, caressing the cover. She made several hand gestures over the book and paused when Cymm's eyebrows rose. "I am checking for glyphs and wards."

Lykinnia must have been satisfied because she lifted the cover with a giddy little dance. After reading the first page, her face turned ghost white, and she peeked at him.

Cymm leaned in, studying the book, but he couldn't read normal words, let alone magic. "What's wrong?"

She continued reading with tears in her eyes, then quickly closed the book before the first tear fell. Lykinnia fell into Cymm with open arms. His body warmed, filling with excitement, which slowly was replaced by guilt. *Stop!* He scolded himself. *She is sad.*

"Lykinnia, I am sorry. I did not intend to hurt you." He gently rubbed her back.

Lykinnia gazed deep into his eyes. "You did nothing wrong. This book is extremely valuable. It is worth a king's ransom, but it is worth even more to me."

"I don't want the gold!" he said harshly before softening his tone. "It is a gift for you."

Her eyes twinkled, and she wiped away the remaining tears. "This book has survived since the Age of Wonder. Sendaria Moonbeam, the most powerful wizard to have ever lived on Erogoth, was the author. She is an idol of mine, but I will tell you more about her later. Are you hungry or would you like to bathe first?"

Cymm strutted like a peacock. He could not have imagined a better reaction to his gift. However, his delight disappeared quickly when he noticed the front of Lykinnia's pure white robes, now smudged with dirt, soot, and old blood.

Oh, no! You idiot, you should have washed your armor. He cleared his throat. "Lykinnia, your robes . . ." He motioned to the front of her.

"What a mess! How about we both clean up before eating."

An hour later, the conversation continued with telling stories from the past two months, talking about religious beliefs, and opining on how to make the world a better place.

He explained the three dragon battles in detail, followed by a comprehensive list of his generous gifts with the dragon treasure. He also told her about his cousin Talo's wedding. He wasn't sure why, but he held back on telling her about his sister's apparition.

She gave him an update on the tavii. They were settling in comfortably, each wearing a bandoleer now. The priestess offered to identify the magic items he had found in the dragon hoard, which he eagerly accepted.

"Lykinnia, did you by chance know a dwarf named Hardre Ironcore?"

"You may have mentioned him the last time you were here. Why?"

"He was a very good friend of mine and a priest of Terazhan like you. Anyway, during my quest, assassins murdered him while he slept." Cymm struggled to make eye contact.

Lykinnia gasped but did not interrupt him.

"If I stayed in Stallion Rise, he would still be dead, but now I can make a difference."

"How is that?" she asked softly.

"I can search for the assassins." Cymm tapped the sword hilt, watching her reaction.

"That would be justice," she replied quickly and vehemently.

"What if I kill several other assassins in order to get to the ones who killed my friend?" he asked tentatively.

"Hmm, I see where this is going. Your sword is very powerful." She spotted it still strapped to his back while he ate. "If you let it control your body and mind, eventually it will change your heart," she provided her sagely advice. "And Cymm, your heart is pure and beautiful."

He thought to himself, *"My heart is beautiful? Is she flirting with me? Aah . . . I wish I understood women better!"* but out loud, he said, "I will keep that in mind. In the beginning, the sword overpowered me, but since the dragon battles, it has been a more balanced relationship."

"Has it?" Lykinnia responded with raised eyebrows.

He had an extremely enjoyable evening, and his infatuation with her grew stronger. They parted ways, and the paladin slept in his favorite spot, about one hundred feet south of the altar.

The following morning, they began a ritual he enjoyed tremendously; they prayed at the altar together, not aloud, but at the same time, before having breakfast. Again, she filled the table with many kinds of fruit and bread with the wave of her hand.

"Cymm, my lifeday is approaching."

"It is? Is it a special lifeday?" he asked, trying to get her to say a number.

"Yes, it is my coming-of-age. I was born in the month of The Initiate on the fourth day. I will have many special guests and hope you will be one of them."

Cymm noticed that she held her breath, anxiously awaiting his response. "I would not miss it for anything!"

She set her bread on her plate, clapping her hands vigorously. "Excellent!"

"I promised to help my uncle with harvest, so I need to leave in the morning. Plus, my cousin's wedding will be right after that." He nervously evaluated ways to invite her as his guest, but his heart pounded like Warhez's hammer, and his mouth went dry. *How can I kill three dragons but not ask her a simple question?*

As if reading his mind, she said, "I am a little jealous that you can come and go as you please. I am not permitted to leave the Pool of Age." She had a sad, distant look on her face.

She did not elaborate, so he did not pry. "Well, how about I come back to visit right after the wedding?"

"Yes! How about a walk in the orchard?"

Kamac or his brother wandered into the area. "Hello Cymm," he growled.

"Hello Kamac!" he responded, then whispered to Lykinnia, "Now that's progress." She burst out laughing while hanging on his shoulder. He was in heaven.

77

World's Collide

L
ykinnia had spent the past few days studying and reviewing the new spell book, intermingled with her clerical duties, research projects, and tending to her taviian wards.

She missed Cymm deeply and thoughts of him distracted her, consuming her mental capacity—his strong jawline, how he loved his horse, the quirky way he crinkled his nose and his sigh when she mentioned the number of languages she spoke.

Maybe I should use the altar to flash-travel to him, but how will I find him? If I do find him, then what? Fly next to him in my golden form? Talk about the trees? She exhaled forcefully.

She drummed her fingers absently on the open book. *Maybe I should spy on him like Solar does?* "Ahhh!" She folded her arms and put her head down. *Now I'm creepy and cringy.*

Slamming the book closed with a groan, she said, "That's it! I need a problem to solve right now." She paced back and forth, processing dozens of ideas.

The voice from the void.

An impulsive plan formed quickly in her mind. *If the hand could touch me, then I should be able to pull the creature through the aperture. If I am standing at the altar, whatever foul denizen comes through will be instantly baked by the holy wards.*

Her plan had several flaws. What if it was another god, an Arch Demon, or Ledaedra herself. She calculated the odds quickly in her head. *Not very likely. What if this thing pulled her into the void? Then I will get baked, literally, for leaving my point of genesis prematurely.*

It took several minutes to walk to the Pool of Age, as she evaluated her impetuous behavior. Her heart rapidly thumped in her chest while her mind evaluated new scenarios. No one was around. She raised her hands to cast the spell of invisibility; they were shaking. She did a little dance shaking her arms and legs to relieve stress; then she disappeared.

She yelled into the void, "Creature!"

"Lykinnia?" the voice replied instantly.

"Why do you harass me?"

"I need your help," the voice said.

"Who are you?" asked Lykinnia, forcefully projecting confidence.

For the first time, there was no answer.

Her voice shifted to a desperate yell. "Who are you?"

"Sendaria Moonbeam."

Lykinnia paused for several seconds, replaying the name over and over in her mind.

"Mother?"

Afterword:

I read my first fantasy novel, Sword of Shannara, in the 7th grade, and fell in love with the genre. Around the same time, I began delving into role-playing games with my cousin Jeff and my friend Todd, which captivated me even more. By my freshman year of college, while trying to destroy the Balrog in the Unix-based game of Moria, I was ready to create my own fantasy world and the storyline for this novel took life. I can still remember laying the graph paper out all across my dorm-room floor to make sure the coastlines and rivers lined up perfectly and hoping my roommate wouldn't return anytime soon. I created the Bard's Hollow Tavern, a roughneck hang-out on the edge of "society" with a back-door alley leading to the even rougher slums. The tavern's proprietor, the renowned Brag Arrowthorn, was a flamboyant cross-dresser that had no problem defending his right to do so (decades ahead of his time). Most importantly, I wrote a two-page story about Cymm and DragonSin, which was the genesis for this entire series.

I couldn't wait to share the new world with my friends from high school, and the nine of us agreed to restart our weekly gaming session over the college summer break. Their adventure occurred during the Age of Wizardry, a time when magic-users were revered, and the creation of powerful relics was possible. They spent most of their time in the City of Mystics and the Lower Darken Wood exploring, battling, and dying. Fueled with Cool Ranch Doritos and caffeine, the gaming sessions flew by. [Cheers to Brian, Bruce, Harv(Mike),

Joel, John, Kit (Chris), Tim, and Todd]

The summer ended and so did our gaming sessions. Unbeknownst to us at the time, that was our last gaming session with the entire group, but I doubled my efforts during my sophomore year of college and developed more story lines, characters, creatures, civilizations, immortals, conflicts, and city maps. This activity continued for the rest of my undergraduate studies at the University of Buffalo (SUNY) with a new gaming group. However, poker, euchre, and fantasy football usually took precedence. [Cheers to Ron, Jeff, Don, and Steve]

After graduating, I hired on with a copier company and 170 other engineers into a technical development program. I made several new friends that also enjoyed role-playing, and we formed yet another new group. This adventure took place during the Age of Frost, with unstable planar travel and vortices that brought new quests and challenges. [Cheers to Ajay, Brian, Eric, Gordon, Kit, Ronnie, Sal, and Todd]

I have had several stints on Roll20 and Fantasy Grounds, but my latest group is proving to be quite appealing. All of you!

I will leave you with one more interesting fact about this world with four moons. It does not spin as it revolves around its sun; it rolls. This creates a dichotomy of extreme climates, one hot blazing pole, the other frigid and dark, but both possess fascinating and exciting new creatures.

Peace my friends!

And long live Cool Ranch Doritos and Baja Blast!

DragonSin

I hid a few. Let me know if you find any.

Do you want to be the first to read Chapter 1 of Book 2?

Do you want to know the name of Book 2?

Or see the reveal for the cover of Book 2?

Head over to CMSurowiecJr.com and subscribe.

DragonSin

Made in the USA
Middletown, DE
04 August 2022